With
HEARTS AND HYMNS
AND VOICES

For Derek Tangye
who inspired me to write
as he inspires others to read

WITH
HEARTS AND HYMNS
AND VOICES
A NOVEL

PAM RHODES

MONARCH
BOOKS
Oxford, UK, & Grand Rapids, Michigan

This edition published in the UK in 2010 by Monarch Books
(a publishing imprint of Lion Hudson plc)
Wilkinson House, Jordan Hill Road, Oxford OX2 8DR, England
Tel: +44 (0)1865 302750 Fax: +44 (0)1865 302757
Email: monarch@lionhudson.com
www.lionhudson.com

ISBN 978 1 85424 975 3

First edition published by Lion in 1996.

Distributed by:
UK: Marston Book Services, PO Box 269, Abingdon, Oxon,
OX14 4YN
USA: Kregel Publications, PO Box 2607, Grand Rapids,
Michigan 49501

Acknowledgments
Verses from 'Be still, for the presence of the Lord' pp 63/64 by David J. Evans © 1986 Kingsway's Thankyou Music PO Box 75, Eastbourne, East Sussex BN23 6NW, UK

The text paper used in this book has been made from wood independently certified as having come from sustainable forests.

British Library Cataloguing Data
A catalogue record for this book is available from the British Library.

Printed and bound in the UK by MPG Books Ltd.

Who's Who

In the village

Reverend Clive Linton Vicar of St Michael's, Sandford

Helen Linton The Vicar's wife

Mrs Hadlow Elderly local busybody. Married to George; their daughter, Rosemary, works occasionally in The Bull Hotel in the village

Ivy Mrs Hadlow's friend and constant companion. She is not very talkative and finds it difficult to walk

Charles Waite Chairman of the Parish Council, Church Warden, local amateur historian

Betty Waite married to Charles, has been the Choir Mistress and Organist at St Michael's for years

Jack Diggens Lonely accounts clerk, who has recently retired

Don Birch Runs the Village Store with his wife, Joan

Anna Birch Their daughter, a very talented singer, still in her teens and at school.

Matthew Gregory sixteen-year-old schoolboy, who is keen on Anna and the technical side of broadcasting

Major James and Marjorie Gregory Matthew's parents. The Major is on the Parish Council, and influential locally. Marjorie is not a regular churchgoer but is desperate to get a ticket for the recording

Margaret Abbot A harpist and music teacher from the neighbouring village of Steepleton, who becomes friendly with Jack Diggens

Reverend Stephen Yearling Baptist minister at Steepleton—he has a wife, Wendy, and children Luke and Stephanie—interviewed on 'Village Praise'

Reverend Norman Oates A larger-than-life local Methodist minister, married to Marion

Reverend Walter Millar Retired local vicar. Beryl is his wife.

Bill and Maureen Proprietors of The Bull Hotel

Stanley and Eric Regulars in the Public Bar at The Bull

Brian and Ellen Owners of Grove House, Bed and Breakfast hotel for the BBC Production Team.

David Hughes Farmer at Dinton, with his wife, Karen, and their five-year-old son, Michael. He owns two donkeys, Doreen and Denis, who are auditioned for the Palm Sunday procession

Bunty Maddocks Active and tireless church worker. Head of the Ladies' Prayer Group and the Ladies' Flower Arranging Group.

Iris Baker Hairdresser and owner of the Hair Salon in Sandford High Street.

Grace and Madge Members of the Ladies' Flower Arranging Group

Dorothy Jolly, cuddly customer at Iris' Hair Salon

Debbie Receptionist at the Hair Salon

Colin Brown Talented organist from nearby Stowmarket who runs his own estate agency

Pete Durrell Editor of *The Herald*, the local newspaper

Bob Evans Reporter on *The Herald*

Dee and Chris Stevens Born-again Christians with two children, Daniel and Naomi, considered as possible interviewees for the programme.

Mrs Hulme Daunting choirmistress of St Mark's Church Choir from Stowmarket

Bill Hewitt Organizer of the Saxmundham Songsters

Sidney West Bad-tempered, bossy elderly man who regularly goes off-shore in a small boat with his friends Frank and Bo, to sing hymns and read the Bible

Mike Hallam Organizer of 'Out and About', which arranges countryside outings for people hampered by disability or circumstances

Mary Denby Disabled young mother. Enthusiastic supporter of the 'Out and About' project. Interviewed for 'Village Praise'

Mrs Rose Smith Patronizing organizer of the Women's Institute Choir

Mrs Gearing Headmistress of Sandford Junior Mixed Infants School

Gregory and Jessica Children at Sandford School

Brenda Member of St Mark's Choir

In the Television Crew

Jan Harding Producer of 'Village Praise'

Sue Production Assistant, who arranges schedules, accommodation, timings for the whole production, and is a regular churchgoer at her home in Salford

Simon Martin Engineering Manager, with overall responsibility for technical requirements, including the lighting of the church

Frank Harris Sound Supervisor

Kate Marsden Researcher

Ian Spence Musical Director

Sarah Ian's girlfriend, a professional flautist

Richard Newham Musical Adviser

Roger Harwood Director of location and church recording

Ros Denham Attractive and efficient Floor Manager

Joe Security Man whose caravan always has tea on the brew and the biscuit barrel open

Michael Sheehan Irish Rigger/Driver

Des and Charlie Riggers

Jim and Terry Electricians (sparks)

Keith Location cameraman

Bob Location sound man

Pam Rhodes 'Village Praise' presenter. Her husband is Paul, and her two children are Max, aged eleven, and Bethan, five

5 *February*

W hen the phone rang, she almost missed it. She was down in the cellar, digging out crepe paper supplies for the Sunday School youngsters, and although she heard it ring, Helen ignored it. Clive was in—let him get it.

By the time she realized he was ignoring it too, and she'd climbed over the cat basket and a line of wellington boots to clamber up the stairs, Helen was breathless as she grabbed the phone.

'Hello, St Michael's Vicarage, I'm sorry!'

'I'm not,' said a woman's voice, with a slightly musical lilt to it. Was it Scottish? 'St Michael's Vicarage is what I'm after. Is the vicar there?'

'Well, he should be,' said Helen, craning her neck to peer into Clive's study, 'but apparently not. What time is it? He's got a funeral at ten-thirty this morning—he's probably gone over to the church. Can I help? I'm his wife.'

'I'm sure you can. I'd like to fix a time to come and chat to him. I'm going to be down your way on Wednesday afternoon—I just wondered if he's got any time free then?'

Definitely Scottish, Helen thought.

'Well, I don't know of anything booked for that afternoon, but that doesn't mean a thing. I'll get him to ring you back, if you like. Can I tell him who called?'

Helen tucked the receiver under her chin as she reached for the pen, attached with sellotape and string to the phone, and searched for a corner of paper that wasn't already written on.

'My name is Jan Harding. I'm a Producer at the BBC. I want to look into the possibility of doing a "Songs of Praise" from Sandford.'

Helen's pen came to a halt in mid-air.

'Can I leave my number, and perhaps your husband—it's the Reverend Clive Linton, isn't it?'

'That's right.'

'Do you think he could ring me later today? I'd like to get things moving.'

Helen seized the pen again, and scribbled down the number. 'I'll pass the message on. He'll probably get back to you in an hour or so. Bye.'

Helen replaced the receiver, and stared at the phone. What an extraordinary call! 'Songs of Praise', here? Sleepy little Sandford, population eight hundred, and shrinking? Sandford, on a road that probably went somewhere once, but no one could quite remember why. This was a backwater, a place seldom found except by accident—and for most of the locals, except perhaps the ones who wouldn't mind a bit more B & B business, that was just fine.

Helen chuckled. Wait till Bunty heard! Think how she'd set up four committees just to organize the summer fête! Something like this would keep her happily harassed and indispensable for weeks!

That reminded her—the Parish Magazine. Bunty had already rung twice, first to remind, and then to demand, that Clive get his intro over to her by yesterday at the latest. This morning, he'd promised he would closet himself in the study first thing, and get it done.

What was the time? Helen glanced at her watch. Five to ten. Wherever was he?

Dear Clive—so well-meaning, so willing to offer, so often to disappoint. For a man whose life was structured by services and meetings, time seemed to have surprisingly little relevance. He just forgot. As his thoughts took him on to heady spiritual heights, the worldly business of getting on with the day simply faded from his mind. He never meant to let anyone down, or cause confusion. He hadn't a hurtful bone in his body. He simply forgot. And what he forgot, Helen—good old reliable Helen—always remembered, and organized around him.

Helen reached for her coat, and glanced at her reflection in the hallstand mirror. Her cheeks were flushed. Simmering frustration always left her that way, and nowadays, it seemed to her that frustration was all she ever felt where Clive was concerned. What an old grouch she was becoming! She gave herself a stern look in the mirror, grabbed the funeral service sheets Clive had probably meant to take with him, and dropped the key, as usual, into the black flowerpot before pulling the front door shut.

Had he been forgetful when she'd first met him, she wondered, as she walked towards the church? He probably was, but it hadn't mattered then. At twenty-four, in his last year of a theology degree, Clive's search for truth, and his certainty of answers in the Christian faith, made him a compelling, mesmerising companion. She admired his clarity of thought, his passion, his vision. She found herself watching him, asking about him, wishing she knew him better. And even before he ever really noticed her among the gaggle of students who often hung around together, she was probably already a little in love with him.

It had been the Christian Fellowship that finally brought them together. He suggested they invite along a well-known evangelical minister to one of their meetings. She volunteered to write the letter, and do the publicity. He had chaired that meeting, and introduced the speaker. She had arranged the tickets, the chairs, and given the vote of thanks from the floor. A week later, he received a card thanking him for organizing such a stimulating and thoroughly enjoyable evening. She was rewarded by the warm glow of friendship in Clive's eyes, a warmth that over the months, steadily grew into love.

'Oh, Mrs Linton!'

Helen's thoughts were jolted back, as she saw the comfortable, coated frame of Mrs Hadlow waiting at the church door.

'Oh, Mrs Linton. I am glad to see you, dear. I didn't bring my key, you see, because the vicar said he'd be here. Just thought I ought to spruce things up a bit, well, for poor John, of course. So sad. Never really knew him well, but he seemed nice. Lonely, I think, all by himself, since Maisie died. His heart must have been broken. I told George, I thought it must have been broken, he missed her so much. Poor John. It's a real shock. We'll miss him.'

Helen smiled to herself, as she turned the key in the lock. 'It's kind of you to bother, Mrs Hadlow. I'll just come and switch the lights on, and light that fire in the vestry. I'm sure Clive will be over in a while.'

'I've brought my own tin of polish with me,' said Mrs Hadlow, as she eased herself through the door. 'I never really think you get a proper shine from a spray. It doesn't smell right. I popped up to take a look in John's garden this morning, to see if his daffs were out. His always seemed to be the first, and I thought he might like his own flowers in church this morning. Too early, though—but he did love his garden! Whatever's going to happen to that garden now? Did he and Maisie have any family, do you know? My Rosemary, she did breakfast at The Bull this morning—well, it's Thursday, so she always does—she said there's a couple staying there, come for the funeral today. Do you think they're relatives? Poor man, kept himself to himself. I never really knew him well.'

Helen headed back towards the door.

'Oh, leave the door on the jar, would you, dear? Mrs Murray said she'd pop over. Did you hear her leg's bad again? Those pills really aren't working. I keep telling her she ought to go back and ask, but you know how she hates making a fuss. Anyway, she'll want to come and pay her respects. We all do, poor man.' And as Mrs Hadlow began a cheerful, tuneless hum, Helen slipped away.

So, Clive wasn't at the church. She headed for the next most logical place.

The Reverend Clive Linton was rarely happier than when he was in his greenhouse. Standing big and lopsided at the end of the long garden, the greenhouse took him out of the rectory, and into another world, a world of endeavour and miracles, of death and resurrection, of peace and perfection. He sometimes thought he felt closer to God here, than he ever did in the pulpit. As his hands busied themselves with planting, pruning and spraying, his mind wandered free. His best sermons were born here. His keenest insights were glimpsed here. Those nagging irritations of jobs to be done faded into comfortable obscurity, as he marvelled again and again at new life, creation at close hand.

'Darling, look!'

He turned a beaming face towards Helen, as she opened the door. 'The amaryllis, you know, the one from last year? It's about to flower again. Do you remember what a splendid colour it was? Would you like it in the house now, the hall perhaps?'

The years have hardly touched him, Helen thought. Oh, he's greyer, more thickset—but his gentle features and warm eyes have hardly changed at all.

'It's lovely. I'll take it through. You'll want to get your robes on, I expect. They'll be starting to arrive for John's funeral pretty soon. The service sheets are on the back pew, by the way.'

Reluctantly, Clive brushed the dirt off his hands.

'Oh, and Clive, when you've a moment, there's a number for you to ring on the pad. A lady from the BBC—she wants to come down and talk to you about perhaps doing a "Songs of Praise" here.'

Clive's eyebrows lifted. 'Well, I never. On the pad, is it? I'll ring right now.'

'You know, there are some people staying at The Bull. They've come specially for John's funeral. I wonder if they might like a word with you before the service. They might do.'

'Oh yes, of course. I'll get ready straight away. His niece, probably, I think. She rang earlier in the week, to talk about hymns. Mrs—what was her name? Oh, never mind. I'll know her when I see her.'

And picking up the amaryllis, Clive headed for the house.

As funerals go, this one was quiet and dignified. There were only a few seats filled, mostly by locals—the Hadlows, next to their friend, Ivy Murray, whose beige raincoat matched her beige hair, and her pale face. Ivy gave the occasional martyred sigh as she tried to find a comfy position for her leg.

Behind her, Jack Diggens sat, slight and wiry, neat and reserved in his best suit. He hadn't needed to wear a suit since he had retired from his job in accounts, but old habits die hard. He was never seen without sharp creases in his trousers, matched by a sharp, precise knot in his tie. At first glance, he looked younger than sixty-six, although slivers of silver gleamed in his thick hair. He spoke to no one. He wasn't one for conversation. He wasn't one for church, either. He was only here because he felt he should be. John hadn't been a 'friend' exactly, more of a companion. Since the death of John's wife, Maisie, Jack, the retired bachelor, and John, the widower, had often teamed up for cards, and the odd pint, just to pass away an evening or two. They didn't really talk, well, not about anything much. John hadn't been a man with a lot to say. They could sit in The Bull comfortably for an hour, and not feel the need for conversation at all. John had seldom mentioned Maisie, or adjusting to life without her. As Jack listened to the familiar words of the funeral service, he wondered whether John was happy now, to be with Maisie again. Somehow, he thought not.

Marriage had never really been an option for Jack. It wasn't that he avoided it, or wouldn't have liked the sense of belonging that he thought must be part of family life. It just never came his way. Did women frighten him? Jack considered this. Not 'frighten' exactly. They intrigued and confused him. Lately, well, for the last twenty years or so, he'd simply kept his distance. Until he left, he had found his accounting job in Ipswich much easier when he kept his door shut—quieter, more orderly. He liked figures. Reassuringly logical.

Jack glanced forward to look towards the three unfamiliar faces at the front of the church. There was an older man Jack had a feeling might have worked with John—his boss, perhaps, at the ironmongers in Stowmarket? Although John rarely spoke about his work, Jack felt he would have been very conscientious in all he did. Jack's gaze moved on to the other two visitors, a man and woman in their twenties. Relatives? John had never really mentioned his family.

It was over. The congregation stood to leave, respectfully allowing the newcomers to lead the way. By the time they reached the door, Clive, now out of his robes, was waiting for them.

'Thank you,' said the young woman. 'We spoke on the phone, I think. Mrs Monro, John's niece.'

Monro, thought Clive with relief. That was the name!

The young woman was still speaking. 'You made it very personal. It sounded as if you knew him quite well.'

'It's a small village, Mrs Monro, so we are inclined to live in each other's pockets. John liked to keep to himself, though, so this whole thing has taken us rather by surprise. He always seemed a fit man. A sad business. Had you seen him recently?'

'Well, no, I'm afraid we haven't. Uncle John was never one for visitors—and we live so far away. The trip from Yorkshire takes three hours, you know, so it's been difficult. I feel awful that we didn't make more of an effort now.'

She looked at her shoes, and in the awkward silence, her husband put his arm around her.

'Come on,' he said. 'Let's get started. There'll be a lot to do. Thank you again, Vicar. Goodbye.'

'Well,' said Mrs Hadlow, as she reached the church gate. 'That'll be his niece then. Come to clear up his things, I shouldn't wonder. It was his house, was it? Now, there's a thing. Whatever will happen to that house now? Poor man. So sad.' She took Ivy's arm, and together they set off down the lane, with George Hadlow, as quiet as a shadow, following dutifully behind.

'Oh, Charles!' Clive called out to the Church Warden as he emerged into the cool sunshine. 'Some news for you. Well, it might be news. Someone from the BBC rang, about doing a "Songs of Praise" from here. I'm just going over to ring her back now.'

At this news, Charles Waite, a large, imposing man, drew himself up until he seemed a whole inch taller.

'"Songs of Praise", eh?' His glasses sank further down his nose as he peered at Clive. 'Well, if that's the case, there's a lot we must take into consideration, a lot to discuss.'

He paused, looking at Clive.

'Would you prefer me to handle the call, Vicar? This really is a matter for the whole Parish Council, you know.'

'Kind of you to offer, Charles, but I can manage perfectly well, thank you. I'll let you know as soon as I hear more about it.'

'Straight away,' replied Charles. 'We'll need a meeting. It must be fully discussed.'

'What must?' Hearing mention of a meeting, Bunty Maddocks'

13

antennae were jangling. The round, beaming woman joined them, pulling her three-quarter length lilac-coloured jacket snugly around her. 'What must be discussed?'

'It seems,' said Charles, 'that the BBC plan to take over our church for a "Songs of Praise".'

Bunty's eyes widened, but before she could open her mouth to comment, Charles went on.

'As you know, I've had experience of television people before. This could be very disruptive. It needs careful handling. It's essential that the PCC are kept informed. We must lay down the ground rules.'

'Oh, but that's wonderful!' Bunty managed to squeeze in at last. 'Wonderful, exciting news! When? When will it be?' She turned to Clive.

'I don't know anything about it, until I get back and make that phone call to the producer. Do excuse me, won't you.'

'Well!' Bunty's eyes were shining, as she turned to Charles' wife, Betty, who had just come out of the church with her arms full of sheet music and hymn books. 'Did you hear that, Betty? "Songs of Praise"—it's coming here!'

'Not necessarily,' said Charles. 'It needs to be discussed.'

'Oh, but Betty, that means you'll be playing our organ on TV. Will they let you choose the hymns, do you think?'

'It's all to be decided. It needs to be discussed,' repeated Charles, and taking Betty firmly by the arm, he led the way home.'

'Thanks for ringing back', said Jan, when Clive introduced himself. Her Scots accent was quite pronounced, especially on the phone. 'I'd like to come and have a proper chat with you. Obviously, we're only putting out feelers at the moment, but we are planning to do a programme from somewhere in East Anglia, and I noticed your church when I was driving around the area a couple of days ago. Sandford is a beautiful village.'

'Well, we like it—and we'd certainly like to talk about your idea. Wednesday? Was that when you thought you might come?'

'That would be best for me,' Jan flicked through her diary. 'About three-ish?'

'Best day to choose. My afternoon off,' replied Clive. 'I'll get my wife to drum up something special for tea.'

10 February

The fact that Jan's glasses were perched on top of her dark, curly hair, as usual, didn't stop her slipping on her sunglasses too, as she turned the car off the main road towards Sandford. This first week in February had been dark and cold, until today, when at last it felt that Spring was really taking hold. Trees lined the way, their boughs shaking off the bareness of winter with new lime-green shoots. Then came fields, dotted with fat sheep, too busy chewing to notice the occasional car that passed by. Over the hedges, Jan could already see the tower of St Michael's, quite out of proportion with the squat, neat houses that mostly surrounded it—but then, that was one of the most appealing oddities of this corner of Suffolk. Back in the Middle Ages, when a thriving wool trade meant that times were good in East Anglia, the most telling sign of an area's prosperity was the grandness of its church. The more ornate the building, the more devout the locals must surely be—the higher the spire, the more likely they were to have the ear of God. Over the years, as the trade in wool became less important, thriving boom towns mellowed into pretty, quiet villages. Nowadays, all that remained of their former affluence was the church—a cathedral-like anachronism of days gone by.

As Jan's car turned into Sandford, St Michael's drew the eye. It filled the side of the High Street, as the road turned a right angle into the main part of the village. Standing at the back of the old graveyard, lined on either side by small pargeted houses in pinks and yellows, the solid grey walls and huge clear glass windows of St Michael's were impressive, and somehow moving. For Jan, who spent so much time in churches of all shapes, ages and persuasions, this was the very epitome of the English country church. For centuries, it had stood on that spot, marking out the Christian year, sharing joy and grief with its neighbours. How many of those neighbours would take a place in the pews on Sunday morning nowadays? Twenty, perhaps, in a building that could seat three hundred?

The vicarage was easy to find. Jan thought wryly of her two-up, two-down terraced cottage in Manchester, and decided that there was a lot to be said for becoming a vicar's wife. This house probably looked older than it was. A coat of paint might make it seem smarter, but it gave off an air of contented decline. No doubt it cost a fortune to heat, and the chimneys lolled at a charming angle—but if ever Jan found the elusive Mr Right, a house like this would do very nicely, thank you. She smiled to herself, as she gathered her bag and bits together. Mr Right! When was there ever time to find Mr Right, when she was constantly on the road, researching this programme, recording the next! If she met Mr Right, the chances are it would be in some far-flung, inaccessible corner of the country where their paths would never cross again! Working in television, and working on your love life—what an impossible mix!

What could she smell, sweet and earthy? Fancy a girl from the Borders not recognizing good fresh air when she met it? I need a holiday, she thought, as she locked the car. In fact, now she really looked at it, the garden was beautiful, even this early in Spring—mature, rambling and obviously loved. Someone had green fingers.

'Hello, need any help?'

The tall man in baggy brown trousers and wellingtons, appeared from round the side of the house, and could have been the gardener—except that the clerical collar at the neck of his black shirt gave him away.

'I'm not too early, am I? We did say three o'clock?'

His expression was blank for a moment before he came towards her, his hand outstretched.

'Miss Harding, of course, you must be Jan. Come to think of it, no one here has got a car that young!'

'A hire car, company issue,' Jan explained, as Clive caught sight of the mud stains on the sleeve of his jacket, and thought better of shaking hands. 'Better not do that. I've been digging, you see—first chance I've had this year. Come on round the back, to the kitchen. Keep to the path, I should!' And he strode off, leaving Jan to pick her way past the rockery, the bins and a rack of milk bottles, to the kitchen door.

Clive's wellies trailed clumps of dirt across the room, as he made for the kettle. 'Helen!' he called. 'Helen, she's here!'

Clive was on the point of opening a third tin, trying to remember which one held the tea bags, when a slim, fresh-faced woman came in. The overall impression you got from Clive's wife was that she was attractive. Her face was more interesting than pretty, framed by a sensible haircut which insisted on curling where it probably wasn't supposed to. Helen held out a hand to Jan, saying, 'I'm so sorry, I didn't expect you to arrive at this end of the house. Tell you what, why don't you two make yourselves comfortable in the front room, and I'll bring the tea in.'

She barely glanced at Clive's boots, but he got the message. He sat down heavily, pulling off first one, and then the other, as he asked, 'Long drive from Manchester? You haven't done it all this morning, have you?'

'Well, no. Actually, I stayed in Ipswich overnight. I think I mentioned to you that we know we want to make a programme somewhere in this area, but what we'd like to find is just the right church and village to base the programme in, a place that's really typical of life round here. We're still at the stage of searching for the right location, so I popped my nose around a couple of other churches on the way here.'

'Oh,' said Clive. It hadn't occurred to him that theirs wasn't the only church to be considered. 'Right, follow me.'

The front room was large, sunny, and packed full of chairs. Obviously, this room was used for more than just family evenings in front of the television. Everything from the Parish Council meetings to tea parties for the local lonely took place in this room, as Jan could tell from the shelves that lined one wall, stacked with assorted pamphlets, books and boxes of knitting. Clive directed her to a comfy, overstuffed armchair near the window, where she sat with a file unopened on her lap.

'How old is St Michael's?' she asked.

'The oldest part, around the altar end, dates back to the thirteenth century—sundry bits and pieces added on after that. The entrance porch is a youngster, built when Victoria was still a slip of a girl.'

'And how big is Sandford? How many people do you count among your congregation?'

'I have just over 800 potential parishioners on the books. Probably less than two hundred of them have ever been into the church for an act of worship, and that includes weddings, funerals and the Candlelit Service on Christmas Eve. I'd say perhaps a hundred would call themselves Christians, and about twenty of those would turn up regularly on a Sunday morning—thirty, if it's nice weather.'

'Do you have responsibility for any other churches besides St Michael's?'

'Well, I take a service on the first Sunday each month at the little church in Dinton—that's about a mile and a half up the road. There are only half a dozen or so houses in Dinton. It's such a nice church, though, that often the service there is quite popular.'

'You don't happen to have a picture of that church, do you?'

'Um, let me think. Hold on, Helen will know.' He stood up, and just outside the door, shouted, 'Darling! Have we a photo of Dinton Church anywhere?'

'I am sure we have,' came the reply. 'If I can lay my hands on one, I'll bring it in with the tea.'

Dinton Church. Have we got any snapshots of it? Helen rummaged through the kitchen table drawer, pulling out packs of photos, trying to remember. Egg rolling on Good Friday last year. Weren't there some pictures from that? Dinton Church stood on the only decent hill around these parts, and it was a favourite tradition for children to race eggs down the slope. But were there only pictures of the green, or was the church included too?

The buzzer on the cooker went. The scones were ready. Homemade, yes, but not by her. These had been left over from the Coffee and Cakes Stall at the Christmas Fayre, ably run, as usual, by the ladies of the parish, under the sergeant-like management of

Bunty Maddocks. Helen pretended not to notice their understanding looks when she agreed to keep the leftovers in her freezer. A vicar's wife who was hopeless at baking? They probably prayed for her!

Found one! A grinning group of youngsters standing at the church porch, clutching eggs lovingly decorated with smiley faces and go-faster stripes. And she found another in the same pack of the altar at Dinton, with the stunning arrangement of catkins that had been so eye-catching. Bunty, and the team of flower arrangers she organized like clockwork, had excelled themselves with that.

She buttered the last of the scones, and placed them on the tray with the photos and tea things. She was halfway out of the kitchen when she remembered the jam. She could never imagine herself making jam, but she was always glad to accept presents from others who could. She opened the cupboard, its top shelf overflowing with jars of pickles, lemon curd and marmalade. Strawberry, she decided, and picking up the tray, she made her way towards the front room.

'This programme would be part of our special Lent series, "Village Praise",' Jan was explaining as Helen walked in. 'We did the same thing last year, and it was really very popular. The whole idea is quite complicated from our point of view, though. You see, "Songs of Praise" has a large production team based in Manchester, who work together in small groups on each individual programme. The technical teams are quite separate though, and may not come from Manchester at all, but from the most convenient base for Outside Broadcast vehicles and technicians. That means that often, both the production and the technical teams working on "Songs of Praise" one week, may well be completely different from the team working on the following week's programme.

'But "Village Praise" is unusual, because for six weeks, the same unit are on the road all the time, working their way around the country from village to village. And last year, that meant a huge circle around the British Isles, covering Wales, Scotland, the North-East coast, and several other places around England.'

'How many people make up a unit?' Helen asked as she put the tray down.

'Well, I suppose there would be about twenty technical people, probably with about three or four large trucks carrying equipment and cabling—and on the production side, let me see...' Jan counted people off. 'There would be me, and my Production Assistant; a researcher; a director to take charge of the interviews and shots of the area; our Musical Director—oh, and the presenter, of course.'

'Gracious me, I had no idea it was such a big operation.' Clive reached for the tray. 'Scone?'

'Not for me, thanks—and no milk in the tea either.' Helen handed Jan the cup, saying nothing.

A sudden appalling thought struck Clive. 'Lent. That starts in two weeks' time.' He relaxed back with a plate of scones balanced on his knee. 'You'll be thinking about us for next year then.'

'No. For Palm Sunday this year actually. A programme to be made during the first week of April, and transmitted on the Sunday, 4th.'

The scone never reached Clive's mouth. He thought for a while before speaking. 'Things move rather slowly around here. I'm not sure that we'd have anything to offer you with so little notice.'

'Well, don't worry too much about that. We're used to organizing these things, and will just need your help to draw together local support, and all the individual elements we need. What you have readily available here is what we need most—a beautiful village, a lovely old church, an area steeped in history, and a local community that must include a few people who have interesting experiences to share, about how their faith has helped them through various aspects of their lives.'

It was Helen who spoke first. 'You know, Jan, we're not a large congregation here. What about the singing? Our choir, if you can call our handful of ladies that—well, they're very enthusiastic...'

'But their style is quite... free, shall we say?' finished Clive. 'Betty, our organist, is excellent, of course, and can handle anything you throw at her—including choir pieces,' he added loyally, 'but she's not...'

'Look, don't worry about that yet. We'll be bringing along our own music expert from the very start, to identify talent in the area, and make sure that the quality of the singing and the music is good enough to keep people entertained at peak viewing time on a Sunday evening.'

Helen and Clive looked at each other. 'Peak time? How many

people are likely to be watching the programme?'

'Viewing figures are usually quite high while the evenings are still dark. About six, seven million, I should think.'

'Right.' Clive sounded doubtful.

'Let's take it a step at a time,' said Jan. 'First, can I have a look around the church? After all, when you're planning to bring in four big cameras, scaffolding to put up the lights, and yards of cabling, it may well be that the church simply isn't the right size or shape to cope.'

'Certainly.' Clive was at the door, before he remembered that he was still in his socks. 'Let me just find some shoes, and I'll join you and Helen in the church in a minute or two.'

The school bus dropped Anna off at the end of the main street, and as she walked past the church gate, she saw her godmother, Helen, and another woman she didn't recognize, slightly built, with glasses perched on the top of her dark curls. She waved, but Helen was deep in conversation, and didn't notice her.

Anna's bag was heavy—lots of homework tonight, too much when there were so many other things she'd rather have time for. Mum was forever nagging about GCSEs coming up, and how she should be thinking about what she wanted to do with herself. Well, she had always known what she wanted to be, and a fat lot of good that did her. Mum didn't think singing was a 'proper job'. Tough, that's what she was going to do anyway—and GCSEs never made any difference once you'd made your first hit record. She'd even write the song herself. You got more money if you did that.

'Hey, Anna!' She didn't turn round. She thought she'd missed him this evening. Too bad.

'Anna, wait!'

'I'm in a hurry, Matthew. Can't stop, sorry.'

Matthew was level with her now, and finding it difficult to hang onto his bag as he ran. 'You're going home, aren't you?'

Anna said nothing.

'Well, I'm going the same way. That's alright, isn't it?'

Anna looked straight ahead as she walked.

'Oh, for heaven's sake, Anna, what's got into you?'

Anna came to a sudden halt, then turned to look at him. 'Look, Matthew, it's no big deal. You're my neighbour, that's all, so stop trying to play big brother, OK? I can walk home by myself. I can look after myself. I like to choose my own company—and you bug me. Right? Now, please, just push off.'

Matthew laughed. With an expression she hoped was one of total indifference, she turned on her heel, and stomped off.

As Helen switched on the church lights, Jan was already walking down the side aisle, obviously deep in thought. Daylight poured through the ornate windows, spilling onto the high wooden pews which gleamed rich red. She looked up to the ceiling of the church. It was a simple criss-cross arrangement of dark beams against a pale painted wooden roof. Where each beam met the wall, a different figure had been carved and painted—angels, cherubs, faces that seemed to grimace more than smile. They would look lovely bathed in light for the close-ups. There was definite potential here.

Jan looked at the width of the aisles—plenty of room there, not just for the cameras to trundle up and down taking pictures of people singing in the pews, but they could tuck cameras out of sight too, for long shots of the congregation. And the gallery arrangement at the back, where the bells were obviously rung, would be just right for one camera to take a complete picture of the whole event. Not bad at all.

'What about the organ? Is that in reasonable shape?'

Clive had appeared at her elbow. 'Well, I'm not much of a judge. It's always seems fine to me. What do you think, Helen?'

'I think,' answered Jan, 'that it would be a good idea for me to come along to the service here next Sunday morning, so that I can hear the organ for myself. And do you think it would be a good time to arrange a get-together for all interested parties? Obviously, we would want to involve members of other churches in the area—all denominations, that is. Could you help me out with names and phone numbers I might need for that?'

Clive looked at Helen, who said, 'I've got all those handy at home. We can draw up a list before you go. And I reckon that as soon as possible after the service on Sunday would suit most people.' Clive nodded in agreement. 'Shall we say, eleven o'clock, at the vicarage?'

'What time does your service start, then?' enquired Jan.

'Half past nine.'

Oh heck, thought Jan. There goes my lie-in.

Helen and Clive both stood at the door to see Jan drive away, her folder now fat with leaflets on St Michael's, a couple of back copies of the Parish Magazine (one of them featuring the article on the history of Sandford that Charles Waite had written with painstaking accuracy), the local newspaper, and the diocesan handbook listing a host of numbers and addresses she might need—and many she definitely would not.

It was only as she closed the door, that Helen realized that the photos of Dinton Church were still on the tray—and that she had no idea why, if Jan was seriously interested in St Michael's, she should have been so curious to know more about a tiny little place like Dinton.

Jan didn't drive straight out of the village. She parked a few hundred yards along the main street, glad to see that the local store was open. It was a shop that defied precise description. Outside, a display of brightly coloured primulas (59p each, or 4 for £2) fought for space alongside magazines, papers, huge bags of potatoes, homemade bird tables, and a large bin for ice cream papers. Every inch of the shop window seemed to be covered, with handwritten postcards advertising pushchairs for sale, or domestic help wanted. There were larger posters too—a notice about a new martial arts club starting up at a nearby village; a bingo night at The Bull, to raise money for Stowmarket Hospice; and, most colourful of all, an unmissable reminder that a few tickets still remained for 'West Side Story', being performed by the Saxmundham Songsters the following week.

As Jan pushed open the door, a bell jangled. A lady working behind the grid of a tiny Post Office counter, looked up and said, 'Just give me a yell when you're ready!' and carried on working. Jan glanced around. There were toys and stationery at one end, next to knitting patterns and wool, fresh vegetables, tinned stuff, bread, free-range eggs and postcards. Sweets were near the cakes and pies at the counter, and cigarettes, medicines and a very small selection of spirits, wines and beers were neatly stacked where they could only be reached by the person serving.

'Do you need any help?' A smiling, middle-aged man came out from the door behind the counter, obviously modelling one of the more homely knitting patterns they sold in the shop.

'Well, yes,' replied Jan. 'You don't have such a thing as a guidebook, do you? Either about Sandford, or about the area in general?'

'Now you're asking!' grinned the man. 'Joan—guidebooks? Have we got any?'

The lady behind the counter looked up. 'Wrong time of year really. Don't get many visitors here until a bit later on.' The bell jangled again. Anna banged the door moodily as she walked in, hitching her school bag higher up on to her shoulder.

'Hello, love,' said the man, 'good day?'

'Not really,' replied Anna, not stopping to look at him.

'If you're going upstairs,' said Joan, 'would you have a look in the cupboard and see if there are any guidebooks there from last summer for this lady?'

Anna kept walking.

'Oh, and a street map of the village, and the area round about. Is there such a thing?' Jan asked.

'They should be up there too, Anna. Be a love and take a look for me, will you?'

Anna glared at her mother, shrugged, and went through the back.

'I think that means yes,' said Joan. 'Honestly, Don, is it me? Am I not speaking English, or something?'

'Teenagers!' Don pulled a comical face at Jan. 'You know what they're like.'

25

Like they could do with a quick clip round the ear, thought Jan.

'Doing a bit of travelling then, are you?' Don asked, opening up a new display box of crisps as he spoke. 'On holiday?'

'That would be nice', smiled Jan. 'But no, it's work, I'm afraid.'

'Hey, you're not the lady from the BBC, are you? The one from "Highway"?'

'Well, from "Songs of Praise"—and news does travel fast! However did you know that?'

'Oh, it's a small place. My next door neighbour does a bit of singing with Betty Waite, the organist. Her husband is Chairman of the Parish Council—well, I think he is the Parish Council really. You probably met him, I expect. Charles Waite?'

'No, I'm just talking to the vicar at this stage.'

Joan chuckled. 'Charles won't like that one bit.'

Don laughed. 'So, have you decided then? Are you going to do a programme from here?'

'Well, I've got a bit of sorting out, and ringing around to do. It's a bit early to say yet, but it's looking quite possible, I should say.'

'That should ruffle a few feathers,' Joan said. 'Wait till certain people around here get to know that there'll be television cameras coming to the village.'

'What cameras?' Anna threw a book and map on the counter, and looked at Joan.

'"Songs of Praise"—it might be coming here. This lady is involved with it.'

Anna looked at Jan coolly. 'Sounds pretty boring to me,' she said, and disappeared into the back of the shop.

14 February

The clock on the mantelpiece was just striking eight-thirty, as Betty Waite pulled her coat on. 'Bye then. I'll see you later.'

Charles flicked the Sunday paper moodily, his lips drawn tightly together.

'Charles?' Betty moved towards him.

'I'll be there at quarter past nine, as usual. And you're a fool, Betty, to be doing anything out of the usual yourself.' Charles' eyes didn't leave the newspaper.

'Look,' explained Betty patiently, 'I'm just popping in early to have a spot of a practice—if I'm going to be playing something a bit special and new on the organ, what's wrong with getting some practice in? I enjoy it anyway.'

'Going in early has got nothing whatsoever to do with you enjoying practice. It's simply to impress that BBC woman when she comes this morning—and it's ridiculous.'

'Why should it be ridiculous to try and make the best impression we can? I simply don't want to let the church down.'

'And running around, trying to get the choir to sing something that's really beyond them? I've never heard such rubbish.' Charles snorted, his eyes still firmly focused on the newspaper.

'Look, Charles, they wanted to try something special. It's not often that we have any visitors to listen to us. We've had fun. We've enjoyed it. It's all been so hurried, and we don't expect to work miracles. We just want to do our very best for the church. Now, what on earth's wrong with that?'

'I'll tell you what's wrong.' Finally, Charles laid down the paper, and with the condescending tone of a parent ticking off a truculent child, he said, 'Number One—there will be no decision about whether "Songs of Praise" can come here, until the whole Parish Council has agreed. No formal application has been made, so no decision can be taken. Number Two—if, and when, it is agreed that a programme can be made here, then it must be on our terms. We make the decisions. Number Three—if the BBC plan to feature Sandford and its church in a programme, then obviously, our choir and organist will be the centrepiece. It's no use pretending to be something more than a village choir. That's the essential charm of it. We are what we are—and it is sheer foolishness to pretend to be something we're not!'

Betty stared at Charles, whose face had become redder and redder as he spoke. There was silence for a while, and then she said, 'You know, sometimes, Charles, I don't understand you at all.' She started for the door, hesitated, and turned back to look at him. 'There's another cup of tea in the pot, if you'd like one. See you about quarter past nine then.' And the bang of the front door echoed around the house, as Charles glared once again at his paper.

It's a funny thing about Sunday mornings, thought Jack Diggens as he put the kettle on in his small kitchen. Mostly, he enjoyed living on his own. He had a routine that was comfortable, and comforting. He was happy to be alone. But somehow, Sunday mornings were the only time when he was aware of feeling lonely. He thought of families having breakfast, husbands and wives listening to the radio, chatting over Sunday papers at the table, doing the washing up. He thought of them talking over their day together—and he thought of his own day, looming ahead. He had planned nothing for today. And the worst thing of all was that nobody minded one way or another that he had nothing planned. If he'd popped off during the night, there was no one who would really notice or care. No one at all.

What a morbid thought! Jack dropped an egg into the pan of boiling water, and wondered why such thoughts had struck him this morning. It was John, of course. This time last week, he'd still been alive, and at Sunday lunchtime, they'd sat in The Bull having a drink together. And now, he was gone, just like that. As if he never was.

Was it just the loss of a friend—well, an occasional friend—that had prompted this feeling of—what was it he was feeling? Was it just loneliness? No, more than that. It was a sort of—emptiness. Yes, that was it—as if he were just like the shell of the egg he was watching, bubbling away in the pan—a shell that enclosed nothing, hid nothing, felt nothing. Nothing—that's what I am—nothing and nobody.

Jack sat down heavily, staring ahead of him. Thoughts tumbled together in his mind. He was just feeling sorry for himself. Of course, he was somebody—well, he'd certainly been somebody when he was working. His accounts had been crucial to the smooth running of the firm. People relied on him. He'd been an important cog in the wheel then.

And now? Now he was retired? Now, he spent all his time in the village that, for several years, had simply been the home he'd commuted from, into Ipswich every day. While he'd been working, he'd never been around during the week to socialize—and at weekends, apart from the odd trip to The Bull, where he'd met John, he'd been happy to potter round the house. And things hadn't changed that much in the year since he'd retired. Keeping to himself had become a habit, and because of it, he had met very few people in Sandford, and really knew no one well at all.

He picked up the egg spoon, and began to draw neat square patterns on top of the sugar in the bowl. Why hadn't he got any friends, then? Didn't he need them? Is that why he hadn't made more of an effort to get to know his neighbours? He thought back to the people who had been in the church for John's funeral. He recognized most of them by sight, but had probably never said more than 'good morning' to them. And these were people who cared enough about John, to come along to his funeral—people that he had that much, at least, in common with; people he had shared sadness with, and yet never bothered to speak to. Striking up conversation took courage—and small talk. He had always lacked the first, and was hopeless at the other.

The timer rang on the cooker. His egg was ready. He glanced up to the clock, and saw that it was a few minutes past nine. At half past nine, the Sunday morning service would start, and people would gather in the church again. Without really thinking about it, he simply knew that he would like to be with them. Until John's funeral, he hadn't been to a church service for years, since his mother was alive. After today, he might never go again. But this morning, his search for comfort and company would take him to St Michael's, for the second time in one week.

Mrs Hadlow, her friend Ivy clutching on to her arm, was just reaching the church porch, when the sound of slamming car doors and unfamiliar voices caught her attention. 'That'll be them, then. The people from the BBC!' Ivy peered round and stared pointedly at the newcomers, without comment. The two of them made their way to their usual seats, collecting hymn books, and a sheet of notices, as they went.

The casual, fashionable dress, and the unfamiliar faces, of the four people who followed them into the church drew curious glances, and whispered comments. The lady who led the small party, a pair of glasses prised in amongst her tight, dark curls, smiled towards the vicar's wife, before all four took their places towards the back of the church. Jan had brought three key colleagues with her for this Sunday service—Sue, her Production Assistant, Simon Martin, the Engineering Manager, whose responsibility it would be to plan and oversee the rigging and lighting of the church, and Frank Harris, the Sound Supervisor.

In less than a week's time, the 'Village Praise' caravan of vans, technicians, and production staff would be taking to the road for the first programme in the series coming from Somerset. One of Jan's colleagues, another producer from the 'Songs of Praise' team, was already hard at work in Somerset, setting up interviews and sorting out ideas, which would be pulled together for transmission in two weeks' time. The schedule would be relentless. In a different village each week, the vans, technicians and the presenter would rehearse and record a programme that not only highlighted the community and spiritual life of the area, but also captured the events, the weather and the topics of the previous seven days. The programme would be edited in a van parked in the village, and the finished product would be shared with six or seven million viewers the following Sunday evening. By that time, though, the team would have moved on to the next village on their list—they would gather around a TV in their new hotel, to watch their programme about last week's location, before getting down to the more immediate business of sorting out how to capture the essence of this week's village in the programme they'd start work on the following morning.

At an office meeting on Friday morning, Jan had reported on her search for a location in Suffolk, which would be for the last programme in the series, to be transmitted on Palm Sunday. Sandford was ideal, not just because St Michael's was such a splendid church, but because it reflected the feel of the whole area so well. There was plenty of potential for variety there—agriculture, and farming people; the Suffolk Heritage Coast close by, with its tourism and fishing industry (what was left of it); plenty of rich history and glorious countryside. Yes, everyone agreed—this could be a lovely programme.

The congregation stood for the first hymn, as a small procession, with Clive Linton at the rear, made its way down the aisle. Jan didn't sing. She couldn't. Anyway, she was too busy listening—to the organ (not bad, needs tuning), the organist (nice lady, but not good enough, definitely needs replacing) and the singing (well, a full church would add volume, harmonies would add depth, a good conductor would add style and feel—careful placing of microphones would probably do the rest).

Simon, the Engineering Manager, wasn't singing either. His practised eyes were scanning the building. Where could he put the lights? How would he fix them up there? Then he considered the shape of the church. Where could they get a camera up high, so that it had a clear view of the whole congregation? Was there space for the other cameras to hide, when that long shot was being taken? Would the pillars get in the way? Quite a nice church really. Nice warm colours, and dark corners which could add mood and subtlety when they were lit properly. Yes, he thought, it would be fine, but the final decisions would have to be discussed with the director of the outside broadcast. At that moment, it was not totally certain which director it would be. Perhaps Jan would have more news on that today.

Standing beside Simon, the Sound Supervisor, Frank Harris didn't even pick up his hymn book, because the words didn't interest him. He was no stranger to churches—he loved them, but not because he was remotely sympathetic to the content of any service. No, it was the acoustics that drew him. Churches were always too high, too empty, too full of bare stone walls to ever make a Sound Supervisor's job straightforward—but nobody enjoyed a challenge like Frank. This one wouldn't be easy. All those pillars, the choir pews so far away from the rest of the congregation, those enormous grey walls, and its ceiling so high you could barely see the top of it. He'd tell Jan when he had the chance, this church was hardly suitable from a Sound point of view at all. Still, if that was what she wanted, she must accept that he and his team could only do their best. To get decent results from this barn of a building would take skill, hard work and serious planning. He couldn't wait to get started...

As Production Assistant, Sue's job was to work with Jan, taking note of all the decisions made, and organizing the details that would make the production run smoothly. Sue had always loved being in church, and if she couldn't be at her usual service in Salford this morning, this was the next best thing. 'Praise My Soul, the King of Heaven' was one of her favourite hymns, and she joined in with enthusiasm.

Jack Diggens sat at the far end of one of the pews, hoping no one would notice how he struggled to find his place in the Service Book. He kept his head bowed, and looked at no one. He barely heard the sermon. The words floated over him. He felt awkward and alone. If he had been overwhelmed with loneliness this morning, at least that was in private. What on earth had possessed him to come here, where his ignorance and nervousness would be obvious to everyone, his embarrassment on show for all to see? He was going to leave. He was going to leave at the first possible opportunity, but his way out was blocked by four people he didn't recognize at all, sitting by the aisle. As soon as he could, he would make his escape.

Suddenly, he was aware that people were moving. He heard someone call him, and he turned to see that the people in his row were standing in the aisle, looking at him, waiting for him to lead the way down to the altar. There was no escape. He couldn't push them aside, and make a bolt for the door at the back of the church. He found himself carried forward, joining the queue, following blindly until he sank on his knees at the altar rail.

His head fell on to his clasped hands. He sensed rather than heard the voice of the minister, as he moved along the line. 'The body of Christ.' 'The blood of Christ.' The words swam in his mind. He felt hot, his hands were shaking. He looked up as the vicar stood in front of him, placing the silver cup to his lips. 'The blood of Christ keep you in eternal life.'

And as Jack drank, a stillness draped itself over him, like a warm, familiar mantle. Dear God, he was home!

'Jan!' Clive finally greeted her, as the last few members of congregation filed out of the church door. 'We're all set up. Some of the people you need to meet might already be at the vicarage. Others have got services to finish first, of course, so they'll be here when they can. Do you want to come over to the house with me now?'

Jan smiled. 'Let me just introduce you to some of the other members of our team—my PA, Sue—you'll probably end up talking to her quite a lot; Simon Martin, our Engineering Manager; and Frank—that's him up near the altar now—Frank is the Sound Supervisor.'

'You're all welcome, very welcome—oh, and Charles, Charles, I'd like you to meet Jan Harding, the "Songs of Praise" producer. Charles is Church Warden here—and Chairman of the Parish Council—a tremendous help to me in every way.' Charles said nothing, and barely slowed down on his way to the door. 'You're coming to our meeting, of course, Charles?'

Charles stopped. 'Is it starting now?'

Clive looked at Jan, who answered, 'Well, if you don't mind, we could do with a proper look round in here, just to sort out what will work for us, and what problems we'll have to take into account. About quarter of an hour? Will that be alright?'

Charles snorted impatiently, as he turned on his heel. 'Well, the quicker the better. For *some* of us, Sunday is an extremely busy day.'

While Jan and her colleagues took their time looking around the church, Helen slipped home to pop on the coffee for the meeting. When eventually she saw them walking down the path with Clive, she opened the back door, and headed towards the church for her usual job of locking up, and making sure that everything was switched off. It wasn't until her final glance around the building, that she became aware of a quiet figure sitting by the window, at the end of one of the pews.

She suddenly felt guilty, that she had been clattering around noisily, without noticing the man, obviously deep in prayer. This was a dilemma. How long would he be likely to stay? They hadn't felt able to leave the church door unlocked for some years now, and she really had to get on this morning.

Making as little sound as possible, Helen walked slowly back up the aisle. The man didn't move. She drew level with him, and tactfully cleared her throat. There was no response. She recognized him now, from the odd occasion when she had passed him in the High Street, or stood beside him in the shop. Jack, she thought his name was— he came to John's funeral earlier in the week, but really she didn't know him well. She could never remember him coming along to a Sunday Service before. Quietly, curiously, she made her way along the pew in front of his, until she stood near him. He wasn't praying. He wasn't doing anything. He simply stared down in front of him, his eyes blank and unseeing.

'Jack?' Please, let me have remembered his name right. 'Jack? Are you alright?'

Slowly, he turned his gaze towards her—and then past her, to the empty church. 'Oh, I'm sorry. I'm sorry, so sorry...'

'No need to be. It's just that I nearly locked you in, you were sitting here so quietly. Are you OK?'

Jack very nearly smiled. 'Stupid, really,' he said at last. 'It's taken me years to get back inside a church—and now, I can't leave. Stupid. You must think me very stupid.'

'No, not at all.'

There was an uneasy silence, neither quite sure what to say next. Finally, it was Helen who asked, 'You used to go to church then? Not this one?'

'No, nowhere near here. It was years ago, when my mother was alive. When she was ill, for a couple of years before the end, she would get very upset if she couldn't get to church—and the only way she could get there was if I took her. It was for her that I went, not me. I didn't go for myself.'

'But you stayed with her, during the service?'

'Not at first. I used to drop her off, and then just pick her up again at the end. But then, when things got worse for her, she found it so painful to walk, painful to sit in those pews too. I'd watch her struggle up the path to the church, see how difficult it was for her to get up the steps, and I'd wonder why on earth she bothered. All I knew was that her visit to church each Sunday was the most important part of her week, and it became more and more important to her—as if she was terrified that if she stopped going there, God would forget her, and then what would happen? She knew she hadn't long to go. I used to kid her about it, used to tell her that it was a kind of insurance for her, that she was building up Brownie points for when she reached the Pearly Gates, just to make sure she'd get in!'

Helen said nothing, glancing quickly at her watch, as she settled herself on to the seat in front of him. He wasn't looking at her. His eyes stared, seeing nothing.

'But she got so frail, I just couldn't leave her, so I didn't have a choice, did I? I had to go. I remember that first time, when I went in with her, I sat holding her hand, and watching her face as she listened. And then I held her as she struggled up to the altar rail—and her face, well, I'll never forget the look on her face. You know, pain does cruel things to a person's face. I could always tell when it was bad for her. It wasn't that she said anything—I could just see it in her expression. But as she looked up from the altar rail, to take the bread and wine—well, it was as if the pain just dropped away from her, as if for those few moments, the burden was lifted. I didn't know what to make of it really. I didn't know what to think.'

'Did you ever talk to her about it?'

'Oh yes. I asked her why she insisted going when it was obviously so difficult for her. Why bother going up for Communion? Surely she could say her prayers just as easily sitting in her seat? Why on earth did she love it so much? And I'll never forget what she said. 'It's not

my love that's important. It's when I receive the Body and Blood that
I know God loves *me*. I just know it. I feel it." That's what she said—
and I remember looking at her, and not being able to think of a word
to say.'

Suddenly, Jack turned his head to look intently at Helen.

'I never took Communion myself, of course. It all seemed a bit
melodramatic to me. When I went up with Mum, well, I just turned
my head away, so that the vicar would know I wasn't interested. I was
just there for her. And then, one day, it wasn't the usual chap—can't
remember why. I took Mum up to the rail as usual, and I remember I
was looking at her face as he offered her the wine—and then he
looked at me, and his eyes sort of locked on to mine. I just couldn't
look away—it sounds ridiculous, doesn't it? I just watched him as he
put his hand on my head, and blessed me—and the whole of my
body came alive at his touch. It was as if it burned me—like an
electric shock, but not painful, not unpleasant at all. I was stunned,
shaken. I remember that I didn't want to move. I remember suddenly
becoming aware that Mum was looking at me, wondering why I
wasn't helping her up. I remember it all so clearly.'

Jack fell silent. Helen thought of all the visitors waiting at the
house, and said nothing.

'Well, that was how it began. After that, I started going along to the
services, because I wanted to. I wanted to learn, wanted to know as
much as I could. The vicar there, he was great really. I even went along
to his Confirmation Classes—I think I was the only one in the class
over the age of fifteen, but I didn't care. I just wanted to understand
and learn. And after that, taking Communion became one of the great
joys of my life—and honestly, there wasn't much joy in my life around
then, because Mum was so ill. It broke my heart to see how she
suffered—a long, degrading illness that sapped her strength, her will,
her very self out of her body. I watched her as she faded away from
me, day by day. And even then, the end for her wasn't peaceful. She
haemorrhaged on the floor of the loo, and died screaming in agony
and fear. And I did nothing, I could do nothing for her. I just watched
and cried and felt useless until it was over. Where was her loving God
then? If he loved her, why let her suffer such pain and indignity?
Suddenly, it was crystal clear to me. She suffered because there was

no God. It was all an illusion. It wasn't true, and I had deceived myself into believing it.'

'We had Mum's funeral in the church, because that was what she would have wanted. But I never set foot in the building again—nor any other, until this week.'

'How long ago did your Mum die?' Helen asked.

'Eighteen years.'

'So, what made you come here this week, after all that time?'

'Duty, really. John didn't have many folk to mourn him, did he? I just felt he would like me to be there. And a funeral would be safe enough. I mean, you can just watch, can't you—you don't have to get involved.'

'But, why this morning then? What made you come back again for a Eucharist Service like this one?'

'I don't know,' Jack answered bleakly. 'Loneliness mostly, I think. Curiosity, perhaps. I just thought it would be alright.'

'And it wasn't?'

'I meant to just sit and watch. I didn't mean to join in. I don't know quite what happened really, except that suddenly everyone was waiting for me to lead the line down to the altar, and I didn't know how to say I wouldn't, I couldn't go, I didn't want to... And then, suddenly...'

'Yes?' Helen prompted gently.

'Suddenly, it happened again—just like it happened when that vicar put his hand on my head all those years ago—that feeling of peace and power—I felt small and wrong—and I knew that it didn't matter, it had never mattered to God—He had been there all the time, just waiting for me to come back.'

'And now?'

'And now, I don't know.'

'Would you pop round to the vicarage later, and have a chat with Clive, my husband?'

'Perhaps. I'm not very good at "chatting" with people. I'm not very sure what I'd say. I mean, he's a professional, isn't he. He'll probably think all this sounds round the twist. He'll think I'm just a rambling old fool,' he smiled wryly, 'which I probably am.'

'I don't,' replied Helen.

'Ah, but you are a very good listener.'

'Then, pop round to the vicarage some time, and have a cup of tea with me. You'll always be welcome—really.'

Jack slowly pulled himself to his feet. 'Thank you. Maybe I will. But what I'd really like now is to go home.' As he reached the end of the pew, he turned to her again. 'Perhaps I'll see you then. And—thanks, just for—well, you know.' And he walked towards the door.

'What do you mean—other singers?'

Charles Waite's voice echoed down the hall as Helen reached the vicarage. She hurried towards the kitchen, only to find that the ladies of the parish, in the shape of Bunty Maddocks and Mrs Hadlow, had already staked their claim to her kettle. Two trays were neatly laid out with cups, milk, sugar and biscuits.

'Seeing as you weren't here, dear, we really thought we ought to get on. Never mind, we've just about organized everything now.' Milking cups as she spoke, Mrs Hadlow barely glanced at Helen. 'We had a terrible job finding the biscuits—you must have run out. I've put a note on your shopping list on the wall, that you need some more. By the way, did you know that one of your cups is cracked? Of course not, or you'd have thrown it away—all those germs! Anyway, it's in the bin now, all wrapped in newspaper. Hold that door open for me, would you, dear—we'll just take these in for you.'

'Oh, Helen—isn't this exciting?' Bunty enthused, squeezing both the tray, and her ample hips, through the door, as she marched towards the front room. Helen leant back against the kitchen table, silently counted to ten—and followed Bunty towards the front room.

'You see,' Jan was saying, 'this programme will be going out on BBC1 at peak time on a Sunday evening. It has to be pleasing in every way—inspiring, of course, but entertaining, informative—a visual and musical feast, that can be enjoyed by all sorts of viewers, for all sorts of reasons. It's all about ratings, I'm afraid. "Songs of Praise" may have been in this slot for more than thirty years, but tradition alone won't keep people watching, unless the quality of what they see is high enough. And if the number of viewers drops, then there's always the danger that the programme will be shifted to another, less accessible slot—perhaps some time during the day on Sunday, when a lot of the people who would like to watch it might be at church anyway!'

'But surely, whatever programme ideas you come up with, you will hardly influence ratings one way or another,' said the hugely overweight, bespectacled Methodist minister, Norman Oates. '"Songs of Praise" will only ever appeal to Christians, mostly in the more elderly age group. What they want is what they've always had—the predictable "Songs of Praise" format?'

'Well,' replied Jan, shaking her head to Mrs Hadlow's offer of tea, 'six million or so people often choose to watch "Songs of Praise". Compare that to the number of people who might be in church on a Sunday morning—how many would that be? A million and a half, perhaps two? So, it's not just churchgoing Christians who are watching. A lot of them may be elderly, perhaps people who find it difficult to get along to church nowadays, who think of the programme as a kind of fellowship. But what about the others? Our research shows that people tune in for all sorts of reasons—because the hymns are familiar, and they enjoy singing along; because they enjoy hearing people talking about how their faith helps them through difficult patches in their lives; because they love looking at beautiful scenes around the country from the comfort of their own armchair. And it's not just elderly people who watch, by any means. We don't want to have only elderly viewers in our audience, any more than you want only elderly people in your churches. We have to make programmes that appeal to everyone.'

'I repeat,' Charles said, his back ramrod-straight in his chair, 'what do you mean by other singers?'

Jan removed her glasses from the top of her head, and popped them on her nose, as she eyed Charles, recognizing a potential enemy in the camp. She'd come across people like Charles on countless programmes in the past. He was used to being in charge. If he wasn't calling the tune, he'd cancel the party! It was important to win him over, to get his support from the very start.

'We will need to find the very best voices from around this area, to create a special choir for the programme. Above all, our viewers expect the standard of music and singing to be the very highest possible, and...'

'And this is a small village,' continued Charles. 'Its very charm is its smallness. Our choir is small—but it's excellent. It has an excellent leader. If you are going to capture the essence of Sandford on television, then you must show it honestly. We would have to consider our position very carefully, if you think you are going to bring in outsiders, and pass them off as if they come from Sandford. I don't think so, Miss Harding—I really don't think so.'

'I must stress to you all,' Jan said, taking off her glasses again, so that she couldn't see the cold stare coming from Charles' direction, 'that the programme we are planning is about this *area*. We have chosen Sandford in which to base our outside broadcast, because it is conveniently placed, it's very interesting, extremely picturesque—and it's typical in many ways of several of the villages around here. Apart from the resources and talents we find in Sandford itself, we will have to draw on the surrounding area too—for our pictures, for our interviewees, for our musicians, for our singers, and probably for our congregation too.'

'Do you mean to say that the people of this parish, the people who actually live in Sandford, may not be able to get into their own church for the recording, because preference will be given to people from outside?' Charles' face was growing steadily redder, as his spectacles slipped menacingly down his nose.

'What I mean, Mr Waite, is that the church must be full on the night, not with people who come along just because the cameras are there—but because they are regular members of church congregations in the area, and they are taking part because they consider it to be an act of worship that they are sharing with our audience of viewers. Tickets will be printed, and distributed fairly around churches of all denominations, providing they're near enough to come along. In fact, distribution of tickets is one of the things we must talk about in detail this morning...'

'Musicians, too? You're planning to bring in musicians from outside?' Charles was relentless, too incensed to allow Jan to change the subject.

'We'd love to use local musicians, providing their standard of playing is high enough. If necessary, we will cast our net further afield, particularly if specialist instruments of any kind are required. We have a first class musical team who will sort all that out. Our Musical

Director, Ian Spence, will oversee the whole series. He usually prefers to work with a professional organist, someone who is based reasonably locally—because the work load, and the level of music required, is so heavy and demanding. And Ian'll be writing any special arrangements we need throughout the 'Village Praise' series—and, of course, he always conducts. That makes most sense, really, when he knows the music so well.' Without knowing it, Jan opened and shut her glasses in her hand. This man is trouble, she thought, real trouble. He could put a spoke in the whole idea.

'Perhaps you haven't been here long enough to ascertain, Miss Harding, that we have a perfectly good organist here already—my wife, Betty, who is also a first-class conductor.' Charles looked around, challenging anyone to disagree with him. 'There is absolutely no need to bring in anyone else.'

'Er, I wonder if we might...' started Clive, desperately trying to think of the right way to cool Charles' obvious anger.

But it was Betty's voice that cut clearly through the heavy silence. 'Well, I can't say how relieved I am that you're not expecting me to play for the programme. Honestly, I could never cope with it all. It's been keeping me awake at night, thinking that everything might depend on me—I just know I'd go to pieces, I'd be so nervous.'

Charles drew breath to speak, only to be stopped as Betty went on, 'But Jan, if it would help at all, I'd be delighted to talk to your Mr Spence about the singers and musicians I'm aware of around these parts. Would that be useful?'

'It most certainly would. Thank you, Betty.'

And as Jan spoke, Charles rose from his chair, and without a word, left the room.

Blast the thing! The lock on the front door of Charles and Betty's salmon-pink cottage had a habit of sticking once in a while. Today, it reflected his fury, as it stubbornly refused to budge.

Charles took a deep breath, and tried coaxing the key to turn, gently this time. As if responding to a bit of understanding and tenderness, the door opened immediately.

He headed for the lounge, but didn't sit down. Instead, he paced the room, mulling over the indignities of the meeting at the vicarage. How could they all be so blind? Those television people, they think they can ride roughshod over everyone. They think we should all be so grateful for our moment of glory on the screen, that we should just accept whatever they thrust on us. Well, they'll have to learn—they can't have it all their own way. Most definitely not if he had anything to do with it!

And Betty! Whatever had possessed Betty to speak out as she did? She must have known the embarrassment, the humiliation it would cause for him? He had made it quite clear what his feelings were on the matter. Where was her pride? Her loyalty?

Well, she might well be bewitched by the idea of television cameras in Sandford—but then, women were susceptible like that. He was a realist. Action was needed. He sat down at last, and picked up the phone.

'Well, that seemed to go OK. What did you think?'

Jan spoke as she turned the car back along the High Street, and headed out of the village. 'They all seem really enthusiastic, don't they,' Sue replied. 'Well, except for—what was that chap's name? The one who stormed out?'

'Charles Waite—and he's someone we must try to win over as quickly as possible. If I had a bit more time today, I'd call in and see him. I'll ring him later in the week, and try and arrange to meet him on Friday when I'm back here again. Or, better still, I think I'll ask Kate to make contact with him when she starts researching the programme. She'll be a lot more diplomatic than me.'

'Why does he matter so much?'

'Well, he seems to wield a lot of influence around here. Someone told me the first day I arrived here that he *is* the Parish Council. He strikes me as the sort of person who likes to be in control—which he probably is, most of the time. We could work round him, of course, especially as everyone else is so very keen to be involved, but I don't want to get his back up. He could be a powerful and disruptive enemy.'

'But the objections he kept coming up with? He wasn't listening to what you were saying at all. If only he'd let you explain before he stomped off.'

'Well, someone must sit him down, and explain properly. Not me though. One more of his patronizing looks, and I might just be tempted to clock him one with my clipboard!'

'Jan! How un-Christian!'

'To err is human,' Jan replied, a mischievous twinkle in her eye.

'Do you need any more of these forms, Stephen?' Clive offered Stephen a handful of sheets to be filled in by local clergy, if they could suggest any local people who might make suitable interviewees for the programme. Stephen was the minister at the Baptist Church in the neighbouring village of Steepleton. He had moved there with his young family only a matter of months before, and his enthusiasm, and his inclination towards 'happy clappy' choruses, had divided opinion. Some thought he brought a breath of fresh air—others thought he heralded a decline in all that was decent in church worship.

'Thanks, Clive, I've plenty here. There are a couple of people who may be interested. It's difficult though, isn't it? I mean, we know that some people have wonderful testimonies to tell, but they'd never share them with a television camera. I'm not even sure that I could— would you?'

Clive grimaced. 'Look, I'm losing my nerve already. Jan asked me if I would do the Prayer and Blessing at the end of the programme—but she was talking about taking me out to some local beauty spot to record it! It's bad enough thinking of what you want to say when you're standing in front of everybody at the altar—at least that's familiar territory. I just know every sensible word will go out of my head if they expect me to *act*!'

Clive's arm was gripped by long, bony fingers. 'Interesting, very interesting, all of that this morning, Clive. Call on me if you need any help, my boy!' Clive and Stephen watched the Reverend Walter Miller, now happily retired, make his slow, unsteady progress towards the door. Without looking back, Walter lifted his hand in what might have been a wave, and stepped outside to be clasped by the matronly figure of Beryl, his wife.

'Poor Walter. What he'd give for a whisky, if only Beryl would let him!'

Stephen and Clive lowered their voices, like boy conspirators. 'Well,' said Clive, 'I hear she has good reason to keep an eye on him. Apparently, before he retired, when he was at his old church, she found out that it wasn't just tea he had in his breakfast cuppa. And she only noticed because his sermons got slower and slower, and longer and longer. In the end, she took to keeping a clock on him—as soon as he'd been up in the pulpit for ten minutes, she'd wrap her knuckles on the pew, and say, "That's enough, Walter. Sit down now!" And he did!'

With the two ministers throwing their heads back with laughter, Bunty wondered if this was quite the right moment to approach the vicar about The Problem. She tidied the mauve-patterned scarf she had around her shoulders for the umpteenth time, and then hovered around the front room, picking up cups and plumping cushions. At last she saw Stephen make his exit, and like a shot, she was at Clive's side. 'Oh, Vicar. Have you a moment?'

'Of course, Bunty. How can I help?'

'Well, it's about the flowers.'

'Flowers.' Clive looked vague.

'The flowers—for the programme.'

'Oh, of course, Bunty—your flower arrangements are legendary, legendary.'

'It's Lent.'

'Yes.'

'Palm Sunday—the last Sunday in Lent—and you know about flowers in Lent...'

'We can't have any.'

'No.'

'It's a tradition. Very bad taste to have any flowers in the church during Lent.'

'Exactly!' At last, Bunty thought, he sees The Problem!

But he didn't.

I'm going to have to spell it out, thought Bunty. Oh, this is so difficult.

'Well, we do want the church to look its best, don't we? And it will hardly look its best with no flowers, will it? It will look bare—and boring.'

'It will look bare and reverential—totally appropriate as we approach Easter, when we remember the death of Our Lord on the Cross.'

There was a note of despair in Bunty's voice. 'But I watch "Songs of Praise" every week, and they always make a point of featuring the flowers. It's the high point of the whole programme for me—and for lots of others. I bet every woman in the country notices the flowers!'

'But not at Lent, Bunty.'

'How about just a few small, subtle displays—something tasteful and sombre...'

'No, Bunty, we couldn't possibly. It simply wouldn't be right.'

'But we're not High Church. This is a small country parish—there are always flowers in country churches.'

'Not in Lent, Bunty. Sorry!' And as Clive's attention was claimed by the overpowering presence of Methodist Minister Norman Oates, Bunty bit her lip to stop it trembling.

In the kitchen, Mrs Hadlow was still in residence. 'Thanks so much for your help, Mrs Hadlow, but you've done enough already,' Helen said. 'You get off home now—I'll finish here.'

'No need. It's almost done now,' was Mrs Hadlow's immediate reply. She was enjoying herself! 'By the way, dear—your cups...'

Helen held her breath—whatever now?

'You know, I'd never hang my cups up under the cupboard by the handles like that. They might fall—and all the dust and germs get right inside them. It's none of my business, of course, but if I were you, I'd keep them in the cupboard. Much more hygienic.'

Helen thought better of the reply that was on her lips—and before she could come up with something kinder to say, the telephone rang. She glanced out the window. She could see Clive was already in his greenhouse. 'Just a minute, Mrs Hadlow. I'll be right back. *Please*, do leave all that now—I'd *like* to do it, really.'

45

A bright, young voice greeted her on the phone—a girl who wanted to know if she could come along to talk to Clive about having her wedding at St Michael's in September.

'Do you live in the area?' asked Helen.

'No, but my Mum does. Does that make me "a spinster of this parish"?'

No sooner had Helen put the phone down from that call, than it rang again—so it was some time before she made her way back to the kitchen.

Mrs Hadlow had gone, and so had the washing up. Helen opened the cupboard. There at the front, handles all parallel, stood a gleaming line of upturned cups, as neat and precise as a line of soldiers.

16 February

When Jack popped into The Bull on Tuesday evening, discussion around the bar was all about the coming of television cameras to the village.

Bill was leaning across the bar, holding court with anyone who'd listen. From the amount of time Bill spent behind the bar, you'd assume he was the barman. But he was, in fact, the owner of the small hotel, along with his wife, Maureen, who often felt overworked and under-appreciated, as she did everything else except run the bar! It wasn't that it was a big place, really. There were only ten bedrooms, but they were always busy in the summer months, especially as the old house stood invitingly on a corner of the High Street, in a perfect position to catch the eye. There was plenty of passing trade for morning coffees and lunches. The visitors mostly sat in splendour in the Lounge. The Public Bar was just a nice sitting room really, with its chintz curtains, and a big log fire during the winter months. It may be called 'Public', but the locals thought of it as private, and all their own.

'What I don't understand,' Bill was saying, 'is why churches are always empty on Sundays, but full to the brim when the cameras are there? It all seems a bit hypocritical to me.'

'That's right,' said Stanley, who thought of The Bull as home, much more than the house he lived in two doors down. 'They just want to be on telly, that's all. They dress up in their Sunday best, go and sing hymns, and get theirselves on telly.'

'Are you going then, Stanley?' The question came from Brian, who had popped out for half an hour to relax at the end of a very busy day. Brian and his wife, Ellen, ran Grove House, 'friendly, comfortable guest house accommodation in a family atmosphere', at the edge of the village. Brian was tackling the renovation of some of the rooms before the summer rush. It was hard, thirsty work, although he couldn't say he wasn't enjoying the challenge!

'Me!' guffawed Stanley. 'Me! Sing? I can't see 'em wanting me in no choir!' He spluttered over his bitter, as he chuckled at the thought. 'What about you, Jack? Will you be singing?'

Jack was just taking the first sip of his pint. 'I don't know really. I might, I suppose.'

'Does all that church stuff interest you then?'

'Well, a bit.' Jack took another mouthful, to conceal his discomfort. 'Anyway, from what little I do know, I don't think it's only people from the village who'll be going along.'

'But it's about Sandford, isn't it?' Bill asked. 'Surely, only Sandford people will be allowed to go.'

'Well, I don't know really, it's only what I've heard, but I think that tickets are being given out through all the churches in the area. At least they'll know the hymns, won't they!'

'Well,' said Stanley, 'I hope they ask me to choose a hymn. I've been thinking about it, giving a lot of thought to the one I'd say. Guess what I'd choose!'

'"Jesus Wants Me for a Sunbeam!"' Bill roared with laughter at his own humour.

'No, no, Bill, I'm being serious for once. I do have a favourite hymn. "The Old Rugged Cross"—I've always loved it. It was my Mum's special hymn, that one—we had it played at her funeral. It makes me cry.'

'Do you know, that's strange,' said Bill, suddenly serious, 'They played that at my Mum's funeral too.'

'All I know,' said Brian, 'is that Ellen is already wittering on about needing a new dress. She says all the guests who've ever stayed at Grove House, watching all over the country, will see her there—and that if she isn't the best dressed in the congregation, they'll think our business must be going downhill!'

Bill threw his head back, and laughed. 'You'd better just give in, I reckon, Brian. Give her the money, and let her get on with it. You don't stand a chance!'

17 February

As the news got round, the possibility of a television programme being made in Sandford was the topic of nearly every conversation in the village. When Helen popped in to the High Street shop the next morning, Don was at the far end, stacking tins, talking to a couple of Mums. One of them was holding the hand of a toddler who had his eye, and—with a bit of luck, if his Mum kept talking long enough—one chubby little hand, on a box full of packets of white chocolate buttons, that happened to be on a shelf that was just about on his eye level.

'Now, here's the lady to ask! Helen, when is this programme going to be? Do you know the date yet?'

'Yes, it's for Palm Sunday—well, that's when it will be on the TV, but they'll be filming bits of it all week before that, and apparently, they need everyone who's singing in the church on two separate nights that week.'

'Two nights! Whatever for? It only lasts about half an hour, that programme, doesn't it?'

'Not much longer than that, I'm sure,' said one of the Mums, as she skilfully prised a packet of buttons out of her son's hand, and picked him up for a cuddle. He burst into tears, but she hardly seemed to notice as he thumped his small fists at her shoulder. 'I only know because it's during that programme that I get him and Natalie into bed, read a story, have a quick clear up—and with luck, I'm back in time for "You've Been Framed".'

'Well,' said Helen, as she gathered a few items into her wire basket, 'I get the feeling it's quite a complicated business. They're arranging half a dozen choir rehearsals over the next few weeks, and then, the first night in the church—that's the Wednesday of that week, the 31st March, I think that must be—is a rehearsal for everyone, I think, so that the congregation can learn the hymns, and the cameras can work out what pictures to take.'

'Learn the hymns?' Joan spoke from behind the Post Office counter. 'What are they thinking of asking us to sing, then?'

'Well, finding the hymns might be the least of their problems, I think.' Helen smiled at Joan. The two women had always been good friends. 'Finding people who can sing them properly will be the hardest bit.'

'Well, there's me, Grace next door, and Betty—and your Clive's not bad, when he's singing something he likes!' chuckled Joan.

'They're going to have to find others from around about, I suppose,' replied Helen.

'Where?' Joan mused. 'There's not a lot around here, really, is there? Well, there aren't a lot of people at all, I suppose! How are they going to start looking?'

'Betty is helping, of course, and anyone in the know at other churches. I think they'll be able to draw together a small group of people who are already singing in their church choirs in the area. But I get the impression they need more than that.'

'How about you, then, Don?' asked the other young Mum, over the din of the toddler, whose shrieks were growing more furious because no one was taking a bit of notice of him. 'Are you a singer?'

'I tell you, the only scales I'm interested in, are the ones I sell things from. But I'm a good singer, aren't I, Joan? I am, Joan, aren't I?'

Joan's shoulders shook with laughter, as she looked down at the Post Office forms in front of her. 'Well, I wouldn't like to be the neighbours, when you start on "Nessun Dorma" in the bath. I don't think Pavarotti has much to worry about!'

Don looked offended, but not for long. 'So Betty's got her hands full then, sorting all that out before she starts working on the music?'

There was a moment's hesitation before Helen replied. 'Betty won't be playing for the programme, or conducting either. They've got their own music director, so he'll be conducting, and apparently, they like to work with professional organists.'

'Well!' Joan's eyes were like saucers. 'That will put the cat amongst the pigeons!'

'Honestly, Joan, I don't think Betty minds a bit. In fact, I think she's quite relieved.'

'Betty might not mind, but what about Charles?'

The question hung in the air—as the toddler's Mum finally grabbed a packet of buttons in exasperation, threw coins on to the counter, and strapped the triumphant youngster into his buggy.

'You see, James,' Charles said, as he and Major Gregory strolled in the garden, the only place that Majorie, the Major's wife, allowed him to smoke, 'this is an invasion! Those blessed BBC people think they can just march in, and call the shots! It's not on—it really must be stopped!'

'You've spoken to them, of course? Explained the situation.'

'Believe me, James, they're not interested in what we think. At that meeting on Sunday morning, it was quite clear that a lot of people there had objections, but they just ignored it all. Mind you, the vicar is besotted with the idea of having his church on television. I think his good sense has just been swept away with the glamour of it all.'

'And people from the village won't be allowed in the church at all, did you say?'

'Well, that was certainly the impression they gave! They're bringing people in from churches miles away. They want to get people who can sing hymns, or some such nonsense!'

'And they've told Betty she isn't good enough to play—or lead the singing?'

'Precisely.'

The Major drew on his cigar, and pondered as he walked. 'It's a sad situation, then—very worrying indeed.'

I knew the Major would understand, thought Charles. A voice of reason, at last!

'What do you suggest, then, Charles? A public meeting, do you think?'

'Perhaps,' replied Charles, 'if we have the time to organize such a thing, before this avalanche of television mania engulfs us. We certainly need a campaign—a well-planned, intelligent campaign.

That's why I rang you. You're just the man for that sort of work!'

The Major's thick eyebrows shot up towards his disappearing hairline, and he turned to look at Charles.

'Well, old chap, I might have been once. My campaigning days are rather a dim memory now.'

'But people respect you, Major. They recognize authority. For heaven's sake, you were a magistrate! If you say that something must be done, people listen to you!'

'Aren't they listening to you, then, Charles? You hold a very well-respected position in the community. You're a Church Warden. You're Chairman of the Parish Council. You surely have much more influence in these matters than I have.'

'You're on the PCC too, James. You have the same obligations to uphold the dignity of the church as I do! We must act! We must nip this nonsense in the bud before it goes too far. We must explain why we object to this onslaught by the BBC, and throw them out! People will understand, if you tell them!' Charles caught sight of the Major's expression. 'If we tell them together—as a Committee.'

There was a long silence, during which the Major was plainly deciding how to respond. At last, he spoke. 'I think I should do a bit of research on this, before I commit myself either way. I'll ring you, Charles.'

Consumed with frustration, Charles managed to keep his face calm, as he asked, 'When? When do you think you'll have decided?'

'Soon. I'll be in touch soon.'

And like a schoolboy dismissed by the Headmaster, Charles shut the garden gate as he left.

'Hello there! Is that Helen?' The soft Scottish lilt to the voice made Jan instantly recognizable.

'Hello, Jan. How are you?'

'Harassed. Understaffed. Overworked. Overwhelmed. In need of a holiday!' Jan laughed. 'Do you wish you hadn't asked?'

'It sounds,' said Helen, 'as if you need to come down to relax for a few weeks, rather than make a programme here. When will you get a break from work?'

'A break? What's that?'

'Well, you know you're always welcome, if you just want to come and hide down here, get away from it all.'

'Thanks, Helen. And you will be seeing me quite soon—but with a huge list, I'm afraid, of things that must be done. Ticket printing is going ahead, by the way. We've settled on 300 people in the church, if we don't use that back corner section. I'm going to need that for cameras at one point. I'll let you have the tickets in a week or two. I'd appreciate it if you could divide them up between the churches as we discussed at the weekend, and get them into the hands of the relevant people.'

'That's fine. Oh, and did Clive manage to talk to you about hymns? He's been singing away to himself in the garden, so I think he's got some suggestions to make.'

'Not yet, but that's one of the top things on my list. I'd like to arrange for our Music Director, Ian Spence, to be with me when I come—on Friday, if that's alright with you. We must sort out the programme, so that we can get the hymn books printed.'

'Can you do that yet? I thought the people you interview choose their own hymns?'

'Well, that happens less and less now. After all these years of ending every interview with the question, "And what hymn have you chosen?", it got a bit predictable. There are about ten hymns that everyone you ask seems to choose!'

'Like what?' asked Helen.

'"Dear Lord and Father", "The Day Thou Gavest"—and "The Old Rugged Cross". Everyone asks for "The Old Rugged Cross"! I'm beginning to wonder if anyone ever has anything else for funerals, because people always seem to want us to include it in memory of people they've lost!'

Helen laughed. 'I suppose it is pretty popular—in a morbid sort of way! Anyway, I'm sure you didn't ring to discuss hymns. Was it Clive you wanted?'

'He's not there, by any chance, is he?'

'You've just missed him. He's out visiting this morning. Can he give you a ring at lunchtime?'

'Fine. In the mean time, I'll get in touch with Ian and arrange for him to meet us on Friday. He's in Somerset today, setting up the first programme. There's only just over a week before "Village Praise" takes to the air. Terrifying, isn't it!'

'Well, we'll be seeing you then—and Clive will probably call you later. Bye, Jan.'

Heavens, thought Helen, as she put the phone down. If she's terrified, what about the rest of us?

19 February

The atmosphere in the Waite household had been decidedly strained since the Sunday morning meeting. Charles wasn't exactly silent, but he spoke no more than necessary. His cold anger was worse for Betty to bear than a good argument, and be done with it! She tried to coax him round. She cooked his favourite dinner. She didn't complain when he left his shoes in the middle of the bedroom floor, so that she tripped over them when she went to the loo in the night. She managed to be busy doing sewing, and so not able to watch television, when a documentary on Egyptian pyramids came on to BBC2. She supposed he never knew that there was a Danielle Steele film on the other station. He probably didn't even know how hard she was trying to patch things up.

But as the days wore on in stony aloofness, Betty realized that it was simply below his dignity to talk about what happened. And his assumption that he must be right, and therefore, she must be wrong, began to irritate her. She couldn't deny her feeling of relief that the burden of playing and organizing the music for such an important occasion had been lifted from her. She knew her limitations as a musician. She enjoyed what she did in spite of them! Thirty-seven years of marriage, and how little he knew her!

It was on the Friday morning, during their customary silent breakfast, that her patience snapped.

'Charles, we must have this out! It's absolutely ridiculous, the two of us living in the same house, and one just not talking to the other. For heaven's sake, let's just get the argument over with, and forget it!'

Charles slowly turned his cold stare towards Betty. 'That's just it,

Betty. I can't forget, and I won't forgive. You humiliated me. I can't forgive that.'

'But you assume too much, Charles. You assumed that I would want to play the organ or conduct the choir for the programme! Believe me, I don't! I never have! The whole idea scared me to bits!'

'Why all the practice then? Why all the special rehearsals before those BBC people came to the service? Oh yes, you wanted to play alright—and so you should! So you should!'

'Look, whatever you think, it really doesn't matter to me. And it shouldn't matter to you either. What does matter is that we have been married for nearly forty years, we love each other—and I can't bear this dreadful atmosphere between us!'

Charles stood up, and moved towards the window. 'At our wedding, you promised to "love, honour and obey". So much for your promises, eh?'

Betty was speechless with indignation. 'Well, if, after all these years, you don't know how much I love and honour you, then the whole of our married life has been a waste of time! And as for 'obey'—no one in their right mind would choose to obey orders from someone who is so full of his own importance, that he can't see when his orders are unreasonable—and wrong, Charles! I can't ever remember telling you that you're wrong before—but because I love you, it's better that I tell you, before the rest of the village does!' And with shaking hands, she picked up his breakfast plate, and slammed the door as she went out to the kitchen.

When Ian Spence arrived in Sandford to meet Jan, it was just on one o'clock, so Jan suggested that they held their discussion over lunch at The Bull—a rare treat for the vicar and his wife. Ian thought that it might be a good idea if their church organist could join them too, and he rang Betty's home, when Helen gave him the number.

'Hello, I wonder, is Mrs Betty Waite there please?'

'Who's calling?' Charles asked.

'It's Ian Spence from the BBC here. I'd like to talk to her about singers and musicians for "Village Praise".'

At that point, Ian thought, there must have been a fault on the phone. There could be no other explanation for the curt way in which the line was suddenly cut off.

They did run into Betty though. She was coming up the path towards the church, as they all left the vicarage for the The Bull. Betty looked flushed. There were two bright red spots in the middle of her cheeks. I hope she's not going down with something, Helen thought. Sunday services revolved around Betty being fit and well.

After the introductions had been made, Betty was invited to join them for lunch.

'Well,' she hesitated. 'I ought to organize something for Charles.' Then, a stubborn recklessness crept up on her. Stuff him, she thought. Let him work out for himself how much 'loving and honouring' he gets, if I'm not there to 'obey' him!

'Thanks, I'd love to,' she said, smiling broadly at Ian. 'Let me just get my address book, and a few bits and pieces out of the church, and I'll join you in the bar.'

'Um, the Lounge Bar,' Clive pointed out. 'We've got visitors...'

Betty smiled to herself. My! What a treat! I'm going to enjoy this.

Over bar snacks, they managed to iron out all sorts of details and potential problems. The discussion about what hymns should be sung took up most of the time. Clive had obviously given the matter a good deal of thought. He wanted the programme to reflect the kind of hymns that the congregation were used to singing, and could cope with well. Ian, it seemed, had more daring ideas.

Clive's list, which he read out aloud, was full of familiar, and well-loved standards.

'"All Hail the Power of Jesus' Name"—we always need a fairly big congregation to tackle that, and there are lots of twiddly bits in the tune— I thought you might like it for that. "Praise to the Holiest in the Height"— good solid tune, a favourite with the older members of the congregation. "O Praise Ye the Lord"—everyone likes that, apart from the high note towards the end. "Come Let Us to the Lord Our God"—that's not quite so well-known, but it goes down well here. "When I Survey the Wondrous Cross"—wonderful hymn for this Easter season—and "Ride On, Ride On in Majesty" is a must, being Palm Sunday.'

Clive looked at Jan and Ian with a mixed expression of confidence and hope.

'Great start. There's some good suggestions there,' Ian replied, pushing his blond hair away from his eyes in a way that was so characteristic of him, 'so good, in fact, that we've already got some of them earmarked for earlier programmes in the 'Village Praise' series. Now, let's see, you're right about "Ride On, Ride On". I definitely think we should start with that—what do you think, Jan?'

'Well, do you traditionally parade into St Michael's on Palm Sunday?' Jan asked Clive.

'Well, I wouldn't describe it as 'parade' exactly—more like a gentle amble from the village green, through the church grounds. Why?'

'Are there any donkeys around here? Preferably very well-behaved, used to children, and desperate to be television stars?'

'As long as you don't expect me to ride on anything with four legs, I think we might be able to find someone who could help there. What about David who runs that farm up near Dinton Church?' Clive turned to Helen. 'I'm sure he's got a couple of donkeys in his paddock, that his children play with. He'd probably help—he's a Methodist.'

'You know, I've been meaning to ask you,' interrupted Helen, 'why were you so interested in knowing about Dinton Church?'

'Well, it's sometimes nice to be able to stage a choir item, or perhaps a solo, at another indoor location—and a pretty, atmospheric little church like the one at Dinton could be perfect. Simon, the Engineering Manager, and I popped in to take a look at it on our way back from here last Sunday. I think a bit of smoke, and some moody lighting could make that a lovely setting for something or another. Don't know what yet. Go on with your suggestions for hymns, Ian. Is there anything that might suit Dinton?'

'How about "O Sacred Head Sore Wounded"—it would be great as a choir item...'

'What, *our* church choir, do you mean?' answered Betty doubtfully.

'Well, it's early days yet, and obviously we're still working on gathering together all the voices we need to provide the core choir for the church recording,' replied Ian, 'but until we know what voices we've got, it's very difficult to select music.' His hand went automatically to his blond hair, which had fallen into his eyes. 'Right,' he said amiably, 'Solos! Jan, you wanted some suggestions. How about "Be Still, For the Presence of the Lord"?' Nods of approval all round—although Clive had clearly never heard of it. 'Or "Just As I Am"?'

'The one that ends with, "O Lamb of God, I come?" I like that!' said Clive.

'Very nice,' added Betty.

'Lovely melody,' agreed Helen.

'Great one to go after a really sensitive interview,' decided Jan.

'That one's settled then,' continued Ian. 'And what about a couple that you can put shots of lovely countryside over—"For the Beauty of the Earth" perhaps, or "Like a Mighty River Flowing"?'

Clive was obviously still trying to place the two hymns, as Jan said, 'Yes, I like both of them. Both—or either—would do.'

'Need one for the children to sing?' Ian continued. '"There Is a Green Hill" would be appropriate for Palm Sunday.'

Clive felt on sure ground with hymns like that one, and encouraged by nodding heads all round, he said, 'Another one that would just suit this season is a great personal favourite of mine. "The Old Rugged Cross"—I've always loved it, especially since they played it at my mother's funeral.'

Ian, Jan and Helen looked at each other—and laughed out loud.

'You're on!' giggled Jan. 'For once, I have to say that's a perfect choice!'

Anna shrank into her seat, when Matthew got on the same school bus as she did. Too late! He practically landed on top of her, school bag and all, when the bus jerked into movement just as he was trying to curl his lanky body into the space beside her.

'Matthew. Babies sit on people's laps. Grow up, and find your own seat!'

'Well? Heard the news then?'

Anna stared deliberately out of the window, but curiosity got the better of her. 'What news?'

'That the BBC are going to make a programme here in Sandford.'

'Oh, that!' An expression of boredom flicked across Anna's face. 'Doesn't really interest me.'

'Why not? They're looking for singers, you know—and you can sing. You're a great singer. You ought to get in there! It might be the break you need!'

'What, singing hymns? Do me a favour!'

'No, Anna, do yourself one! Stop being so negative all the time! You've always said you want to be a singer. Well, how else are you going to be noticed, living in a backwater like this? Talk to Helen about it—she's your godmum, isn't she? I bet she could put in a word for you.'

Anna was quiet for a moment, and then said, 'I've got some revision to do. There's a History Test tomorrow. Push off, would you, Matthew.'

'OK. But promise you'll think about it!'

Anna's face was indifferent, as she began to dig into her bag, and draw out a book. Her eyes were fixed on the pages—but for the rest of the journey, her thoughts were plainly elsewhere.

When the group in The Bull were finally ready to leave, Ian was armed with a lamentably short list of contacts for singers and musicians. It was important, he knew, to draw in as many local people as possible. Of course, at the end of the day, through his own contacts, he knew he could call on quite a few professionals, or good amateurs, from further afield, if that was the only way to achieve sufficient quantity and quality.

'It would be nice to find a soloist who lives in the village, though,' he said out loud, just as Helen's eye was caught by a wave from her goddaughter, Anna, who was getting off the school bus in the High Street outside her Mum and Dad's shop.

'You know,' Helen suddenly thought aloud, 'I think I might just be able to suggest someone. Young Anna over there has a superb voice—and she's had proper training too.'

'Bring her over then,' said Ian, 'let's meet her!'

Curiously, Anna crossed the road towards them, when she saw Helen beckon. 'Anna,' Helen said, with her arm round the girl's shoulders, 'I'd like you to meet some of the production team from the BBC, Jan Harding, the producer, and Ian Spence, who's in charge of the music.'

And as Anna shook Ian's hand, she looked up into the face of the most goodlooking man she had ever seen.

19 February

For days after that first meeting with Ian, Anna was in a dream. She recalled over and over in her mind, the way that they had all gone into the church, so that Ian could try out the organ, to see if any work was needed on it before the recording. She cursed herself now for the way in which shyness had overcome her. He must have thought her so naive and tongue-tied, as he chatted away to her, explaining about the programme as they walked towards the church.

She did manage to ask one thing, she remembered. 'So what do you do then?'

'Anything to do with the music, really,' Ian replied. 'My job as Music Director on this series is to work with local people and the production team in deciding what hymns to include in the programme, and then to prepare any special arrangements that might be needed. There may be pieces of incidental music that the Producer would like me to compose, to cover a sequence of pictures she has in mind—or perhaps, it might be a good idea to include a particular instrument that is traditional in the area. I come up with all the dots on paper—and I conduct on the night.'

'Oh,' was all Anna had been able to manage in reply, as she thought what a marvellous job his must be. Fancy being able to write music all day long—and be paid for it! Wow!

'I hear you enjoy singing?' Ian prompted gently. 'What kind of material are you involved with?'

'Oh, anything really,' replied Anna. 'I've had singing lessons for ages now, and because of Aunty Helen and Uncle Clive being at the church here, I used to sing in the church choir too.' She hesitated awkwardly, trying to work out how best to continue. 'I have a lot of homework now—GCSEs, you know, so I don't have time to go to church much any more.'

'Helen tells me that you sing solos in the church sometimes though.'

'Yes, for special occasions, you know, like weddings, or at Christmas.'

'Well, we need to try out the organ now, and it would be really useful to hear the acoustics for singing at the same time. Would you do me a favour, and help us out with a hymn or two?'

'Sure I will.' Anna tried to sound casual, although her stomach was churning with dread and excitement.

Ian sat down at the organ and ran his fingers over the notes. Anna had never heard the trusty old instrument sound so wonderful! His fingers seemed barely to touch the keys, as the church resounded with rich, majestic music. Suddenly, the mood changed, and Anna recognized one of her favourite hymns, 'Be Still For the Presence of the Lord'. She found herself mouthing the words, as Ian's voice over her shoulder said, 'Don't be afraid. Sing out! It would be a great help to us.'

So she did. She forgot the audience. She forgot her nerves. She simply heard the music, and felt the words.

Be still, for the presence of the Lord,
The Holy One, is here;
Come bow before Him now
With reverence and fear:
In Him no sin is found,
We stand on holy ground,
Be still, for the presence of the Lord,
The Holy One, is here.

Pale Spring sunshine poured through the stained glass windows, as her sweet, strong voice echoed round the church.

Be still, for the power of the Lord
Is moving in this place:

He comes to cleanse and heal,
To minister His grace,
No work too hard for Him,
In faith receive from Him,
Be still, for the power of the Lord
Is moving in this place.

The final notes reverberated round the building, as Ian put his arm around her shoulder.

'You'll do!' he said, hugging her. 'You'll do nicely!'

SUNDAY

21 February

'Good morning! You must be Miss Marsden!'

It was Ellen who opened the door of Grove House to Kate, as she arrived on the following Sunday at about four o'clock that afternoon, the long drive from Wales finally behind her.

'That's right. Kate's the name—and I can't believe I'm here at last. What a journey!'

'You'll need a cup of tea then. I'll just get Brian to take your bag— um, bags,' Ellen corrected herself, as she eyed the great heap of holdalls, books, computer and printer that stood on the doormat, 'up to your room, while I put the kettle on.'

As Kate filled in her details in the Visitors Book, she took in the homely surroundings of Grove House. As a 'Songs of Praise' researcher, she spent most of her time on the road, and from experience, she had learned that staying in hotels can be a lonely, and sometimes precarious, business for a woman travelling by herself. She had developed an eye for reading between the lines in the Accommodation Guide, seeking out homely Guest Houses where she could spread out, come and go at irrational hours, pop her smalls in the washing machine, and not feel she was putting anyone out! She could tell from the first few minutes spent in Grove House that this was going to suit her nicely!

A tall, smiling man was wiping his hands on the sides of his trousers as he came down the stairs. 'Sorry! I'm Brian. Welcome to Grove House!'

Kate smiled. 'You're painting, I see. Don't let me stop you working!'

'Believe me,' grinned Brian, 'I'm glad of the break. I'm trying to give a new lease of life to the skirting board down behind a wardrobe,

65

and because it's such a big, heavy old thing, I've not moved it out very far. I need arms like Twizzle—and I didn't know a back could ache so much! Here, let me take that bag for you!' He led the way up to the landing, which divided in several different directions. He showed Kate towards the front of the house, and opened the door to a delightful, cosy room with fresh flowers on the windowsill, and a pile of clean pink towels on the counterpane.

'Do you want to come down for your tea?' Brian thought better of the question when he saw the real exhaustion in Kate's face. 'No, don't worry! Ellen will bring it up for you. You just make yourself at home!'

The moment the door was shut, Kate fell back on to the soft, inviting bed. The start of yet another programme! She had only just come to the end of weeks of work on two particularly challenging editions of 'Songs of Praise', one of them coming from a town in Europe, which had taxed her schoolgirl Spanish to the full! And now, she had been assigned to two of the six 'Village Praise' programmes— this one, here in Suffolk, which was the last in the series—and Programme Number Two, based in Wales to coincide with St David's Day. If she thought Spanish was difficult, that was nothing compared to Welsh! The programme was set in a part of Wales where more than half of the locals spoke Welsh as their first language. It was disconcerting when suddenly, the conversation took off in a language she was excluded from, and her pronunciation of names and places was little better than when she started! The people were wonderfully welcoming though, accepting her attempts at Welsh in good humour and some amusement. It promised to be a great programme, especially as the beautiful scenery of Wales would be matched by wonderful music and singing! Kate sighed. Certainly, as far as the singing was concerned, things were hardly likely to be as easy here.

She was almost on the point of dozing off, when she became aware of a soft knocking on the door. She leapt to her feet guiltily, and opened up to find Ellen there, a beautifully laid tray of tea in her hand. 'That looks wonderful!' Kate said, as she drew the tray into the room—and it did look inviting, especially as next to the teapot, Ellen had placed a plate that was barely visible beneath an enormous piece of chocolate cake! 'I shouldn't eat that, you know—but I will! You don't care about my waistline, do you!'

'Not a bit!' replied Ellen, with a grin. 'If you're working hard, you need some extra calories inside you—give you energy! By the way, do you want to eat here tonight?'

'That would be lovely, if it's not too late to include me. I've got quite a lot of sorting out to do this evening. There is a phone in my room, isn't there? Well, I'll just spend this evening getting a few visits organized for tomorrow, and a bit of home cooking will go down a treat. Thank you.'

'About eight suit you?'

Kate nodded.

'See you then,' Ellen called over her shoulder, as she started towards the stairs.

Right, thought Kate. I'll run the bath, eat the cake—and drink the whole pot of tea while I'm soaking!

22 February

The knock at the front door was so timid, that Helen almost didn't answer it. Then, she saw the figure of someone standing beyond the frosted glass panels, and went to see who it was.

Jack Diggens stood there, looking ill at ease and hesitant. 'I've probably come at a bad time. I'll pop back later, if you're busy.'

Helen was pleased to see him. 'You've come just as I was about to put the kettle on for coffee. Come and join me.'

'The vicar's not here, is he?' asked Jack, before stepping inside the door.

'No, he's got a busy day today—all sorts of visits and meetings booked. I don't expect to see him until teatime. Come on through. Oh drat!' The telephone rang. This morning, it never seemed to stop ringing. 'Would you mind putting the kettle on, Jack? I'll only be a minute!'

'Mrs Linton,' said a friendly male voice on the phone. 'Simon Martin here, Engineering Manager—we met last weekend?'

'Of course, Simon. Nice to hear from you.' Helen remembered the businesslike but very pleasant man at Sunday's meeting.

'Can I pop down and see you tomorrow? I'll be bringing my Lighting Gaffer, so that we can draw up some proper plans. We'll need to get into the church for a couple of hours, at least. Will that be OK?'

'What time are you thinking about? Clive has a Pram Service about eleven o'clock on Tuesday mornings, so the place will be full of screaming toddlers until midday!'

She could almost hear him shudder on the phone. 'We'll avoid that then! Around two suit you?'

'Fine, see you then!'

When she reached the kitchen, the kettle was steaming, and Jack was perched on a stool as near to the back door as he could manage, as if he was planning a quick escape.

'It's a busy time for you, I can see,' said Jack. 'I won't stay long.'

'Honestly, I'm glad of the diversion. I promised Clive I'd think about who in the parish we could suggest to be interviewed on the programme. I thought it would be easy, but all I can think of is reasons why people would prefer not to bear their souls in public! I started off with six possibles on my list, and one by one, I've crossed them all off again!'

'Do you wish the programme wasn't happening then?' asked Jack, helping himself to a spoonful of sugar as she passed over his coffee.

'Yes. No.' She caught his bemused expression. 'It depends when you ask me, really. No, I'm not being fair. Of course, I'm pleased the programme is going to happen. It will be a great occasion for the church and the village—and I must say that all the BBC people I've met so far have been very nice.' She grinned. 'So far, anyway!'

'They were talking in The Bull the other evening about needing singers.'

'Yes, well, that's another headache. I'm supposed to be delivering a pile of posters that arrived here from the Producer this morning. Look, here they are—giving details of the programme, and the times of rehearsals.' She lifted up the pile of yellow papers that were stacked on the kitchen floor. 'They're looking for anyone who can read music, and sing either Soprano, Alto, Tenor or Bass lines. You can't sing, I suppose?' Helen eyed Jack hopefully.

He laughed. 'Definitely not—but do you need a hand delivering that lot? I'm not doing much today.'

Helen's eyes shone with gratitude. 'Oh, Jack, would you? That would be such a help!'

'Where have they got to go? Anywhere in particular?'

'Anywhere, and everywhere,' Helen replied. 'In every shop, every front window, every pub, on every noticeboard that you manage to find. And not just in Sandford—we need to spread the cover as widely as possible, so it's important to deliver some to all the neighbouring villages too, even if it means just dropping a handful off to the homes of the various ministers in the area.'

'Well,' said Jack, starting to rise from his seat, 'I reckon it would be better to deliver each one personally, just to make sure that piles of notices don't end up gathering dust somewhere. I'll start right away!'

'But, Jack, you've only just arrived—and we ought to talk, didn't we, about the other morning. Have you had more thoughts about all that?'

'Yes—and probably I should talk about it, but right at the moment, the idea of delivering posters seems much more appealing! I'll let you know how I get on. Bye!'

And before Helen could manage another word to stop him, Jack had scooped up the pile of posters, and slipped out the back door.

23 February

Bunty had had a miserable week. Nothing could lift the cloud that seemed to surround her. The only consolation had been the fact that her faithful group of Flower Ladies were all feeling as wretched as she was.

'The problem is that the vicar simply doesn't see there's a problem at all!' Bunty lamented that afternoon, when the Ladies gathered for their weekly 'get-together' at her house. 'Why, oh why, did they decide to make a programme here in *Lent!*'

'So he won't allow any flowers at all—not even some small arrangements on the windowsills where they won't be seen much?' asked Madge, a slight, wiry figure, well into her seventies.

'Who wants to do arrangements that "won't be seen much" anyway?' said Iris, well known in the village for her artistic creations in the small hairdressing salon she ran in the High Street.

'Well, is there any way we can dress the church that he will accept?' ventured Grace, as she tried to balance both a cup of tea, and one of Bunty's Burmese cats on her lap. 'What about banners? We could make up some lovely banners.'

'That would be nice but, you know, Clive even covers up the cross during Lent. He's a bit of a stickler, isn't he?' replied Bunty, adding loyally, 'It's one of his most admirable qualities. We're fortunate to have a vicar who feels such commitment to what is right and proper.'

'Um,' agreed Grace, rescuing her bourbon from the Burmese, who obviously had a penchant for chocolate.

'What's this I hear about them doing something or another at Dinton Church?' asked Iris, who was always in the know where gossip was concerned. When she had people at her mercy in the hairdressing chair, it was amazing how much they liked a natter!

'Yes, I've heard that too,' said Madge. 'Perhaps Clive would let us organize flowers to go in there—something very tasteful, of course.'

'Oh, of course,' agreed the others.

Conversation stopped. No one really thought that Clive would relent in any way, as long it was Lent.

'Lent starts this Sunday.' It was Iris who spoke. 'No more flowers for six weeks then.'

'No,' said Bunty, and they sat in companionable silence to mourn this sad fact.

❧

As Kate knocked on the vicarage door, it was well past the six o'clock appointment that she had arranged with Clive.

'I do apologize that I'm so late. I'm Kate, the researcher, and I should have been here quarter of an hour ago!'

'Don't worry,' said Helen, 'and it's me who should be apologizing because Clive isn't here.'

'Oh.' Kate looked crestfallen. 'I really do need to talk to him soon, and he said he had no time earlier today.'

'To be honest, I'm not quite sure where he is. He had several people he needed to see today, but I did remind him before he left this morning that you were coming this evening. He must have got held up, perhaps with a parishioner. You know how it's sometimes very difficult to get away...'

'Of course. Well, I'm staying at Grove House. I'll go back and get on with a few phone calls, and perhaps he can give me a ring there if he comes back later.'

If he comes back later, Helen repeated to herself as she closed the door behind Kate, and went to take another look at the wilting, overdone shepherd's pie in the oven—*When* he comes back later, I'll wring his neck!

❧

At that precise moment, the Reverend Clive Linton was sitting in Dinton Church. It was dark, and he had only put on a single light at the back of the building. He was sitting in a pew in the semi-darkness, looking at the gleaming cross above the altar. He loved this place. He loved its simplicity, its solidness, its peace. He felt God here—not that He wasn't everywhere, of course, but here, he felt His presence so keenly, that it was almost as if he could stretch out a hand and touch Him. Often, when life became too busy, parishioners too demanding, problems too exhausting, he saught the sanctuary of Dinton Church.

He had had a hymn recurring in his brain all that day. 'Forty Days and Forty Nights.' To himself, he thought of the words.

Forty days and forty nights
Thou wast fasting in the wild;
Forty days and forty nights
Tempted, and yet undefiled.

Oh yes, Christ knew the need for peace and solitude. He thirsted for moments of silence to be alone with his Father. Time to listen. Time to accept: 'Thy will be done.'

What was God's will for him, Clive Linton, vicar of Sandford? What did he expect of him? Did he have a divine purpose, in which Clive had his role to play? 'It just seems, Lord,' Clive spoke aloud, 'that although I try to do the best I can, and try to be there to minister your Word to all who'll listen, that my efforts are so—so—small, so—meagre.'

The silence engulfed him, responding, listening.

'This television programme—the producer says that millions of people will be watching, more people than I've ever met in my entire life. She says we must think of the programme as an act of worship, fellowship to be shared by everyone who sees it around the country. And she has asked me to do the prayer and blessing.'

He fell silent for a while, before sinking to his knees, his head dropping onto his clasped hands.

'Dear Lord, I have a thousand prayers in my heart—but the one I want to say for that programme must be a prayer that can touch other people's hearts, that brings your Word alive for them!

My head is empty. Fill it for me, Lord! Father, inspire me with words that can inspire them! Give me the instinct, the knowledge, the courage to make the very most of this opportunity—for Your sake, O Lord, and for the sake of your Son, Jesus Christ—Amen.'

And as he prayed, Clive felt the warm mantle of silence caress and enfold him.

SATURDAY

27 *February*

'That you, Vicar? Gregory here!'

'Major, how nice to hear from you!' Clive had recognized the clipped, gruff voice straight away.

'I'll come right to the point, Vicar. This television business...'

'Ye-s.' What's coming now, thought Clive?

'Bit pushy, are they, these television people?'

'In what way, exactly, Major?'

'Dictating who should be involved, and who shouldn't?'

'Not at all, Major. They have worked with us every step of the way so far. Can't complain at all really.'

'Heard that some people were complaining—that the locals aren't necessarily going to get the leading roles, so to speak!'

'Of course they will. Betty is very busy helping their music people to draw together a choir in the area. Their researcher was here for hours the other evening, picking my brain about possible people to be interviewed. Young Anna—do you know her? Of course you do— your son, Matthew, is quite a pal of hers, I think—Anna is to sing a solo.'

'And Sandford people will get priority for seats on the night?'

'If they are regular churchgoers, of course they will—as will other regular churchgoers of all denominations around here. You'd agree, I'm sure, Major, that the recording in the church is primarily an act of worship. We don't want people coming in merely because the cameras are here...'

'Of course not. Of course not!' replied the Major, whose wife, Marjorie—only ever seen in church grounds for the Annual Fête—had threatened him this morning with all sorts of dreadful repercussions if her "Village Praise" ticket hadn't arrived by the end of the week!

After a moment's pause, Major Gregory asked, 'Good for the area, then, do you think?'

'I think our hotels and guest houses will be fit to bust this summer, after wonderful publicity like this,' replied Clive, knowing that one of the many committees the Major sat on, was for the development of tourism in this corner of Suffolk.

'Champion. Carry on then. Morning, Vicar!' And Clive was left with the receiver still in his hand, as the line went dead.

On Saturday morning, Kate was packing her bags again, at the end of an exhausting, but in many ways, fruitful week. She had done the groundwork of research for the programme—meeting most of the local ministers, and gathering together what had turned out to be more than a dozen suggestions for people who might make suitable interviewees. She had spent hours in the library in Saxmundham, digging out books on the history, geography and industry of the area. She had folders full of brochures following her visit to the Tourist Information Centre. She had spent a very happy evening having a meal at the home of that larger-than-life character, Norman Oates, the Methodist minister, and his wife, Marion. She didn't glean much useful information from that—but the gossip was fascinating! She'd even managed finally to track down Clive Linton, who had proved most elusive. His suggestions were slightly vague and general, but his wife, Helen, seemed to be a mine of information. And Kate had managed to meet up for a drink in The Bull not just with Simon Martin, the BBC Engineering Manager, and his Lighting Gaffer, but also Roger Harwood, the 'Songs of Praise' Assistant Producer who had been given the job of directing the programme. Chatting with them all that evening, Kate had discovered that Simon had booked every room The Bull could offer for the technical crew, just as she had booked every room at Grove House for the production team.

And now, back to Wales! The first 'Village Praise' programme in the series, from Somerset, would be on the air the following evening. Any of the BBC team who weren't involved in the editing of that programme, which was done in a van at whatever village they were based in for the week, would already be on the road, heading for the next location—*her* location, in Wales! And in six or seven hours, she'd be there too!

The silence in the Waite household was stonier than ever. Meals appeared on time; shirts turned up ironed; messages were taken—but neither Betty nor Charles said one word to each other.

If Charles hadn't been so furious about the whole affair, he might have mused that Betty had never cold-shouldered him in this way throughout all their years together. As it was, his indignation on her behalf, for the terrible insult she, and therefore the 'Waite' name, had been dealt, coupled with her own betrayal in the way she had ignored and insulted him, made him more furious than ever.

The final straw came on Sunday evening, when he walked into the lounge at twenty-five past six, to find Betty staring at the television, as that blonde presenter, the one with the lisp, stood in some village in Somerset, talking about the start of the new series of 'Village Praise'. And to top it all, she even mentioned Sandford by name, as one of the villages to be visited later in the series!

He could have kicked the television—but he didn't. With all the dignity he could muster, he marched out of the lounge, and out of the house.

And his ire wasn't only aimed at Betty. He'd like to stick pins in Major Gregory too! That pompous old fool! It had been a whole week and a half since their meeting—and so much for his promise to 'do some research' and ring Charles with his plans.

Well, it seemed he alone saw the dangers that lie ahead. Just wait till the whole caravan of television people arrived in the village, taking over the place, dictating the terms! There'd be a different tune in Sandford then! Well, he wasn't going to take this invasion of their privacy lying down. No! He had a plan—and all he had to do to get it started was to post the letter that he had safely stored in his jacket pocket!

1 March

W hen the first 'Village Praise' programme came on the television, it caused quite a stir in Sandford. The village that was featured was slightly bigger than theirs, and, of course, the countryside around was nowhere near as beautiful as Suffolk, but really, it had been a very enjoyable programme indeed, in spite of all that!

Certainly, Mrs Hadlow approved of what she'd seen, as she told her friend, Ivy, when she came to meet her at the end of her weekly appointment at the Hair by Iris Salon in the High Street.

'Oh, Mrs Hadlow!' called Iris, who was halfway through a blow-dry. 'Do you want to book in for your perm the week of the recording? My appointments are nearly full for that week already, and I don't want to find I can't fit you in!'

'Nearly full? Really?' replied Mrs Hadlow. 'Why's that then? Surely no one knows who's going to get tickets yet?'

'Oh, I think they're all getting spruced up, just in case!' chuckled Iris. 'I mean, you never know when one of their cameras might catch you, when you're just round and about the village, do you?'

Dorothy, a cuddly beaming woman, sitting in the chair in front of Iris, parts of her hair still wet, and hanging in tendrils around her face, swung her seat round, and announced to anyone who'd listen, 'Anyway, I'm going to make sure of my seat. I'm joining the choir!'

Mrs Hadlow turned on her. 'Are you an accomplished singer then, dear, with plenty of experience in that sort of thing?'

'Nope!' replied Dorothy. 'But I'll give it go! I've heard they're desperate for singers, so I'm going along. The first rehearsal's a week on Thursday, in the Village Hall—that's what it says on the notices!'

'Of course, I know that,' retorted Mrs Hadlow, as she turned towards the reception desk, where Debbie, the glamorous young receptionist, was engrossed in reading a magazine. 'Excuse me!' Mrs Hadlow's knuckles wrapped impatiently on the desk. 'Will it disturb you too much to make an appointment for me? Saturday at the start of that week would be best...'

'Sorry, Mrs H. All booked for that day.' The receptionist's long, painted fingernails tapped their way over the Appointments Book. 'How would the Thursday before, about four-thirty, suit you?'

'Four-thirty?' squeaked Mrs Hadlow. 'So late? I always come in the mornings, always,' she said emphatically, as she pulled her coat on.

'Sorry, Mrs H. That's all we've got left. You do want the usual, I suppose. Cut and perm?'

Mrs Hadlow was flustered—not just by this break in routine, but by the irritating way in which Debbie insisted on calling her Mrs H. No respect for their elders and betters, these young people!

She turned to Iris. In future, she had no intention of dealing with anyone less than the owner herself. 'I'll check with my calendar, Iris,' she said, indignation written all over her face. 'And I'll let you know. Come along, Ivy!'

No sooner had the two women made their dignified exit from the shop, than Iris sat down on the nearest seat, her shoulders shaking with laughter. 'Debbie! You are so wicked! You wound her up deliberately, you little minx! You know how she hates being called Mrs H!'

'Well, she deserves it,' grinned Debbie, 'there's just no pleasing her! She's so blessed pernickety about everything, always sticking her nose in, and telling everyone how to do things! She drives me mad! Anyway, what am I supposed to call her? It's so old-fashioned to call anyone "Mrs", nowadays! We always use Christian names for everyone else who comes in here—and I don't even know what her Christian name is!'

'Do you know,' replied Iris, 'neither do I!'

Dorothy giggled, as Iris coaxed the last of her curls into place, 'I don't reckon she's got a Christian name—and if she ever had one, she's forgotten it!'

'But then,' continued Iris, suddenly serious, 'Mrs Hadlow comes from a generation when it was considered impolite to call people by their Christian names, until you were invited to use it. It's all a matter of respect, really—and in many ways, perhaps it's not such a bad thing, to have a clear idea of what's proper and right.'

'Right, Mrs Baker!' Debbie replied, as she rose from the Reception Desk, her eyes twinkling at Iris. 'With all due respect, I could do with a cup of tea. How about you? One biscuit, or two?'

❧

'Honestly!' huffed Mrs Hadlow, 'Iris is going to find herself losing customers, if she doesn't take that girl in check.'

'That's right,' agreed Ivy, as she adjusted the fine beige scarf she had fastened over her hairdo, whilst trying to negotiate the uneven paving stones along the High Street.

'And she shouldn't be allowed to read magazines all day long, just ignoring the customers like that. It gives a very bad impression.'

'Oh, I know,' said Ivy, clutching tightly to her friend's arm.

'And that Dorothy! I don't believe for one minute that she can sing a note, do you?'

'Oh no, not for a moment. Certainly not!'

'The cheek of it, then. Going along to join the choir, just to get a seat in the church. It's not right—not right at all!'

'Not at all!'

'For heaven's sake, I can probably sing better than that Dorothy! At least, I used to sing in a church choir, when the children were small, you know!'

'Really? In a church choir, were you?'

'Oh yes, an Alto—that was what I was. And Altos are very hard to come by, you know. There's always a shortage of Altos!'

'Goodness, yes!'

Arm in arm, they drew level with the village shop. This was one place they could never pass without having a good look at all the notices—it was fascinating to know who was selling what—and why—around the village.

Right in the centre of the cluttered window a yellow poster caught their eye.

'Village Praise'

On Sunday, 4th April, the last programme in the series 'Village Praise' will be centred around the village of Sandford. The BBC 'Songs of Praise' team will be recording the programme in the village, and in the surrounding area, during the week prior to transmission. The recording of the hymn-singing in St Michael's Parish Church will be at 7.30 p.m. on the evening of Thursday, lst April, with a full television rehearsal for all choir members and congregation at 7.30 p.m. the previous evening, on Wednesday, 31st March.

In order to include music and singing that is of the highest possible quality, we would be very pleased to hear from any local people who would be interested in forming a special choir for the recording. We are looking for SOPRANOS, ALTOS, TENORS AND BASSES—who can cope with harmonies, and who are able to read music. We will be holding a series of rehearsals in preparation for the week of recording. If you are interested in being involved, please come along to the initial rehearsal in Sandford Village Hall on Thursday, 11th March

'I see they're looking for Altos, then,' commented Ivy, 'just like you said they would.'

Mrs Hadlow turned away from the poster thoughtfully, and offered her arm once again to Ivy. 'Yes, well, if they need me, I suppose I'll have to get involved. I'd have no choice, would I, if the reputation of the village is at stake.'

'None at all!' agreed Ivy.

'Well, we must get on, dear. George will be wanting his dinner.' Mrs Hadlow began to walk more briskly. 'Let's walk home past poor John's house. Did you see they've put a FOR SALE notice up outside it? Such a nice man—so sad! I wonder how much they are selling it for...?'

11 March

Ian Spence arrived back in Sandford halfway through the following Thursday afternoon, exhausted by the long haul he had just driven from the Lake District. It had been a difficult recording in the church there the night before. The building was charming, but small and awkwardly shaped. From the conductor's point of view, it was a nightmare, because there were whole sections of the congregation who weren't able to see his baton at all. The aisles were narrow, with uneven flagstones, so the cameramen had found it difficult to move fast enough to get out of the way of each other's shots. Three times throughout the evening, the congregation had been asked to sing a hymn yet again because one camera had ended up taking a beautiful, if unintentional, picture of another!

The programme from the Lake District, the third in the 'Village Praise' series, would be on the screens that Sunday evening—well, at least, Ian hoped it would! When he had left the team earlier that morning, they were bemoaning the fact that it hadn't stopped raining all week, and that they were lamentably short of pictures of the area. The hills had disappeared beneath thick blankets of cloud, and everything—from the sheep in the fields, to the locals battling their way through the downpours—looked miserable! Even the spring flowers, which would usually be in full bloom by now, looked as if they had no interest in making an appearance. To top it all, Pam, the presenter, was thick with cold, sounding terrible, and looking even worse! Everyone seemed to be suffering from mid-series blues—exhausted by the gruelling schedule of nearly three weeks on the road, with the prospect of so much travelling and hard work still ahead of them.

Quite a few of the team managed to get home for a day or two during the 'Village Praise' run. Ian wasn't one of them. He never seemed to be out of the car these days, rushing not just from one recording to another, but one rehearsal to the next. Trying to prepare for six programmes all at the same time was enough to cross your eyes, and have you jibbering like an idiot! As it was, he spent all of these long journeys working out arrangements and new themes in his head. It had been quite an embarrassment earlier that day, when he had stopped at traffic lights somewhere around Huntingdon, and taken the opportunity to conduct with both hands the piece of music that was marching through his head—only to look up into the faces of a lorry driver and his mate, parked next door to him at the lights, both almost in tears with laughter as they watched him in action!

One thing that had become abundantly clear to him over the past few weeks was how much he was missing Sarah. It was a funny thing that they had known each other for years, ever since they had started at college together. They had belonged to the same group of friends, while Ian studied the piano and organ, and Sarah specialized in the flute. Surprisingly, during those college days, there had been very little pairing off amongst the group—mostly, they had preferred to do things as a pack, studying together, drinking together, playing music together and planning their glittering careers together. Ian recalled that, even then, he had noticed Sarah's dark hair, and pale, classic face—he remembered how moved he had been when he had seen her play a solo in the End of Term Recital. She had talent, without a doubt—but her quiet confidence, and the self-contained air that surrounded her, made her slightly unapproachable and challenging. It wasn't until his three years of study were nearly over, when he was asked to accompany her for a performance which was to be judged as part of their final degree, that they had the chance to get to know each other better. Their shared passion for the music brought them to the unspoken agreement that their performance of the piece would not only be more technically brilliant, but more breathtakingly beautiful, than it had ever been played before. The time spent closeted together as they practised, the hours over coffee at the end of their rehearsal as they talked about their hopes and doubts, the tension they understood so well in each other as the performance loomed—all combined to build a comfortable understanding between them. And when their performance was hailed as a wonderful success, with the applause still ringing in their ears, they fell into each other's arms at the side of the stage. He remembered looking down into her laughing face, her eyes shining with tears of relief and triumph, before his lips found hers. Everything faded from his thoughts, as he sank into the surprise and pleasure of that kiss. Her passion and need were an unexpected delight, her body moulding into his as they clung together. For a few precious seconds, the world slipped away from them—until Ian felt himself slapped on the back, as the Stage Manager said something about doing their snogging somewhere more private! It was a coarse, embarrassing intrusion—and yet, when he looked at Sarah, he knew that she felt the magic too.

'I love you,' he thought in amazement, as he held her close. Whether he said the words out loud or not, he was never sure—but when he looked into her eyes, he knew that she had heard him, loud and clear.

And that was the start. After years of seeing each other daily, when they worked and studied in the same building, they had only really found each other with four weeks to go before their degree courses were over. The intense pressure of revision for exams was matched by the intensity of their feelings for each other. Every possible moment was spent together—and even when it should have been impossible, her sweet face swam into his thoughts. He was lost, engulfed and drowning in the wonder of loving her.

And then, all too soon came the end of term—and the end of their time at College. Sarah was going home to Exeter, and had plans to spend several weeks in France over the coming summer months. Ian already had a job lined up, organizing the music for a Christian youth organization. He went with her to the station, as she piled her mountain of bags and books on to the train. She held him close, her face wet against his neck, until the train slowly pulled away. They would write every day, they promised. They would telephone every hour, if they could. They would find a way to be together always.

And as he watched the line of the train grow thinner and more distant, all Ian could think was, dear Lord, don't let me lose her! Don't take her from me!

Ian's thoughts were jogged back to Sandford, as his car turned finally into the High Street. While he kept his eye on the road, watching for the sign for Grove House, he mused on how things had turned out for Sarah and him.

She had become a great success. Before the end of that summer, she had been asked to audition for the Birmingham Symphony Orchestra. He had met her in Birmingham as she arrived by train that morning, and held her hand tightly as they made their way to the rehearsal room. Her face, as she emerged two hours later into the Autumn sunshine, said it all. The audition had gone well, the remarks from those who were judging her had been positive and encouraging—and Ian had felt the first disturbing doubts that today would change everything.

He was right to worry. She was offered a position with the Orchestra two weeks later. She was no longer a talented, penniless, hopeful student. She was an accomplished, professional musician, whose talent was fast recognized by other professionals around her. She travelled a lot. She was rarely at home. Often, when Ian rang her flat beyond midnight, there was no reply. When she rang him, she was full of excitement about the pieces she was playing, the venues they would be visiting, the conductors who had made a point of speaking to her. She was slipping away, slipping away.

His own career, too, was busy, although hardly in the mainstream of professional music. His job took him round the country, encouraging young people to sing, play and enjoy church music. He had also taken over the helm of an amateur national orchestra and choir for young people, that had already gained a reputation for wonderful, enthusiastic musical evenings at huge halls in various corners of the country. These were time-consuming, sometimes frustrating affairs, but they did allow him to indulge his passion for composing and arranging.

As work claimed more of their time and thoughts, it became more and more difficult to dovetail their timetables so that they could see each other more than once every couple of months. The phone calls became less frequent—and when Sarah told him that she was growing fond of someone up in Birmingham, Ian accepted the inevitable. The early intensity of their feelings had mellowed anyway.

Their last few meetings had been strained and awkward. For both of them, there was a sense of release that they were free to move on to other relationships without the niggling worry that they would be hurting someone very dear to them. It was over.

They promised to keep in touch, but they didn't. Once in a while, Ian would spot Sarah playing in one orchestra or another on television. Occasionally, he heard news of her on the musicians' grapevine. He was glad she was doing well. He was proud of her—but he never tried to make contact. He was never short of girlfriends. He liked them. He dated them. One girl seemed to be a permanent feature, for a short while. But he never really got involved. He always said that music was his first love. Perhaps it was.

In the mean time, his own career had gone from strength to strength. The world of Christian music is a relatively small one, and it wasn't long before his ability and work was noticed by the media. It began with radio, when they broadcast a special Remembrance Service from his own church in London. It was a beautiful service, made all the more haunting by Ian's moving, evocative arrangements. The Producer of that programme often asked for his help after that— creating specially written theme music, or atmospheric arrangements. And when that Producer moved from radio to television worship, Ian's contacts grew. He would often be called in to conduct the choir for live Morning Worship broadcasts coming from various parts of the country—and it was only a small step from there for him to become an unofficial resource for the 'Songs of Praise' team. When a conductor and arranger was needed for the first series of 'Village Praise' the year before, he was the obvious choice. That series made his name, and his reputation. He had never looked back.

It was just before Christmas, five years since he had last seen Sarah, when he met her again. He was working on a 'Songs of Praise' programme in Stratford, and had prepared some special arrangements that needed a solo flautist. There was no one in the immediate area who could cope with the difficult and last minute musical demands. A professional was needed—and a quick check with those in the know showed that the obvious professional to use was the one who lived less than fifteen miles away. Sarah.

He sat for some minutes with her phone number in his hand, before he finally picked up the receiver. She answered almost immediately. Her voice was just the same, and a shiver of anticipation and foreboding surprised him as it coursed down his backbone. She was plainly taken aback to hear from him, but there was pleasure and affection in her reply. Yes, she'd love to help. Fine, it did look as if the date would suit her. Certainly, a chance to meet up and take a look at the music before the television recording would probably be a good idea.

They met in the lounge of his hotel, as he waited with tea and sandwiches for the two of them. He saw her, before she spotted him. Her hair was shorter, stylishly cut, surrounding the face that had never left his dreams from the moment he first met her. She was confident, attractive, seemingly unaware of the effect she had on those around her. As she came towards him, and he stood up to greet her, he forgot everything he had meant to say. He forgot the disappointment and pain of all that had gone before. He forgot the loneliness of the years in between. He simply opened his arms, and she walked into them.

They never really got round to talking about the music that day. The evening drew in, as they sat, their hands touching, catching up on so much, with so much still to talk about. And finally, when he thought he couldn't bear another moment without holding her again, it was Sarah who leaned across, and cupped his face in her hands. There were no words. None were needed. The love in her eyes said it all.

'Ian, welcome back!' said Brian, strolling out of the back door of Grove House, as Ian unloaded his car. 'Just a quick visit, this time, is it?'

'Certainly is,' Ian replied, as he tried to manoeuvre out his overnight bag, without disturbing the electric keyboard he had balanced in the boot. 'I'm just here for the first choir rehearsal this evening—then back to the grindstone tomorrow morning. They've got a rehearsal tomorrow night in Northern Ireland—that's where not this week's programme, but the next one is coming from!'

'No peace for the wicked, eh?' chuckled Brian. He took a good look at Ian's tired face. 'Why is it that all you BBC types always arrive here looking so dreadful? Don't they let you have time off for sleep in your job?'

'Sleep? What's that?' grimaced Ian, as he signed the Register, and made his way up the stairs. He turned the key, and let himself into the now familiar homely room, its double bed spread in a chintzy cover. He looked longingly at the bed, and smiled. Then he picked up the phone, and dialled Sarah's number in Stratford. Her answerphone was on. He knew it would be.

'Hello you!' he said, when it was time for him to speak. 'Good news! I think I'll be free on Saturday night. How do you fancy stroking the fevered brow of an overworked, underpaid, desperately tired musical director? I promise I'll try to stay awake this time! Love you— give me a ring when you can.'

He replaced the receiver, and was probably asleep before his head hit the pillow.

To call the first choir rehearsal in Sandford a disappointment was an understatement. When Ian arrived, Betty was already trying to get everyone into the right groups, according to their voice range. It wasn't a difficult job. There were barely forty people there—and more than two thirds of them were sopranos, or so they said!

Most of them knew each other, at least vaguely. Nearly all of them were members of one church choir or another, and it became clear very early on that there was a keen sense of competition between one group and another, or perhaps, more particularly, between one choir leader and another. There was one complete row of about eight people who had obviously come as a result of the poster asking for volunteers. Seven of them were women, the broad smiling figure of Dorothy at one end, and the neat, tidy, slightly disdainful Mrs Hadlow sitting apart from everyone else, right at the window end of the row. There were six men in all, and none of them were basses.

When Ian arrived with his arrangements, and handed out parts and music to everyone, it was clear that sight-reading was not the strong point of this gathering.

He never let his smile drop once. His enthusiasm and patience was an inspiration to them all. No one would have guessed about the niggling voice of panic in the back of his brain, as he wondered if finally, the 'Village Praise' campaign had met its Waterloo.

Sitting in the front row of the Sopranos, Anna gazed at Ian with barely concealed adoration. Even with the mismatched choir the village had managed to muster, the skill and beauty of Ian's musical arrangements were plain to see. He cajoled and bullied, persuaded and coaxed, until the harmonies fought their way into clarity. The atmosphere of the group, which had started off with uncertainty and detachment, became warmer and more enthusiastic. They responded as best they could, charmed by Ian's warmth and humour—and for Anna, it was simply the best experience of her life.

The rehearsal had been going for about half an hour when Jack passed the church on his way to return the spare posters to Helen at the vicarage. A small red Metro pulled up at the side of the road, and a woman peered out uncertainly at the notice at the front of the church.

She wound down the window as she saw Jack approach. 'Excuse me!' she called. 'Could you help me?'

Jack stooped down until their heads were level. The woman was probably in her sixties, elegant and attractive, with pale white hair, and glasses.

'I'm looking for the Village Hall. Someone said it was near the church, but I'm blowed if I can find it!'

'Well, it's actually around the back of the church, and from where you are now, it would be quicker to leave your car here, and just walk through the church grounds.'

The woman eyed the gravestones nervously.

'Look,' said Jack, with a speed that surprised him, 'I'm going that way. If you don't mind stopping for a second or two while I just drop something into the vicarage, I'll be with you.'

Margaret considered the wisdom of accepting his offer of help, but only for a moment. He looked friendly and harmless enough— especially if he was on his way to the vicarage! Throwing caution to the wind, she grabbed her handbag, climbed out of the car, and locked the door.

'You're going to the rehearsal then, are you?' asked Jack.

'I'm late, I know I am,' admitted Margaret, 'but I teach piano most weekday evenings, and my last pupil on a Thursday doesn't leave until seven-thirty.'

'Where do you live, then?' asked Jack.

'About three miles the other side of Steepleton. It's not far really, but somehow, I never come into Sandford. I don't usually have any reason to, so I don't know my way around here at all.'

'It's funny,' said Jack, 'there are lots of places around here I don't know either. I suppose with working away from here for years until I retired, I never really had the time to get to know the place. And now I've got the time, I don't really have the inclination to go hunting around on my own.'

Margaret laughed. 'The dreadful thing is that I've spent a lifetime teaching youngsters, telling them to make the most of all the opportunities around them. I don't practise what I preach though. It's amazing how the last people to visit important landmarks are the ones who live right next door!'

Their conversation was interrupted as Jack made his way up the path towards the vicarage. He rang the bell, and when there was no reply, he left the leaflets on a neat pile on the doorstep.

'So you teach music?' he asked Margaret, as she waited for him by the garden gate.

'Music—plus anything else that was needed. I'm retired too, but I used to teach at a private school for eleven- to eighteen-year-olds, just outside Saxmundham.'

'Do you miss it?'

'Yes, very much—and no, I'm glad to have a bit more time to myself—time to get involved with things I really want to get involved with. Like this rehearsal, for example—I was quite excited when I saw the poster. I just hope I'm not too late to be included.'

They were practically at the door of the Village Hall. The sound of a far-from-beautiful rendition of "For the Beauty of the Earth" reached their ears from inside the building.

'Thank you, for coming to the aid of a damsel in distress.' She held out her hand to Jack. 'I'm Margaret Abbot, by the way.'

'Jack Diggens—and our paths might cross again. I'll probably be involved in stewarding on the big night.'

'That will be nice. Thanks again, then. Good night.' And as Jack watched Margaret disappear inside the door, he suddenly realized that, for a man who found small talk difficult, that had been a very pleasant conversation indeed.

The next morning, Ian loaded up his car again, and called into the shop in the High Street to buy some man-size hankies on his way out—it looked as if he was about to succumb to the 'Village Praise' cold, along with the rest of the team.

By that night, he would be in Northern Ireland, at yet another choir rehearsal. That one, he wasn't worried about. The core choir for that programme promised to be about one hundred strong, and they were all enthusiastic, experienced singers.

But Sandford, oh Sandford, what on earth could he do about Sandford? How was he going to produce a reasonable sound with so little available to him—no basses, a handful of tenors, some very questionable altos, and sopranos who were mostly decidedly shaky on anything above top E?

He opened the door of the shop, found the hankies, and headed for the counter.

'You don't know me, of course,' said the man behind the counter. 'Don Birch, Anna's Dad.'

'Oh,' smiled Ian. 'Good to meet you. A talented young lady you have there.'

'Well, she's very keen, always has been. Her Mum and I have never really been sure how much to encourage her, what with her school work and all.'

'It's difficult, I'm sure—but she's got a delightful voice.'

'And will she be—I mean, are you planning to use her for the programme?'

'Certainly. I'll be in touch when I back here, probably next week some time, to arrange a proper rehearsal for her.'

'How did it go last night?'

'Not bad.' He caught sight of Don's amused expression, and grinned. 'Not good either. We're very short of voices—and there were virtually no men at all! Aren't there any choirs around here?'

'There must be, I suppose, but don't ask me how you find them! I wish you luck, mate!'

'I think I'm going to need it—and these!' replied Ian, as he grabbed a pocket-sized pack of Paracetamols from the counter, and gave Don a five-pound note.

He pulled the door to as he left the shop, but when the wind caught it, the door flew open again. As Ian turned to shut it more firmly, he came face to face with a faded notice to one side of the door. He looked thoughtful as he read the notice, and then, took out his pen, and made a note of the phone number on a clean page of his notepad. And at the bottom of the page, he wrote just one word—EUREKA!

15 March

Luckily, Betty had just left the house when the phone rang.

'Charles Waite.'

'Oh, Mr Waite, it's Pete Durrell here, Editor of *The Herald*. Got your letter. Have you time for a chat?'

At last! A response at last! 'Yes, of course,' Charles replied, his voice calm in spite of the knot of triumph in the pit of his stomach.

'We've heard quite a bit about this television programme in Sandford, of course—but your letter is the first inkling we've had that not everyone is delighted at the prospect. We got the impression that most people think it will be very good not just for the village, but for the area....'

'I think it will bring great pleasure to a very small number of people—the people in the little clique who will be allowed in for the recording,' interrupted Charles. 'I wonder how many people in this village realize that on that night, they will not be allowed into their own parish church, unless they've got a ticket.'

'Who will be there then?' Pete Durrell's pen was scribbling furiously, as he took notes.

'A good question,' said Charles. 'Outsiders. People chosen at the whim of the Producer, no doubt.'

'But why not use local people? Surely, that would be simplest...?'

'Of course it would. But these BBC people have decreed that our choir mistress and organist are not up to scratch, that our church choir is simply not competent enough, and that our congregation are really not of sufficient standard for their blessed programme—and unless you're a singer, you don't get a ticket!'

'And the poster you enclosed with your letter—this is being widely circulated, is it, to try and attract singers in?'

'Correct.'

'Have you any idea what sort of response there was at the first rehearsal?'

'Abysmal, I should think.'

'Your wife wasn't there, then? She is the organist at St Michael's, isn't she?'

Handle this carefully, thought Charles. In truth, although he had been longing to know how the rehearsal went, he certainly hadn't been prepared to break the silence with Betty by asking anything at all about the programme. As if he was remotely interested!!

'My wife is indeed the organist at St Michael's, although whether she will choose to remain so, having been snubbed so insensitively by the BBC, I really can't say. After all, her work has been quite good enough for the church for the past seventeen years—with all she does for the choir, and the way she turns up to play the organ for practically every service—and yet now, just because these television people are moving in, her services are no longer required. Suddenly, she's not considered worthy enough!'

'She must be very upset about that,' coaxed Pete, writing faster than ever.

'She most certainly is—and so are many other people here in Sandford, on her behalf. Her treatment has been shameful, shameful!'

'What's the vicar's view about all this?'

'A very holy man, our vicar,' replied Charles, 'wonderful, in a pastoral sense—but not always as worldly as we would wish. Sometimes, those of us who work with him, as Church Wardens and PCC members, have to protect him from pressures and influences that he's not best equipped to deal with.'

'So the Parish Council is right behind you on this, are they?'

'To be frank, Mr Durrell, the Parish Council have had no say at all. This whole affair has been steamrollered through, without any proper discussion or preparation. These things take careful planning—and what were we given? Two months from the moment we first heard about this hairbrained scheme until the programme goes on air! It's ridiculous! Impossible! No wonder people are so incensed about it!'

A small pulse at the side of his throat throbbed visibly, as Charles warmed to his subject. 'And another thing! St Michael's is an old building. What are the safety implications of having all these people tramping about in it—cameras, vans, lights, cables? None of that has been looked into. And what about the people in this village who don't want cameras poking into their homes, watching them as they go about their business? It's a gross intrusion, that's what it is—of our hospitality, our privacy and our community!'

'So what are you planning to do about it, Mr Waite? Have you made an official complaint to the BBC?'

'A fat lot of good that would do! They listen to no one. They haven't so far—why should they change now?'

'Well, Mr Waite, it's certainly a very interesting viewpoint, and frankly, if things are as bad as you describe them, I suggest that this is such an important issue that it should make a front page article, probably for next week's edition.'

Yes! thought Charles.

'I take it I can quote you on all of this.'

'I stand by every word of my letter to you. Quote me as you wish.'

'And I can come back to you for further comment...'

'Please do.'

'Fine, then, Mr Waite. Thank you very much for all your help. Goodbye.'

And as he put the phone down, Charles Waite—usually so conservative and stately—whooped for joy as he punched the air!

The sudden flurry of snow that morning didn't make the house any easier to find. Her research notes perched on the back seat, Kate gingerly turned the hire car round yet again, and tried to peer at the map as she drove back down the road she had just been on. Norman Oates, the Methodist minister, who had suggested these people, had said the path was off here somewhere, but she must have driven right past it. She was about ten miles out of Sandford by now, in an area that didn't seem to have a proper name, as there were so few houses around.

Suddenly, she spotted the sign—or what would have been a sign, if it hadn't been coated in snow. This was the landmark she needed, and minutes later, she drew up outside a tiny cottage that was a picture right off the top of a chocolate box this morning—but Kate suspected that what looked quaint and charming today, might revert to being run down and delapidated tomorrow, once the snow had melted.

There was nothing cold about the welcome though. No sooner was she out of the car, than a huge, indescribable dog bounded out to meet her, his paws on her shoulders, his tongue lapping her face. 'Boris! Down, Boris! Boris, I said, get down!!' A strong, tanned hand stretched in front of her face to grab the dog's collar, and as Boris reluctantly compromised with the lesser tactic of simply sniffing her thin, fashionable boots, a casually dressed, bearded man looked anxiously at her.

'Sorry. He loves visitors.'

'For lunch?' asked Kate, eying Boris nervously. 'What sort of dog is he exactly?'

'A big one,' answered the man with a grin. 'Don't ask me about his pedigree—he hasn't got one! I'm Chris Stevens, by the way. Come inside and meet Dee!'

And as if he understood every word, Boris made a bolt to be first in the house, turning at the front door to make sure they were following.

Quarter of an hour later, a huge mug of coffee perched on the arm of the faded, comfortable settee that stood to one side of the Aga, Kate got down to business. She already knew quite a bit about Chris and Dee, from everything that Norman had told her, when it was suggested that they might make suitable interviewees for the programme. It was immediately clear that the couple were anxious to share their story with her.

They had both lived in London some years ago, when their mutual addiction to drugs had brought them together. They had gone through a desperate, frightening time—alienated from their families, stealing to get enough money to buy what they needed, getting through each day by lying to themselves and everyone else. Finally, Chris had ended up in prison for burglary, leaving Dee with a small baby that, quite often, she was hardly aware of. The detail of how she got picked up, and taken along to the rehabilitation centre, was lost to her now. All she remembered was waking up one morning in a room that was somehow familiar to her, and yet she didn't know where she was. She was alone. There was no baby with her, and she had felt relief that he wasn't there, yelling at her, looking at her with those demanding, disapproving eyes.

It was much later that she realized that this room had already been her home for two weeks—and it took months for her to recognize that The Red House quite simply saved her life. With patient, sponge-like tolerance, the small group of professionals who ran it listened and held her, listened and supported, listened and prayed. They listened to her, as if what she said was important. They listened to her, when she shouted and screamed and cried. They listened to her, when she was childlike and frightened. They listened as her thoughts became more coherent, her anger less overwhelming, her plans more defined. And as she became aware of those around her, she realized that these people who were always so strong for her, drew their own strength from their unshakeable, unquestioning Christian faith. The closeness of their relationship with God—the everyday way in which they included him in all the events of their lives—were a revelation to her. Although there was never any pressure on her to accept their beliefs, nor commit herself in any way, she began to find comfort in the rhythm of their day, that began with prayer, was filled with a thousand small prayers, and ended in quiet, companionable prayer before the day drew to a close.

One night, as she lay wakeful and restless in her bed, she suddenly stood up, and turned her face to the ceiling. 'Here you are then, God!' she shouted. 'You said you wanted sinners! How about me? Would I be too much of a challenge for you?' And she fell to her knees, and sobbed until exhaustion left her drained and empty.

'I can look back on that now,' Dee said earnestly to Kate, 'and see that it was a turning point. I didn't really seriously believe that God could do anything for me—but I had invited him in, and he came. He just came.'

'What difference did that make?'

'Are you a Christian, Kate?'

'Yes.'

'But you haven't been born again, or you couldn't ask a question like that.'

'The thing is,' interrupted Chris, 'when I got out, and managed to track down Dee again—and that was some months after all this—I couldn't believe the change I saw in her. She had a kind of peace about her, that made her almost unrecognizable to me. She was together, she was happy, she talked about a future—none of that fitted the Dee I knew when we'd lived in London together. And I suppose a lot had happened to me too. Prison had been pretty dire—they're not very sympathetic to drug addicts in there. I just felt that I had been to hell and back again—so to see Dee like that, so different, so—complete, I suppose is the word I'm looking for, well, it just wrecked me, wrecked me...'

'So he was invited to stay.' Dee took up the story. 'He had nowhere else to go anyway, and they seemed to feel that I would never really get my life together if I didn't face the problems I shared with Chris—like Daniel, for example. Daniel was nearly one by this time, and with foster parents. I'd been a lousy mother—but I knew I wanted him back, and that if I managed to get him, I would make up to him for his rotten start in life.'

'I was there for about six months in all,' continued Chris. They sat close together, Dee in an old armchair, Chris with his arm round her shoulders, as he perched to one side of her, on the edge of the seat. They finished each other's sentences, holding hands tightly, drawing on each other as they spoke. 'And when we left, it was together. We had both found the Lord by then. He blessed us so much. He helped us to find a home—just a couple of rooms at first, not far from the Centre. He found me a job, only labouring, but it was regular money coming in.'

'And finally we were able to have Daniel back with us, praise the Lord!'

'How old is he now?' asked Kate, peering towards the array of photos on the sideboard.

'He's seven, and Naomi is three. She's at playgroup this morning.'

'What brought you to this part of Suffolk to live?'

'My Mum lives in Stowmarket,' replied Dee, 'in fact, I grew up not far from here really. I just wanted to come back home—and this was the only place we could find that we could afford to run.' She grinned at Chris. 'I don't think anyone else wanted it!'

'And are you very involved with other Christians around here?'

'Well, we don't go to church here very much, because the style of worship isn't what we want really. We do keep in touch with a small circle of like-minded Christians, and we get together in each other's houses at least a couple of times a week, for prayer and Bible study.'

'You have to understand,' interrupted Chris, 'that Jesus Christ is our life. There is nothing that matters to us except him. Our lives are devoted to him. We exist because of him. We never stop worshipping him, and thanking him for saving us, praise the Lord!'

'We thank you, Lord, thank you, Lord, Alleluia!' added Dee. Suddenly, she turned to look Kate full in the face. 'Your presenter? What's she like? Is she born again?'

'I don't think so,' replied Kate. 'She is a Christian, of course—she has always been a Christian—but I don't think she'd describe herself as "born again".'

'Thanks be to God for bringing her to us, then. If she's not born again, she'll go straight to hell.'

❦

17 March

Snow still lay in grubby patches along the side of the High Street, as Bunty made her way towards the church that morning. She realized the door must already be open before she could see it, from the strains of organ music that echoed across the graveyard. Perhaps one of the BBC people was here, practising? Her pace quickened. Perhaps, she could make them really welcome, get them a cup of coffee maybe—and then, well, it would be so easy to get into conversation, wouldn't it? She might have the chance to ask how other places managed to make their churches as welcoming as possible, even through Lent? Didn't they find just a few flowers, tastefully displayed, worked rather well...?

She stepped into the darkness of the church porch, and the moment she moved into the aisle of the church, she realized that a voice accompanied the music.

Ride on, ride on, in majesty,
The last and fiercest strife is nigh!

There was no doubting Betty's voice. Bunty's disappointment that it was only Betty was soon forgotten as she hurried up the aisle to talk to her friend.

'Sorry to disturb you, Betty—just popped in to see if there are any messages left on the noticeboard that I ought to deal with. Don't stop—that was lovely!'

'Do you know,' Betty turned her back to the organ, as Bunty settled herself into the seat behind her, 'the music for this programme is really special. That chap, Ian, has done some beautiful arrangements—I can't resist having a bash at them. They're all such old favourites, I've played them for years, but they just sound different.'

'Honestly, Betty,' Bunty's face was suddenly serious. 'Tell me honestly, are you upset about not playing for the programme?'

'Honestly, Bunty,' Betty's expression matched her friend's. 'No, I'm not!' She laughed. 'And honestly, Bunty, I'm really enjoying helping out in the background. I'm an Indian, not a Chief.'

'How's it going then? I heard not many turned up for the first rehearsal.'

'No, we were a bit thin on the ground. We're desperately short of men—and really, our ladies were... how can I put this?' Her eyes twinkled. 'Enthusiastic, that's the word! Ian's looking for more than that, though. We really do need some good, strong voices, who know what they're doing when it comes to holding harmony lines.'

Bunty moved in closer, and in a conspiratorial whisper, asked, 'Is it true that Mrs Hadlow was there?'

Betty hooted with laughter. 'I couldn't believe my eyes! I've never seen her so quiet! She just sat there, all by herself at the end of the row, doing what she was told! It made my night, I can tell you!'

'But whatever was she thinking of? She's never shown the slightest bit of interest in singing before—has she?'

'Well, I did have a word with her after, just quickly. She said something about singing in a church choir years ago.'

'When she was a pupil at Sunday school, more than likely!'

The two women giggled like schoolgirls.

'Can she read music?' Bunty asked.

'It didn't look as if she could—and she'd sat herself in the Altos, where it's really important to be able to read the notes of the harmony lines. Still, at least she turned up, and had a go. Quite frankly, we were grateful for anyone that night!'

'So what are they going to do, Betty, if they can't find some more voices?'

'I really don't know. It's men we're desperately short of—and where do you find a load of men who can sing and read music? If they're not singing in church choirs already, where do you look?'

Bunty looked thoughtful. After a few moments, she said, 'Of course, there is the Women's Institute Choir...' The two women looked at each other. 'Not a lot of men, of course,' Bunty grinned, 'but if it's just good voices they're after, they are reasonably local—well, Saxmundham—no, that's probably too far away...'

'Still,' said Betty, after a moment, 'to be fair, they would be good. And they do sing the right kind of music...'

'They're not my cup of tea,' replied Bunty nonchalantly, 'but I suppose they have a go at anything, really. Songs from the shows, light operatic...'

'And hymns,' added Betty thoughtfully. 'Well, spirituals, and carols at Christmas. They are quite good... and there are a lot of them, forty or so.'

'Umm.' Bunty's reply couldn't have been more offhand.

'I ought to let Ian know.' Betty paused for a moment. 'I suppose Rose Smith is in charge...'

'Ah-ha,' agreed Bunty.

'Not someone I ever really warmed to, I must admit.'

'Oh, nor me,' agreed Bunty again. 'A bit too fond of blowing her own trumpet for my taste.' There was silence—and then, Bunty added, 'I don't think anyone from Sandford is involved in her choir.'

Their eyes met.

'It would be a shame, wouldn't it,' Bunty continued, 'to bring in people from outside, when we haven't really exhausted the search in our own village yet.'

'I do see what you mean,' said Betty. Slowly, she turned back to the organ. 'I'll not mention them just yet then. Better not to interfere...'

In spite of the weather, Kate was getting on quite well, working her way through the list of people it had been suggested she should meet. She was looking for perhaps five or six interviews for the programme, and in all, she had about fifteen possibles to talk to. She would draw up notes on each of them, with her recommendations, but in the end, the decision would be Jan's, as the Producer. It wasn't just a matter of choosing the six who came across as the best talkers. They needed to work together on screen, giving an overview of the area, its past, its problems, its community and its pastoral life. What they needed was a combination of people who painted the most appealing, inspiring and informative picture of village life around here.

At the moment, though, it wasn't people she was hunting at all. It was donkeys! One donkey, in particular, of course, because that was all that was needed for the triumphant procession into the church at the start of the Palm Sunday programme. Clive Linton had mentioned that a local farmer, David Hughes, had a couple of donkeys that usually did their bit for the Village Fayre in the summer months, and it was David she was on the way to visit now. Not with much enthusiasm, though. She had learnt from long experience as a researcher that anything with four legs and no brakes could be trouble! All she knew about donkeys was that they had sharp teeth, and deadly aim with their hooves! Please, she thought, let this one be a docile donkey—biddable, well-mannered, with a sense of occasion!

David's farm backed right on to Dinton Church, so it was quite easy to find. David was younger than she had imagined him to be— tall, with straight brown hair that fell over a face that was plainly used to an outdoor life. She was ushered into the kitchen—where the warmth of the stove matched the warm atmosphere of the room. This was obviously a family room. Children's works of art adorned the walls—'I Love Mummy', said one; 'My Cat by Michael Hughes, Age 5' said another. Plastic alphabet letters plastered the fridge door, holding up bills, and bits of paper with scribbled notes on. Wellington boots were lined up by the door, next to a huge wicker basket, overflowing with an even more huge pile of ironing. And to one side of the stove, tucked away in a dark corner, was a battered cardboard box, where two sleepy, tiny lambs watched her with clear, worried eyes.

'Don't mind the mess,' David apologized. 'It's always chaos during lambing. Just move that pile of books, and sit down. Karen helps out at the village school a couple of mornings a week, so she's not here right now. Can I get you a coffee, or something?'

'Only if you're having one,' replied Kate. 'Don't bother just for me. You must be busy.'

'Never too busy for a coffee though,' grinned David, 'and the good thing about an Aga is that the kettle is nearly always boiling!'

'Great house!' said Kate, looking round her. 'How long have you lived here?'

'As long as I've been around!' replied David, pulling down two mugs from hooks above the working surface. 'My family have always lived here—four generations of them, anyway. You ought to take a look at the graveyard at Dinton Church—it's full of Hughes! I find it rather comforting to see them there, and know that one day, my name will join them.'

He caught sight of Kate's surprised expression. 'Oh, there's nothing morbid about it. I'm not planning to make my exit for a good few years yet! I just like the thought that I'm carrying on, working the farm, as my father, and his father, and their fathers, did before me. There's a rhythm to it—just like the countryside, really. There's no part of the year that I don't enjoy. Every month brings something new—new life, new responsibilities for someone like me that farms the land—but every farmer that's gone before me must have had the same sense of fascination, wonder even, as I have.'

'I would have thought that the "wonder" soon wears off when you're working at the pace you are now—what with the weather, and the lambing in full swing?'

'Do you know, I'm shattered at the moment. I was up twice in the night for lambing, and it's been like that for more than a week. But I wouldn't change my job for anything. I love it.' He chuckled, 'Well, you'd have to, wouldn't you? Why else would you put up with all the rules and restrictions they're putting on farmers at the moment?'

'Tough, is it?' asked Kate.

'Tough? It's nothing short of murder—and I don't mean just killing off a whole, traditional way of life. I mean "murder" quite literally. Some blokes are finding it so much of a strain, trying to make ends meet, when they keep cutting back on prices and how much we're allowed to produce, that it's killing them! Did you know that more farmers commit suicide than almost any other profession?

'Oh, well, that's blown it,' said Kate, 'I'd always rather fancied marrying a farmer, because I thought they were rich, as well as rugged!'

David roared with laughter. 'More "rough" than "rugged", I should think! And you've no chance if you're after his money! They're poorer than vicars these days!'

'What about your wife? Does she worry about the pressure on you—and what it means for her and the children?'

'Well, Karen's a farmer's daughter herself. She knew the score when she took me on—and she still married me anyway! You're right about the pressure though—and I honestly don't know how I'd get through it, sometimes, if I didn't have...'

His voice faded, as he eyed her.

'Well, if I can't tell you, who can I tell? Without my belief that God has a hand in it all—that's what I was going to say.'

'Even in the bad times? You can see God at work then too?'

'Oh, the mess and muddle is none of his doing—we can manage to create that all by ourselves! But when I'm out there on my own, all I have to do is look around me, and he's there. I feel him. I can see his handiwork. Oh yes, I feel his hand in my life every moment of the day. Sometimes I talk out loud to him, and he listens. Sometimes, I do the listening—to the sounds of the countryside, to his world around me, to answers that I know he puts in my mind. He's there alright!'

Suddenly, the telephone rang—shrill and unwelcome. David reached for the receiver. His end of the conversation was short and monosyllabic. As he put the phone down, he grimaced. 'Triplets! One of the ewes is in trouble. Got to go. Walk over with me, and I'll show you the donkeys as we go through. It depends really, if you're looking for brains or beauty. We've got Doreen Donkey (sorry, Michael chose the name!), who's as pretty as a picture, but daft as a brush—or there's Denis, who's old and wily. He looks as if he's a simple soul, but don't you believe it! He's only eying you up, while he works out what's in it for him! You've not got wellies, then? You'll have to sort some out for yourself, you know, if you plan to catch a farmer...'

18 March

It was about half past five that evening, when Helen answered the door of the vicarage, to find Ian, the Musical Director, standing there. He looked dreadful. 'For heaven's sake, come in!' said Helen, leading him through to the kitchen. 'What do you need first? Lemsip, or a cup of tea?'

'Both! Either! Or perhaps I'll just swallow a whole bottle of Nightnurse, and have done with it!' he groaned, his blond head in his hands.

'It wasn't just a cold then, that you started last week?' Helen glanced at his flushed cheeks and watery eyes, as she filled the kettle.

'Well, I think it was then, but it just never got better, only worse. I think this is full-blown flu now.'

'And where have you travelled from today?'

'Only Birmingham.'

'So you've just done a four-hour drive feeling like that?'

'It's all a blur, Helen, all a blur. I'm here now anyway—and I've just got to get through this rehearsal tonight, and then *sleep*! Wonderful sleep!'

'Until when? When have you got to leave again?'

'Well, as long as I get to the Cotswolds for their rehearsal tomorrow night—how long should that take me? I reckon if I leave after lunch, I'll be alright. You know Jan's coming down tonight, do you?'

'Uh-huh, she rang earlier in the week. She's meeting up with your researcher, Kate, I think, so she said she'd pop in here sometime in the morning.'

'Big Decision Day tomorrow,' mumbled Ian, his head still buried in his arms. 'We've got to get the shape of this Sandford programme finalized. Interviews, hymns, music, choir... Oh no, the choir! What am I going to do about the choir?'

'Well, we've been putting out the notices everywhere we can think of, but there haven't been many more phone calls here this week,' Helen replied. 'I did have a word with Mrs Hulme, the Choir Mistress over at St Mark's in Stowmarket. They've got a very strong, almost professional, choir there (well, Mrs Hulme would say it was anyway!)—but I know they're often busy with bookings. She said that she'd put it to the group when she saw them on Monday, and she'd ring back. Nothing so far, though.'

Ian lifted his head. 'Well, that sounds hopeful. Should I ring her, do you think?'

'You could do—but they may just turn up this evening, who knows?'

Ian's head sank again.

Helen handed him two steaming cups—one with tea, one with a fragrant honey and lemon mixture. 'It's men's voices, though, that you really need,' she said, 'and heaven knows where you'll find them!'

When Ian's head shot up this time, his face was transformed by a beaming smile. He cheekily tapped his nose twice with the end of his forefinger, 'Aah! Well now, I might just have cracked that one! We'll have to wait and see!'

❧

Jack was on his way to The Bull, when he spotted the red Metro, pulling up exactly where he'd met Margaret the week before. He glanced as his watch. It was twenty-five past seven. He walked over to the car, as Margaret climbed out, her smile friendly and welcoming as she saw him approach.

'What happened to your pupil this evening? Did you let him off easy?'

Margaret laughed. 'Well, I've rearranged my lessons for the next couple of weeks—I should be able to get to the rehearsals on time from now on. Nice to see you, Jack. I didn't expect to bump into you so soon. You're not going to the rehearsal too, are you?'

'Well, I could pop along, I suppose. I seem to have volunteered myself to organize the seating in the church on the big night—don't know quite how I managed that really! Anyway, I've got a few questions I need answers to, and I hear the BBC lot are there in force this evening. Come on! You can lead the way, now you know where you're going!'

'How's your week been?' Margaret asked as they walked. 'Has this programme kept you busy?'

'Not really. Not for me, anyway. Everyone's very excited about it though. Nothing like this has ever happened to Sandford before!'

'I love "Songs of Praise",' said Margaret, as they turned into the church gate. 'I never miss it. I don't go out much in the evenings now. Tonight is quite an exception really. I get a bit nervous, being out on my own, especially while the evenings are still so dark.'

'Do you miss the company of the people you worked with at school?'

Margaret eyed him shrewdly. 'Only someone who is retired themselves could ask that question, and understand my answer. Yes, I miss their company dreadfully—and yet, I don't miss working. I've had enough of the nine to five routine of it all. From now on, I'd rather pick my own times to work—and when not to! But it's the conversation I miss most of all. There are days when I simply don't talk to a soul, from the moment I get up, until I go to bed. And then, when you've been on your own for a while, you find the art of conversation slips away from you. I spend all my time longing for someone to talk to—and when I get the chance, I can't think of anything interesting enough to say!'

'You sound pretty interesting to me!' said Jack.

'That's because you're very easy to talk to!'

They both turned their eyes to their feet as they walked, each one taken aback not just by the ease of their conversation, but the direction in which it was taking them.

The silence was broken by Jack, whose next suggestion took him as much by surprise, as it did Margaret.

'How about coming over a bit early for the next rehearsal—in time to join me for tea and cakes at The Bull? They do a good tea there, so they tell me.' He faltered, suddenly unsure of how he sounded, what she'd think.

Her reply was instant. 'Thank you, Jack. I'd like that very much.' And together they walked up the path towards the Village Hall.

'Ian, you're a genius! How on earth did you do it?'

Jan and Ian were standing at the front of the hall, as people filed in for the rehearsal. There were at least thirty more faces there than the week before—and most of the newcomers were men!

'"West Side Story"!' grinned Ian. 'I noticed there had been a production of "West Side Story" around here a few weeks ago, by some group called the Saxmundham Songsters. There was an old notice about it on the shop door when I called in the other week. Well, any group brave enough to put on that musical has to have a really strong men's chorus—all those Jets and Sharks! I gave the phone number on the poster a ring—and Bill Hewitt, their Producer, was really positive about helping us out. They're all good experienced singers, most of them can read music—they'll even dance for us, if we give them half a chance!!'

'And whistle, click fingers, and stab people in the back too?' laughed Jan. 'I'm not sure how well that will go down on "O Sacred Head"! Hang on, who are this lot coming in now?' A mixed group of twenty or so men and women were making their way to seats, lead by a formidable hatted lady, in a severe grey coat. She looked towards the front of the hall, obviously made up her mind that Ian and Jan were in charge, and headed straight for them.

'Another one for the men's chorus?' whispered Ian out of the side of his mouth, which had Jan hiding a smile behind her hand as the woman approached.

'Dorothy Hulme,' she announced, 'Leader of St Mark's Choir. Now, what exactly is going on here? Have you music? My choir will only work from music.'

'We have all the music they'll need, Mrs Hulme,' replied Ian, his face perfectly straight. 'We're delighted to see you. I've heard good things about St Mark's Choir.'

Mrs Hulme peered at him. 'Of course you have. Now, before we start, what are the dates? We're very busy already, you know. I have to be sure that your booking doesn't clash with any others!'

'Jan,' said Ian, turning to his Producer so that only she could see the twinkle in his eye, 'perhaps you would be kind enough to talk over the dates with Mrs Hulme, while I get this rehearsal under way.'

19 March

They all sat round in their makeshift 'office' in Grove House, balancing papers in one hand, and cups of coffee in the other. Ian had been banished to an armchair on his own by Jan, who told him in no uncertain terms that if he passed on whatever 'bug' he was harbouring to anyone else in the team, she'd personally throttle him! Kate was doing most of the talking at the beginning, as she went through her research notes, reporting on the people she had met.

'I've had a chat with the headmistress of Sandford Junior School, and she's quite happy for us to film their egg rolling afternoon—that's on 1st April, the Thursday of that week.'

'How many children are likely to be involved?'

'All the school—about fifty pupils, from the little ones who are just five, up to eleven. Oh, and apparently, they have a competition to paint and decorate their own eggs, and they want to know if Pam would judge the winners for them. She would, wouldn't she?'

'I bet she'd love that—providing we don't have to whip her off straight away to do more recording. Tell them we'll confirm that nearer the time. Right, let's just think about how we'd use that egg rolling piece. Are we likely to want to talk to anyone about what's going on?'

'Maybe some of the kids—a couple of vox pops?'

'Mmm,' said Jan, chewing her pen, 'it's worth a try—otherwise, we could just have Pam tell us to camera what it all represents as the eggs roll behind her. How far do they go, by the way—and how fast are they?'

'Well, the hill is quite steep, but not very high—and the grass is long, so I'm not sure that they get up much of a speed.'

'Are they chocolate, these eggs?' asked Ian, who was poised on the point of blowing his nose.

'No, real, I think.'

'Raw?' asked Ian again.

Jan groaned. 'That sounds like a stupid question, but it probably isn't. You'd better check that, Kate. If anyone is going to end up with egg all over the face, it will be me! Especially on April Fool's Day!'

'Right,' said Kate, 'donkeys! I've got the offer of two—one I'm told is pretty but dopey—the other is bright as a button, but can be bad-tempered. Take your pick—Doreen or Denis—they both belong to the same farmer.'

'Perhaps that's what we should do, then,' said Jan thoughtfully, 'literally "take our pick", and include the choosing of the donkey in our programme. That's something we could do at the school that Thursday lunchtime, before the egg rolling—get the children to "audition" them both, and then select which one will have the starring role in the Palm Sunday procession. When are we recording the exterior of that procession—early Thursday evening, isn't it, before the church recording that night?'

'That's what we've planned so far—and don't forget that we've got to record the *end* of that sequence too, as the procession comes through the door, and up the aisle, when the congregation are there during the church recording. So, Doreen—or Denis—won't have much time to prepare for their big moment!'

'Make a note to remind the headmistress that we'll need all the children in the church that evening, in full costume. Have they chosen a Jesus yet?'

'Apparently, the most suitable child is the only one who's had experience with donkeys—and that's a girl. Her hair's quite short though, so her teacher reckons that with her headdress on, and perhaps a beard, she'll look the part.'

'Fine. Now, Ian, what about "There Is a Green Hill Far Away"? The school do know that the children are singing that on the night, don't they?'

'Yes,' replied Ian, 'I popped along to see them, when I was here last week. They're OK—loud, very loud, but quite sweet. There are some lovely faces amongst the little ones.'

'The other hymns are fairly straightforward, I think,' continued Jan, "For the Beauty of the Earth", and "The Old Rugged Cross". You know we're planning to use "The Old Rugged Cross" over what I hope will be old rugged fishermen. Have you met them yet, Kate? What are they like?'

'It's a lovely story,' said Kate, flicking through her notes. 'I've only met one of them so far—that's Sidney, who seems to be the one who organizes everything. I don't know how old he is—he may even be in his eighties now—but he's a real old character. He's pottered about on water all his life, and now he's retired, once a week he meets his mates, Frank and Bo (heaven knows how old they are, I've not seen them), and they all take a little rowboat about half a mile off the coast, and sit there fishing, as the sun goes down. And as they wait for the fish to bite, they read the Bible out loud to each other, and sing hymns—and "The Old Rugged Cross" is one they're sure to know.'

'That sounds perfect,' said Jan, making a note in her file. 'He'll be alright for an interview, will he, Sidney?'

'Well, what he says is fine. How he says it may be a bit of a problem. He's got a really broad Suffolk accent—we might need subtitles...'

Ian spluttered into his cup of coffee, his fair hair falling over his eyes.

'No, I'm serious,' grinned Kate, 'I had to ask him to repeat everything, because I didn't understand a word of his answer! But the other two fellas may be just as good, and perhaps easier to understand. I'll try and track them down during the next week, and let you know.'

'Have you come across anyone who can fill in the history of the area, and why the churches are so huge in little villages like Sandford?'

'No, I've not got far on that yet. I've been meaning to have a chat with Clive Linton about it—he said he would try to think of someone. He's not the easiest person in the world to get hold of, though. I don't know where he disappears to, but he never seems to be where he should be, when he should be!'

'I hope he's been giving some thought to the prayer and blessing,' said Jan. 'It's important that we get the words right for that. What do you think about recording him doing the prayer outside somewhere nice? Do you think he could manage that?'

'I should think so,' replied Kate, thoughtfully. 'Do you want me to mention it to him?'

'No, I've got to see him later today, to sort out a few arrangements for the outside broadcast. Leave that to me. Now, other interviews? Are there any?'

'Well,' said Kate, thumbing through her notes again. 'I've come across a great idea to get disabled people exploring the Suffolk Heritage Coast—and this area is all part of that, really. Because it's considered to be of outstanding natural beauty, the various organizations involved in protecting the coastline have got together to organize a scheme called—hang on a minute...' Kate flicked over pages furiously, '"Out and About". Basically, they organize an outing at least once a month, where they lay on transport to collect anyone who would normally find it difficult to get out at all, because of illness, disability, or perhaps lack of opportunity. Then, they usually end up with a group of about thirty, a mixture of disabled and able-bodied, and they take a slow stroll—or push—to somewhere different each time. The chap who runs it, Mike, is great—he talks about the great outdoors, and feeling at one with God—all good stuff for us, really. It could make a nice piece.'

'Sounds very promising. Now, we could record that on Monday afternoon, couldn't we?'

'Yes, that would work out well, providing the weather's OK.'

'Anyone else?' asked Jan.

'Well, talking about the great outdoors, I came across someone quite by accident, that honestly, I think would give a terrific interview, if I can persuade him to consider it. David Hughes, the farmer who owns the donkeys—he's a wonderful speaker. His family have farmed around Dinton Church for generations, half the graveyard is filled with his ancestors, his family still go along to services there now. And he talks very movingly about the pressures on farmers nowadays—and how he draws comfort and strength from what is obviously a very deep, but simple, faith.'

'We could do with someone who comes from the farming community,' commented Jan, 'because it's obviously a way of life around here. Have a proper chat to him, Kate—see if you can talk him into it.'

'That reminds me,' Kate changed the subject abruptly. 'I need wellies. I forgot mine on this trip, and I got my shoes coated in something very unsavoury when I went to see him this week...'

'That's three interviewees,' continued Jan. 'We could do with a strong Christian testimony—have you come across anyone for that yet?'

'Well, I did go to see a couple the other day—Dee and Chris were their names—it's a very gritty, tough story they tell about being addicted to drugs in London when they first met—he ended up in prison, she found herself in a drug rehabilitation centre, separated from their young son, who was only a few months old at the time. And at that centre, she found God—and when Chris joined her there later, he did too.'

'That sounds very strong—and not what you'd expect in a programme in a rural area like this,' said Jan.

'Ye-s, that's true...' Kate started.

'But...' prompted Jan.

'But—I'm not sure that they wouldn't scare the bulk of our "Songs of Praise" audience to death. They're devout born-againers, and they come out with rather a lot of pat phrases—you know what I mean. They even said that Pam would go straight to hell, because she wasn't born again herself! I think they can't wait to get their hands on her, to save her soul!'

'It's a difficult one, that,' agreed Jan. 'I mean, we've had some really inspiring interviews with born-again Christians on the programme in the past—but some of them can be very dismissive of people who've been Christians all their lives. We'd just have to be really careful that we didn't exclude a lot of our viewers who haven't had a "road to Damascus" experience! What do you think, Kate? What about Dee and Chris? Are they worth pursuing?'

'Well, I did meet someone else, who in many ways can provide just as gritty a story, but perhaps would be able to express his faith in a way that most of our viewers would feel more at home with. I'm thinking of Stephen Yearling, the new Baptist minister in Steepleton. I had a smashing chat with him the other day. He was based in Birmingham for several years before coming here, a very tough, challenging job for a minister—so to be posted to a rural ministry now is quite a change for him. He's very good at talking about the pain and suffering he was used to seeing around him in the big city, and he talks about how people still have problems here, but they're different. And I especially liked the way he talks about his sense of smallness and inadequacy, even though he believes all things are possible through God. It struck me that his could be a great interview to go into "Just As I Am".'

'And have you decided on a soloist for "Just As I Am" yet, Ian?'

'Yes, well, Anna, I think. You heard her. What did you think?'

'I think she's charming—young and pretty. Not keen on the way she dresses though. You might have to have a word with her about that. Black can be very unflattering on television, particularly on a young girl.'

Ian put his hands up, in mock horror. 'Don't ask me to get into discussions about fashion. That's definitely women's talk. I leave that totally to you!'

'I quite fancy the idea of beginning "Just As I Am" inside the church, during our outside broadcast—but continuing it like a kind of pop video, with Anna singing in some nice locations outside. Do you think she could cope with that?'

'I reckon so,' replied Ian, who hadn't had much time to give Anna any real thought at all, since he first heard her sing. 'I meant to organize a rehearsal with her this week, but didn't manage to fit it in. I've given Betty the music though, and she says she'll make sure Anna knows it well enough by next week. I'll meet up with her when I'm next down, to fine tune it. Actually, that reminds me—did I tell you I've found someone absolutely perfect—and local—to be our organist on the night?'

'Good!' said Jan. 'How?'

'Fell into my lap, really! I was at college with a chap called Colin Brown, who's a much better organist than I'll ever be! I've kept in touch with him over the years, and he's based in Stowmarket now—not far away really. He's organist at the big parish church there, but oddly enough, he's only a semi-pro, and seems to think of playing as just a pleasant hobby! I couldn't believe it when he told me that his day job is at an estate agency! He seems to be doing very nicely out of it, and of course, he's a family man now—but it's a real shame when I think how much talent he's got.'

'And he's the right man for our recording? He's experienced enough?'

'He can play anything. He'll even be able to make the old organ at St Michael's sing! And talking of singing, I'll get him to meet up with Anna to go through her piece during the coming week, and he's happy to take the local choir rehearsals that I can't get to.'

'Right, make a note, Sue, to draw up a contract for him. What was his name again?'

'Colin Brown. Nice bloke. You'll like him.'

'One last thing,' said Jan. '"O Sacred Head". I'd like that to be a choir piece, recorded at Dinton Church. Now, what are the chances of us having a choir that can cope with that?'

Ian looked thoughtful. 'Well, I have no doubt at all that St Mark's Choir will be wonderful for it. They really do perform to a very high standard—although I don't think they have much chance not to, with Mrs Hulme in charge. I tell you, that woman scares me rigid! I'm more worried, in a way, about the general balance of the choir we're gathering together. Those men were great last night, but they're a bit undisciplined as singers. I could still do with some strong lead voices, sopranos and altos—a good women's choir is just what we need.'

'And you've not come across one locally?'

'Not a sausage, so far. I may have to look farther afield. Anyway, I'm working on it.'

'Well, keep looking. I've scheduled to record "O Sacred Head" in Dinton Church on Friday morning, by the way. It would be nice to know if we've got anyone to do the singing!'

'I'll speak to Mrs Hulme as soon as I can,' replied Ian, 'but, of course, I'm off to the Cotswolds now, for their rehearsal this evening. I'll give her a ring while I'm on the road.' He scribbled a note in biro on the back of his hand, then glanced up at Jan's worried face. 'Don't worry about it, Jan. Have I ever failed you yet?'

Jan looked straight into his watery, cold-laden eyes. 'There's always a first time!'

❧

Anna had found the disappointment of not hearing from Ian almost unbearable. What he'd said, the way he'd looked at her, when he heard her sing that day—it had all been so... so positive. He had talked to her as if she was a fellow professional. He had spoken of future rehearsals together. His whole manner was one of promise—he acknowledged her, he rated her, he was attracted to her—wasn't he? Had she just imagined the warmth in his eyes? Was it only her heart that had been pounding when they shook hands? Had he felt nothing, when he hugged her after she'd sung to him—for him? Had she played it wrong? Did he think her immature? Why, oh why, had she been so tongue-tied? And why, for heaven's sake, had she been in school uniform when he met her? That couldn't have helped much.

Before the two rehearsals in the Village Hall, she had closeted herself into the bathroom and then, her bedroom, for a couple of hours, before she was finally satisfied with the way she looked. Her long, tight black skirt, black socks, black boots, a black polo neck and a long black waistcoat—she glanced at herself in the mirror. She looked good—fashionable, and sophisticated. Why then, at that first rehearsal, had Ian barely said more than 'hello', with a casual wave across the room in her direction? And last night, he'd spent all his time pandering to the new people who arrived, and didn't actually get round to speaking to her at all!

She loved the rehearsals, though. It had nothing to do with the music, or the singing. It was just him—being able to watch him at work, admire his skill and patience, and stare at his face, his dear face, with its curtain of fair hair that always seemed to be falling in his eyes. She wondered how old he was—mid-twenties, perhaps? Nothing wrong with that. For two people like them, who had such a love of music and singing in common, there was nothing wrong with that.

Anyway, he would have to see her soon. She already knew that she was going to sing 'Just As I Am', and she'd been practising hard at home, to make sure that she knew every word perfectly. He'd have to make time to see her, so that he could hear her sing, and be sure she was doing it just right. Perhaps there would be some word from him today, especially as he had been here for the rehearsal in the village hall the night before?

She had been home for more than an hour, and was curled up in the armchair watching television, when her Dad came up from the shop, a letter in his hand. 'Sorry, love, I meant to give you this earlier. That chap, Ian, dropped it in.'

'Oh, Dad! For heaven's sake! It might be really important! The least you could have done is given it to me immediately!' She was up, and went to snatch it from his hand, as he withdrew his arm, and held the letter away from her. 'Look, Anna,' he said, 'let's get one thing straight. Your Mum and I are busy. We're working, you know, to pay for all the million and one things you keep saying you need and must have. You might be a star for the television people, but in this house, you just a family member—and you either start behaving like a decent member of this family, and take other people's feelings into account, or you can feel the back of my hand! You're not too big for a clip round the ear, you know!'

Anna said nothing. Her face was black and indignant. She waited.

'Do you understand what I'm saying?' Anna was silent.

'Well, do you?' Don shouted straight into her face.

'Of course, I do,' Anna replied, staring back. 'Come on, Dad, give over. Just give me the letter.'

'Well, I expect to see an improvement, missie. I mean what I say!'

They glared at each other, neither speaking—then, slowly, he handed her the letter. She grabbed it.

'Thank you!' shouted Don. 'It's polite to say *Thank you!*'

'Thank you. Thank you. Thank you. Is that alright?' Anna's pose was cocky and furious. 'Can I get on and read my letter in private now? Please!'

Anna waited until Don had left the room, before she marched over and banged the door behind him. She tore open the envelope.

Dear Anna,

Sorry I haven't had much chance to sort out your solo yet. I seem to be forever on the road between one programme and the next at the moment.

I've left the copy of the actual arrangement for 'Just As I Am' with Betty, and I've asked her to contact you to run over the arrangement with you. I may not make it down here now until the actual week of our recording, but Colin Brown, the organist, will ring you within the next few days, to organize a proper musical rehearsal.

Hope school is going well. All the best,
Ian Spence

Anna tore the letter up into four pieces, and screwed it into a tiny ball, before flinging it with all her might across the room.

Ian was well on his way to the Cotswolds by the time Anna opened his letter. He glanced at the time, reached over to the dashboard, and switched on his mobile phone. Sarah might be home by now. He hoped so.

She picked up the receiver almost immediately, and her pleasure at hearing his voice was plain.

'You are still coming, aren't you? You've not had to change your plans?'

'Listen, you're talking to a man who's in dire need of some tender, loving care. I'm ill, you know, desperately ill. I'll expect a lot of sympathy.'

'I'll have a big pot of Vick ready, to rub on your chest...'

'You hussy!' chuckled Ian. 'Can't wait to see you! I reckon if this rehearsal in the Cotswolds finishes on time, I should be near Stratford about eleven. That OK?'

'And you can still stay tomorrow? You haven't got to rush off anywhere?'

'Tomorrow,' he replied. 'I intend to sleep all day. How about you?'

Jan and Kate planned to travel back to their base in Manchester together that evening, where they hoped to grab at least one day at home before they made their way back to Sandford again. For Kate, that day meant a rare day at the family home she still shared with her Mum, and younger brother—a chance to wash the smalls, catch up on the television soaps she'd missed, and sleep—glorious sleep!

It would work very well if the two girls travelled back together, because they lived within three miles of each other. Jan's terraced two-up, two-down was cosy and cluttered. When she moved in four years ago, she came up with a master plan for the decoration and renovation. She still had the plan—but sadly, never the time! The walls and paintwork remained exactly as they had been when she bought the house, and somehow she had stopped noticing the dated colours, and faded paper. It was home, somewhere to unwind and hide, when the work piled up on her.

But before they could hit the road for home, there was still so much to do. With barely a week to go before the vans started arriving, and the recording in the village began, there were a million and one small details to finalize. Many of the arrangements for the recording in the church could be settled by getting down to brass tacks in a conversation with Clive Linton. All they had to do was pin him down to a meeting, and hope he'd turn up to it!

It was with great relief, then, that they were greeted at the door of the vicarage by Helen saying, 'He is here! He's just finishing what he's doing.'

'Don't tell me,' laughed Jan. 'He's in the garden!'

Jan noticed that there was no laughter in Helen's reply. 'However did you guess? Come through to the kitchen. I'm just making tea— only sandwiches, but if you fancy joining us, you're welcome!'

Jan and Kate looked at each other, and grimaced. 'We're supposed to have a pact,' Jan explained, 'to eat less while we're away! The trouble is that it's so easy to eat too much when you're working. If you've ever seen the size of the breakfasts at Grove House, not to mention the slab of cake that arrives with every cup of tea, you'd know what I mean. And when you've been out filming in the cold and rain all morning, it's somehow comforting to sit down at lunchtime in front of a meal that someone else has cooked! And then, in the evenings, sometimes the only thing you can do when you're away from home is find somewhere to eat—again!'

'No,' said Kate, 'the real trouble is that both of us have willpower like a blob of jelly. I'd love a sandwich, Helen! I'll diet tomorrow.'

Jan grimaced, gave in, and pulled up a stool in front of the breakfast bar. 'Can we help?'

'Nothing to do really!' replied Helen, as she emptied tea leaves from the pot.

Just then, Clive swept through the kitchen door, his apologies profuse.

'I had your engineering man, Simon, on the phone earlier on, by the way. Just a few last-minute details he needed to check. He says the first vans should be arriving late on Friday evening.'

'Yes, the outside broadcast for the Cotswolds programme is on Thursday night,' replied Jan, 'so once they've de-rigged the church, and loaded up the vans, most of the vehicles—except for the scanner and the generator van that are needed to complete the editing for the Cotswolds programme—will start the journey here. Have you finally agreed with Simon about where they should be parked?'

'Well, we've had to get the Council's agreement, but it's all been settled now that the vans will be parked in the lane which leads round towards the Village Hall.'

'That suits us fine. What a relief that's settled at last,' said Jan.

'Oh, by the way, Clive,' interrupted Helen, 'I meant to tell you earlier. I had a very strange phone call this morning from that Pete Durrell—you know, the one who edits The Herald newspaper?'

'Oh, good,' said Jan, 'I've been meaning to follow up the press release we sent all the local papers. Is he going to give us some coverage, do you think?'

'Honestly, I'm not sure what he was after. He asked some most peculiar questions—about how old the church was, and then what sort of insurance cover we had! And then he started talking about Betty, asking how long she'd been our organist—oh, it was all friendly enough, but it was a very odd conversation...'

'How did you reply?' It was Clive who asked.

'Well, I felt uncomfortable about the tone of his questions pretty early on, so I just said that I didn't know any details, and that really he should talk to you.'

'And me, by the sounds of it,' added Jan. 'Give me his number, and I'll ring him. Now, any news on how the tickets are going?'

Helen buttered slices of bread as she spoke. 'Well, Bunty Maddocks seems to have her finger on that, along with Jack Diggens, who's turned out to be a born organizer. Basically, we've given out tickets to each of the neighbouring churches, along the lines that you and I talked about. Nobody's let us know that they can't find homes for their tickets—in fact, a couple of them have come back and asked if there are any more to spare.'

'I have kept back twenty,' said Jan, 'just to make sure all the people we select for interviews have seats, and for emergencies. You know, don't you, Clive, that we aren't able to use that front right-hand corner block of seats, because we'd like to put scaffolding tower there?'

'Oh, right!' said Clive, who didn't look at all sure that he understood which seats she was talking about.

'It's the perfect place we can get a camera up high, to see the whole of the congregation at once,' explained Jan. 'Perhaps you and I could take a walk over to the church in a minute, so that we can discuss the seating arrangements properly. Do you think Bunty should be in on that chat, too?'

Helen smiled. 'I'm sure she'd love to! Shall I give her a ring, and ask her to pop round here in the next quarter of an hour, or so, if she can?'

'That would be great,' said Jan. 'How are you getting on with stewards for the night, by the way?'

'Well,' said Helen, as she mixed together contents of a tin of tuna and some mayonnaise, 'Jack's the one you need to talk to about that—he's sorting out all the seating arrangements too. He's not been involved with the church for long, but he's got time on his hands, and he seems very organized. Do you want to meet him, while you're here?'

'Not necessary tonight,' said Jan, 'but I would like to have a chat to him in the early part of next week. And talking of having chats with people, you and I must get together quite soon, Clive, to go over the wording of your prayer and blessing. Have you planned what you'd like to say?'

Clive closed his eyes, as he replied. 'I'm still giving it some thought. I want to make sure the words are absolutely right.'

'Well, I'd appreciate your suggestions by—what shall we say—Monday, sometime? Then, we can make any adjustments necessary, and work out how and where to record it. I'm thinking of asking you to do the prayer out of doors somewhere. Would that be appropriate, do you think, bearing in mind that I hope your prayer is going to be about giving thanks for the beauty of the area in which you live, and for loving, caring community life?'

Clive opened his mouth to reply, then closed it again.

'Clive?' prompted Jan. 'Is that OK?'

'Oh, fine—yes, absolutely fine,' agreed Clive.

'How's the rest of the programme shaping up?' asked Helen, as she piled tuna and cucumber sandwiches on to a plate. 'Have you found all the people you need to interview now?'

'Mostly, yes,' said Kate, 'except—well, come to think of it, you might be able to help with the one person we could do with finding. You don't know anyone who can explain the history of why churches are so large and imposing in this area, do you—someone who could put it all into a Christian perspective, and perhaps link right up to church life here at the present time?'

Helen looked thoughtful for a moment, then, 'You know, I think I do know someone who might be able to help. Come to think of it, there's someone who'd be just perfect!'

When Bunty arrived, she reached the vicarage door at exactly the same moment that Betty walked up the path, on her way to see Helen. They joined the group in the kitchen, who were through with the sandwiches, and on to chocolate biscuits and their second cups of tea by then.

'The rehearsal went well the other night, didn't you think so, Betty?' asked Jan.

'Honestly, I think that Ian is a marvel—so good with people, and a lovely sense of humour!'

'That's one of Ian's most endearing qualities,' agreed Jan, 'to keep smiling, even though sometimes his job is an extremely hard one. We're not quite there yet, are we, with the choir? We really do need some more ladies' voices—and heaven knows where we're going to find them!'

Bunty and Betty glanced at each other.

'It just sounds so unbalanced, as it is,' continued Jan. 'Ian's arrangements could sound much nicer, if the ratio of one kind of voice to another is just right.'

It must have been warm in that kitchen. Betty looked flushed—not that Jan appeared to notice. 'Of course, we can do quite a lot of tweaking the sound by planning precisely where we place our microphones, and by mixing it all carefully in the scanner—but there really is no replacement for getting it right in the first place. If only we could find a really good ladies' choir around here somewhere...'

'Do you know,' interrupted Helen, 'I do believe the Women's Institute have a quite a good choir, don't they, based in Saxmundham? If anyone knows, you would, Betty—have you ever seen them? Are they any good?'

'Well...' mumbled Betty, looking to Bunty for inspiration.

'What a great idea!' exclaimed Bunty immediately, 'I had completely forgotten about them, hadn't you, Betty?'

'Umm...' said Betty, her head down.

'I bet,' continued Bunty, in full swing now, 'I bet that I could lay my hands on a number for Rose Smith, the County Organizer for the Institute, when I pop back home! I'll go right now—back in a tick! How clever you are, Helen! That's a wonderful suggestion!'

And with that, she rushed out of the house, leaving behind her in the kitchen a variety of expressions that ranged from disbelief to total bemusement!

21 March

In most ways, Betty had never felt happier. Getting involved with the preparation for the 'Village Praise' programme had become an exhilarating and exciting treat. Any embarrassment she'd felt at first about her lack of experience and limited musical knowledge had disappeared once she met Ian, and realized that he was competent to organize everything. All she had to do was to suggest, encourage and be around. She felt necessary and indispensable—part of the team.

As she looked into the bathroom mirror to brush her hair that Sunday morning, she found herself blushing again at the scene at the vicarage on Friday about the Women's Institute Choir. Why, oh why, had she ever allowed herself to be swayed by Bunty, about not mentioning that choir, the moment they had thought of them, days before? It was all because of an old, almost unspoken sense of rivalry. Bunty and she belonged to the Town's Women's Guild, whose branch met in Sandford Village Hall. Their meetings were small, but informal and friendly. The Women's Institute was much stronger in the region, headed by the highly efficient, highly charming Rose Smith. Whenever their paths crossed, their smaller club seemed to come off at a disadvantage. At flower shows, it always seemed that a Women's Institute member walked off with the biggest prize; at sponsored events, the Women's Institute seemed to be better connected, drawing in larger, more impressive sums of money. Not a word was said—and Rose Smith was never anything but sympathetic and conciliatory—but frankly, it got right up the noses of the TWG in Sandford! The thought of Rose and her band of ladies rushing to the rescue of the good name of Sandford would take a bit of swallowing—but the deed was done.

Bunty had made the call, the scene was set, and the Women's Institute Choir were all ready to save the day by coming along to both the music rehearsals scheduled for the coming week.

Betty closed her eyes, as she stood at the bathroom mirror. 'Forgive me, Lord, for failing to offer all the help I could. Forgive my pride and arrogance. Help us all to work together, for the glory of thy name, Amen.'

There was a loud thump on the door. 'Betty, how much longer are you going to be in there?'

She sighed. Charles was at last acknowledging that she lived in the same house as him, but his conversation was never more than absolutely necessary. He became more bitter and isolated as each day went by. He went out of his way to avoid anyone who was involved in the forthcoming programme. He hadn't spoken a word to the vicar, who frankly hadn't seemed to notice much. Charles continued with his duties as Church Warden with a minimum of words and commitment. What, Betty wondered, was Charles thinking, as he knelt to pray during the service each Sunday morning? Was he asking for forgiveness and understanding too?

'Betty!' Charles' voice roared from outside the door. 'Betty, you're not the only one who has to get out this morning! Kindly allow other people to use the bathroom, apart from yourself!'

Betty opened the door, and came face to face with him. 'I'm ready now,' she said. 'I'm just going to put the kettle on, and make some toast. Can I get you some?'

'I'm quite capable of making my own, thank you,' Charles snapped, as he pushed past her, shutting the door firmly behind him. She stood there for a while, her forehead against the doorframe, a wave of sadness and despair coming over her. And then, slowly, she made her way downstairs.

Once inside the room, Charles stood silently for a while too. He heard Betty at last move away, and his breathing relaxed. Poor Betty. She really didn't understand. Her heart was in the right place, he never doubted that for a moment—but she was so easily led, so quickly engulfed by other people's ideas and enthusiasm. He knew that he should sit her down, and explain why it mattered so much to him that she had gone against his will—but then, if after so many years of marriage, she didn't know him well enough to understand how much the humiliation and her disobedience had offended him, then was there any point in trying to explain now?

He sat heavily on the side of the bath, and thought about her downstairs in the kitchen. He knew she was sad. He knew she was trying to offer olive branches. Why couldn't he accept them? Well, perhaps in a few days, he would be able to.

Wednesday. That would be the day when the whole matter would be out in the open, for proper public debate—the day *The Herald* appeared with *his* article on the front page.

Charles found himself smiling. That would get people talking! His warnings would be listened to then! Betty would have to see that he had been right all along, on Wednesday! Then, she'd understand alright! And then, he'd be able to forgive her.

It was a strange thing, mused Clive, as he made his way down the aisle to begin the service that morning, that since it had been announced that the BBC were going to make a programme from St Michael's, pews had been unusually full each Sunday morning. Of course, he wasn't naive enough to think that it was the charisma of his sermons that was bringing them in. It was all about tickets. It had been made clear from the outset that only regular church-attenders would be allowed tickets for the recording. Over the past few weeks, the number of 'regular attenders' had almost tripled.

Never mind, he wasn't complaining. Whatever it was that brought them back to the house of God, it was his duty to make sure that they found truth and peace within these walls. God's hand had brought them here—he had to make sure that they came back again and again, long after the programme had come and gone.

But it wasn't just the size of the congregation that had changed. There was a subtle difference in the atmosphere too. There had been an almost club-like fondness between the small group who had always attended on a Sunday morning. Each of them found comfort in the routine, the expected, the predictable sameness of the service. But when the programme makers came, presumably seeing something precious in the simple, devout worship at St Michael's, local people began to look at their church with a fresh eye too. It was true, as it was of so many things—that you don't always value what you've grown used to, until someone from outside recognizes the treasures you have on your own doorstep.

Praise to the Lord! O let all that is in me adore Him!
All that hath life and breath, come now with praises before Him!

Clive had always loved singing, and this hymn had been a mainstay of his worship life for as long as he could remember. As he walked, he sang without a moment's hesitation about the words. And as he moved towards his seat at the top of the church, he glanced at the faces to either side of him in the pews. Major Gregory was there—he had come less frequently in recent months, because his hip was playing him up badly these days. And Marjorie was beside him—now, there was a surprise! Clive couldn't remember the last time he had seen her in St Michael's, but he was pleased to see her here today. He must make a point of having a word with them both when the service was over. And that chap, Jack! Helen had mentioned that he might appreciate a quiet chat sometime, and yet, although Clive had noticed that he was following the service with great concentration at the back of the church where he'd sat for several weeks now, Jack always seemed to have left the church before Clive could get his robes off, and down to the door. Come to think of it, Clive thought for a moment—I don't believe he comes up to the altar rail for Communion either. I'll keep my eye on him this morning, Clive decided, and make a point of talking to him very soon. Perhaps I'll catch him at home one evening.

From Jack's viewpoint at the back of the church, he could watch and listen, without anyone making demands on him. He still felt an outsider, as if everyone but him knew where to find the words of the service, how to track down the readings, which book the next hymn was in—all the things he had forgotten. At least, he was prepared for the part of the service where Communion was taken now. He simply kept his head down, and avoided all eye contact as rows of people began to move towards the altar. He wasn't ready for that yet.

He had been frightened, shaken, even shocked by what had happened last time. If he ever took Communion again—if he ever felt the time was right—he would hold his head up to take the bread and the wine, knowing that for him, this was total commitment. Until he had sorted out a few more answers for himself, until he felt more sure that this was what he wanted, he preferred to stay in the background, watching, listening, learning. He knew the vicar had been trying to catch his eye, and because he sensed that Clive would seek him out at the end of the service, he always made his escape early. He knew he couldn't talk to Clive, not about his questions and uncertainties, not yet. What Jack needed were answers to the kind of questions that children probably asked in confirmation class. His doubts were too basic, his knowledge too sketchy, his faith so tender and new that he wasn't ready to talk to someone as knowledgeable and sure as he knew Clive to be.

He looked around him. Sometimes, he still couldn't believe that he really was sitting in a church again, after all these years. And although he held himself distant from the rest of the congregation during the service, he had made a commitment to himself to try and give something, some small amount of time and effort, so that he wasn't only taking from the church, but giving back too. That's why he had so readily offered to help Helen with distributing the posters. And that's why, when she mentioned that someone reliable was needed to organize seating and stewards on the rehearsal and recording nights (something about it usually being Charles Waite's domain, but for some reason, he wasn't able to help on this occasion), Jack had volunteered without hesitation. Funny, looking back on it. He had spent years in this village avoiding involvement and commitment, and now, well now, he knew he needed to be part of what was around him. It was almost like wanting to be part of a family again. Over the years, as he had pushed people away, loneliness had crept up on him. He knew that he couldn't change his shyness overnight; he still knew how hopeless he could be at small talk, especially in a crowd, but he was trying. He was trying.

He found himself smiling. How on earth had he ever found the courage to talk to Margaret in such a—such a—forthright way? His behaviour, and his boldness at asking her to have tea with him before the rehearsal on Tuesday, still had him reeling. And perhaps, even more of a surprise—she had said yes! Unbelievable! Since then, Jack had gone over that conversation time and time again in his head. Perhaps she thought him too forward, even insincere? Perhaps he would be able to think of nothing at all to say to her? Perhaps they would both feel awkward at being in each other's company by arrangement, rather than by accident?

But she had said yes! She had said yes, and because of that, Jack recognized for the first time in as long as he could remember, a small, unfamiliar flutter of excitement stirring in him.

⁂

Helen caught sight of Bunty's mauve-coloured cardigan, and rushed to head her off before she reached the church door. 'My!' she said, grabbing Bunty's elbow to stop her. 'You're anxious to get away this morning!'

Bunty smiled back at her. 'Just a few ticket details to sort out with Jack. He's been marvellous really. He's more or less taken over the whole thing, but people keep ringing me, because I suppose they always have rung me about everything! Anyway, the Catholic Church have returned ten of theirs, and the Methodists rang last night to ask if there were any spares. I thought I'd just grab a word with him, before I go back and put the dinner on.'

'Well,' said Helen, as they walked together towards the church gate, 'believe it or not, I wanted to ask you something which is not about the programme at all—well, not really. I just wondered if we're organized with enough supplies of Palm Sunday crosses. You're making them again this year, are you?'

'Yes, we're well under way with them,' Bunty replied. 'We thought that perhaps we should do quite a few extra because we'll need them for two services really, won't we—for the recording which will look as if it's actually happening on Palm Sunday, and then for our real service that Sunday morning.'

Helen laughed. 'I bet you've got to the point where you never want to see another palm leaf as long as you live!'

But Bunty didn't answer. Her eyes had glazed over into a distant stare.

'Bunty?' Helen's voice was full of concern and curiosity. 'Bunty, whatever is it?'

Suddenly, Bunty snapped out of her reverie, her face breaking into a broad grin. 'Helen, you're brilliant!' And with that, she clasped the astounded Helen to her ample lilac bosom—then she was gone, hotfoot out of the gate, and down the street in the direction of her home.

Sunday lunch was always a snatched affair in the Linton household. Helen stood at the sink, washing up the coffee cups she should have washed up more than an hour before, and sighed as she watched Clive, hard at work, cocooned and totally content, inside his greenhouse.

She should have sat him down, across the kitchen table from her, to drink that cup of coffee, she thought. There was so much to discuss, so many loose details that needed to be settled, so many phone calls that should have been returned. Clive forgot them all in his hurry to get back to his beloved seedlings. Correction, Clive did not forget—how could he forget things that had never registered in the first place? And he had the freedom to ignore whatever didn't interest him enough, because of her. She was his memory. She was his diary. She was his secretary. She was his conscience. She was always there, so that he could choose not to be. And, Helen realized with an unwelcome stab of self-pity, she was tired—she felt overwhelmingly tired, put upon, and—lonely. Being married to Clive was like being married to a shadow. His mind was always miles away, on some lofty plain, that excluded her. It wasn't exactly that they had grown apart, because in fact her life was mostly spent making the life *he* chose possible for him. But what about her? About *her* life? Why didn't her needs and wishes matter to him?

She dried her hands, and sat down heavily, her head slumped over her arms on the kitchen table. Whatever's the matter with you, she told herself sternly. Stop feeling so sorry for yourself! For heaven's sake, you took him on 'for better or worse'. You knew exactly what he was like when you married him. Twenty-four years, and two grown-up children on, don't pretend now that his behaviour takes you by surprise!

No, she thought, there was no surprise—just sadness, and a gaping, empty loneliness. It was as if she were invisible, as if he simply didn't see her as someone at all special any more. She organized his life around him. She supported, encouraged, walked and slept beside him—and he simply didn't see her at all. At least, that's how it felt. Their lives ran along parallel lines, with no friction, no passion, no touching. She didn't doubt the love between them, but that had changed over the years they had been together. They were loving but not in love. Together, but rarely intimate. Like friends and business partners, not husband and wife.

Are all marriages like this, she wondered? Isn't it inevitable that the passion fades, and you're left with what remains—friendship, if you're very lucky; companionship; the worries and joys of children to share together; love?

Her head still buried in her arms, Helen thought about love. Did they still love each other? She loved him, of that she was quite certain. She didn't always find herself able to like him, when his forgetfulness and selfish lack of thought hurt and embarrassed her, or perhaps worse, other people. She knew, though, that she loved him, not simply because she had promised to, but because he still had the power to make her heart skip a beat, just as he had in those heady student days when she first watched him from afar. There were moments now, when she would be sitting in the church, hearing him preach, and she would find herself lost in love and pride for him, marvelling at his insight, his deep unshakeable faith, his ability to create such an atmosphere of worship that to doubt God's presence there would be simply unthinkable. But what about him? Did he love her? There would be long days when he simply didn't touch her—not deliberately, she felt sure, but he would be so engrossed in his own thoughts and plans, that he just didn't notice her. And then, as she reached the point of exploding, rehearsing the angry words she wanted to fling at him over and over in her head, suddenly, for no reason at all, he would put his arms around her, look warmly into her eyes, and say, 'You look tired, darling.' And she would sink against him, all the anger and resentment flooding from her.

That was all she needed. She loved him—and in his own way, although he never said so, he must love her too. He must, mustn't he?

Clive was thinking about love too—God's love, and the wording of the prayer and blessing needed for the end of the 'Village Praise' programme. All the while, as phrases and thoughts came to his mind, then faded as others took their place, Clive's hands busily potted, planted and pruned. The routine of the work on the plants took no thought at all on his part. Years of practice made this a mindless, pleasurable chore. His fingers flew, whilst his thoughts soared. He began by praying—well, perhaps it was a prayer, but it took the form of a conversation with God, trying lines out on Him, asking, discussing, discarding. The words of this prayer had to be just right. They had to speak of this village, of their life and their faith, and yet, at the same time, they had to say something to every single person who happened to hear them, as they watched the programme. And if just one person was moved, comforted, or perhaps even brought to faith by his words, then he would have succeeded. Years of experience in the pulpit had taught him that sometimes great truths were stronger and more inspiring when they were simply expressed. At last, he stopped working on the plants, stood back from the table, closed his eyes, and let the words come.

Lord of our World—you lived on earth, and know its beauty
Lord of our Homes—you know our hearts, our hopes, our fears
Lord of Forgiveness—you heard their cheers turn to derision
Lord of the Heavens—you died on the cross that we might live

Open our eyes to the wonder around us,
Open our minds to the beauty within,
Be there, in our homes, in our thoughts, in our loved ones,
Lord of all love, our praises we bring.

22 March

When Kate and Jan drove back into Sandford at lunchtime on Monday, their car was loaded. In their one short day at home, they had both prepared themselves for the coming two weeks, with an ample supply of clean, warm clothes, and plenty of home comforts (for Jan, top on the 'Comforts' list was a soothing pink bottle of Badedas Bath Foam—for Kate, one huge bar of Fruit and Nut!). The boot was packed out with portable computers and printers for producing scripts, boxes full of specially designed hymn books, stationery of every description imaginable, copious supplies of tea bags, coffee, sugar and biscuits—and a comprehensive medical kit! In short, they'd brought an office, which is exactly what they intended to turn the downstairs back room at Grove House into—the 'Village Praise' Production Office. And they had an extra passenger—Roger Harwood, the loud, jovial, red-haired director, who had visited Sandford earlier, because he would be taking responsibility for all the interviews and items that were to be recorded throughout the week, as well as directing the outside broadcast in the church itself. That would leave Jan in overall charge of the content, and finished look of the programme.

It took them some time to unload all their bags and bundles from the car, and it was probably an hour later, before they sat together in their newly organized office, over a cup of Ellen's excellent tea. And, as usual, the tea was accompanied by slabs of mouthwatering lemon cream cake. Jan and Kate, in mutual support, had left theirs. Roger was already halfway through his second piece, with his eye on the third.

'Right!' said Jan. 'I've got a whole of list of phone calls to make, and then I think, Roger, you and I should walk over to the church, to make some final decisions on camera shots and moves, before you start work on the script for the recording.'

Roger leapt off his chair, and headed for the door. 'I've got my notes upstairs. I'd like to do a bit of work on them, before we go over.' He got up and headed for the door.

'I'm off too,' said Kate. 'There's someone I really must chase up this afternoon.'

'OK, how about four o'clock to go over to the church, Roger? And then, let's rendezvous back here about six-ish, and we can pop down to The Bull for dinner about seven-thirty. Alright with everyone?'

Roger's head immediately popped back round the door. 'Oh, I'll certainly be there for that! See you at four!' And raising his hand in a casual salute, Roger closed the door behind him.

❧

Kate found the house with little difficulty, and made her way up the path towards the front door. The solid ring of the doorbell raised the sound of footsteps.

'Good! At least he's in!'

Charles Waite opened the door to a stranger, a young woman he didn't recognize. 'Yes?' he said.

'Mr Waite? I'm Kate Marsden, the Researcher on the 'Village Praise' programme. I'd very much appreciate a chat with you. Are you free for a few minutes? Could we talk now?'

They've heard, thought Charles. They know about the newspaper report, due for publication the day after tomorrow. She's come to smooth things over, to get me to take back all I've said. Well, she can apologize all she likes, but I shall still feel exactly the same about the shabby way that I, my wife, and the village, have been treated.

That's what he thought. What he said was, 'Come in please.' And he stood back to allow her through to the lounge.

He didn't show her to any particular chair. He simply sat down himself in his own armchair, and left her to sort herself out, while he spied at her over the edge of his glasses, his clasped hands cupped in front of his chin. He said nothing. Let her say it all! Let her squirm! He wouldn't change his mind. After all, they hadn't even had the courtesy to send the Producer—only a Researcher! No, they would get no change from him!

Kate smiled. 'Mr Waite, you know about the forthcoming "Village Praise", of course. We're anxious to produce a programme that gives as truthful, as informative and as inspiring a production as we can manage...'

Huh! he thought. But he said nothing.

'Things are going very well so far,' continued Kate, slightly unnerved now, wondering why his eyes were so cold. What a strange man! 'Everything seems to be falling into place quite nicely—and of course, the technical team will be arriving at the weekend. We record everything in the week before transmission, and then the programme will be edited here, ready to go on the screen on Sunday evening, Palm Sunday.'

Still, he did not reply. Why should he? What did he care about their arrangements? They could all be in tatters by Wednesday morning, when the article came out. Her apology would have little meaning then.

'Well, I'll come straight to the point, Mr Waite. I'm told that you are quite an historian, and that when it comes to explaining the style of church buildings here, their historical context, and their role in worship today—there's no one to match you! We need a key interviewee who can appear right at the top of the programme, to set up the village and the area. Mr Waite—we would consider it a great honour if you would agree to take part!'

Jack was ironing, when the phone rang. This was the third shirt he'd got out, ironed, and then decided against. He felt worse than a teenager, unable to make up his mind what to wear for a first date! For heaven's sake, he was sixty-six years old, and this was hardly 'a date'! He was simply keeping company with a charming lady over a cup of tea, because they were both on their way to the same event.

What possible harm could there be in that? So, why the panic—because panic it surely was!

When it rang, the phone was a relief really, as well as a surprise. He had never been in the habit of receiving many phone calls, and yet, since offering to get involved with this BBC programme, it seemed he was suddenly in demand! As his hand stretched out towards the receiver, a sudden dreadful thought struck him. It was Margaret, ringing to tell him, ever so nicely, that she wouldn't be able to make it after all! His throat was dry as his picked up the phone.

'Yes? Jack Diggens speaking.'

'Oh, Jack!' Helen's voice was instantly recognizable. 'So glad I caught you in! I'm just passing on a message. Jan, the BBC Producer, has asked if you could meet up for a word with her about the final seating and stewarding arrangements. She'd going to be at the church for quite a while this afternoon, and I said I'd ring you to see if you could pop in sometime? Do you think that's possible?'

Jack glanced at the ironing board, then laughed out loud.

'Helen! I'm standing here ironing—and if there's anything in the world I hate more than ironing, I can't think of it! It will be a great pleasure to close the door on this lot! I'll be over at the church in a couple of minutes!'

Charles shut the door behind Kate Marsden, and then made his way automatically back to the lounge, where he sat down heavily in his armchair, staring ahead of him with unseeing eyes.

What a mess! What a tangled, awful mess!

Did he know much about the history of the area? It had been a passion of his since first becoming fascinated as a boy. Was there anyone more appropriate and knowledgeable than him, who could perhaps do the interview better than he? In short, no—certainly no one he knew of. Could he put the history of the area into modern context? Yes. Could he talk about old religious traditions that were still upheld today—like egg rolling down Dinton Hill? Yes, yes, yes!

Did he want to do the interview? More than anything in the world. Would they let him, once they had read his views in *The Herald* on Wednesday? Almost certainly not. Urgent action was needed—if it wasn't already too late! His hands trembling, he fumbled for last week's copy of *The Herald*, to find the editorial number, and dialled.

'News Desk!' answered a brisk, businesslike voice.

'Oh, good afternoon.' Charles' voice was unusually hesitant. 'Good afternoon. Is Pete Durrell in, by any chance?'

'Nope, 'fraid not,' was the curt reply.

'Is he contactable this morning?'

'Not sure really. Don't know quite where he is. Why? Who wants him?'

Charles was reluctant to leave his name. Instead, he asked, 'Are you expecting him back soon?'

'No idea, I'm afraid.' Charles thought desperately, then tried another tack.

'Can you tell me, please, what time do you settle on the final copy for the front page of this week's edition of *The Herald*?'

'Depends really. We're always prepared to change the front page right up to the last minute—but the deadline for everything is eleven o'clock tomorrow morning.'

'Then I must speak to Mr Durrell before then. Is he likely to be ringing in?'

'Probably. Almost certainly, I should think. Look, is this anything I can help with?'

'To whom am I speaking?' asked Charles, uncertain whether to talk candidly to this abrupt, rather unhelpful man.

'Bob Evans here. I'm a reporter on *The Herald*.'

Must go straight to the top, thought Charles. No use speaking to someone as junior as a reporter. 'Please ask Mr Durrell to ring me urgently, and I mean *urgently*, as soon as he possibly can. I'll be at home—he knows the number. Just ask him to ring Charles Waite.'

'Charles Waite?' Bob Evans' attention was roused by the name. 'Charles Waite? You're the one who's come up with all those allegations against the BBC, and the programme they're making in Sandford, aren't you? It will make quite a story! Are you sure I can't help you?'

'No,' replied Charles. Something told him not to trust this man. 'Just ask him to call me, will you? Urgently!'

Charles slammed down the phone, and for the first time since he was a small boy, without even thinking, he began to chew his nails.

Bunty popped her head around the door of Hair by Iris, and in a whisper that would have been quite in place on a stage, she beckoned Iris over. Curiously, Iris excused herself from her customer, and went over to join Bunty, who had backed herself into the front corner of the shop, as far away from Debbie at the counter as she could possibly manage to be.

'I've thought of something!!'

'You what?'

'I've thought of something! You know, 'the problem'! I've thought of a way round it!'

'Hold on a minute,' said Iris, who plainly hadn't the faintest idea what Bunty was talking about. 'Slow down. You're losing me...'

'Oh, you know!' whispered Bunty. 'The little problem with the vicar and it being Lent.'

'Oh,' said Iris, catching up at last. Bunty looked triumphant. 'Well?' added Iris. 'Aren't you going to tell me what you've thought of?'

'I can't—not here!' Bunty replied mysteriously. 'I'm calling a meeting of the Flower Ladies tonight, eight o'clock at my place. Can you make it?'

'I'll be there!' replied Iris, who was so curious by now, that wild horses wouldn't keep her away. 'And Grace is popping in here for a cut in quarter of an hour or so—I'll tell her too.'

'And I'll tell Madge,' said Bunty, as in true 007 style, she slid silently out through the shop door.

In the end, it was Roger who was the last to arrive in The Bull. Jan and Kate were already poring over the menu, which they had perched on top of a pile of papers and clipboards. Roger was carrying papers too. Obviously, he'd got down to some detailed inspection of Kate's research notes, bringing him up to date with the interviews and features Jan hoped to include in the programme.

'How did you get on today then, Kate?' Roger asked as he brought over fresh drinks for the girls.

'Well, I think I've found someone to do the interview about the history of worship in the area. Charles Waite? Do you know him, Jan?'

Jan's eyes narrowed in surprise, as she took a sip from her glass. 'Can't say I do, really. I have met him though—and a very frosty meeting it was too! How was he with you today?'

'I have to admit that it was really hard work at first,' admitted Kate. 'He didn't say a word to me—he just listened and stared! But when I told him that he had been highly recommended to us (you remember, Helen was the one who mentioned him? She said that no one knew as much about the history of the place as he does), he looked really strange, as if he couldn't believe he was being asked! And after that, he was charm itself. Funny old boy, really!'

Jan was spluttering into her drink, perhaps with amusement, perhaps with shock. When she recovered, she explained, 'Right back at the beginning, when I came down to meet everyone to chat about the possibility of us coming here to make this programme, Charles Waite was at that meeting. He was really difficult to talk to from the very start. He seemed to think that he should have been the one who was approached, not Clive Linton. I gather Mr Waite is Chairman of the PCC, and he sees his status as very important. Anyway, Clive Linton just seemed to get on with doing things his own way, and as he didn't appear to take the ranting and raving too seriously, neither did I! Charles Waite actually stormed out of that meeting—and I did mean to go and have a proper talk to him, to clear the air, but never got round to it.' She paused for a moment. 'I wonder...'

'What?' asked Roger, peering over the rim of the menu.

'Do you remember that Helen passed on the number of the editor of the local paper, who had rung up asking all sorts of rather odd questions? Well, I rang him today, and he dropped everything to pop over and have a chat with me in the church this afternoon. He was very interested in everything—seemed pleasant enough, but from the tone of some of the things he asked, I got the feeling that he had come along with a list of questions that had come from someone wanting to cause as many problems for us as possible! I may be wrong, but the questions he was asking seemed very much along the same lines that Charles Waite was thinking when I last spoke to him at that meeting.'

'So, are they going to print anything about the recording in the paper this week?' asked Kate.

'Pete Durrell certainly gave me the impression that he would be writing something. I suppose we'll just have to wait and see what he says. Wednesday morning, I think it comes out.'

'Well,' replied Kate, 'all I can say is that there was no doubt today that Charles Waite was delighted to be asked to take part in the programme—and if he has been trying to put the boot in, I bet he'll be sitting under his letter box in fear and trepidation, when the newspaper boy arrives on Wednesday morning!'

Curiosity plainly got the better of the Flower Ladies, because one by one, they arrived at Bunty's house well before eight o'clock.

By half past eight, they were all huddled in Bunty's living room, in earnest conversation.

'Well, what do you think?' asked Bunty at last.

'I think we've cracked it! I really do!' said Madge.

'But will the vicar agree?' Grace's voice was doubtful. 'You know what a terrible stickler he is...'

'But we won't be breaking protocol at all,' interrupted Iris. 'We will be playing it completely by the book—except we'll be using our imagination to bend the rules—just a little!'

'Right then,' announced Bunty, relishing her role as decision-maker, 'I suggest that we go ahead and make our plans, but for the time being, we'll keep those plans under wraps, until we're absolutely ready! Agreed?'

'Agreed!' they all replied in unison.

'I wonder...' ventured Grace, as they all beamed at each other, 'I wonder if it might be a good idea to take Helen into our confidence— you know, try our idea out on her?'

Bunty and Iris looked at each other, and then nodded at Madge. Finally, Bunty answered, 'I think, Grace, that would be an excellent idea. Helen would probably instinctively know what Clive's reaction would be.'

'And she loves flowers!' giggled Iris. 'I think she would be an excellent ally!'

23 March

The phone rang in the flat above the High Street shop at five to eight, just as Anna was leaving to catch the school bus.

'Anna!' her Mum yelled down the stairs. 'Pick up the phone, would you?'

Anna, who had loaded herself up with school and sports bag, and her violin, all of which she needed that day at school, sighed dramatically as she untangled herself, and made her way over to the phone.

'Sorry to hold you up, Anna,' said a cheerful, familiar voice. It was Ian. Anna was so surprised to hear from him, that she had to grab hold of the counter to steady herself. 'Just wanted to make sure you got my note.'

'Yeah, thanks, I did,' said Anna, cursing herself for the way in which every sensible word went out of her head when he spoke to her.

'I'm just passing on a message from Colin Brown, the organist for the programme, really. He's coming over to take the rehearsal for me tonight, because I need to be up here in the Cotswolds for the next few days.'

'OK,' said Anna, who thought this was a particularly depressing bit of news.

'Anyway,' continued Ian, 'Colin wondered if you could meet him at the church about four o'clock today, to go through your piece. Would that be alright for you?'

'Oh, I have violin practice after school on Tuesdays, so I'm not usually home until about quarter past four.'

'I'm sure a few minutes later won't matter. I've got to speak to him a moment, so I'll let him know.'

'Alright.' If only she could think of something witty and interesting to say to him, to make this call last as long as possible...

'That's all, then, Anna. Have a good day at school. Bye now!' And before Anna could word her goodbye, he was gone.

It had been arranged that Kate and Roger should meet up with Sidney, and his fishermen friends, outside a pub between Thorpeness and Aldeburgh. From that point, there was a dirt track which would take them down to where they kept their small boat. Usually they would take to sea (if you could call taking the rowboat about 500 yards off the shore 'to sea') in the early evening. Because of the choir rehearsal planned for that particular night, Sidney, Bo and Frank had made a special concession to invite Kate and Roger along with them in the morning, for a change.

Sidney and Bo were sitting in a battered beige-coloured Morris van, when Kate drew their spanking new, bright red hire car up alongside them. Frank was just arriving too, haphazardly making his way towards them on a bike that looked older than he was!

'You're late!' Sidney was hissing at Frank, as Kate got out of the car. 'I knew you'd be late! You're always late!'

'You said ten o'clock, and it's only five past now,' puffed Frank, as he pulled himself off the ancient bike. 'By, that's a long hill, that!'

'Why didn't you come in the van, like I told you!' Sidney went on. 'You'd have been on time then. I told Bo you'd be late—and you were!'

'Hello there,' Kate interrupted, holding her hand out to Sidney. 'Nice to see you again.'

But Sidney was too indignant about Frank's tardiness to bother much with Kate. 'He's always the same, you know. He never gets here on time. Bo and me, we always have to wait around for him.'

'Well, you're all here now,' said Kate, soothingly, looking towards the two men she had not yet been introduced to. 'Now who's who?'

Bo, who had now got out of the van, grinned at her, displaying considerably more gums than teeth. 'Bo's the name. Glad to meet you.'

'And you must be Frank!' said Roger, grabbing the bike, as it started to slide away from the wall on which Frank had leaned it. 'I'm Roger Harwood—I'll be directing all the interviews for the programme.'

'Oh, 'sthat right?' replied Sidney, who plainly thought that all facts and instructions should be channelled through him. 'Well now, let's be goin' then, or we'll miss the tide!' And with that, he marched off empty-handed, leaving Frank and Bo to wrestle with the misshapen back door of the Morris, grabbing out three fishing rods and a delapidated, almost square black wooden box, the contents of which Kate and Roger could only guess at. Hurriedly, they reached for their lifejackets, notebooks and wellies from the boot of their car (Kate's were green, and gleamingly new), and followed Sidney's disappearing figure towards the sea.

It was quite a walk. Quarter of an hour later, as the path became increasingly sandy underfoot, they rounded a corner to find a boathouse which had obviously seen better days. Sidney yanked open wide the door, which hadn't quite been shut in the first place, and together, he and Bo began to pull out 'Star of the East'—an optimistic name for their small, peeling, grey-green boat.

'Frank!' barked Sidney. 'You come here, Frank! You come and pull too!'

Frank, who now Kate could see was walking with quite a pronounced limp, was still making his way down the lane, dragging the old black box behind him, as Sidney shouted at him. He grimaced at Kate—then, with a lopsided grin, he ambled off towards the boat, arriving just in time to see it emerge fully from the shed.

'Right then, Frank! You grab that end—and push!' Sidney's beady glare never left Frank, as together, with Roger and Kate giving a hand, they finally got the boat down to the shore.

Roger eyed the little boat thoughtfully. 'How many can you take in this boat, Sidney? Are you sure five of us won't be a couple too many?'

Sidney looked at Roger as if this was a particularly stupid question, which needed no reply. 'Right then,' he ordered to everyone and no one in particular. 'Everyone in! Hold it still, Frank, while the lady gets aboard first!'

Rather gingerly, Kate picked her way through the shallows, to clamber into the boat in a most unladylike manner. A twitch of Sidney's eyebrows in Roger's direction indicated that he was next— and once Bo and Frank had passed over rods and boxes, and pulled themselves in too, Sidney—looking splendid in his waders—finally took up his Captain's position at the front of the boat. Nervously,

Kate watched the boat sink lower as each new passenger came on board. She put her hands in her pockets, and crossed her fingers. Seconds later, her hands were out again—grasping hold of the side of the boat to steady herself, as Frank and Bo wrestled with the oars which were lying flat on the bottom of 'Star of the East', trying to get them into position. This task, which would have been simple with just three people on board, was positively terrifying as Kate and Roger dodged from side to side, trying to keep out of the way.

'Oh, for heaven's sake, why on earth didn't you sort this out before you got in!' Sidney snapped at Bo and Frank, as they valiantly fought to get both oars, and themselves into position. 'Come on, we're going to get stuck here, if we don't cast off soon! Get rowing!'

Frank winked at Kate. "E does go on. 'Is bark's worse than 'is bite though!'

'Where we headin' then, Sidney?' asked Bo reasonably.

'Where we always go, of course,' replied Sidney, his eyes gazing seawards. 'Round in the direction of the point, and out a bit!'

'You're obviously well used to being on water, Sidney,' commented Roger, trying to make polite conversation. 'What was your job before you retired?'

'I was a bookbinder,' replied Sidney curtly. 'Steady now, Frank. Keep your rhythm steady!'

Kate's fingers never loosened their hold on the side of the boat. Neither did her eyes—she watched as the water lapped over the top of the boat with each pull of the oars. Her feet, neatly tucked into her now splattered wellingtons, were sitting in water. Where was that water coming from? From above—or, perish the thought—below?

'Nearly there!' barked Sidney. 'Keep going—just a few more yards, then we'll tie up on that buoy.' Obediently, Bo and Frank pulled the boat towards the buoy, where Sidney reached out, and secured the line.

'Right!' he said. 'Let's get the fishing tackle sorted first, before we get the Bible out!'

'What are we going to sing today, Sidney?' asked Bo, as he tried to man-oeuvre out the fishing rods. 'It's my turn to choose this week, you know.'

'Well...' started Sidney, as Roger spoke up. '"The Old Rugged Cross" is the hymn we were hoping you'd sing, because that's scheduled to be in the programme.'

'Oh, I've changed my mind about that one,' replied Sidney, as Bo started to speak. 'A bit hackneyed, that hymn, I think. No, I reckon we should sing "Eternal Father Strong to Save"—the words are much more appropriate!'

'That's certainly a very popular hymn,' said Kate, joining in with the conversation as one way to take her mind off the precariousness of the boat, 'but our programme does go out on Palm Sunday, so "The Old Rugged Cross" would be just right for us.'

'No, I don't like the idea of that one,' said Sidney again. 'We prefer "Eternal Father", don't we, boys?'

Bo and Frank looked at each other noncommittally. Roger decided it was time to take charge. 'Look, just pretend we're not here. Just do what you would normally do, so that we can see what goes on. We can decide about the detail after that.'

'Get the Bible out, then, Frank!' said Sidney, and they all watched as Frank dug down deep in the battered black box, and from amongst the spare hooks, lines and thermos flask, he drew out an oblong cardboard box, which he opened up to reveal what was obviously a well-used and loved Bible. With due reverence, he handed the Bible to Sidney, who cleared his throat, as he thumbed his way through the fragile pages to the passage he had selected.

'The reading today...' Sidney's voice boomed, as he made sure he could be heard above the lapping waves, and what was obviously a rising wind. 'The reading today is taken from the Gospel according to St Matthew, Chapter 8, Verses 23 to 27.

And when he was entered into a ship, his disciples followed him. And, behold, there arose a great tempest in the sea, insomuch that the ship was covered with the waves: but he was asleep.

Not far from the truth, thought Kate, as she tightened her lifejacket, and wondered why she had ever allowed herself to be persuaded to take her place in this rickety, overpacked boat in the first place.

And his disciples came to him, and awoke him, saying, Lord, save us: we perish. And he saith unto them, Why are ye fearful, O ye of little faith? Then he arose, and rebuked the winds and the sea, and there was a great

calm. But the men marvelled, saying, What manner of man is this, that
even the winds and the sea obey him!

The wind carried Sidney's words away from him, across the water.
No one spoke as he finished. They were all caught in the spell of the
moment—the sea around them, the whistling wind, the motion of the
boat, the haunting familiarity of the much loved words. Suddenly,
Sidney raised his face to the sky, his arms outstretched. Kate and Roger
watched, as Bo and Frank, with one accord, lowered their heads.

'Our Father, who art in heaven!' boomed Sidney, his prayer shouted
out towards the heavens. 'Look down on us in our small boat of life!
Keep us anchored to your ways, steering our endeavours along your
channels of goodness! Help us to ride the storms of everyday troubles,
and bring us safe into the harbour of your love and care. We ask this
in the name of your son, Jesus Christ our Lord—Amen!'

Everyone sat silently, lost in the sounds around them. Then, Sidney
started singing, his voice breaking with emotion, his eyes glistening.
One by one, Bo and Frank added their own voices to his:

Eternal Father, strong to save,
Whose arm hath bound the restless wave,
Who bidd'st the mighty ocean deep
Its own appointed limits keep:
O hear us when we cry to thee
For those in peril on the sea.

Kate slowly turned her gaze towards Roger, to see that his face
registered the same amazement that she felt. Words failed her. These
three old men—bumbling and cantankerous—had touched and
moved her in a way that she had never experienced before.

By half past ten that morning, in spite of two phone calls to the
Newspaper Office, Charles had still not made contact with Pete
Durrell. He was beside himself with worry. He hadn't slept a wink that
night, tossing from one side to another until finally he gave up, and

stopped pretending that there was any chance at all that sleep would come. Trying not to disturb Betty, he quietly slipped out of bed, found his dressing gown and slippers, and tiptoed downstairs to the kitchen. Out of habit, he reached for the kettle and teapot, to make a cup of tea that frankly he had no appetite for. The kettle boiled. He ignored it. He sat at the kitchen table, his arms clasped in front of him, and simply stared. How long he had been sitting there, he was unsure, but suddenly, he became aware of Betty. She was sitting opposite him, her face full of question and concern. In front of them both stood two steaming mugs of tea.

'Charles?' she asked quietly, as if afraid of his reaction to her presence there. 'Charles, love, what is it?'

Slowly, he focused his gaze on her face. And just as slowly, he reached across the table for her hand, lowered his head, and sobbed. His body shook as the first tears fell, and he sucked in breath in painful gasps. Betty, shocked and appalled to see this proud, decent man so distraught, stood up, and came round to stand beside him. Gently, she cradled his head against her, stroking his hair, rocking him in her arms as if he were a small boy. For minutes, the sobbing was uncontrollable—and then, he relaxed in her embrace, until the only sound was an occasional gasp for breath, as in exhaustion and defeat, he clung to her.

At last, still clasping his hand, Betty reached out to bring her chair round to sit beside him. 'I love you,' she said simply. 'Whatever happens, I'll always love you.'

'Oh, dearest Betty, I love you too. I can never apologize enough for what I've been putting you through. I can't think what came over me.'

'Ssshh...' Betty's voice was soothing, sensing he was dangerously near to tears again.

They sat in silence for a while, both looking at their hands, interlocked and stroking. At last, Betty spoke. 'Something's happened, hasn't it? Tell me what brought this on.'

So he did. He began with his anger, his sense of rejection and humiliation that no one else supported him, not even her. She listened as he tried to find the words to explain the feeling of betrayal, that she, his wife, had blatantly and publically slighted him. He told her about his visit to Major Gregory, and his annoyance that the Major had dismissed and ignored his appeal for help. Then, he told her about his idea, his plan to discredit the whole concept of the programme through the paper. He remembered the wording of his letter to the News Editor perfectly. She held his hand even tighter, as she listened to the vitriol, the bitterness, the cold condemning logic of the words he had written. He told her about his conversation with Pete Durrell, and about the promise that they would be printing a front page article based on his letter in the paper to be published on Wednesday. Then, he told her about Kate's visit, and her request that he should be an interviewee. He didn't need to tell her how delighted and flattered he was to be asked to speak on a subject he loved passionately. She knew. She listened, she understood—and she knew why he was in such turmoil. She knew—and when he'd finished, wordlessly she drew him to her. And in the still silence of the early hours of the morning, they held each other close, lost in the comfort, the trust, the love that had bound them together for so many years.

When Pete Durrell finally did ring, it was gone twelve o'clock. Charles was sitting in the lounge, absently staring at nothing in particular, when the shrillness of the phone startled him. 'Hello?' he said into the receiver. 'Charles Waite here.'

'Mr Waite! Pete Durrell—I gather you've been trying to get hold of me.'

Charles was immediately alert. 'Yes, I have—but I think I might be too late now. The article you planned to write, following our conversation the other day?'

'Yes?'

'Have you written it?'

'Yes.'

'And will it be in this week's edition of *The Herald*?'

'On the front page, as we planned.'

Charles felt his mouth go dry. 'You see, Mr Durrell, I was wrong. I didn't fully appreciate all the details of the situation...'

'Really, Mr Waite?' Pete Durrell was very cool, not helping Charles at all.

'I'm terribly worried that I hadn't checked my facts thoroughly—perhaps wasn't in possession of all the salient points before I spoke to you...'

'Well, Mr Waite, it's a very dangerous thing, not to check your facts.'

'But is it too late for you to reword the article? I could give you a very different story now!'

'Far too late, I'm afraid, Mr Waite. The final copy went down more than an hour ago.'

Charles was crushed. 'Oh, oh, I see. And is there any chance of having a preview of what the article says, any chance at all?'

'Not the faintest possibility, I'm afraid, Mr Waite. Against company policy. You'll just have to wait and see the article for yourself, tomorrow morning. Thanks for your help. Bye now!' And with that cheery greeting, Pete Durrell signed off, leaving Charles with the receiver still grasped in his sweating palm.

That afternoon, Jan was hard at work on the word processor, her glasses perched on her head, when Kate and Roger returned, bursting to report back on their trip out with the fishermen.

Jan gave up trying to work, and listened in on their conversation. 'Honestly,' Roger was saying, 'when I first met those three old boys, I couldn't believe they were for real! Sidney, the one who organizes everything, is a real old boot, isn't he...?'

'And he looks like an old boot too,' said Kate, taking up the story. 'His face is leathery and lined, and he doesn't look a day under ninety. Heaven knows how old he really is!'

'But the thing is,' Roger interrupted, 'he's so objectionable! He just moans at the others all the time, bossing them about, treating them like naughty children...'

'And they don't seem to mind,' said Kate. 'They just let him get on with it.'

'But the boat!' Roger spoke with his hands, painting a picture. 'I couldn't believe it when I saw how small it was. I really didn't think we could all get in it, did you?'

'And it was so old—I'm sure there was water seeping in from the bottom somewhere. My feet were soaking!'

'And then when Sidney flatly refused to sing "The Old Rugged Cross"...!'

'Hold it! Hold it!' Jan laughingly threw her hands up in despair. 'Do I gather then, that you don't think they are going to make an interview for us?'

Roger and Kate looked at each other, their faces suddenly serious. 'I think,' said Roger at last, 'that they will be impossible to interview, dreadful to organize, and that they'll probably drown the lot of us—but I am quite convinced that their story will make one of the most memorable and inspiring items we've ever seen on a "Songs of Praise" programme!'

It was gone half past four before Anna opened the church door, to find Colin already seated at an electronic keyboard and stand. Through music circles, they already knew each other slightly, in fact, Colin had accompanied Anna at a church recital a couple of years earlier.

'Well, let's get cracking then!' Colin smiled. 'Ian has come up with a lovely arrangement for "Just As I Am". See what you think of it!' He ran his fingers across the keys, producing a sound that was at first mellow and light, then with orchestral richness. 'This is it. Eight bars in—they tell me this intro will go over some pictures, to ease the viewer away from the interview we've just had, and into you singing. You'll know when to come in.'

The arrangement was beautiful—haunting, evocative and moving. Anna closed her eyes, and sang:

Just as I am, without one plea
But that Thy blood was shed for me,
And that Thou bid'st me come to Thee,
O Lamb of God, I come.

'Great!' said Colin. 'Carry on—we're missing out verse two, so straight on to verse three.'

Just as I am, Thou wilt receive,
Wilt welcome, pardon, cleanse, relieve,
Because Thy promise I believe,
O Lamb of God, I come.

'Watch your breathing on that verse. Take note of where the commas come. And you're losing the first note of every line just a fraction. Think of your consonants! Attack each line as it comes. Carry on—next verse!'

Just as I am, Thy love unknown
Has broken every barrier down;
Now to be Thine, yea, Thine alone,
O Lamb of God, I come.

'Fine! That verse starts very positively, but that third line needs to be more melodic—think about the words you're singing. Bring out the emotion a bit more. Keep going—build this last verse!'

Just as I am, of that free love
The breadth, length, depth, and height to prove,
Here for a season, then above,
O Lamb of God, I come.

The music came to an end—but Colin had only just started. By the time the rehearsal finished, more than an hour later, Anna's performance had been dissected note by note. She felt exhausted, exhilarated and breathlessly excited for the task ahead.

The upstairs sitting room at The Bull Hotel was only used in the afternoons, when Bill and Maureen opened it for the steady trade they had built up in high teas. They had earned themselves a mention in *The Good Teashoppe Guide* which was produced for the whole of East Anglia, and because of that, The Bull had become a popular haunt for visitors to the area, especially during the summer months. At this time of year, before the season really got under way over the Easter weekend, trade was slow—but still they opened, to offer sandwiches, homemade cakes and endless pots of tea for locals who cared to pop in. That afternoon, when Jack arrived, only one other table was occupied. A couple of elderly ladies were quietly talking, and munching their way through a plate of assorted sandwiches, as he chose a table next to the window. He tugged at his shirt collar. Either the shirt had shrunk, or he had put on weight since the last time he'd worn it. His shoes were uncomfortable too. They were his best brown ones, chosen because they picked up the tan fleck in his jacket. He hadn't found occasion to wear those shoes for perhaps a year now—and he remembered that they had been stiff and uncomfortable then. He carefully sat down, in a seat where he had a clear view of the street below. Margaret wasn't due for ten minutes yet. Ten minutes to wait. He read the menu. Then he read it again. Then he turned the card over, and stared for some time at the picture on the front, until he could stare at it no longer.

'Can I help you with anything?' Jack recognized the girl who was serving as Rosemary, Mrs Hadlow's daughter. He only knew her by sight, and she probably wouldn't know him at all, so he said nothing, except, 'I'm fine thanks. I'm waiting for someone—um, a lady.'

Rosemary smiled. 'Fancy a cup of tea while you're waiting?'

'No, no thanks. I'll wait, if you don't mind.'

'Give me a call when you're ready to order,' said Rosemary, and she disappeared back down the stairs.

Jack stared around him, looking in detail at every picture on the wall, studying the displays of flowers, working out the pattern on the carpet—and it was while he was reading the menu for the third time, that he heard her car. He looked out of the window, to see the familiar red Metro pull in towards The Bull, and disappear down the side of the building towards the car park at the back. Jack's mouth was dry. He felt hot. His hands were clammy. He rubbed his palms against his trousers, and wished he'd called in at the Gents before he'd sat down.

Then, suddenly, she was there, arriving at the top of the steps in a cloud of fresh, flowery perfume, genuine delight on her face as she spotted him at the table. 'Jack!' she called. 'Am I late, or are you early?'

Jack grinned back at her, his nerves fading as he looked at her friendly, open smile. 'I just wanted to make sure we could get a good seat.' He looked around at the rows of empty tables. 'Well, there might have been a rush!' And they both laughed like children.

Bunty called in to the vicarage, just as Helen was unloading the car from a supermarket trip. She grabbed a couple of bags, followed Helen through to the kitchen, and as she helped Helen unpack and put away, Bunty poured out what was on her mind—how upset the Flower Ladies were that they wouldn't be able to contribute in their own special way to the success of the programme, because it was Lent, and Clive flatly refused to consider having any floral decorations at all. And then, she came to The Plan. Helen listened, and she considered, and finally she said, 'Well, it's certainly worth a try! Why not?'

'But what will Clive say? What do you think Clive will say?'

'Honestly, Bunty, I don't know—but I think your idea is a good constructive one, and if you need any help, count me in!'

'Helen, you've made my day!' enthused Bunty, and she threw her arms around Helen before striding out the door, ready to get to work.

'You mean, you play a harp! An enormous instrument like that!' Jack laughed at Margaret. 'However do you get it in your Metro?'

'Oh, I don't get much call to play in concerts nowadays, and when I was very busy with performances, I had a bigger car.' Margaret chuckled. 'A much bigger car!'

'Do you still play much, for your own pleasure, I mean?'

'Every day. I think of it as my first instrument, even though I suppose, over the years, I've had more need to play the piano than the harp. It's just such a beautiful sound though. I love it because it's so soothing and lovely all by itself. It doesn't need any other instrument to make it complete.' She smiled again. 'Good job I have nice tolerant neighbours. I play for at least an hour each day—although I try to make it during the morning, when they're both at work.'

'Do you live in a house that shares a wall with your neighbours?'

'Yes, I do, and I regret that really. I've often thought it would be nice to find a nice cosy little cottage that stands on its own—not too big, with a garden that wouldn't mind the meddling of an enthusiastic amateur! I'd like that.'

'Roses round the door,' suggested Jack.

'Of course!' replied Margaret. 'Oh, it's silly even to think about it really, because I'm perfectly comfortable where I am...'

'But...' prompted Jack.

'But,' Margaret went on, 'it's a fairly new house, with practically no garden to speak of. I thought I'd like that when I bought it. I was working such long hours at school, it seemed a good idea to cut down on the work I'd need to put in, to keep the house tidy. And in that respect, it's suited me nicely. It's just that now, now I have more time on my hands, I yearn for a house with a bit more character. A house like me—seen a lot, battered a bit, in need of loving care and attention!'

Jack thought for a moment. Then he said, choosing his words carefully, 'When you come on Thursday, there's a place I'd like to show you. A friend of mine very sadly passed away a few weeks back, and his cottage sounds just exactly what you're after. It's on the market too at the moment.'

'Heavens!' said Margaret, taken aback. 'I'm not sure I'm serious. It's just a dream really. I don't know that I could honestly face the upheaval of moving. I'm probably not serious at all.'

'Then we can just window shop!' replied Jack. 'You should take a walk around that part of Sandford anyway, if you've not been there before. It's beautiful, so close to the river, very peaceful. I'm just beginning to appreciate where I live, in a way I never could when I was at work all day.'

'Takes a bit of getting used to, doesn't it,' commented Margaret, 'this business of being retired. I'm not quite sure how much I want to be busy, or whether I really should just put my feet up and vegetate!'

'I think,' said Jack, 'what I miss most is being needed. At work, someone always seemed to be chasing me for something or another. Until this TV thing came up, months went by when no one seemed to need me for anything at all. At work, I used to long for people to leave me alone so that I could get on with my job. Now, I sometimes find that I don't have the chance to speak to anyone all day.'

'I know exactly what you mean,' agreed Margaret, 'and I tell you what I think we should do. I think we should talk to each other. Talk to each other about things that matter, and things that don't. I think, Jack, that you and I are embarking on a friendship—a friendship I value very much indeed. And, my friend, if we don't watch the time, and get some cake and tea down us, we're going to be late for that rehearsal!'

❧

The Village Hall was comfortably full when they arrived, and unlike the previous week when people had been inclined to sit in the separate groups they had come with, it was clear immediately that the atmosphere was warmer, as sopranos chatted to basses, and West Side Story cast members mingled with St Mark's choristers. And right in the middle, obviously very pleased to be there, was the Women's Institute Choir—all thirty of them—every single one wearing a neat black skirt, and rich turquoise-coloured silk blouse. And, at the centre, sat their conductor, the charming and benevolent Rose Smith. 'Coo-ee!' she called, as she spied Betty making her way towards the piano. 'Betty! Over here!' And she waved so conspicuously, that Betty had no choice but to pin on a broad smile, and go over to greet her.

'Rose, how lovely to see you and your ladies in Sandford. We couldn't possibly have "Village Praise" here without you!'

'Oh, my dear, how kind!' enthused Rose, planting a tasteful kiss on each of Betty's cheeks. 'We're raring to go. We practised the music all weekend!'

Over Rose's shoulder, Betty caught Bunty's eye. Bunty's grimace would only have been noticed by the most observant—and Betty had to smother a grin, before replying to Rose, 'You must make yourself known to Jan Harding—there she is, over by the stage. She's the Producer.'

'Oooh,' commented Rose, her expression confident and knowing, 'that's Jan Harding! We've seen her name so many times, of course, on television. Such a talented person! Such a pleasure to work with a real professional!'

Actually, Jan was having trouble. Mrs Hulme was very hot under the collar—and it was collars and clothing which were the problem! She was incensed when she saw that the Women's Institute Choir had come 'in costume'! 'And, Ms Harding,' she stated, stabbing her finger in Jan's direction, 'if they are going to wear costume, then so shall we!'

'Really, Mrs Hulme,' said Jan, with as much sympathy as she could muster, 'it would be most helpful to us if no one dressed in any group style at all. Just imagine if every group here decided that they must wear a uniform dress for themselves—it would look very distracting on screen...!'

'Our robes are not distracting! They are dignified and gracious— and most important of all, they identify us as St Mark's Choir. We have a reputation to think of. People expect to see St Mark's Choir looking like St Mark's Choir!'

'Really, Mrs Hulme, it would be much better if...'

'St Mark's Choir will not be taking part at all, unless they are seen in their robes—and that's final!'

Jan looked at Mrs Hulme's indignant expression for a second or two, before sighing deeply. 'Sit down, please, Mrs Hulme. I need to talk over another matter with you.'

Mrs Hulme wasn't sure what to make of this change of tone. With suspicion written all over her face, she slowly sat down. 'Well?' she asked.

'One of the hymns we are including in the programme is "O Sacred Head", for which we have written a special arrangement to be sung not by the congregation in general, but by a choir.'

Mrs Hulme's expression had changed from indignation to avid interest. 'Yes,' she said, encouraging Jan to say more.

'Our Musical Director, Ian, thinks it's an arrangement that would suit St Mark's Choir admirably. Would you consider looking the music over, and perhaps, if you are interested, we could keep the choir behind for a while after the general rehearsal is over this evening, to try the hymn out?'

'I don't think, Ms Harding,' said Mrs Hulme, turning a warm, gracious smile full power towards her, 'that there is any doubt that St Mark's could do justice to any arrangement you give us. Please do leave the music with me, and we will consider your suggestion straight away.'

'And,' added Jan, with great emphasis, 'and—for that choir number, which will be recorded at Dinton Church on Friday morning next week—it would be absolutely appropriate for the choir to be dressed as they are best recognized, in full church robes. Will that be acceptable?'

'Perfectly!' agreed Mrs Hulme, feeling she'd won both the battle and the war.

After that, the rehearsal went very smoothly. All in all, there must have been around one hundred people present, and the sound was wonderful. True, the basses were a little loud, the tenors a little scarce, some of the sopranos a little shrill, and a lot of the altos a little lost when it came to the harmonies—but everything considered, it was a most encouraging sound. And when, finally, Colin dismissed everyone except St Mark's Choir, so that they could have a run-through of "O Sacred Head", Jan privately heaved a sigh of relief. You had to hand it to Mrs Hulme. A tyrant she may be, but the choir was disciplined and expert. She had no doubt that by the time Ian saw the choir again, the arrangement would be note- and word-perfect.

As the choir at last made their way home, and just a few people were left tidying things up for the playgroup who'd be using the hall in the morning, Colin was chatting to Betty and Jan, as he collected together his pieces of music. 'They're impressive, aren't they, St Mark's Choir?'

'They certainly are,' agreed Jan. 'It's a beautiful hymn, and I think they'll put it over with great skill and emotion, especially if we see them in the setting of Dinton Church. We'll put a smoke machine in, to create a peaceful, timeless atmosphere. It should look lovely.'

Colin was thoughtful. 'I'm not absolutely sure about this arrangement though, not now I've heard them sing. I think the accompaniment could be much softer—perhaps just a single instrument, but not an organ or keyboard. I don't know. I'll talk to Ian about it, but maybe a horn... or a harp.'

'Not much chance of finding someone to help with either of those round here,' said Betty, just as Jack, who was stacking chairs to one side of them, hesitantly spoke up. 'I know someone,' he said.

All eyes turned to him. He felt awkward that he had been eavesdropping. 'Sorry, I didn't mean to interrupt, but you had a very accomplished harpist here in the choir this evening. Margaret Abbot. You know, the music teacher from over Steepleton way. She played the harp in concerts for years, and I know she still practises every day.'

Colin and Jan exchanged hopeful glances. 'It would certainly be a good idea to talk to her, just to see what her standard of playing is. Do you know where I could reach her?'

'Certainly,' said Jack, digging into his inside pocket for his diary, where he'd made a note of Margaret's telephone and address. Jan wrote down the number, and asked, 'Do you want me to mention that you suggested her?'

Jack grinned. 'I have a feeling she'll probably work that out for herself!'

24 March

Matthew lowered himself into the seat opposite Anna's on the eight o'clock bus the next morning. He didn't seem a bit surprised when she turned and smiled happily at him.

'No wonder you're so chipper! I hear you've been discovered! Congratulations!'

'It's all happened so fast really,' said Anna. 'But yes, I am going to sing a solo in the programme.'

'Are you nervous?'

'Not nervous exactly, although the Organist, Colin, really put me through it, when I had a rehearsal with him last night. Every single detail has to be perfect, so I am a bit worried about getting it all right. But I can't say I'm nervous—just excited, really.'

'What are you singing?'

'It's quite an old hymn, called "Just As I Am". Do you know it?'

'Can't say I do. What do you think of it?'

'It's a bit slow, but the arrangement Ian has come up with—oh, you won't know Ian, but he's great! He's conducting our programmme! The arrangement he's written is beautiful, very easy to sing!'

'So you'll have to sing it in front of everyone the night they're recording the hymns in the church, will you?'

'Yes—but I think they're also planning to record some shots of me singing around the ruins over at Haycliffe—do you know where I mean?'

'What? That old church there? Is it safe?'

Anna giggled. 'I suppose I'll soon find out!'

'And do you have to wear something special?'

'Funny you should ask. The producer, Jan, came up to me last night, and nearly tied herself in knots, trying to be tactful about suggesting what I should wear. She seemed to think I shouldn't wear black—but that's my favourite colour, the only colour I ever wear! I'm not going to dress up to look like someone I'm not!'

'Well, stick to your guns,' said Matthew. 'You must feel comfortable, or you won't perform as well as I know you can!'

There was a pause. Anna looked down towards her bag, and then shyly glanced up towards Matthew.

'Matthew. Thanks. Thanks for giving me the push I needed. You're a pal.'

Matthew laughed—a big, happy sound. Then, his face became more serious as he said, 'I've done nothing. You've done it all yourself. Just make us all proud of you!' He stretched out his arm, to touch her hand. She immediately pulled her hand back in alarm. 'Look, you! Don't go getting any ideas, OK? This doesn't mean I like you!' But this time, when he laughed, she laughed along with him.

❧

Of all mornings for the paper boy to be late! Charles had been watching the road since seven o'clock, and at quarter past eight, there was still no sign of him.

Betty brought him another cup of tea. 'I don't think, you know, that he ever comes before this time. I'm sure the paper will be here soon.'

'And in every other house in the village! Oh, Betty, whatever am I going to do? This could be the end of me!'

'Charles, people get misrepresented in newspapers all the time. Everyone takes newspaper reports with a pinch of salt. If it's terrible, you can always deny it all...'

'If it's terrible... if it's terrible... oh, Betty, I know this is all my own stupid fault, but 'terrible' is exactly how I feel!'

Betty couldn't think of a word to say. Instead, she picked up the full teacup, and offered it to him. He was too distracted to notice.

'Do you think I ought to ring Clive, now, before the paper arrives? Sort of sugar the pill? What do you think?'

'I think you may be worrying about nothing. Better to know exactly what you're dealing with, and then ring him, if you feel that's best. Always better to deal with facts!'

Charles laugh was hollow. 'That's more or less what that Pete Durrell said yesterday. Always check your facts, he said. And he did, didn't he! He rang me—and I really told him, didn't I! Boy, did I tell him...!'

At that moment, there was a click of the letter box. 'It's here!' shouted Charles, covering the ground between the front room and the door in no time at all. And there it was, *The Herald* lying on the doormat. Charles stared at his fate.

Margaret answered the phone almost immediately when Jan rang. She recognized her straight away, and if she was surprised to get a phone call from her, it didn't register in her voice.

'Well, yes, I do play the harp. I played for years with the East Anglian Orchestra, and often gave concerts on my own in years gone by. Recently, especially because of teaching music at school, I've concentrated on the piano, but I have never stopped playing the harp. More often than not, nowadays, I simply play for my own pleasure.'

'Well, do you think we could meet up, with Colin Brown, the organist, this morning? Really, it should be our Musical Director, Ian Spence, who does this, but he's up to his eyes in this weekend's programme over in the Cotswolds at the moment. He'd like to try out a few new ideas for the arrangement of "O Sacred Head", and it would be interesting to have your thoughts about how a harp could fit in.'

'That would be fine. I'm afraid you'll have to come here, though. I can get the harp in the car, but only just and I may never get it out again!' Jan took down the directions, and promised to be with her about half past ten.

Margaret whistled softly to herself as she put the phone down. That was a call she had certainly not expected, but the prospect of playing her harp for such an important occasion was both daunting and exciting. Before she could stop herself, she rang Jack's number.

'Jack Diggens.'

'Jack Diggens, I've got a bone to pick with you!' Margaret tried to sound gruff, but her voice tinkled with delight. 'Who have you been telling tales to?'

'You didn't really mind, did you?' asked Jack, worried that he might have offended her.

'Of course not! I'm flattered—and flabbergasted! That chap, Colin, and the producer, Jan, are on their way over this morning, to talk over ideas for the arrangement!'

'You'll be wonderful!' said Jack, reassuringly. 'I've not even heard you play, but I have great faith in you!'

'Well, I tell you what, I'll give you a ring after they've left, and let you know if I'm still standing!' Margaret paused for a moment. 'And, Jack, if it goes well, you know, I'll have my time cut out, getting all the practice in...'

There was silence at Jack's end of the phone.

'So, I could do with a candid opinion of what it sounds like. If I have the kettle on about three-ish this afternoon, would you come and lend an ear?'

'Well, I never!' Charles could hardly believe his eyes. From the very start of the lead article on the front page of *The Herald*, which began with the headline:

SANDFORD CHOSEN FOR TELEVISION GLORY

right down to the last word, Pete Durrell's article didn't mention the name 'Charles Waite' once! Not only that, but there was no hint of the grumbles and reservations that the two men had discussed. Instead, there was an enthusiastic statement from Clive Linton, talking about how honoured and thrilled they were that millions of viewers all over the country would be able to worship along with the congregation in Sandford on Palm Sunday. Then, there were some programme details from the producer, Jan Harding, talking about their success in drawing together a very creditable choir (mentioning St Mark's Choir, the Saxmundham Songsters and the Women's Institute, by name), about how seats were being allocated through the churches, and about the tone and aim of the series in general. And the article ended with the promise that there would be interviews with the presenter, Pam Rhodes, members of the television crew, and a double page spread of photos to look forward to in *The Herald* next week!

'He was right, then,' said Charles, as relief flooded through him. 'It is important to check your facts—and that's exactly what Pete Durrell did!'

Betty was beaming from ear to ear, as she hugged Charles to her. 'Do you know, my love?' she said. 'I think you ought to ring that nice lady researcher, Kate, and find out when they'd like to record your interview!'

'Better than that! I think I'll stroll over to Grove House, to see if the production team need help with anything! If they need any strings pulled locally, then...'

'Then, you're their man!' finished Betty, her eyes shining with pride and love.

'Iris! It's for you!' Debbie yelled up the length of the shop, to where Iris was in the middle of pulling strands of hair through a rubber hat covering her customer's head, ready for highlights.

'Is it urgent?' Iris called back. 'Can it wait?'

Debbie spoke once again to the caller, then clamped her hand across the mouthpiece, and said, 'No, she says it's quick, but it's urgent. It's Bunty Maddocks!'

Iris quickly extricated herself from the rubber hat and crochet hook, and ran to take the phone call.

'Just a quickie!' said Bunty, urgently. 'They're delivering everything we talked about today. The only thing is that I'm not going to be at home myself—I've got a few problems to sort out, so I've asked them to make the delivery to you!'

'Oh, Bunty! Where on earth am I going to put them?'

'In your back room? In the boot of your car? Please, Iris, I'm desperate!'

'And you'll be able to collect them tonight?'

'I'll pop round as soon as I've finished—probably about four o'clock this afternoon, and take them back to my front room. We'll work on them there!'

'Righty-ho,' said Iris. 'Must go!' And ignoring Debbie's curious stare, she hurried back to her highlights.

Jack found Margaret's house quite easily. It was part of a new estate, built on the outskirts of the old village of Steepleton, a neat, cream coloured house, with a matching beige door, which was open even before Jack began to walk down the path. 'Well?' he asked, 'How did it go?'

'Alright, I think!' Margaret closed the door behind him, and showed Jack into the living room which was pretty well full of harp!

'My goodness!' exclaimed Jack. 'I didn't realize just how huge harps are!'

'Come into the kitchen, and I'll rustle up some tea and ham sandwiches,' said Margaret. 'Actually, I need to ask you a favour.'

'Ask away!'

'I couldn't help noticing as you arrived, that you've got an estate car.'

'Yes.'

'How would you feel about giving a harpist in distress, and her very large harp, a lift to the rehearsal tomorrow night?'

'One very lived-in estate car, and matching driver, reporting for duty, ma'am!' Jack's face beamed. 'Margaret, I'd be honoured!'

25 March

Mrs Hadlow was early for her four-thirty hair appointment with Iris. This was the first time she had ever had her hair done by Iris at anything other than ten o'clock in the morning. This break in her usual routine was deeply upsetting. She was flustered, and out of sorts. Nothing was quite right for her. The perming lotion was 'too acid'. The tea was 'too strong'. The salon was 'too stuffy'. And Iris was 'too rough', as she pulled the short wiry hair on to the perming curlers.

But Iris was well used to handling Mrs Hadlow. She ignored the grumbles, and smiled sweetly as she sympathized and cajoled. She knew it was Debbie who really got Mrs Hadlow going. Debbie left her post at the counter, and wandered up the salon to sit in the seat next to Mrs Hadlow, handing perming papers to Iris as she worked.

'How are the rehearsals going then, Mrs H?'

Mrs Hadlow glared at Debbie, and then looked back towards the mirror, ignoring the question.

But Debbie was not easily put off. She raised her voice a notch, almost shouting, as if to someone who was hard of hearing, 'The rehearsals—how are they coming along? You are in the choir, aren't you?'

Mrs Hadlow looked pointedly at Iris. 'Iris,' she said, very slowly, as if controlling her temper, 'will you please explain to Deborah that I am neither deaf, nor stupid. And if she wants me to answer her question, then she must address me correctly!'

Iris looked at Debbie, silently pleading with her to return to her desk. Reluctantly, a secret smile on her face, the young woman strolled back to her own end of the shop.

'I'm sorry, dear,' explained Mrs Hadlow, 'I find that girl very offensive.'

'She's young, that's all,' replied Iris. 'She's got a few years to go, before she catches up with us, eh!' She chuckled, and in spite of herself, Mrs Hadlow almost smiled too.

Iris carried on working, while Mrs Hadlow handed her the perm papers. 'How is it going then, Mrs Hadlow? Are the rehearsals working alright? Have they managed to find enough singers at last?'

'Well, dear, I was a bit worried that first night. Honestly, I was practically the only person in the Altos, with any voice to speak of at all! Things have got much better now, though. The Women's Institute singers have come along, and, of course, that very good church choir—St Matthew's, isn't it, in Saxmundham? Very professional, they are! So it means that now, it's not just the first few of us who are carrying all the responsibility.'

'Oh,' said Iris, 'that's good. And is it very hard? Don't you have to be able to read music, and everything?'

'Oh, of course! How could you take part in a performance like this, if you couldn't read music. Oh no, dear, we'd be drummed out straight away if we weren't all completely conversant with music.'

'My, I never knew you could do that! Wherever did you learn to read music?'

'I can't even remember exactly how and when. It's just something I've always been able to do. I never needed to be taught.'

'Oh,' said Iris again, her face doubtful. 'So, you're going to be on the telly then. What are you going to wear?'

'Really, dear, I haven't given it any thought at all, none—except, well, they did say the other night that plain striking colours work best, so I thought perhaps my dove-grey jacket, you know, the one I wore to Rosemary's wedding? Did you see it? Well, I thought that would team very nicely with that pale blue blouse of mine, and my grey skirt. I might need to get some new shoes though. The heels are going on my black court shoes. Mind you, perhaps I might be more comfortable in flatties? They say there is going to be a lot of standing up, and sitting down, and I don't want to have to worry about blisters, if my shoes are too new. And I wondered about some earrings? What do you think, dear? Do you think earrings would suit me, with this new perm?'

Iris smiled at Mrs Hadlow with affection. 'Wear those little pearl clusters you had on the last time you came. They'd be just the job!'

It had been raining steadily all week—March had proved to be a bleak, cheerless month, at the end of a winter that felt as if it would never end. But that afternoon, the sun came out—weak, watery, but warm. For the first time in months, people at least thought about leaving their anoraks at home, and digging out lighter jackets that they usually reserved for summer.

Margaret had only ever driven through and out of Sandford previously, until that first rehearsal in the Village Hall. She'd never had reason to leave the main road, and take a look at the quieter, prettier spots towards the edge of the village, where the river meandered over boulders and small rocks, and under ancient old bridges. One of those bridges was just a few yards away from Jack's small house, and that Thursday afternoon, the two of them strolled in the sunshine, chatting as if they had known each other for years. The ease of their company still surprised them both. Both felt their friendship was a fragile, precious thing—but neither wished to analyze their feelings too much, nor discuss their private pleasure in knowing each other, for fear of tempting fate.

'You're obviously pretty involved in the church, Jack.'

Jack thought for a moment before answering. 'Well, no, not really. They just needed someone to help out with the running around and stewarding for the recording, and I couldn't think of a reason why I shouldn't help, quickly enough!'

'You're not enjoying it then?'

His face creased into a wry smile. 'Funnily enough, I am. It's frustrating and it's driving me mad—but I suppose I am quite enjoying it really.'

She looked at him as they walked. 'Nice to be needed, eh?'

'Yes. Yes, it is. And I've had so little to do with anyone here in the village until now, I'm quite enjoying getting to know people at last.'

'Do you go along to the church services yourself?'

'Sometimes.' He considered saying more, then thought better of it. 'And you? Are you a churchgoer?'

'Oh, yes. I've always gone to church, for as long as I can remember. It's always been such a comfort and strength to me, the most important thing in my life really—well, that, and music, I suppose.'

There was a pause. Then, Jack said, 'Haven't you ever had doubts? Wondered whether it was really true? I mean, how do you know? How can you know that a God exists that you can't touch and you can't see?'

Margaret smiled. 'Because he does. Look, I've been a teacher all my life, and over the years, I've had to turn my hand to teaching anything and everything. And I remember how I used to answer that question whenever a youngster asked me. Suppose you are travelling along in your car at night, where everything is dark, except for the panel of light you can see ahead of you in your lights. Now, you recognize everything you see in that light—you know what you see, and you know without question that what you see is true. But what about the darkness on either side of you? Are you saying that because you can see nothing, there is nothing there? Doesn't your good sense tell you that there are all sorts of things going on, even though you can't see them? Don't you know instinctively that there is life out there—that there are houses, with people and problems, people who argue, people who doubt, people who love life, and each other? And isn't that what faith is? For me, it's instinctive. I know God exists. And I know that when I share my thoughts with him in prayer, He listens. No, Jack, I have no doubts. Loving God comes as naturally to me as breathing.'

They walked on in silence, each with their own thoughts. Finally, Jack spoke. 'You know, Margaret, I think you are going to be very good for me.' She simply smiled in return, and without thinking, looped her hand through Jack's arm.

'Well, that's the meaning of life out the way! What next? How about that house you wanted to show me?'

FRIDAY

26 March

Shortly after four o'clock on Friday, Helen was sitting at the typewriter at the table in the front room window, hoping to sort out the Diary section for that month's edition of the Parish Magazine, when she looked up to see a massive grey lorry skilfully manoeuvring its way up the narrow path towards the Village Hall. Before the letters 'BBC' came into view, she knew that this was the first of the trucks needed for the programme.

She was undecided what to do. Should she try and contact Clive— not that she had the faintest idea where to find him at this precise moment? Should she leave them to get on with whatever it was they had to do? Perhaps they would need to talk to someone, to know exactly where to park, who's in charge, where the loo is? That did it! She scooped her coat off the stand in the hall as she hurried through the front door, dropped the key in the flowerpot, and made her way down the path.

Michael climbed down from the van, and stretched. This vehicle was fine on long, straight roads. Somehow, it got tiring once the roads became narrow and winding, and there were plenty of those on the last leg of the journey between the Cotswolds and Sandford. He was looking around, trying to get his bearings, when he saw a slim, smiling woman hurrying towards him.

'Hello there!' she called. 'Can I help?'

Clear grey eyes twinkled down on her, from the tall, slim man who now approached her. His Irish accent somehow took her by surprise. 'I'm not sure. I was just wondering if I'm the first here, and if I'm parked in the wrong place.'

'You are—and you're not!' She laughed, thinking how daft her answer sounded. Michael laughed too, and from the lines around his eyes, Helen thought that this man's face had great warmth to it, as if smiling came easy to him.

'What do you need? Do you want to unload? Do you need the church open? Do you need to contact anybody?' She hesitated, trying to think what else she should ask. 'Would you like a cup of coffee?'

He laughed again, not at her, but with her. 'Now you're talking! I'd love one. I'm Michael Sheehan, by the way.' He held out his hand towards her. She returned the handshake, and then led him towards the vicarage, as she explained, 'And I'm Helen Linton. Clive, the vicar of St Michael's, is my husband.'

❖

Jack's phone was ringing as he stepped inside the front door. Before he had a chance to reel off his telephone number, a clipped voice said, 'Oh, Mr Diggens! Charles Waite here!'

'Mr Waite, how nice to hear from you.'

'Just wanted to thank you for stepping into the breach when I was indisposed—um, unable to get involved in the preparation for the recording.'

'No bother at all. I'm enjoying it.'

'Well, I can relieve you now. I'll take over organizing the stewards on the night, and I'll drop around in a few minutes to pick up any papers you need to hand on to me.'

Jack was astounded. He had no intention of relinquishing his new responsibility without a fight. 'Oh, that won't be necessary, thank you, Mr Waite. I'm very much on top of things. There really is little for you to do at this late stage.'

'Well, Jack,' Charles continued, his voice persuasive and charming, 'As you know, I am Church Warden, and there is certain protocol that needs to be followed. It would be much easier if...'

'If I continued with the job I started, Mr Waite,' said Jack firmly. 'Most of the arrangements are in my head, you see, and it would be very unwise to change horses midstream, so to speak. Thank you for calling, all the same. I promise I will call you if I need any help.

173

Goodbye now.' And with the sound of Charles' sharp intake of air at the other end of the line, Jack firmly replaced the receiver.

'Where are you staying?' Helen asked over her shoulder in Michael's direction, as she filled the kettle.

'Somewhere called The Bull, I think,' Michael replied, fishing in his inside pocket for his schedule. 'Do you know it?'

'Oh, everyone around here knows The Bull. It's just up the High Street a bit, after the bend in the road, so you can't quite see it from the church. You'll like it there. The couple who run it, Bill and Maureen—they'll look after you!'

'Oh, I could do with that, a bit of looking after,' Michael agreed, his twinkling grey eyes never leaving her. Very Irish, she thought, as she unhooked two mugs, and reached for the tin of coffee. Very Irish, with the gift of the blarney! She smiled to herself, as he went on. 'It's been a long haul, this trip. We're on the road for six complete weeks with "Village Praise"—and the lads on my team, the riggers—we don't manage to get home at all. It gets a bit tiring after a while, although I must say there's a really good atmosphere on this programme! It's been a good laugh—but hard work, and I don't think any of us will mind when we get to the end of this week—and the end of the series.'

'Six weeks. That's a long time to be away from your family. Have you got youngsters at home that you're not managing to see much?'

'I'm not married,' replied Michael.

'Oh,' said Helen. 'Sugar?'

Once the business of getting coffee was organized, Helen sat down at the opposite end of the table from Michael, and asked, 'So how many vans will there be? It looked at bit tight for you, making your way down that narrow lane?'

'Well, there should be another arriving shortly after me—that's the lighting van. It's not a BBC lighting crew, but freelancers—and their van is as big as the one I'm driving, but it's maroon coloured. Then, some time tomorrow, probably in the evening, or maybe even the next morning, the scanner will get here. That's the mobile control room really, with an editing machine on board. They're still using that in the Cotswolds at the moment, finishing the editing for this Sunday's programme.'

'I had no idea that it took so much organizing, and so many people, just to get thirty-five minutes of programme on the screen,' said Helen, offering him the biscuit tin.

'Well, I haven't finished the list yet,' said Michael, helping himself to a hobnob. 'Then there's the generator—very important that, so that we've got enough power to run the lighting in the church. And the scaffolders—now, they're a law unto themselves. They're outsiders too, so they'll be fitting in other jobs around this one. They'll probably arrive on Sunday, or Monday, and start putting up the scaffolding for the lights.'

'And what do you do?'

'Apart from driving, do you mean?' replied Michael, with a smile. 'Well, I'm the Rigger Supervisor, which means that I work with a team of riggers laying out all the cables for the cameras, and making sure that everything is working OK. Then, during the actual recording, we keep an eye on everything, and make sure that none of those cables get into shot. And we also act as what they call 'grips'. In other words, some of the cameramen are perched on top of moving platforms, that can be raised or lowered to get the best shots—and we're the people who do the raising and lowering.'

Helen grinned. 'It all sounds very technical! It will certainly provide great interest and entertainment for everyone here in Sandford, to see how it all goes together.'

'Well, I'll tell you now,' said Michael, rising from his chair, 'that the whole thing runs on cups of coffee—and if you go on making cuppas as good as that, you're in for a busy week! I must go.'

'Of course,' said Helen, getting up too. 'See you about, then!'

'Oh, you will,' said Michael, his gaze direct and unnerving, 'and I'll look forward to it.'

SATURDAY

27 March

W hen the scanner finally did trundle its precarious way up the narrow lane, late on Saturday night, Matthew was waiting to greet it. Since he'd come home from school the evening before, and seen the first van had arrived, he had hardly been home, except to eat, and very briefly, sleep—and only then because Marjorie Gregory was the sort of mother for whom mealtimes were an occasion. Matthew was there to see the doors open on Michael's camera van, and it wasn't long before his offer to help with showing the way and holding doors open had been graciously accepted. He was there when Joe, the Security Man, arrived, in his small motorized caravan. His job was to keep an eye on the vehicles throughout their stay in Sandford. During the day, that wasn't too much of a problem, because usually there were so many technical people about—but at night, he went on his hourly patrol, watching and checking, just to make sure that no important little pieces were spirited away as 'mementoes' by local youngsters.

Matthew was not considered to be a nuisance though, because his keenness to help, and his quick understanding of what bit of equipment went where, and who did what, were recognized with good humour and encouragement. Besides that, he was always willing enough to pop along to the shop to pick up drinks, chocolate and packs of sandwiches and biscuits, when no one else had time to make a trip. This proved to be particularly useful for Joe, whose caravan was an open house during the programme making. His kettle was always on, his biscuit tin always full, and his table always covered in the daily newspapers. On cold, wet mornings, there could be half a dozen people crammed into that van, and it would take nothing less than a bomb—or a few sharp words from Simon, the Engineering Manager—to entice them out again!

But because work on the church didn't need to get going in earnest until Monday, after the scaffolders arrived, the weekend was a chance for the riggers to relax, and get their breath back after five weeks of being on the road. Very quickly, the bar at The Bull became home. Bill behind the bar was always glad of extra customers, especially a crowd as friendly and willing to settle in as these were—even old Stanley, who didn't always take kindly to new faces, was won over, when Des, the broad, stocky Cockney comedian on the crew, let him win—twice—at darts.

They soon discovered the potency of the local brew, Adnams, and enjoyed downing a few pints knowing that their beds were waiting for them just up above the bar. Only Michael was different. He didn't drink alcohol. He never drank anything but coke. Bill, behind the bar, wondered if that was because at one time in his life, Michael had enjoyed alcohol too much—but Michael said nothing, and Bill didn't ask.

And because it was Saturday, and because they were demob happy, with the end of the long stint on the road almost in sight, what began as a quiet beer and darts night in the pub, became a sing-song. Des, and his pal, Charlie, both of whom had been everywhere, done everything, and knew everyone throughout long years of being riggers, started to sing, and as they downed more pints, their voices got louder, and their repertoire more entertaining. It was as Des and Charlie (Des with an old mop head draped over his head, under which he flashed his eyes like a baby doll!) were right in the middle of their rendition of 'Delilah' that Bill got his camera out to record the moment—and that photo stayed in pride of place over the bar for a good many years after the Sandford 'Village Praise' programme had become a distant memory.

SUNDAY

28 March

It had been Margaret's suggestion that she come along to St Michael's that Sunday morning for the Family Eucharist. She hadn't ever seen inside the church, and as she would be performing there that coming week, she thought it would be a good idea to become familiar with her surroundings. Besides, the Mothering Sunday service was one that she'd always loved, even though she had never been a mother herself. That had been a huge regret in her life—that she'd never married, and had a family of her own. Somehow, her work in an all girls' school had brought her mostly into contact with other women, and her love and commitment to music had taken over so much of her time. It wasn't until she was almost forty that it really registered with her that the idea she'd always had firmly rooted in her mind, that one day she would leave teaching to raise a family of her own, was probably not to be. Instead, she threw herself into the care of other people's children, and gradually, the sadness faded as acceptance of her single status became a way of life.

It was Margaret who managed to entice Jack away from his seat in the far back corner of the church, to sit with her much nearer the front, where she could see and hear better. She smiled happily about her, nodding to familiar faces that she had come to know through taking part in the rehearsals. And when the service began, she looked around her, taking in the gracious, high stone walls of the the old building, and the pale spring sunshine that poured through the clear glass windows. Next to her, but much further along the pew, sat Mrs Hadlow, sitting unnaturally upright. She tried to catch Mrs Hadlow's eye, to say hello—but the older woman sat stiffly, staring straight ahead. And Margaret hadn't actually set eyes on Clive before this morning. What a wonderful speaker! His sermon was clever and absorbing, tying in modern-day family life and motherhood, with the thoughts of that most loved of mothers, Mary, as she watched the crowds cheering her son, all the while sensing that sadness and pain were yet to come.

And then, the Sunday School children came back into the church, bringing with them small, bright bunches of daffodils to give not only their mothers, but all the ladies in the congregation. With delight, Margaret accepted her flowers from a small, long-haired girl who appeared to have no teeth at all at the front of her mouth. And Margaret watched the youngster move down the line, to offer another posy to Mrs Hadlow, who seemed ill at ease as she took the two daffodils lovingly wrapped in silverfoil.

Then, as the bread and wine were consecrated, the congregation moved into position to take their places in turn at the altar rail. Margaret glanced at Jack, and seeing the hesitation in his eyes, held out her hand to him. At first, she thought he was going to refuse. Then, slowly, he took her hand in both of his, and allowed himself to be guided to the end of the line, to the front of the church, to the rail itself. And as the minister moved towards him, Jack raised his eyes to greet him. And when Clive offered him the wine, with the words, 'The blood of Christ', Jack's 'Amen' rang out around the altar, as he drank in both the wine—and the moment.

❧

'Oh, Charles!' Clive called out, as Charles and Betty left the church. 'I hear you're to be interviewed on the programme. Congratulations!'

'Yes, well, they seem to want to get an overview of worship in this area in a historical sense,' said Charles, 'and they tell me that I am the most obvious expert in that field.'

'When are they coming to see you?'

'Well, actually, we're meeting here at the church, tomorrow morning, so I understand. I don't know how long these things take, but I've set an hour aside.'

'Well, I'm very pleased to see how enthusiastic you are about this little project now,' said Clive, walking with Charles towards the church gate. 'I wasn't sure at the start. I meant to pop down and have a chat to you about it, but somehow, time seems to have gone so quickly lately.'

'Yes, well,' said Charles, reaching up to push his glasses more firmly on to his nose, 'I've had a lot on my mind lately too. But I'm back now, and am able to take the reins for the arrangements this week. The seating, for example? There is a plan, I presume.'

'Oh, most certainly, and that excellent chap, Jack Diggens, has got that well under control. Can't say I've had much chance to get to know him, but I must say he's turning out to be a real asset. Do you know him?'

'No,' answered Charles stiffly.

'Well, I think you should make a point of saying hello. It's quite likely he's got a job or two he'd like you to help him with!'

Charles was silent, his eyes cold. Then he turned on his heel. 'Come on, Betty!' he snapped over his shoulder, and he strode off towards home.

Helen had gone on ahead, and was almost at the house when Bunty caught her. 'Helen!' she hissed. 'Helen, stop!'

Helen looked round in surprise, to find her arm firmly clasped by Bunty, who drew her over to one side of the path. 'You must come and look!' said Bunty urgently. 'We've almost finished, but we don't want to do anything, until you've taken a look. We need to know what you think, if you feel it's still a good idea. We don't want to get Clive's back up...'

Helen smiled at Bunty, and nodded her head. 'OK, I'll come. Now?'

'Please!' said Bunty, and together they hurried off towards the High Street.

It was much later that morning that Kate let herself into the church, to drop off the specially printed hymn books. She made her way to the front of the building, and deposited the box at the side of the organ—and it wasn't until she was practically back at the church door, that she noticed a small light on in the vestry. Wondering if at last she had tracked down Clive, after several abortive phone calls she'd made to the vicarage, in the hope that he could provide answers to her growing list of questions about arrangements this week, she made her way towards the vestry door, and peered around it. No one was there.

And then, the slightest of sounds—a sigh, a breath—caught her attention, and she looked again at the corner behind the door, where the old wooden cupboard that held everything from hymn books to bleach and dusters, stood alongside a row of hooks, draped in choir robes. And there sitting quietly in the haphazard array of mops and buckets, clutching a small bunch of daffodils, was Mrs Hadlow.

'Hello?' Kate called softly. 'Hello, it's Mrs Hadlow, isn't it?' There was no reply. Kate moved towards the still figure. Perhaps she was sleeping? 'Are you alright?'

Slowly, the older woman turned her head, bringing her gaze into focus on Kate's face. She said nothing. Then, she lowered her head towards her hands, and the daffodils, that were tightly clasped on her lap, and as she did so, Kate saw that her cheeks were wet, glistening with tears.

Kate moved into the room, and knelt quietly in front of the distraught woman. She wasn't sure what to say, how to start—when very low, her voice barely more than a whisper, Mrs Hadlow began to speak.

'It's Mother's Day. I always find it difficult on Mother's Day.'

'Why?' asked Kate softly. 'You're a mother yourself, aren't you?'

'Oh yes,' replied Mrs Hadlow, her face inclining towards Kate, although her eyes stared blankly ahead of her. 'Oh yes, I'm a mother. Rosemary—you know, she got married this time two years ago, and John—he lives up north now. Very good job, he's got, dear. Very good job.' She fell silent again. Kate watched as a slow tear coursed its way down her cheek. 'And then... and then, there was the other one.'

'The other one? Another child?'

'Yes.'

There was silence again, until Kate ventured, 'A child you lost?'

Mrs Hadlow turned to look Kate fully in the face. 'Not lost,' she said bleakly. 'Oh, no, I didn't lose him. He was taken away. He had to be taken away.'

'Why?'

'Because I was eighteen years old, not married, and my parents couldn't face the shame. They couldn't—and neither could I.'

'And the father?'

'He never knew. A soldier, he was. The first proper man I ever knew. He was based near us for about six months, and I loved him. I loved him, and I proved it to him, just as he said I should, if I really meant what I said. I loved him, and I proved it.'

She looked back down to her hands. 'But he was moved on before he ever knew I was expecting. He said he'd write to tell me where he'd be. That's what he said.'

'But he never did?'

'No.'

'And your parents?'

'Well, I couldn't tell them for a long time—how could I? I was their only daughter. They had high hopes for me. I didn't know what to do really. I couldn't talk to them. What could I say? It was just so difficult to be at home, trying to pretend that everything was normal, as if anything could ever be normal again. So I stayed out at much as I could, just hanging around, doing nothing in particular. And then, one day, this woman appeared. She just came up to me, and started talking. And sometimes it's much easier, isn't it, dear? It's easier to talk to a stranger.'

She looked again at Kate, someone she had only ever seen at a distance before that day. Kate moved closer, and settled quietly, waiting.

'Well, I told her. I told her that I thought I might be going to have a baby, and she just held me while I cried. She held me, and rocked me, like I was a baby myself. And then she told me it would be alright, God would make it alright, and that I wasn't to worry, because she would help me sort everything out.

'And He did—or she did, I don't know. But she came home with me, and talked to my Mum, before my Dad came back from work. And by the time he arrived, they had decided on everything. It turned out she was from the Salvation Army—Mrs Brightman, that was her name. Her husband was the Captain at the Citadel. I was to go away, up to Yorkshire, to a Salvation Army place up there, where I could have the baby, and nobody would know. And they could arrange for my baby to be taken away, taken away and adopted by parents who couldn't have a child of their own. It was all arranged, that very afternoon.'

'And how did you feel about all that?'

'It didn't really matter how I felt, did it, dear. I had no choice. No choice at all. I had done a shameful thing, and I had no choice but to go along with what was arranged.'

'So you went to Yorkshire?'

'I was there for five months in all. I can hardly remember much about it now, except that it was cold, and I didn't feel at home there. I missed my Mum—but she couldn't come to see me. She couldn't cope, and I knew that. But I especially missed her, when my boy was born. I was frightened. I didn't really know what was going to happen. It was so painful, and I was frightened. I wanted my Mum so much—but she couldn't come. I knew that.

'And then, he was there. A perfect little boy. A sleepy little chap, with blue eyes that looked at me, and knew I was his own special person. William. I called him William, his father's name—although of course, it wasn't my place to choose a name for him at all. He stayed with me for a whole week. I nursed him, and fed him, and changed him. And then, the lady from the Adoption Agency came to say it had all been arranged, and to make sure I hadn't changed my mind. Changed my mind! Was there ever any doubt in my mind that I wanted to keep my baby more than anything I've ever wanted before or since? But I had no choice. I had no choice.

'So, I dressed him up in the best clothes I had for him. And I held him close, and talked to him. I told him that I would always love him, and that I would never forget him, and that I would pray for him every day of my life—especially on Mother's Day. This day is my special day for thinking of William.'

Without thinking, Kate moved to take hold of one of her hands, as once more tears began to slide down the older woman's cheek. Suddenly, Mrs Hadlow bent down to get her handbag. 'They wrote to me, you know! William's parents—or David, that's what they called him. I've still got the letter. Look, dear, here it is...'

She went to a small pocket in the front of her purse, and pulled out a faded piece of paper, tightly folded into a small square. She handed it to Kate, who peered at the writing in the fading light of the vestry.

Dear Miss Travers,

We could never find the right words to tell you how much joy your son has brought us. He is the child we have longed for. He is the child we will love and care for all the years of our lives.

You have been through so much. And you have given us a greater gift than you could ever know. In time, we will tell David how brave his real mother was, and how much she loved him too. And none of us will ever forget you.

Be happy.

Yours sincerely,

The signature was illegible, at the bottom of the piece of paper which was yellow and crumbling. Kate refolded the note, and handed it back.

'It's nice, isn't it?' Mrs Hadlow said, putting the paper carefully into her purse. 'I thought they sounded nice. I think they will have looked after him. He'd be forty-eight years old this year. I wonder where he is. I wonder if they ever did tell him about me? I wonder if he thought I had been shameful too? I wonder if he was ashamed of what I did? I think about him a lot.'

'And your husband, does he know about William?'

'I told him once, right at the beginning, when he first asked me to marry him. I told him, and he listened, and he said nothing. And he's said nothing about it ever since, and neither have I. It's in the past. It's gone. He's gone.'

She opened her handbag again, and took out a neat, white hankie. She unfolded it, wiped her face, and put the hankie up her sleeve.

'I like being in church. God took care of me. And so I like to take care of Him, you know, look after His house, keep it nice.'

Suddenly, she stood up, smoothed down her skirt, and almost absent-mindedly rearranged the mops into neat order. 'Right, dear. This will never do. George will be wanting his lunch.' And with that, she pulled on her coat—and the bright, brittle face she showed the world—and walked quickly towards the door.

❧

For Pam, the fact that the last programme in this year's series of
'Village Praise' happened to be in Suffolk was quite a relief. At least,
that was only a couple of hours' drive from home—and unlike many
of the production team, she had managed to get home throughout
the series at least a couple of days each week. If it hadn't been for that
chance to get back and see the family, she probably would have found
the series impossible to do at all. As it was, she arrived back each week
drained and exhausted, spending most of her time at home washing,
ironing, catching up on letters (oh, so many letters!) and cramming
her head full of facts from the research notes for the coming week's
programme. Whoever said being a television presenter was
glamorous!

She always felt better once she was on the road, and on her way.
The hours leading up to the moment when she had to say goodbye to
her husband, Paul, and their two youngsters, Max who was eleven,
and Bethan who was just five, were always the worst. It wasn't that
they minded her job, or even that their routine changed one bit
because Mum wasn't always around for them. In many ways, she was
the one who got the worst of the deal, recognizing that she missed
them, much more than they missed her. And nothing ever altered the
fact that first and foremost, she was a wife and a Mum. After that, she
was a television presenter, a job she loved—and a job that, in many
ways, allowed her a great deal of freedom with her time.

She had been presenting 'Songs of Praise' for six years now,
alternating programmes with a team of other presenters. But to have
been asked to present a complete series of six programmes of 'Village
Praise' totally on her own, and for the second year running, was both
an honour and a thrill. She loved the programme—loved the chance
to meet so many varied and inspiring people, and spend time with
them and their neighbours in their village homes. And whereas 'Songs
of Praise' was often very formal, with a style that was predictable,
evolved over the thirty or so years that it had been on the air, 'Village
Praise' was able to establish a personality of its own—informal and
friendly—a style of presentation that came very comfortably to her.

As she drove into Sandford, she dug around in the file on the seat
beside her to pull out the sheet with the hotel details. Grove House—
look out for the sign on the left, towards the end of the High Street.

Minutes later, she was driving through tall wrought-iron gates, to park her car alongside others that over the past five weeks had become very familiar to her.

A tall, friendly man came out to greet her, as she dragged bits and pieces from the boot. 'Brian's the name, glad to meet you! Quite a few of your lot are here already. Get yourself settled, and we'll have a tray of tea waiting for you downstairs in the lounge in ten minutes!'

'This place,' thought Pam, as she tucked the Sandford Research Notes file under her arm, 'I'm going to like!'

The tradition was that as many of the team as possible would arrive at the next village location on a Sunday evening, in time to watch transmission of the 'Village Praise' that most of them had been working on the week before. They abandoned their 'office' at Grove House for the occasion, and piled into the more comfortable settees and chairs in the lounge. Pam was, in fact, the last to arrive. Jan, Roger and Kate had been in Sandford for some days; Sue, the Production Assistant, had driven down from the office in Manchester the day before, arriving at almost the same time as Simon Martin, the Engineering Manager, who was actually booked in with most of his crew down the road at The Bull.

The noisy chatter in the room almost drowned the sound of the News finishing, the weather forecast, and the long promotion that followed for the coming evening's programmes. And then, it was on—and a hush fell over the room, as the familiar strains of the 'Village Praise' theme music announced that their programme was starting. For all of them, this was the first viewing of the completely finished programme, which had been edited by the another director in their team right up until the last possible moment in the Cotswold village that was featured. They all watched with hungry interest— noting what items had made the final programme; bemoaning the terrible weather they had had; commenting that they wished that had been changed, this put in, the other left out!

And as Pam came up on the screen at the end of the programme, saying that for the last programme in the series, she was heading off to Suffolk, and the lovely Heritage Coast village of Sandford, to join the locals for their Palm Sunday celebrations—a cheer went up around the room.

'Not a bad programme! Not bad at all!' said Simon. He looked at Jan. 'Right! On to the next!'

29 March

Monday morning dawned dry, but probably not for long. The sky was grey, and heavy with rain clouds. Charles insisted on wearing his favourite, pale blue shirt for his interview, teamed with his very dark grey, best suit. He looked splendid, and Betty told him so—although she did venture to suggest that perhaps a suit might be a bit formal for a chat in a graveyard... He looked at her, and thought about it. 'No! No, I am representing Sandford. It is important that, as an ambassador for the church and our community, I dress in an appropriate way.'

He sat at the breakfast table, spooning Betty's homemade marmalade on to thin white toast, glancing once again through his assortment of reference books on churches in Suffolk. They'll be surprised, he thought, at just how much there is to say on the subject. He had his speech more or less worked out in his mind. He would start back in the twelfth century, and move through the years until the present day. He kept reading as the telephone rang, and Betty answered it.

'Charles, dear,' she said, her hand over the mouthpiece. 'Charles, it's for you. Kate, from the BBC.'

'Right,' said Charles, slowing replacing his books into a neat pile, and making his way to the phone. 'Charles Waite.'

'Oh, Charles, glad I caught you! Kate here! We're not sure this weather is going to hold today, and as the forecast doesn't look great for the rest of the week, we're going to take this opportunity to nip out and get a few general shots of the countryside, before the heavens open. Don't know quite what time the crew will get back, but shall we say that we'll put your interview back an hour or so? Around eleven-thirty—will that suit you?'

Charles' reply was little more than a grunt of assent.

'Oh, and Charles, I don't need to tell a country person like you, of course, but we're all dressing for warmth today—jerseys and anoraks—and I should bring your wellies, if I were you!'

Pam, Roger and Kate walked down to the scanner, to meet the camera crew. Keith, the cameraman, and Bob, the Sound Recordist, were still unloading gear from the camera van, but they gave a cheery wave to say that they'd only be a few minutes, and they'd be ready to get on the road. 'Right,' said Roger, 'we'll just go out and get a few general views in the crew car—no point dragging everyone along! So, Pam, that will give you the chance to talk the interviews over with Kate.'

'Fine,' Pam agreed, and because poring over research notes always worked better with a cup of coffee in hand, she made her way towards Joe's security caravan. She pulled open the door, to find it packed and smoky, full of riggers, reading the papers and keeping out of the cold.

'Here you are, then!' she grinned at them, pulling out four Yorkie Bars from her coat pocket. 'Your supplies for the week!'

'You're a good girl,' said Charlie. 'We've just got you trained, and we're coming to the end of the series! Thanks, love!'

It was then that Pam noticed a new face in the crowd, a young, tall blond boy, probably about sixteen years old. 'Hello! Have you taken on a new rigger?'

'We have!' replied Des, slapping the youngster on the back. 'This is Matthew. He's home from school for the Easter holidays now, so he's going to give us a hand. Good local knowledge, you see!'

'Well, Matthew,' said Pam laughing, 'just two things—don't lend them anything you'd like to see again, and don't believe a word they say!'

Five minutes later, two cups of Joe's coffee in hand, Pam went off towards the church, to discuss the coming week with Kate. After she'd gone, Joe reached up to a high cupboard above the sink, and got down a white paper bag. In it were a dozen Yorkie Bars, to which he added the four Pam had just brought in.

'You know, Charlie,' said Des, 'you've got to tell her, you know. You've got to tell her we're sick of Yorkie Bars.'

'I will, I will,' said Charlie, 'I've just got to wait for the right moment.'

'Just tell her,' said Des, a look of exasperation on his face, 'tell her we're on to licorice allsorts!'

'Right,' said Kate, taking her cup as Pam settled herself into the pew. 'I've got a few more notes here for you—you got the others, I see.'

'Um,' said Pam, taking a gulp of coffee at the same time. 'Is there a Running Order yet?'

'Yes, Jan drew this one up last night. This is the order we think the programme will go in at the moment. Open to discussion, of course!'

Pam read through the sheet Kate gave her.

RUNNING ORDER—SANDFORD—FIRST DRAFT
'VILLAGE PRAISE' TITLE SEQUENCE
PAM—INTRO, INCLUDING DONKEY AUDITION
RIDE ON, RIDE ON IN MAJESTY—TO INCLUDE PROCESSION, LED BY DONKEY, FROM THE VILLAGE GREEN, THROUGH CHURCHYARD, AND TO THE FRONT OF CHURCH
INTERVIEW—CHARLES WAITE TO COVER CHURCH HISTORY, AND CONTINUITY OF WORSHIP AND TRADITIONS
EGG ROLLING SEQUENCE—WITH COMMENTS FROM CHILDREN ABOUT WHAT ROLLING EGGS DOWN HILL SIGNIFIES
THERE IS A GREEN HILL—SUNG BY SANDFORD JUNIOR SCHOOL CHOIR
INTERVIEW—DAVID HUGHES—LOCAL FARMER, ABOUT THE STRESS OF MODERN-DAY FARMING, AND THE STRENGTH HE DRAWS FROM FAMILY AND CHURCH LIFE IN DINTON; LINK INTO SOLITUDE OF HIS JOB, AND HOW THE BEAUTY OF THE COUNTRYSIDE INSPIRES HIM
FOR THE BEAUTY OF THE EARTH
INTERVIEW—MIKE HALLAM, CO-ORDINATOR, 'OUT AND ABOUT' PROJECT, ABOUT WALKING TRIPS THEY ORGANIZE FOR PEOPLE WITH VARIETY OF LIMITATIONS AND DIFFICULTIES
'JUST AS I AM'—SOLO, ANNA BIRCH

INTERVIEW—FISHERMEN (SIDNEY, FRANK AND BO)
THE OLD RUGGED CROSS (1ST VERSE FROM FISHERMEN, OTHERS FROM CHURCH
CONGREGATION)
INTERVIEW—REVEREND STEPHEN YEARLING
O SACRED HEAD—CHOIR ITEM (ST MARK'S?)
DEEP PEACE—CHOIR —OVERLAY PRAYER (REV. CLIVE LINTON—TO BE
RECORDED AT HAYCLIFFE)
BLESSING, ALSO FROM CLIVE—TO BE RECORDED IN THE CHURCH
WHEN I SURVEY
PAM—WIND-UP PIECE FOR THE END OF SERIES
END CREDITS

Pam sifted through her research notes. 'I seem to have everything I need here, except any real details about the fishermen. Which one will mainly do the talking, do you think?'

Kate grinned. 'You won't get a choice there. Sidney is in charge, and he won't let you forget it! The trouble is that it is very difficult to get a real conversation with him. He's so busy bossing the others about, that it's not easy to know just how to handle an interview with him.'

'When are we recording their piece?' Pam asked, searching for her recording schedule.

'Tomorrow afternoon, quite late,' Kate replied. 'We're meeting them at four-thirty, and with a bit of luck, we should be able to record their reading and prayer just as the sun is setting.'

'Do you think there's a chance that one of the others...' Pam looked down to check their names, 'Bo or Frank, might be good at sharing their faith, if Sidney wasn't breathing down their necks at the time?'

'It's possible, quite possible. They're both real charmers, with a nice sense of humour. They're just a bit overshadowed by Sidney, I reckon. Anyway, while you're out filming this afternoon, I'm going to meet them, to sort all the details out for tomorrow. So, are you OK with everything today?'

'Charles Waite—he's first this morning, isn't he?' Pam asked, searching out the notes on him. She looked up at Kate. 'What's he like?'

'Well, a bit of a stuffed shirt, I'd say. I'm not quite sure if he's glad to be involved, or not. I gather from local gossip that he was dead against the programme coming here at all—at least, he was in the first place. I wouldn't say he's that enthusiastic now, but he is keen to share his knowledge of the history of the area. That's obviously a passion of his, and I get the feeling that he has a mission to tell the country every little ounce of information he knows!'

Pam groaned. 'Difficult to keep him to time then, do you think?'

'Impossible, I would say. Good luck!' Kate grinned, and went on. 'And this afternoon, you're going walkies—with the "Out and About" crowd. They organize outings, mainly along the Suffolk Heritage Coast, for people who would normally find it very difficult to arrange trips like that for themselves. I gather there's a real mixture of walkers—some are able-bodied, but have particular problems or responsibilities at home that make it difficult for them to get out at all. The rest have disabilities of one sort or another—everything from blindness to people in wheelchairs.'

'How many are there likely to be today?' Pam asked.

'I'm not sure really. It may well depend on the weather, but Mike Hallam—he's the one you'll be talking to—thinks there should be about twenty or so. Mike's great, by the way. He obviously loves this area—he's lived here all his life—and although it's clear his Christian faith is very important to him, I think he might be quite shy once he thinks about the camera on him. He may need a bit of help to find the right words.'

'That's fine. Gosh, I hope the weather holds for this afternoon. I don't fancy a long hike in the rain!' Pam sighed. 'You'd think we'd shrink with all the rain we stand out in!'

'No such luck, I'm afraid!' laughed Kate, as the church door opened. 'Brace yourself! Here comes Charles Waite now!'

Charles stepped smartly into the church at exactly twenty-five minutes past eleven.

Kate stood up to greet him. 'Charles, how nice to see you again! Do come and meet Pam!'

He recognized at once the girl with the lisp that irritated him so on Sunday evenings. She seemed friendly enough though, as she moved along the pew to shake his hand.

'Good morning, Charles. Good to meet you. We're going to have a bit of a wait, I'm afraid. The crew are taking advantage of the fact that it's not raining yet, just in case we don't have enough chance to get good pictures of the countryside around here later in the week. Never mind, you and I can sort out what we're going to talk about, before they get back. Come and have a seat—would you like a cup of something? We could probably rustle up a tea or coffee?'

'Not in the church, thank you,' answered Charles tersely, as he made his way along the pew to join her. Kate caught Pam's eye over his shoulder, and grimaced, before saying, 'Well, I need to sort out tomorrow's filming—and I must try and catch up with the vicar... I'll leave you to it!'

Charles sat down, and put his briefcase on his knee. Meticulously, he dialled the figures needed to release the security locks, and then opened the case with a flourish to reveal three large reference books, and a sheath of neatly written notes. Before Pam could say a word, he began. 'Of course, it all depends how far back you want to go. This area is rich in history, and the church has always had its part to play in the story.'

'You know, Charles,' interrupted Pam, eying the pile of books and papers he was neatly spreading out before him. 'What we need to do is to tell the story as briefly as possible...'

It was as if Pam had never spoken. Charles was warming to his subject. 'Of course, even before the first stage of the building of St Michael's, this had been a holy place. It's thought that monks had a small community here over nine centuries ago. This book—' he turned the pages of the largest of the three, 'gives details of extensive archaelogical research that has been undertaken in the area...'

'Charles!' Pam broke in, the note of despair only barely noticeable in her voice. 'Charles, we're talking about an interview that will only last about two minutes on screen. There won't be time for much specific detail. Broad brush strokes, that's what we're after, so that it's nice and clear, and easy to understand. We must keep it brief!'

'All the more reason for you to appreciate the total picture,' retorted Charles. 'As I was saying, this book explains how archaeologists have unearthed evidence of a monastic community that probably flourished here for about two centuries...'

Kate, who had just reached the end of the church, looked back at the two of them, and chuckled as she shut the door behind her.

❦

A few minutes later, Helen closed the door of the vicarage, and began to walk up the garden path, and along the back lane towards the church. As she picked her way past the line of huge vehicles that stood there, she was intrigued about what they all actually did. The back of one van was open, and hoping that no one would notice, she slowed her pace, so that she could peer inside.

And it was like that—walking one way, and looking another—that Helen collided with Michael. His face creased into laughter, the Irish lilt in his voice more pronounced than ever. 'Don't look so guilty! Come and have a proper look!' And his hand reached out to take hers, as he helped her up into the camera van.

Curiously, she looked around her, at what seemed to be a van packed full of shelves and cables, some hanging from the sides, some laid on the floor in coils big enough to sit on. There were cameras too, although, like everything else, these seemed to be in bits, and surrounded by yet more cables. Michael made himself comfortable on a pile of silver boxes, and she did the same, perching herself gingerly on a convenient black carton.

'Would you like to know what everything is?' He smiled again. 'Of course, you should, but do you really want to?'

It was her turn to smile. 'No, you're right! You'd lose me the moment you got technical! As long as you know how it all goes together, that's all I need to know!'

They fell silent, grinning at each other across the van.

'So,' he said at last, his grey eyes fixed on her, 'you didn't come to see the equipment then! You must have come to see me...'

This man is flirting with me, she thought in amazement. Me—a harassed, married—very married—mother of two! And because the idea was so absurd, she threw her head back and laughed.

'Not unless you're any good at taking funeral services! It's a man of the cloth, I'm looking for—my man of the cloth, my husband, Clive. I've had a call to say that one of his elderly parishioners out at Dinton died in hospital this morning, and we need to fit in a funeral service. There are just so many complications this week, with all of you here, I thought I should pass the message on immediately. I don't suppose you've seen him, have you?'

'You're the second person to ask me that in as many minutes,' replied Michael. 'Our researcher, Kate, was looking for him too.' His shrewd eyes never left Helen's face. 'Does he often go missing then?'

Helen hesitated. How easy it would be to say yes, yes, Clive is always disappearing, sometimes for hours at a time, and I have no idea where he is or where he goes. He's a private man, someone who needs peace and solitude for his thoughts, for God. Time to draw strength. Time alone. Time away from me. A life apart from me...

Her answer, when it came, was no mirror of her thoughts. 'Well, he's a vicar. Constantly in demand, always needing to be in two places at once. You know how it is!'

'Yes,' said Michael, gazing steadily at her. 'Yes, I see exactly how it is.'

Helen felt her face redden. To cover her embarrassment, she spoke quickly. 'And you? You're never at home either, are you? Don't you get tired of being on the road all the time?'

'Funnily enough, I don't really. I suppose, because there's no one waiting for me, I'd just as soon be away working.'

'How come you've never married? Lack of opportunity, or lack of inclination?' Such a personal question, Helen thought. How insensitive of her to ask!

'A bit of both, I think. I've had my moments, of course...' Those grey eyes twinkled at her again, 'but I've never been tempted to let anyone move in on a permanent basis. In the end, I've just never felt sure enough to commit myself solely to one person. Not met the right woman, I suppose—not yet, anyway.'

His gaze held hers for a moment, before she looked away. Just then, their attention was claimed by an elderly Volvo estate that drove up just behind the van. There was a flash of lilac-coloured sleeve waving out of the driver's window, as the car came to a halt. Michael looked at Helen. 'You've been spotted!'

'Oh, that's Bunty Maddocks,' replied Helen, adding, almost under her breath. 'If you want to know anything about anyone in Sandford, Bunty's the one to ask!'

'Helen!' called Bunty, her eyes on Michael. 'Whatever are you doing in there?'

'Waiting for you, Bunty. I thought you'd call by this morning. This is Michael, by the way.'

Michael nodded in Bunty's direction, then got up to climb down from the van. 'I see the scaffolders have arrived,' he said, looking towards the group of three men who were just coming out of Joe's security van. 'We'll get things started now.'

'Scaffolding?' asked Bunty. 'What do we need scaffolding for?'

'Well, to put lights up right at the top of the church,' replied Michael, both arms held out to Helen, as he lifted her from the van. 'If we tried to put all the equipment up without proper scaffolding, we might damage the church structure.'

'Oh,' said Bunty, plainly impressed. 'And how long does it take, this scaffolding?'

'All today, and then tomorrow we finalize all the lighting, and the camera and sound cabling.'

'Does that mean the church should be free tonight?' asked Bunty innocently.

'Don't know,' said Michael. 'Probably, if everything goes OK.'

'Right!' said Bunty again, casting an urgent glance at Helen. 'Can I have a word?'

'I'm off,' said Michael, and with what Helen thought, just for a moment, was a wink in her direction, he walked away, whistling softly.

'About tonight!' Bunty spoke urgently, as she slipped her arm through Helen's and drew her into a conspirators' huddle. 'The ladies and I will do it—you know, get everything done—well, as much as we dare! Then, can you think of some reason to bring Clive along to the church, say about nine o'clock? We should have things straight by then.'

Helen smiled at Bunty's worried face. 'I'll do my very best, Bunty, I really will. I'm not sure what Clive is doing tonight.' In fact, she thought to herself, I don't know what Clive's doing at all! 'But I'll do my darndest to get him there at nine—promise!'

By the time the crew arrived back at the church, pleased with the shots they'd collected of sheep, babbling brooks and new buds bursting into colour on the trees, Charles had only reached the seventeenth century in his saga of everything you could ever possibly want to know about churches in Suffolk! Pam had given up trying to interrupt him. She had made a few notes about exactly what was needed, and decided that he was plainly enjoying his lecture so much, that until the crew came back, he might just as well go on enjoying himself! For the past ten minutes, she had been reading the research notes on the other people to be interviewed this week, and she only looked up when the director, Roger, called to her from the church doorway, to say that the crew were setting up around the back of the church, and could she bring Charles out in five minutes?

Pam packed away her notes, and got to her feet. Curiosity made Charles finally stop speaking. 'Charles, that was really interesting. Thanks so much for filling me in. I've made a few notes, and I think it would be best if, as this is near the start of the programme, I begin with a short piece where I talk to the camera, just to set the scene a bit about where we are, and something about my first impression of the churches you see around here. That should lead in quite naturally into my first question—why are the churches around here often so huge and cathedral-like?'

They were out of the church by now, heading round the corner towards the small graveyard that lay at the back of St Michael's.

'Perhaps your answer could cover the wool trade here in the Middle Ages, and how it brought great prosperity to the successful merchants in these parts. Then we could go on to talk about how the richer they were, the bigger the churches they built, with spires reaching up to heaven.'

Charles opened his mouth to comment, when suddenly he caught sight of the camera being carefully positioned just in front of him. Recognizing this familiar reaction to the reality of seeing a television camera, Pam slowed her pace, and drew closer to him. 'Don't worry about the camera, or anyone else who's with us. Just forget they're there, and talk to me. The more conversational and friendly we can make it, the better it will come across to the folk watching at home.'

It was probably a cloud passing across the watery sun that made Charles' face seem suddenly greyer.

'And perhaps we could finish up by talking about the continuity of worship here, and how comforting and inspiring it is to know that

St Michael's has been marking the occasions of the Christian calendar, like Palm Sunday, over the centuries, in much the same way as we are this week.'

Charles' throat was dry. Something had happened to his voice.

'OK, Charles,' said Pam. 'Are you ready to have a go?'

His hands felt clammy and hot. He glanced again towards the camera, and nodded slowly.

Ian was still a couple of hours' drive away from Sandford, as he headed towards Suffolk from the Cotswolds. He had his electronic keyboard safely installed in the boot of his car, so it had been arranged that his rehearsal with young Anna should be held at her home, above the High Street shop, rather than the church, which was likely to be full of scaffolding and cables that afternoon. Ian planned to meet up with Jan first of all, over a cup of tea at Grove House, to have a final chat about the hymns for this week's programme, and to let her hear the incidental music he had written the day before, which could link hymns and interviews in an atmospheric and imaginative way.

Ian was tired. The Cotswolds programme had been difficult, and frankly, he was worn out. He knew his musical imagination suffered when he was exhausted. He didn't think that Mozart himself could come up with masterpieces, if he'd been as drained as Ian felt today! He knew what he should say to producers who expected too much, too soon—do you want it good, or do you want it now? Silly question. They wanted it all—and they had a right to expect nothing less. There were always dozens of others who would happily step into his shoes.

He glanced at the clock. Quarter past twelve. With so much driving still ahead of him before he reached Sandford, he decided that as he hadn't arranged to meet up with Jan until three, perhaps he could allow himself the luxury of a coffee and a bacon sandwich in an hour or so. Maybe that would wake him up.

It wasn't just that he was tired though. When he thought about it, his melancholy was deeper than that. He had never minded hard work; in fact, the more pressure, the more he liked it. With his stare fixed on the road, he made himself think about what was at the root of this emptiness, this dissatisfaction.

In spite of his thoughts, a smile crept up on him. Probably too many bacon butties and cups of coffee at wayside cafes! But there was more, so much more than that. Too many miles in too many different cars. Too many hotel rooms, too many different room numbers to remember. Too many snatched meals, too many meals missed altogether. Too many nights spent burning the midnight oil, scribbling out hurried manuscripts of music, and laying track upon track onto the electronic keyboard. Too many bags of dirty washing, and not enough clean shirts. Too many bills waiting on his own doormat, and not enough time to sort them out, even if he could. Too few nights in his own bed. Too little time with Sarah. Not enough of Sarah. Never enough of Sarah.

Sarah. She was the heart of it. It wasn't his home he missed. That was just bricks and mortar. Sarah was his home. Wherever she was, that's where he wanted to be.

A new feeling this. Here he was, happily single and busily employed for all these years, and now—now, this yawning emptiness that only disappeared when Sarah was near enough for him to stretch out his hand and touch her.

Sarah—who calmed and warmed him. Sarah, who shut out the world and its worries by drawing him close to her. Sarah—so talented, with musical ambitions that were as dedicated as his own. Her life was a merry-go-round of hard work, and concerts up and down the country too. The very fact that they ever managed to meet up at all, was a minor miracle in itself!

He shook his head to clear his vision. With both of them living at such a frantic pace, what hope was there that their relationship could survive this time, when their careers had torn them apart before? He loved her, of that much he was sure—but what of her feelings? She said she loved him too. But did she need him, the way he found himself needing her? Was he always invading her thoughts, when her concentration should have been elsewhere? Did she find a dozen occasions every day when she wished he was there to share a thought, a joke, a worry? Did she long for him, with the physical ache that he so often felt when he thought of her?

Had she ever wondered, as he found himself wondering now and then, what it would be like to live together—in the same home, planning a future where they would always come home to each other?

Whatever was he thinking? About living together? Simply that—no rules, no obligations? Or did he really want, and need, more than that? Commitment to her. A commitment from her...

A sign for a coffee stop loomed up at the side of the road. Just as well, he thought. It's dangerous to think and drive at the same time.

'Right!' said Roger. 'If you start off right back at the wall, Pam, and do your piece to camera walking across the graveyard, can you make it just the right length, so that when you get to the bit when you're talking about the cathedral-like churches, St Michael's is well in shot behind you? Keep walking, and Charles—you wait over here, Charles—that's it—just a bit further to your right—Charles should come into view just as you ask him the first question...'

'The first question,' mumbled Charles. 'What is the first question?'

Pam smiled at him. 'I'll ask you why there are so many huge churches like this one, in tiny villages in this part of Suffolk. Does that sound alright to you?'

'Why are there so many huge churches...?' Beads of sweat spread themselves in a thin shiny coat across Charles' forehead.

'And just vaguely, so that I have an idea what's coming, what is your answer likely to be?'

Seconds of silence hung in the air. 'What is my answer likely to be? My answer...' Charles drew his neatly folded hankie out of his pocket, and patted his nose and forehead. 'My answer, well, my answer could be...'

'How about us deciding on your opening line? Sometimes that helps. It just gets you going, and somehow everything falls into place then.' Pam looked at Charles encouragingly. 'What about something like, "Well, this area might look very quiet and rural now, but back in the Middle Ages, this corner of eastern England was especially convenient for exporting goods to the Continent, and because of that, Suffolk became extremely prosperous in the wool trade..."'

'The wool trade,' repeated Charles, fingering his hankie. 'Yes, the wool trade. And how did you start again?'

'Well, you decide what seems most natural to you, but perhaps something about the area looking quiet now, but back in the Middle Ages...'

'Yes, yes,' agreed Charles suddenly, pocketing his hankie. 'That's fine. I'm fine.'

Roger shot a quizzical look at Pam, then turned towards the cameraman, Keith. 'Are you ready, Keith? How's the light?'

'Patchy,' replied Keith, shading his eyes to look towards the sky. 'The clouds are moving so fast across the sun, that we're just going to have to grab the light while it's there. The church does look so much nicer with the sun on it.' He scanned the sky, then peered at the sun again. 'Let's give it a go. We might have a bit of a break in the cloud, if we do it right now.'

'Let's go for it!' decided Roger. 'Sound, OK?' Bob the sound man, his ears encased in headphones, nodded in agreement. 'Back to the wall then, Pam. OK, Charles? Turn over please!'

Pam waited several seconds, to make sure the tape was recording at speed, and then began to walk slowly through the graveyard, speaking to the camera as she went.

'Some people have described this part of Suffolk as a forgotten corner of England. Wander round here, and you feel that you're taking a step back in time—where thatched roofs and pargeted cottages, sturdily built around their ageless timberframes, have watched over village life for centuries. Sandford is typical of many villages in these parts—small and friendly, where some of the family names have appeared on the parish register here at St Michael's, for generations. But just take a look at St Michael's! At first sight, it's more like a cathedral than a humble parish church—and yet large, towering churches are a regular feature of this part of Suffolk. Charles Waite is a local historian—tell me, Charles, why are there so many huge churches in this area?'

Pam looked expectantly at Charles. He looked back at her. Moments passed, and then Charles turned to Roger and asked, 'Should I have answered then?'

Roger's expression didn't change at all. 'Well, yes. Hang on a minute. Can we tack your answer on?' He looked over towards Keith, the cameraman.

'Well, I wouldn't mind having another go at that anyway,' replied Keith. 'St Michael's had disappeared from my shot before Pam got round to talking about it.'

Pam had moved over to Charles, and smiled at him in encouragement. 'You're right, Charles. That's where you give your answer. You were going to start off by talking about how quiet it is here nowadays, but that back in the Middle Ages, this was the heart of the wool industry... Does that still sound OK to you?'

Charles cleared his throat. 'Fine,' he agreed.

'Please don't feel under any pressure at all,' Pam said quietly, so that only Charles could hear. 'There are plenty of technical reasons why we may need to stop—it's much more likely to be us that need to repeat something, than you. Anyway, it's tape, and we've got plenty of that. Just relax, and enjoy talking about something I know is a favourite subject of yours...'

'Fine, yes, fine,' said Charles, reaching once again for his hankie.

'Right, let's go again. Keith, alright for light?'

'Yep. Running up...!'

And Pam began again. 'Some people have described this part of Suffolk as a forgotten corner of England. Wander around here, and you...'

'Sorry!' yelled Keith. 'Sun's gone!'

'Back to your places, everyone!' called Roger. 'Be ready to go again as soon as the sun comes out...'

They all stood, intently looking towards the sky. Charles brushed his hair back into place, and stared at his shoes.

'Here we go! Turn over!'

Pam began to walk, and talk to the camera again. It was just at the point where she said, 'But just take a look at St Michael's...', when the cameraman interrupted.

'Have to go again!' said Keith. 'St Michael's isn't quite in shot yet. Can you speed your walk up a bit, Pam?'

'But keep the timing of the words the same length, or you'll reach Charles too early,' added Roger.

Digesting this as she went, Pam went back to her starting position.

'Sun's in,' said Keith.

'I don't believe this!' said Roger.

'Are you alright, Charles?' asked Pam.

'Fine,' replied Charles. 'Just fine.'

'Sun's out!' said Keith.

'Right, let's go!' said Roger.

'Hold it! Is that a lawnmower I can hear?' All eyes turned on Bob, the sound man, who was holding one piece of his earphones away from his ear.

'Oh, for heaven's sake!' exploded Roger. 'Where's that coming from?' He looked meaningfully at Sue, the Production Assistant, as if she should know.

'Over there, I think,' said Sue, putting down her clipboard, and heading over to a corner of the church wall. She had got as far as clambering over the wall when Bob stopped her. 'It's gone! Sound ready!'

'OK!' shouted Roger. 'Let's do it! Places everyone!'

Pam, who had been standing near Charles, squeezed his arm and smiled as she moved back towards her starting point by the gate. Charles wiped his damp palms on the side of his trousers.

'Camera ready?' Roger turned to Keith. 'Right, action!'

And Pam began again. She went right through the piece, until the point when she drew level with Charles. She smiled towards him as she continued. 'Charles Waite is a local historian—tell me, Charles, why are there so many huge churches in this area?'

'Well', said Charles, finding her stare uncomfortable. 'Well, it was the wool industry, you know. There was a lot of it here in the old days...'

'Can we cut it there?' Keith turned to Roger. 'Charles is looking at the camera, I'm afraid.'

'OK,' said Roger patiently. 'Look towards Pam, could you, Charles? Just try and forget that the camera's there—imagine there's just the two of you standing and chatting here, because that's what it will look like to the people watching at home. If you look towards the camera, you'll give the game away. Go again, everyone!'

Glancing at Charles' ashen face, Pam moved towards him again. 'It's a funny thing,' she said, 'but if you let your eyes slip towards the camera, you'll look really shifty! And that would never do for a church warden, would it?'

He nodded without comment. A bead of sweat rolled down his back, inside his shirt.

When the camera was running again, Pam started to walk and speak. 'Some people have described this part of Suffolk as a forgotten corner of England. Wander around here, and you feel as if you've taken a step back in time... Oh heck! hold it! I've forgotten what happens when you take a step back in time!'

And she turned on her heel back to her starting position, mumbling her words out loud to herself as she went.

'Camera still rolling!' yelled Keith.

'Hold on a bit!' added Bob. 'There's a plane going over.' They all stood quietly and looked towards the totally empty sky. The very distant sound subsided. 'OK!' said Bob.

'When you're ready, Pam!' shouted Roger.

Once more with feeling, thought Pam—and preferably, this time, she'd get the words right! She did, and it was with some relief that she once again reached Charles, where she smiled encouragingly towards him. 'Charles Waite is a local historian—tell me, Charles, why are there so many huge churches in this area?'

This time, Charles' eyes stayed resolutely glued to Pam's. 'Well, this area—this area may look fairly quiet now, but—um—some time back, well, a long time, around the Middle Ages actually—there was a lot of wool here.'

He stopped—and after a second's hesitation, Pam asked, 'Was there a particular reason why the wool industry was centred in this area?'

'A reason?' asked Charles.

'A geographical reason perhaps?'

'Oh yes, well, it's near Europe, you see—good for exports.' Charles stopped again.

'And did the wool industry have a bearing on the building of all these large churches?'

'Yes, it did,' replied Charles.

'In what sort of way?' prompted Pam.

'Hold it!' said Keith. 'There's someone in the back of the shot.'

They all turned to see Bunty Maddocks, waving the few fingers she could release from her grip on a large mysterious-looking box.

'Hello there!' she shouted. 'Well done, Charles. You're doing splendidly! Mind if I watch for a bit?'

'Actually,' said Roger, smiling pleasantly through clenched teeth, 'actually, you're just in the back of our shot there.'

'Oh!' said Bunty. 'My goodness, I'm in your way, of course. I'll go then. Just popping in to the church to—well, just to, er—well, I'll be off then!' And she disappeared into the side entrance, and banged the door behind her.

'Will she be coming out again in a minute?' asked Bob, the sound recordist. 'Only that door makes an awful din when it closes.'

'Charles.' Pam took Charles to one side. 'I'm having to ask a lot of questions to get the complete answer. I wonder if we can have another go at it, and perhaps you could string several facts together in that first reply. It's quiet here now—but this was the hub of the wool industry back in the Middle Ages—important area for wool because of being so near to Europe... along those lines? Is that possible?'

'Of course it is!' snapped Charles. If only his hands would stop shaking...

'Will I have to do the opening piece again?' Pam looked at Roger hopefully.

'Afraid so,' was the reply. 'If we can just get the first answer on the end of this shot, we can move the camera round for a close-up on Charles for the rest of the interview. Right, has anyone else got any more problems they can possibly think of? OK, from the top then!'

All went well as Pam began her piece, and made her way across towards Charles. It crossed Pam's mind, as she walked towards him, that he had the look of a rabbit caught in headlights. This isn't going to work, she thought—but she kept talking and walking, and eventually was standing beside him.

'Tell me, Charles, why are there so many huge church buildings in this corner of Suffolk?'

'It's the wool trade—well, it was in the Middle Ages. We're close to Europe here, you see, so it was a good area for exporting the wool. And they built churches—the rich merchants—they thought that the grander the church, the more God would appreciate it.'

'Cut!' sighed Roger. 'Let's move the camera in for a closer shot for the rest of the interview. Well done, Charles, that was fine!'

A look passed between Pam and Roger. No words were exchanged.

Pam turned to Charles. 'So let's move on, Charles, to the last piece of our interview. About what it's like to worship in a church which has shared the joys and sorrows of village life here for centuries...'

'Yes. What do you want me to say?' Charles had his hankie in his hand again.

'Whatever you truly feel,' replied Pam. 'We are making a Christian programme, and we would be very glad if you could put your answer in Christian terms—share your own faith with us, perhaps? Tell us what it means to you personally, to worship in such an old and much loved church, and how important the continuity of worship and tradition is to Sandford.'

'Are we set?' said Roger. 'We need to hurry. Look at that sky. Those clouds moving in now look very black.'

'This won't cut, you know,' said Keith. 'We shot the first bit in sunshine. It's really dark now.'

'Can we rig up a little light to help?' asked Roger, glancing at his watch. 'I just want to get this done. We must meet those walkers— the ones we're filming this afternoon—at two, or they'll go off without us!'

'Give us a minute then,' replied Keith, and he strolled off towards the crew car, reappearing a few minutes later with a small hand-held battery operated light.

'Can you hold this, Roger? Just there, so that it gives Charles a gleam in the eye...'

'I can't see the monitor from here,' said Roger, straining his neck to see the picture on the small television set they carried with them, on which they could look at the picture the camera was seeing. 'Does this look like daylight? Will this cut with the first bit?'

Keith looked at him, and shrugged. 'Well, not really—but I reckon we should just record it like this before the rain comes down, and work out how we use it later.'

'Um,' replied Roger doubtfully, 'let's do it, everyone! Keep your eyes on Pam, Charles. Don't look at the camera.'

'Just a moment,' interrupted Pam. 'Charles, would you like to just wipe your handkerchief over your forehead—it's the light, you know—it accentuates the shine.'

Sure enough, Charles' face had now changed from dull grey to glowing red. He hastily wiped his forehead. 'And a wee bit higher too—just there!' Pam pointed to the patch of thinning hair right at the very top of his forehead, which flushed even redder as she spoke.

'That's better,' said the cameraman. 'Camera rolling!'

'And what does it mean to the people of Sandford today, to worship in a church that is steeped in so many years of history?' asked Pam.

'St Michael's means a lot to us,' replied Charles. 'It's a central part of village life here in Sandford. And I'm Church Warden, so I am at the service every Sunday, and I'm Chairman of the Parish Council too. I take my responsibilities towards the parish very seriously.'

'Can we try that again, Charles?' Pam suggested. 'I wonder if you could make it a bit more personal. It's not so much your responsibilities we want to hear about—but what worshipping at the church means to you. When you're at the service on a Sunday morning, do you find yourself thinking of generations of worship that have gone on before in St Michael's?'

Charles looked at her blankly. Then, he nodded wordlessly, and Roger gave the signal for recording to begin again.

'And what does it mean to the people of Sandford today, to have a church which is steeped in so many years of history?'

'People have worshipped here in St Michael's for centuries, and we remember them every Sunday—at least, I do—when I come to the Sunday service. Yes, the church means a lot to us.' Charles' eyes darted towards the director, Roger. 'Is that OK?'

Roger looked as if he was about to answer, and then changed his mind. Finally, he said, 'Charles, that was splendid! Thank you so much for your patience and time this morning. It has been a great pleasure to meet you.'

'That's it then—finished?' A suggestion of a smile crept across Charles' face, as he realized the ordeal was over. 'There's so much more I could say, of course. Are you sure you don't need more than that?'

'Honestly, Charles, that's fine. We're still building up the opening section of the programme. We need to keep our options open, which means we're recording more material than we'll probably have time for. It's not until we get into the edit that we'll know for sure what

207

we'll be able to use—but your contribution is a great start! Thanks again!'

Bob, the sound recordist, had taken hold of Charles' jacket, to remove the tiny microphone, and transmitter that had been hidden inside his suit. Then, Pam held out her hand to Charles. 'Thank you so much, Charles. I know how busy you are, so we do appreciate the time you've given us this morning. I'm sure we'll be seeing you on several occasions during this week.'

'Oh, certainly!' As his confidence returned, Charles seemed to grow an inch or two. 'Well, if there's anything you need—anything at all! I'm overseeing all the arrangements for this week—in the background, you know—I don't like to push myself forward. But if there's anything—any facts you need to check—I should be able to make myself available to smooth your way for you.'

'How kind,' replied Pam. 'We'll just finish clearing up then, and we'll be on our way to the next location.'

And with a stately wave of his hand, Charles collected his briefcase and headed for home.

There was a silence as the BBC group watched him go, and once he was out of earshot, Roger was the first to speak.

'OK, I reckon we've got a couple of minutes before the heavens really open. Be a love, Pam, and cover all that material again. Just rejig your piece to camera to cover all the history bit. We might be able to salvage something from his last answer. I'll have to see when it comes to editing.'

'It's strange,' said Pam. 'He seemed so confident. I was really surprised at how nervous he was. Now, what am I going to say here...?' And she wandered off, back to her starting position, mumbling the words out loud to herself as she picked her way across the graveyard.

As usual, Iris was busy cutting the hair of a customer when Bunty's call came through. Debbie, the receptionist, managed to pick up the phone and answer it without taking her eyes off her magazine once.

'Iris,' she called. 'It's Bunty—needs a quick word. Can you come?'

'Not really!' grimaced Iris. 'Tell her I'll be a minute.'

In fact, it was longer than that before Iris was able to get to the phone. 'Sorry, Bunty—things are really mad here this week. I've never been so rushed off my feet!'

'Well, I just had to let you know that it's all on for tonight. I've arranged it with Helen, and she's going to bring Clive into the church around nine o'clock.'

There was a moment's silence while Iris mouthed signs to Debbie that she needed to take the perm solution off the lady at the end.

'Iris?' Bunty's voice was sharp and anxious. 'Iris—you are still alright for tonight, aren't you?'

'I may be late, Bunty. I'm so busy here, and my last customer isn't in until six o'clock. I'll get there, but I will be late.'

'Oh, Iris,' wailed Bunty, 'don't let us down. You're the most artistic one of the lot of us. We'll never pull this off if you don't come!'

'I'll do my best. I'll be there as soon as I can. Just leave the difficult bits for me!' Iris laughed. 'I'm looking forward to it. What a giggle! Supposing he doesn't like it? What will we do then? All that work, and he might not like it?'

'I tell you,' retorted Bunty, 'if he doesn't like it, he can blooming well write his own Parish Magazine! I'll resign!'

Roger, Pam and the crew made their two o'clock deadline for meeting the 'Out and About' group by the skin of their teeth. They had grabbed sandwiches and soft drinks when they stopped at a garage to fill up, and munched them on their journey towards the coast.

It always surprised Pam that this wild, uncluttered coastline was so deserted. In the summer months, visitors did make their way here, but never in large numbers. Mile upon mile of beaches lay themselves out to the battering of the sea, and the wind whipped across the flat expanses of scrubland, catching the breath of any soul hardy enough to brave the elements so early in the year.

The group had arranged to meet at a youth hostel building about a mile back from the coastline. A friendly hum of chatter and laughter greeted the BBC visitors, and they were shown into a large canteen, where a motley crowd of people, some obviously experienced walkers, others with varying degrees of disability, discussed their plans for the afternoon over coffee and biscuits.

Roger pulled Pam to one side. 'I gather they're going to start the walk in about five minutes, so I want the crew set up outside, ready to see them leaving. They'll walk pretty slowly, I imagine—but as soon as they're underway, I'd like us to jump in the car, and leapfrog ahead of them, so that we can pick up shots of them en route. We'll do the main interview with Mike when they take a break in the middle of the walk. They'll be stopping about a mile and a half down the road, at a little tea shop that's opening specially for them. I took a look at the place when I was here last week, and there's a great view from the veranda at the back. I think we'll do Mike's bit there.'

'Right,' agreed Pam. 'And do you want any general chat with people who are walking?'

'Vox pops? Yes, a couple would be good. Can you sort out a few people, while we go and set up outside?'

'Fine!' said Pam, and she headed off towards the canteen. Mike Hallam was the first person to spot her, and he made his way over to say hello. They found themselves a corner of bench, and sat down to discuss what they both felt the interview should cover. Eventually, they agreed that Mike would begin by explaining how 'Out and About' came into being. He worked for the local council in a job that often brought him into contact with people who coped with a variety of different disabilities. He was a keen walker himself, and it occurred to him that some of the folk he met through work would never be able to take advantage of the lovely countryside on their doorstep, without help and organization. He talked to a few like-minded friends about the idea—and two years later, 'Out and About' was arranging a walk almost every month of the year, for as many as thirty walkers a time. When Pam said that she'd like to ask how his faith fitted in with the project, Mike said that he would explain that this was one practical expression of Jesus' commandment that you should 'love thy neighbour'. Also, he would like to say that he believed that Christians all have a responsibility of stewardship towards God's creation, and this was one way of sharing the beauty of the countryside with people who benefited in such a positive way from the experience.

Mike spoke with simple sincerity and commitment. In spite of the events of the morning, when Charles Waite had suffered from such a dreadful bout of nerves, Pam had no doubt that Mike's interview would come across with strength and confidence. This was going to make a moving and interesting contribution to the programme.

'You know the group here well, Mike. Can you think of anyone in particular who might be able to talk to me about what these outings mean to them?'

Mike scanned the room. At last, he said, 'Henry might be a good bet. He's a good talker. In fact, I don't think he manages to get out much at all these days, so I think he saves it all up for us! He's the one over by the window, with the guide dog. Hold on, I'll nip over and have a word with him, just to see how he feels about the idea.'

Pam turned her attention back to her notes, when she became aware of a young woman, probably in her early thirties, gripping a walking frame as she backed onto the bench beside her. Pam reached out to guide her safely down.

The woman smiled with relief once the docking manoeuvre was complete. 'Thanks a lot! I almost sat on your lap—I'm sorry! I just couldn't stand up a moment longer though. It's not so bad when I'm moving. Standing still for too long—that's my problem! Are you walking today too?'

'Yes—and no,' replied Pam, explaining about the 'Village Praise' filming.

'Oh, I love "Songs of Praise". We always watch it at teatime—in fact, the kids and I compete to see who can sing along the loudest!'

'They're not with you today then?'

'No, these afternoons are all my own! My Mum is going to meet them from school, and get their tea today. She knows how much these walks mean to me.'

'How old are they?'

'Joe is the baby—he's three; then there's Amy, she's five and just started school—and Mikey's eight.'

'It must be very difficult for you, with three lively youngsters to look after.'

'Well, my husband is really good—and, of course, I've not always been like this. The accident was only eleven months ago.'

'What happened?'

'The silliest thing, really. Nothing dramatic at all. I just slipped—
on a wet patch on the pavement. I'm not sure if I hit an uneven
paving stone, or if I just fell awkwardly. Anyway, I crushed two
vertebrae—and the doctors say that there's not a lot they can do to
correct the problem. So, here I am—thirty-three years old, lovely
husband, gorgeous kids—and I'm practically a cripple...'

Just for a moment, her eyes shone with tears—only a moment,
before she was smiling again. 'I used to love walking—well, I've lived
in these parts all my life, and always loved it. And now, things that I
never thought twice about, simple things that everyone normally
takes for granted—I can't do them, not without a lot of help. It's so
frustrating. And the kids don't understand—why should they? I'm
still Mum, and they just want me to be the way they've always known
me. They don't know how to cope with a Mum who's doesn't join in
any more—who's always bursting into tears. But then—look around
you! I come here, and I take a look at a few of these poor souls. Some
of them have never been able to move or walk without pain. How
many of them have got a lovely home and family, like I have? So I have
to give myself a good kick now and then. Count my blessings, you
know.'

'And you can manage these walks OK?'

'Usually I can. It depends. Depends where they go, and how fast
they walk. It depends how many able-bodied helpers there are around
too. But I love them. I can't wait for these afternoons to come
around.'

'I'm Pam, by the way. And you?'

'Mary,' she grinned. 'Mary Denby.'

'I wonder, Mary, if you would be kind enough to let me record a
little chat with you—about these walks, and what they mean to you.
It doesn't have to be too long, but you could just tell us about the
difficulties you have with your back, and why you come along to "Out
and About". What do you think?'

'What? And it will be on the telly?' Mary's eyes were like
saucers.

'Probably, if you don't mind.'

'I'd love to. Now? Where do you want to do it?'

'Well, give me a minute, just to have a chat to our director. He and the crew are setting up their gear outside, so they're ready to see everyone moving off. Perhaps we can quickly record your interview before things get going.'

'Great,' said Mary, 'that's great. I'll wait here then.'

It was some minutes later that Pam returned. Roger was with her, and together they helped Mary to her feet, and walked slowly alongside her as she made her painful way just outside the building, where the crew was waiting for her.

'Just talk to me, exactly as you were inside, Mary,' said Pam, as the camera started rolling. 'Why are you joining this walk today?'

'I crushed the vertebrae in my back about a year ago, and I'm constantly in pain nowadays. It's particularly hard, because I am the Mum of three small kids, and it's so difficult to be the Mum I want to be, when every movement is painful. Before my accident, we all enjoyed walking around here—we'd often come out for the whole day, and walk wherever the fancy took us. I'd begun to think I'd never be able to get out and be in the countryside again.

'But this project is wonderful. They understand my difficulties. They're patient. They organize everything. And I meet such nice people—people who have their own problems, that somehow seem to put mine into perspective.

'And I always go home thinking, thank God. Thank God for all the blessings I do have. I'm alive—and I'm surrounded by love. Thank God—that's what I think...'

This time, there was no mistaking the tears in her eyes. There was a moment of stunned silence—and because there was nothing more to say, Pam simply put her arms around Mary, and held her.

Moments later, Mary's head came up, a brave attempt at a smile on her face. 'What a fool you'll think I am—blubbing all over you! Look, I must join the gang, or they'll go without me!'

The walkers were moving off in a ragged line away from the house, and along a path that disappeared into trees. The crew jumped into action, taking wide shots of the group as they moved, then running alongside the walkers, gettings close-ups of feet, wheelchairs, walking sticks and faces. Then, they ran on ahead, and took several pictures of the group walking through the trees, talking and laughing as they went.

It was probably ten minutes later that the crew headed back towards the house, to load the equipment into the vehicles, ready to drive on to a rendezvous point further along the way. That was where they hoped to pick up another interview, with Henry and his guide dog—a chat done on the move. Pam hunted in her coat pocket for her notebook, and then remembered where she had left it on the canteen table. It was when she was coming back out of the building, that she saw her. Mary—making her slow way, on her own, back up the path towards the house. Pam ran down to meet her.

'Mary! What's the matter? Are you OK?'

'Yes. Don't look so worried! It's just that they're moving a bit fast for me today...'

'What do you mean? Isn't there anyone who can give you a hand?'

'There probably is—but there isn't anyone else on a walking frame, like me. The wheelchairs can be pushed so much faster than I can manage, and I know that I'd only hold everyone up.'

'Oh, Mary. Can't we help? We could give you a lift further up the road—you'd be ahead of them then.'

Mary rested her arm on Pam's. 'Look, it doesn't matter. Really, it doesn't. I'm missing the kids, anyway. If I hurry, I might just be in time to join them for tea.'

'Pam!' yelled Roger. 'Come on! We'll miss them, if you don't get a move on!'

'Mary...' Pam began.

'Go on. You'll be late. I've got the car. I'll be fine. I will. You get going.'

'I hate to leave you like this. Are you sure...?'

'Yes! Go on now. And thanks—I mean it—thanks.'

And as Pam was driven away in the back of the crew car, she could see Mary still climbing the path back to the house, step by painful step.

Ian and Jan sat over a pot of tea in their 'production office' at Grove House, and talked their way through the music for the Sandford programme. Jan listened to Ian's ideas for incidental music to link different parts of the programme together, like the end of one hymn into the start of the next item. Then, she heard the music Ian had written to lead into 'Deep Peace', which would be sung softly by the congregation while Clive spoke the words of the prayer and blessing. The final arrangement for 'O Sacred Head', the hymn that would be sung by the St Mark's Church Choir at Dinton Church, was also ready for Jan to decide upon. At first, she hadn't been sure about the idea of keeping the accompaniment simple, but once she had heard Margaret play, it had soon become clear that she was an experienced and sensitive performer. The arrangement Ian had written for her was haunting and lovely. With the clear, disciplined singing of the St Mark's Choir, Jan had no doubt that 'O Sacred Head' would be one of the most memorable items in the whole programme.

'I'm rehearsing with St Mark's tonight, did you know?' asked Ian. 'Colin assures me they're sounding fine with the arrangement, but I'd like to go along and tighten the performance up a bit before we record on Friday.'

'Are you generally happy with the choir you've gathered together for the church now?'

Ian shrugged. 'Well, you come to a small village in Suffolk, and you get the sound that a small village in Suffolk can raise. It could be better—but it could lose some of its charm if we try to make it sound too professional. We really need about three weeks' more rehearsal time, and we've got three days! It's very ragged in places, but then enthusiasm makes up for a lot, and they've plenty of that! It'll be alright, I reckon.'

'And the solo? Anna? How's she coming along?'

'I'm going over to rehearse with her at four o'clock today.' He glanced at his watch, and gulped at his tea. 'And I'll be late if I don't get a move on! Basically, she's fine! Considering she hasn't had any real voice training, she's a wonderful talent. Actually, I must have a word with her Mum while I'm there this afternoon, to see if they'd consider finding a good classical teacher to coach her. She could go a long way, if she wants to.'

'And does she want to?'

Ian grinned. 'Well, I think she'd rather be appearing on "The Word" than "Songs of Praise"—this won't do her street cred any good at all! But yes, I think a career as a singer would be just what she'd like—but honestly, her talent could take her a lot further than a few chart records. She's a natural.'

'Are you going to tell her that?'

'Well, I thought I'd just have a word with her parents. I'm not very good with bolshie teenagers.'

Jan was silent.

'Why? Do you think I should have a word with Anna myself, then?'

'Honestly, Ian, you men can be so thick! Haven't you noticed that she never takes her eyes off you? Of course, she'd like to hear from you that she's got natural talent! Of course, she'd love it if you encouraged her singing! It's quite plain the girl has an enormous crush on you!'

Ian stood up, and replaced his teacup on the tray. 'Don't be so daft. Anna's just a kid!'

'Right,' said Jan. 'Whatever you say. But can you use your influence to suggest that she wears something other than that awful black outfit she usually turns up in? I know all teenagers look like that these days, and I don't want her to wear anything she is unhappy in—but I can't help thinking an outfit in a warmer colour would work much better on screen.'

'Oh, Jan, I don't know anything about what women should wear! What do you mean, a warmer colour?'

'Anything that isn't black, really—or white, of course! Blue, perhaps, or a rich plum colour? Use your imagination—you know what looks good on television as much as I do!'

'Can't you ring her, and talk to her about it yourself?'

'Ian, I'm up to my eyes with a million and one things at the moment. For heaven's sake, you're seeing the girl this afternoon. Just tell her! Drop it into the conversation! She's much more likely to respond to the idea if you suggest it!'

Ian looked doubtful, as he gathered up his papers. 'See you later then. What are you doing about eating tonight?'

'I'm just meeting up with Simon Martin, the Engineering Manager, to go over a few things with him in the church about six-ish, then I suppose we'll move on to The Bull, probably about eight o'clock?'

'Well, my rehearsal with the St Mark's lot shouldn't take long—I'll see you in the bar about half eight, I expect. Bye then!'

As Ian made his way up to his room, a deep weariness overcame him. Knowing he was already late for Anna, he knew he should collect his things, and head straight out. Instead, he sat down heavily on the bed, and laid his head back against the pillow. What he'd give to be able to close his eyes, and give in to sleep!

His mind was too active for sleep, though. Disjointed refrains of music darted through his head; hymn titles—was it 'Like a Mighty River Flowing' this week, or was that last? Had he sent the latest arrangements to Mrs Hulme, the Choir Mistress at St Mark's, or was he thinking of another set of arrangements, another choir mistress, another choir in another village? And what colour should Anna wear? What did he know about colours? What did he know about anything, when he was so tired...

A moment later, he turned, and switched on the lamp on the bedside table. He picked up the phone, and slowly dialled Sarah's number. She was out. He knew she would be. The sound of her voice on the recorded message both soothed and frustrated him. When the tone sounded, he didn't speak immediately. Then, at last, his voice unusually hesitant, he said, 'Sarah, if I were to ask you to marry me, what would you say?'

He looked as if he might say more, but changed his mind. Quickly, he replaced the receiver, picked up his papers, and left the room.

It was well gone four o'clock before Margaret laid her harp away from her shoulder. She had practised 'O Sacred Head' so much that the notes had become second nature to her, and she was able to close her eyes, and let the harp speak from her soul. She had always felt it was no accident that angels were often pictured playing golden harps. There was something about its lilting, tumbling voice that lifted and restored the spirit. Many a time, she had sat down to the harp, worn and battered at the end of a frustrating day—and the skill of her fingers had brought healing in her heart.

Her fingers touched the letter in her pocket. She drew out the envelope, and looked once again at the papers inside. She smiled as she read, but put the letter hurriedly back in her pocket as she glanced up at the clock. Four-forty-five, the man had said. She was to meet him at four-forty-five. He had sounded nice on the phone, sympathetic and understanding. She was looking forward to meeting him. If she left right now, she would be a few minutes early—a few minutes in which to collect her thoughts, and ponder on the huge, and potentially, reckless step she was thinking of taking.

The most important thing was that Jack should not know. She had no idea what his reaction would be, but she knew that this decision was hers, and hers alone. She had no wish to share it, at least, not yet.

As she pulled on her coat, she caught sight of herself in the mirror above the mantelpiece. There was a sparkle in her eye, a gleam of excitement and anticipation. Suddenly, she laughed at her reflection. 'You silly old fool!' she said out loud to herself, and with a spring in her step, she picked up her car keys, and closed the door behind her.

❧

Joan had left Don to hold the fort downstairs in the shop, and made her way upstairs to the kitchen, to make a cup of tea. From there, she could hear Anna singing more clearly. At first, she had sung just one line, or a verse, before Ian's voice interrupted. Then, a minute or two later, Anna began again—over and over the same line, until it was absolutely perfect.

There'd been a time when Anna had been only too pleased to share her love of singing with her Mum, a time when Anna had been open, and enthusiastic in a way that drew her parents into her hopes and ambitions. All that seemed a long time ago now, as Joan realized how much she missed sharing her daughter's secrets. In recent years, Anna had closeted herself inside a shell, hugging her thoughts to herself.

Joan couldn't remember when she had last heard Anna sing. She rarely sang at home nowadays. It was such a treat to hear her now, her voice sweet and moving. Joan stopped, her hand in mid-air as she filled the teapot, her eyes suddenly misty with tears.

Just as I am, without one plea
But that Thy blood was shed for me,
And that Thou bid'st me come to Thee,
O Lamb of God, I come.

As Joan waited for the tea to brew, arranging biscuits on her best cake plate, she wondered how a daughter that she and Don had produced, should have the gift of such a voice. And when finally, the music stopped, she poured the tea, and made her way towards the lounge, tray in hand.

'Thought you two might need a cuppa, after all that hard work.'

Two faces turned towards her—Ian's open and friendly; Anna's alight with achievement. Just for a moment, Anna's guard was down. Just for a moment, Joan glimpsed the little girl she knew—a youngster whose face shone with elation and triumph. And then it was gone.

'Mum, you know I'm dieting. Why do you bring biscuits, when you know I'm dieting?'

'Because she knows that Musical Directors always have a sweet tooth,' grinned Ian, 'and talent needs feeding. Do as you're told, and have a biscuit!'

Without a word, Anna reached out towards the plate, and then, suddenly coquettish, she looked at Ian.

'Talent? Do you think I have talent then?'

'Yes, I do,' Ian replied, 'but I think it needs a lot of work to achieve its full potential. You have a lovely voice, a young girl's voice. With maturity and discipline, you could have an outstanding voice. It needs to be trained.'

'Trained? What for? I don't want to be an opera singer.'

'What do you want to do then?'

'I want to do what you do. Write music, only not for everyone else to sing—just for me. I want to write my own songs, record them, and be a great big star!'

'For how long? A one-hit wonder? For as long as you are part of a group, until that group splits up? The world of popular music is full of fads—styles come and go. I'm sure you could be part of that, if you're lucky. But you have a voice that could take you much further! I'm not the sort to give praise easily, but you have a tremendous gift,

Anna. You can waste it—or you can use it, to bring pleasure to others, and great fulfilment to yourself. The choice is yours.'

Anna simply looked at him, her expression unreadable.

Ian took a final sip of tea, and stood to collect together his music. 'I must go. The formidable Mrs Hulme awaits! If anyone dares to be late for a St Mark's Choir rehearsal, woe betide them!'

'You think I'll be OK then? You think I sound alright?' Anna's confident expression didn't reach her eyes.

Ian looked up and smiled. 'I think you'll be wonderful. I'm very proud of you.' As he reached the door, he turned, almost as an afterthought. 'Oh, by the way, wear something blue or deep plum coloured. It would suit you!' And with that, he was gone.

❦

'For heaven's sake, Clive,' said Helen, taking a cup of tea into the bathroom to her husband, as he lay idly in the bath. 'You've been in the bath for ages. There are three phone messages for you—and one of them is from Charles Waite, who sounds very put out that you didn't ring him back after the last time he called! And Jack Diggens is waiting for you downstairs...'

'Do you know, Helen,' mused Clive, as he reached out to take the cup, 'I think this television programme is going to be good for us. Can you think of any other single event that has brought all denominations around here together with such enthusiasm? For the first time that I can really remember, Christian unity is alive and well in Sandford! This could be the start of a new spirit here—God is challenging us, I'm sure of it!'

'The greatest challenge right at the moment, Clive,' said Helen deliberately, stooping down so that her face was level with his, 'is just to organize the whole thing so that it happens at all! You've got to keep on top of it! You've got to take more of a lead, make sure it all happens as you want it! There are so many loose ends...'

Clive turned his head slowly, staring vaguely at her. 'Loose ends?'

'Yes!' retorted Helen. 'The phone never seems to stop ringing with questions you should know the answers to—are all the local clergy going to robe up? Is that what the BBC want? Are there any spare tickets? Someone wants to bring a wheelchair—will that be OK?

Will the outside loo be in working order? Should people bring a flask of coffee during the rehearsal? If people take their coats off, where will they put them? What should they wear? Oh, I don't know—a million and one things, and I don't know the answers to tell them, Clive— but you should!'

'Why? Surely the television people should be the ones to answer that lot. I'm a priest. It's the spiritual content and relevance of the event that interests me. That's my job.'

'It's not my job, Clive, to spend all day chasing round after people trying to get decisions and answers to issues that you should be in the know about. You're the vicar! This is the biggest event ever to happen in St Michael's Church! Of course they want answers from you— you're in charge of the church! They expect you to know!'

'Well, I don't know, and I don't want to know. I need to keep my mind clear, to make sure that God is at the heart of all of this. And honestly, Helen, you know you're so much better at sorting out details like that than I ever could be! I'm sure that everyone in the village feels that the arrangements are in safe hands, if you're in control!'

He turned away to take a sip of his tea, while Helen stared at him in exasperation. Finally, she got to her feet. 'Do you want Jack Diggens to wait? He's been here ten minutes already, and I know he's got a lot on his plate today. How long will you be?'

'I'll just finish this,' said Clive as he looked into his cup, 'then I'll be down presently.'

Helen's hand was on the doorknob, as she casually looked back at him. 'You haven't forgotten about the meeting in the church tonight, have you?'

'Meeting?'

'Clive, you do remember. Bunty, and a few people from around about—they're very anxious to pin you down for a little while, just to sort out a few last-minute queries. You will be there, won't you?'

'Remind me nearer the time, will you, Helen? You know what my mind's like...!'

'I certainly do!' thought Helen. 'Unfortunately, I do!'

❧

If the church clock had worked—which it hadn't done for years—it would have said half past six, as Bunty cautiously put her head around the church door. The coast was clear. Her head disappeared behind the door again, as she beckoned to the rest of her party.

'It's alright!' she whispered. 'I don't think there's anyone here! Let's bring the stuff in!'

A huge carton made an appearance around the door, clasped to the matronly bosom of Grace. Madge came in next, dragging a long thin box along the floor behind her. Bunty was last, stooping down to help the tail end of the box over the doorframe, while clutching a huge bulging black bag upright in her other arm.

They made their way, with difficulty, up the aisle, and eventually deposited all the boxes and bags in the centre of the church.

'Right!' said Bunty, in a voice that would have done credit to a Sergeant Major. 'The time is six-thirty. Clive will be here at nine. To work, girls! We've got a lot to do!'

The Bull was packed when Ian finally arrived just before nine. Peering into the dimly lit saloon bar, Ian realized that most of the people there belonged to the BBC. It took him a while to get to the bar, as he said hello, and caught up on the news of several of the riggers and technicians on the way. He called over to the fireside table that had been commandeered by the production team. Jan, the Producer, Sue the Production Assistant, director Roger, Kate the researcher, and Pam, had papers strewn all over the table, with plates of lasagne perched on corners and laps. They shouted their drinks orders across to Ian, and carried on with their discussion.

By the time he joined them with a tray, they were deeply involved in planning the next day's recording.

'Stephen Yearling, the new Baptist minister, the one who's just arrived here from Birmingham,' said Jan, looking at Roger. 'What plans have you got for his interview in the morning?'

'Well,' replied Roger, shovelling another forkful of lasagne in as he spoke, 'his church is in a lovely location, so weather permitting, I'd like to record his chat with Pam while the two of them are strolling down the lane that runs away from his church.'

Pam interrupted there. 'But the tail end of what he's got to say—about his very personal relationship with God—I think we need to have come to a halt by then, so that the conversation can become more intimate.'

'I've been thinking about that,' replied Roger. 'There's a little wall at the bottom of the lane, that looks out over quite a panoramic view of the fields. If you can get him to talk at that point, about his feeling of smallness in comparison with the power of God and his creation, the background would be absolutely appropriate.'

'Fine,' said Jan, 'and before we move on to the afternoon, the local paper want to have a chat with you sometime in the morning, Pam—in fact, they've asked if they can send a reporter out to watch as we record that interview. What do you think?'

'I'm always a bit wary of having too many people around when we record interviews, especially when they're very personal and sensitive. It's hard enough for people to bare their souls to me and a television crew, especially when they're probably talking about things that they've perhaps never even mentioned to their best friend! I just feel we have to treat them with care and respect, and to have extra people looking on is unfair.'

'Couldn't agree with you more,' said Jan. 'Right, I'll contact the reporter and tell him he can come along to tomorrow night's choir rehearsal, or come and see the crew setting up in the church—and that you'll meet him here in The Bull at lunchtime tomorrow, if he wants to talk to you. Will lunchtime be OK, Roger? What time are you all meeting Sidney the fisherman?'

'The tide won't be right until about three o'clock, and of course, the light is going by five,' replied Roger. 'I plan to get a few more general shots of the area after Stephen's interview in the morning, so Pam should be free from about twelve until, say, two-ish.'

'That's agreed then,' said Jan, scribbling in the large hardbacked book in which she kept every scrap of information relevant to the programme. 'Now, the choir rehearsal!' She looked at Ian. 'Is everything OK for that?'

'Seems to be,' replied Ian. 'I had a rehearsal with St Mark's Choir this evening, and they really are very good. "O Sacred Head" sounds lovely, especially with Margaret accompanying them. But tomorrow night, all the singers who've been rehearsing will be in the church, and they're very familiar with the hymns, and their parts, now.'

Jan continued to scribble. 'Sue and I will come along tomorrow night then, to listen, and time all the hymns. Kate, how are you getting along? Any problems?'

'Apart from being nervous about how the fishermen will behave tomorrow, do you mean?' grinned Kate. 'No, basically everything seems to be going to plan. I'm just sorting out the Donkey Audition with the local school, for lunchtime on Thursday. We're hoping to do the interview with Doreen and Denis' owner...'—she caught sight of Ian's questioning face—Doreen and Denis—our hopeful contenders for the starring role of the donkey, that carries Jesus into the church for the Palm Sunday procession at the start of the programme. We're going to let the youngsters at the school choose which donkey should have the honour!' Kate looked back towards Jan. 'And David Hughes—you know, he's the farmer who owns Doreen and Denis—has agreed to do an interview, after a lot of persuasion. I think he's quite nervous about it.'

'Not surprising, really,' said Pam. 'It's not easy to talk in public about something as personal as faith. Will I have the chance to have some time with him on Thursday morning, do you think, before we do his interview?'

'Actually, there are a couple of lovely views of the area that are very close to where his farm is. What we could do is to drop you off to have a cuppa and chat at leisure, while we go out and record them to use as overlay during one of the hymns.'

'That sounds great, thanks.'

'Alright,' said Jan, 'anyone else got any problems?'

'Yep,' replied Sue, 'my glass is empty, and it's Roger's turn to get them in.'

Watching them from the other side of the room, The Bull's most regular customer, Stanley, was leaning over the bar to talk to Bill, the barman.

'You know,' said Stanley, 'I never expected to see that Pam Rhodes in a bar. It doesn't seem right really.'

'Be fair, Stanley!' said Bill. 'She's only drinking lime and lemonade—in fact, I thought I heard someone say she's teetotal.'

'Why?' asked Stanley, who couldn't believe that anyone could be that daft.

'I don't know,' laughed Bill, 'perhaps she doesn't like the taste. Some people don't, you know!'

Stanley grunted, contemplating the unthinkable.

'Have you got your ticket, then, Stanley, for the television recording?'

'Me? No!' guffawed Stanley. 'You won't catch me dead inside a church! It's all those men wearing frocks that puts me off! No, there's a good match on the telly that evening. I think I'll come here, and watch it in the Public Bar, over a pint and a plate of chips.'

'Well, I reckon the bar will be deserted that night. It makes me laugh really. All those people who haven't been in the church for years, all scrabbling for a ticket! It's old Jack Diggens they have to chat up, you know. We haven't seen much of him in here, since he got involved in all this going-on!'

Stanley lowered his voice, and drew his head close to Bill's. 'Oh, I don't think it's only the television that's keeping him busy. I hear he's got other things on his mind!'

'The lady, you mean?' Bill nodded knowingly. 'They were in here, you know—upstairs in the tea room, just the other afternoon. Laughing and chatting like they'd known each other for years!'

'Never thought he had it in him. Who'd have thought?'

The two men looked into their drinks, in silent agreement.

'It's caused such an upheaval, all this business,' mused Stanley sadly. 'Will Sandford ever be the same again? Will we ever get back to normal?'

Someone was trying to attract Bill's attention at the other end of the bar. It was Roger, the BBC director, obviously anxious to order drinks.

As he moved away, Bill nudged Stanley's elbow. 'Oh, I do hope not! It's blooming good for trade!'

It was about ten past nine before Helen managed to prise Clive out of his study, where he was leaning back in his chair, walkman on, the music of Taizé mellow in his earphones. He was put out to be disturbed, especially as he couldn't quite recall what this late-night meeting in the church was all in aid of, and Helen was un-characteristically reticent in helping to jog his memory.

Helen walked up the path to the church, fearful of what she would find when she opened the door. Clive came reluctantly, several paces behind her.

They reached the door. Helen pushed it open, and ushered Clive in before she stepped inside herself.

Every light in the church was on, illuminating the scaffolding, and piles of television lights, poles and cables that were neatly stacked around the walls. But it wasn't the equipment that drew Clive's eye. He slowly made his way down the church, until he stood at the top of the aisle and gazed around him.

The church was full of intricate, beautiful arrangements of dried grasses and palm leaves. At the end of each pew was a small posy of palm crosses and dried ferns. Taller palm leaves stood on every windowsill, interwoven with delicate grasses and seed pods— beautifully shaped, but colourless—hauntingly sad and gaunt.

And beside the altar—a stark wooden cross, made from the trunk of an old tree. The only colour came from simple red berries, like drops of blood, on the crown of thorns that hung at the centre of the cross. At its base, reaching out from a silken cloth of darkest purple, was an array of leaves and stems that seemed laden with sadness and pain.

Helen grasped the side of a pew. The effect was breathtaking—subtle and emotive. But what would Clive think? What would Clive think?

A movement caught her eye. Bunty, Grace, Madge and Iris slowly appeared from the vestry, unsure what to say, how to behave. At last, it was Bunty who spoke.

'Well?' she asked. 'Clive?'

When he finally turned towards her, Bunty was astounded to see that his eyes were glistening with tears.

'It's lovely,' he said at last, 'simply lovely.'

And as Bunty and her ladies whooped together in sheer relief, Helen found herself walking down the aisle, putting her arms out to him, and drawing him close.

❧

When Ian tumbled into bed that night, it was so late, that he almost forgot to check for messages left on his mobile phone. The disembodied voice informed him that he had one message. Suddenly, it was Sarah's voice that he heard. Her message was short and direct. 'If you really want to know what I'd say, ask me properly.'

It wasn't until minutes later, as he lay back on the bed, that he realized the whole of his body was shaking. Whatever had he done?

As soon as she woke up just before seven, Pam rang home. Her son, Max, had to catch a very early school bus each morning, and this was the best time to speak to him.

It was her husband, Paul, who answered. 'Hi, how's it going?'

'Not bad yesterday, although the weather is pretty miserable. I'm out at sea with some fishermen this afternoon, so I'm expecting a downpour!'

'Well, there's not much news this end. Bethan has got a bit of a cold, and wouldn't go to her ballet class last night.'

'Her heart's not in it, I suppose. I know I shouldn't be disappointed, just because I always loved ballet so much! I think she's moved on to horses at the moment—well, for this month, at least!!'

'Hang on a minute, Max has just come down.' Pam could clearly hear Max's heavy footsteps thumping down the stairs—at eleven, he was at the age when his feet seemed to be disproportionally big for the rest of his body! 'You know I'm filming in London today, don't you?' Paul was saying. 'I should be back around eight-ish this evening, I think, so your Mum will be here for the youngsters after school. Speak to you later, shall I?'

'That'll be lovely. Have a good day then!'

'Mum,' Max's voice came on the phone, 'where's my PE kit?'

'Good morning, Max! How nice to hear from you! I'm fine—how are you?!' Pam grinned at the familiar way in which Max dispensed with the niceties—and the equally familiar assumption that she should know the whereabouts of everything he possessed!

'Oh, hi, Mum! Where's my PE kit?'

'I don't know, Max. Where did you leave it?'

'I put it in the wash, and now I can't find it.'

'Have you looked in the airing cupboard?'

'It's not there.'

'Behind the door in the kitchen?'

'Mum, I didn't leave it there. I put it in the wash, and now it's gone!'

'So, if you put your shorts and vest in the wash, what happened to the bag with your PE shoes?'

There was a silence at the end of the line. Finally, Max said, 'I think I left that at school.'

'With your PE shorts and vest still in it, do you reckon?'

'Mum, I don't know! I might have!'

'Max, it's ten past seven. Your bus goes in fifteen minutes. Your white shorts and PE vest from last year are upstairs in your drawer—take them, in case you can't find your others at school. And you can take your white trainers instead of your gym shoes. Has Dad signed your homework book?'

'Oh, no. I'll ask him. I've got to go then, Mum. Speak to you tonight!'

'Tell Bethan I'll ring her after breakfast! Love you!' But Max had put the phone down so fast, that Pam realized she was talking to thin air.

❧

In the Waite household, the routine at breakfast time had returned to its usual pattern. Charles sat at the table, reading his paper, while Betty made the tea and toast in comfortable silence.

'It's the final choir rehearsal tonight,' Betty said at last, not really expecting a reply. Charles carried on reading.

'I do hope it will be alright. The singing sounds much better now.'

She spooned marmalade on to a slice of buttered toast.

'Colin is really good on the organ, much better than I ever could be. You remember Colin, don't you? The organist from St Mark's? He was sitting next to us in the restaurant after that concert we went to last Christmas. He's the one who works in the Estate Agents in Stowmarket. He's very talented though. Do you remember him?'

Charles reluctantly drew his eyes away from his paper. 'No. Can't say I do. Any more tea in the pot?'

Betty reached out for his cup, and poured in milk and tea as she spoke.

'He's going to need help though. There's so much music. I'm going to sit beside him and turn the pages.'

Charles looked up instantly. 'What do you mean? You aren't going to sing with the choir?'

'Well, I might sing along just because I want to, but I'm not going to sit with the choir, no. I want to make sure that Colin is alright.'

'But that means you won't be seen on camera.'

'No, I suppose not.'

'But it's important that you are. People will expect it. You've been in charge of music here at St Michael's for years. It's important that you take your rightful place on the programme.'

'Not to me, Charles. It's more important that I help Colin with his organ music, so that everything runs smoothly. Anyway, seats in the church are at such a premium, I hardly need to take up a space I really don't want.'

'Well, they've got no one to blame for this unseemly rush for seats except that chap, Jack Diggens. It's been organized all wrong!'

'Oh, I don't know, dear,' said Betty, soothingly. 'He seems to have everything very well under control. The only thing that's unseemly is the way people who haven't been seen inside the church for years, are suddenly ardent believers, anxious to take their seats for this occasion! People like the Major's wife, Marjorie, for instance. I see the Major popped a note through the door yesterday, asking you to organize a ticket for her. You're not going to, are you?'

'The Major is a most important and influential member of this community. He's on the Parish Council. Why shouldn't he be able to take his proper place, with his wife at his side?' Charles retorted.

'Because there are other people who deserve to come much more than Marjorie! Anyway, it's Jack you'll have to talk to about it, not me! I gather he's being pretty strict about last-minute requests. Well, he's got to, hasn't he!'

'I don't intend to speak to that man about anything!' snapped Charles. 'I have my own contacts. I shall go straight to the BBC.

After all, I am their main interviewee. They are in my debt. I shall speak to the Producer. She'll sort it out.'

Betty looked at him as she munched her toast. No answer seemed necessary. Then, in a way that totally infuriated Charles, she detached the front couple of pages from his newspaper—the ones she knew he'd already read—and searched for the horoscope column.

When Pam arrived at the Baptist Church, with Roger and the crew, to meet the minister, Stephen Yearling, he was waiting at the door to greet them. 'What do you need first?' he asked, smiling broadly, his hand outstretched in welcome to them all. 'To look at where you want to do the interview—or a cup of coffee?'

'Tell you what,' replied Roger, 'you and Pam go and put the coffee on, while I take Keith, the cameraman, off to take a look at where I suggest we do our recording. We'll give you a yell when we're ready!'

'This must be quite a change for you,' Pam said, as they walked towards Stephen's house, through a huge garden full of apple trees that were already showing signs of being in bud.

'Coming from Birmingham, do you mean? We didn't have any garden at all there. This is so much better for the children. It's great to see how well they've settled down here, although we've only been here a matter of months. They disappear off for hours at a time, and we really don't need to worry about them. The furthest they ever go is to play with the family about half a mile down the road. And they've really become children again—you know, not so worldly-wise, the way all the youngsters seem to be in a big city.'

'How old are they?' asked Pam, as he held the front door open for her.

'We've got two—the youngest is Luke, he's eight; and Stephanie is eleven.'

'What made you want to come?'

'Good question. The actual reason is that David, who used to be the minister here, is—was—an old family friend. He used to be our minister, in fact, when we lived in Ipswich when I was a boy. He died, you know, about eight months ago, and we came down for the funeral. The church was really run down, and the congregation numbers had dropped—well, he'd been ill for the best part of two years, so that wasn't surprising. But I walked into this church, and just felt—how can I explain it? At peace, really, I suppose. As if I'd come home.'

'So when the job came up, you applied?'

'The funny thing was that it wasn't me who first noticed the advert—it was Wendy, my wife. Afterwards, she told me that she had been touched by this place too, although we'd never talked about it. We just felt that we were being called here—so it wasn't a surprise when we applied for the post, and got it. We somehow never doubted that we would!'

'It's a very different ministry though.'

Before Stephen could answer, the kitchen door swung open, and in came a small, round-faced woman, with blond curls, and huge blue, smiling eyes. She was carrying a large plastic basket of dirty washing, and as she headed for the machine, she called out over her shoulder.

'Has Stephen got the coffee organized? And the biscuits? I told you I bought some special biscuits, Steve—in the new red tin.'

And so, a quarter of an hour later, when Roger and the crew arrived in the kitchen, they found Stephen, Wendy and Pam huddled over cups of coffee and biscuits, deeply engrossed in a discussion about the problems of parenthood—and the joys of family life!

'Right, we're ready when you are!' said Roger, eying the coffee pot.

'The coffee won't keep—have a cup now to keep the cold away, and the interview is sure to go more smoothly!' grinned Pam. Sue, the Production Assistant, didn't even wait for Roger to reply, before she pulled up a chair. 'You take sugar, don't you, Bob?' she called to the Sound Recordist, 'and Keith, you like yours black, I think. Biscuit, Roger?' Knowing when he was beaten, Roger shrugged good-naturedly, and took his place at the table.

Ten minutes later, they were all outside the church gate, standing at the top of path that led away from the graveyard, down a slope towards a small tumbledown wall that separated the church from the farmland.

'Now, don't walk too fast,' said Keith, as he hoisted the camera up on to his shoulder. 'Just remember I'll have to walk backwards in front of you, so I can hold the pair of you in shot as you speak.'

'And see if you can come to a natural break in the conversation as you approach the wall—at that point, Pam, just lead Stephen up and past the camera, and make a seat for yourselves on the wall. Then we'll reposition the camera, and finish the chat there.'

'Right, I'm rolling!' said Keith as he began slowly to walk backwards, the camera on his shoulder.

Pam waited until she and Stephen had taken a few paces, before she began the conversation.

'What a wonderful setting for a church!'

'Yes, and so different from the church I left in Birmingham, to come here. That was right in the middle of a large council estate, alongside quite a major road. We lived next door to the church, so seemed to be on call morning, noon and night. It was a challenging job, serving the needs of a lively, diverse community—but there were a lot of problems to deal with.'

'Like what?'

'Unemployment—that was the main one. Too few jobs for the people who wanted to work. Too many people who didn't want to work, even if a job did come up. And that puts a strain on families, of course. We had our share of single parent families too, who often needed practical help, as well as moral support. We ran a family centre in our church hall for them, with a toddler group, and a counsellor, on hand. And unfortunately it was an area with a real drug problem, and a major part of my ministry was to be there for young people, meet them wherever they happened to be—be available if they felt like chatting, or were under pressure.'

'So you were always busy. Not much time for yourself, and your own needs.'

'My greatest need was to have time to build my own relationship with God—but I was so busy being busy—indispensable, or so I thought—that I simply didn't realize that I was running myself ragged, being practical, supportive and generally, everyone's idea of a jolly good minister! And what I was neglecting was my own prayer life—the part of my life that's absolutely fundamental if I am to do my job as a minister as it should be done. I was so obsessed with *doing*, I never allowed myself time just to *be*!'

'So, what happened?'

'My old friend died—the man who was minister here at this church in Suffolk. My wife and I came here for the funeral, and there was something about the peace of this place that struck a very deep chord with me. I suddenly realized how much I longed for peace, God's peace—time to think, to listen, to just *be* with God...'

'And have you found that peace at last, now you're settled here?'

'Every morning, I take the dog out before anyone else in the family is up. I walk down this pathway, and feel totally alone in the world—but content in God's presence. That's my private time for prayer, a time of peace. I have found purpose and meaning in my life, which helps me to recognize how important peace and meaning must be to others too. I may be a different kind of minister, but I believe that I'm a better one.'

'Hold it there!' interrupted Roger, as Pam and Stephen reached the wall. 'Settle yourselves down, and, Keith, do you want the legs to put the camera on now?'

'They're just up on the other side of the gate,' yelled Keith, as he walked up the hill to retrieve them.

'That's going really well, Stephen,' said Roger. 'Just the tail end now, nice and relaxed, with the rolling meadows behind you.'

'Was it alright?' Stephen looked at Pam anxiously.

'I thought what you said was very moving, and very human,' Pam smiled back. 'And we'll just pick up from where we left off. By the way, the piece of music that comes up in the programme straight after this is a solo voice, singing "Just As I Am". Do you know it?'

'Certainly, it's one of my favourite hymns.'

'Well, you might bear the words and sentiment of that hymn in mind, when we come towards the end of our chat, just so that we can use what you say as a strong, and appropriate introduction to the hymn.'

'Right,' said Keith breathlessly, as he fixed the camera to its legs, and manoeuvred the base into position. 'Camera ready!'

Silence descended again, as Pam began, 'But don't you miss the challenge of all the big-city problems you were called upon to deal with at your previous church?'

Stephen smiled. 'Don't think for one minute that being a minister in a rural parish is any less of a challenge that having a city patch. The number of people I meet may be less, and the problems may be different, but in a small community like this, the church, and its minister, are fundamental in so many aspects of everyday life. We can't avoid each other here, as you can in the city. I've really got to know these families, shared their joys and their worries. I'm always around for them. I have more time for them, to care and to listen. Time to encourage each and every one of them in their spiritual journey through life.'

'Do you think that people living in country communities are more aware of that spiritual journey, because of where they live?'

'Well, just look around you. How could you not believe in God, when you're surrounded by countryside like this? When you live with the seasons, when you live with the cycle of life that is so much part of God's creation—yes, I think it's a natural instinct to recognize that God's hand is in all things.'

'And these days, you don't feel the need to solve everyone's problems yourself, make such a personal impact, like you did before?'

'I look around me here, at the vastness of the land I live in, and I feel small and incapable. And then, I realize that all things are possible, because of God. No, I don't have to change the world and all its problems myself. I can only change myself, be myself—and, by example, show something of God's love to everyone I meet.'

Pam caught Roger's eye, as he stood behind the camera. With the slightest of nods, they agreed. Stephen's interview was perfect.

'Hello, Margaret.' Jack's voice was unmistakeable. 'How's the practice going?'

Margaret chuckled. 'Pretty well, I think. Ian, the Musical Director, seemed really pleased when we rehearsed last night. I thought I would be nervous, but I enjoyed it so much in the end. We've got a final rehearsal tonight, when all the choir will be there too, practising the hymns through. Are you coming to that?'

'I might pop in at the end, just to see you back to your car safely!'

'That would be nice.'

'But I wondered if you'd have time to pop in here for a cup of tea before the rehearsal?'

Margaret hesitated for barely a moment before she spoke—but it was a hesitation that Jack noticed.

'I think, Jack, that might be difficult this evening. I've a few things to do this afternoon, and I think I might be running a bit late for the rehearsal.'

'Are you still trying to fit in your pupils with their music lessons?' Why am I asking her all these questions, thought Jack. She probably has much better things to do than have tea with a crusty old bachelor like me!

'Something like that,' said Margaret evasively. She's seeing another man, thought Jack, as despair clasped him unexpectedly by the heart. 'But I'd love to see you later, at the end of the rehearsal,' continued Margaret. 'Perhaps I could have that cup of tea then?'

'Oh, it doesn't matter,' said Jack with a voice that, to his surprise, hardly shook at all. 'It really doesn't matter at all. I won't hold you up then. Bye!'

Margaret replaced her receiver carefully, feeling mean and deceitful. Why didn't she just tell him? Why did it have to be such a secret?

Because it's special, and it's exciting, and for the time being at least, until I know exactly where I stand, I want to savour the thought of it all by myself!

And then she thought of Jack. 'Jack Diggens!' she shouted out loud, to no one in particular. 'Jack Diggens, why do you have to be so—so *hurt*?!'

❧

The first person Pam saw when she arrived at the church to meet Pete Durrell, from the local paper, was her favourite Rigger Driver, Michael. Travelling the length and breadth of the country for a period of weeks, as this unit had throughout the recording of 'Village Praise', had forged deep friendships between them all. Michael wrapped Pam in a huge bearhug, and then pushed her back away from him, to look at her closely.

'You've got a twinkle in your eye. Has that got anything to do with the fact that this is your last week on the road?'

'Yes, yes, yes!' smiled Pam. 'It's been great, this series, but I've been away from home too much, and for too long. I just feel like going home, and being nothing but a Mum for ever more!'

'Ah, you'll soon get over that,' teased Michael, in his lilting Irish way. 'You'll miss us, and you'll be back! What are you up to now, anyway?'

'I'm supposed to be meeting a gentleman of the press here—a chap called Pete Durrell. You haven't seen him, have you?'

'Yep, he's been hanging around here for an hour or so, asking all sorts of technical questions about the vehicles, and our equipment. Young Matthew is looking after him now—you know, the youngster who seems to have adopted us this week! They're in the church, I think.'

'Right, see you then!' said Pam, and as he gave her one last squeeze around her shoulders, Michael watched as she headed towards the church door.

Helen had been slowly making her way towards the church too, when she had spotted Michael and Pam. She looked on from a distance, as he hugged Pam with such obvious affection. He's a flirt, she thought, an outrageous flirt! And I must remember that! She changed her direction so that she could go in to the church through the side door, without the need to walk past Michael. She kept her eye on him as she walked, but he didn't turn round in her direction. When she reached the side door, it struck her with a pang of surprise and regret, that she wished he had.

Pete Durrell was deep in conversation with Simon Martin, the Engineering Manager, when Pam walked in. Rather than disturb him, she made her way over to where Anna's travelling companion on the school bus, Matthew, was standing slightly apart, totally engrossed in the technical details that Simon was explaining to Pete.

'You're hooked, aren't you!' she whispered to Matthew. 'What are you going to be, then? An engineering manager? A sound recordist?'

'I'm not sure yet.' Matthew turned an earnest face towards her. 'Something technical, I'm sure of that. Perhaps in Sound. I really do fancy that.'

'Do you know how you'd go about getting a job like that?'

'Well, I've been talking to Frank Harris—you know, he's the Sound Supervisor. He says it's not so easy to get taken on for training nowadays, because there are so many freelance technicians on the market, that they don't need to train so many. He reckons it would do me no harm to get a degree to start with—well, I was going to do that anyway—but he's given me some suggestions about what kind of course would be most relevant. He's given me the address for the Institute of Broadcast Sound, too—and he even says that the BBC sometimes take students on for Work Experience, and that he'd be happy to put my name forward. That would be so brilliant—it really would!'

'Are they letting you help out much here?'

'A bit. Mostly, I'm just watching, especially what the sound engineers are doing. But everyone is so nice, especially the riggers! They said if I keep on making their coffee, and getting newspapers and things for them from the shop, that they'll let me help as much as I like!'

'Ummm,' agreed Pam, 'that sounds like them!' She noticed that Pete Durrell was making his way towards her. 'Got to go, Matthew—and good luck! I hope it all works out for you!'

At that moment, Helen let herself in through the vestry door, and was not at all surprised to find Mrs Hadlow was already there, a candlestick in one hand, and a huge wad of brass cleaner in the other. 'Do you know, dear,' Mrs Hadlow said, as if she was already halfway through a conversation with Helen, 'I only cleaned these candlesticks last week, but they're filthy already? It's those men traipsing in and out, bringing all the dirt and dust with them. And they won't keep the main door shut! What with all that equipment they're bringing in, no wonder everything is getting grubby!' Helen smiled in agreement, and tried to move on into the church—but Mrs Hadlow was still in full swing. 'The problem is—how are we going to get all that dust off those beautiful grass arrangements?' She emphasized her point, by waving her hand, complete with brass wadding, in front of Helen's face. 'What I'd like to know is how Clive felt about there being arrangements in the church at all? During Lent? Clive's a stickler for protocol, we both know that, dear—I'm just so surprised that he allowed it!' She looked meaningfully at Helen, waiting for her opinion, or at the very least, an explanation—in vain.

'You'll have to ask him, if you see him.' Helen hesistated. 'Have you seen him, by the way?'

'The vicar? Not this morning, no.' Mrs Hadlow turned back to her candlestick. 'Lost him, have you?'

'Of course not!' retorted Helen sharply. 'Must rush, sorry!' She turned on her heel, and walked quickly out of the vestry door towards the body of the church. Too quickly. Her foot caught on an uneven flagstone. In panic, she groped out wildly to stop herself falling, just as a strong pair of arms caught and steadied her. She looked up into smiling grey eyes, as Michael made no attempt to release her from his hold.

'I'm fine now. Thank you,' she stammered, disengaging herself from his clasp.

'You look harassed,' Michael replied, his shewd eyes still on her. 'Can I help?'

'You already have. Thank you again.' Helen gathered up her hymn sheets, now scattered all over the floor. Michael kneeled down level with her, and helped her to pick them up.

'You're upset,' he said at last. 'I know you are. I'm a good listener, you know, if you want to talk about it.'

Helen stood up abruptly. 'Upset? Whatever have I got to be upset about? I'm just shaken by the fall, that's all.'

Michael stood up, and slowly handed back the hymn sheets he'd collected. 'No, that's not all. You *are* upset. I can see it. And your husband should be able to see it too.'

Helen looked at him wordlessly.

'He can see it, can't he?' Michael went on quietly. 'He does know how unhappy you are. Doesn't he?'

Helen felt her eyes fill with tears. Aghast with embarrassment, she looked down, trying to think of a reply, and finding none.

Michael gently put his hand under her chin, and lifted her gaze up towards him.

'Helen, we're friends. I'm here if you want to talk. Any time. I'm here.'

Helen nodded dumbly, her eyes fixed on his. And then she broke away. Without a backward glance, her back stiff, she walked on into the church.

Michael watched her as she moved. And from the vestry door, candlestick still in hand, so did Mrs Hadlow.

❧

In the end, Kate didn't go with Pam, Roger and the crew when they set out later that afternoon to meet Sidney, Frank and Bo, the fishermen, for their interview. As researcher, Kate still had several details to organize and establish for filming later in the week, and she was glad for the opportunity to spend an hour on the phone. Her shoulders felt stiff and aching, as she replaced the receiver for the last time. She hung her head for a moment, rubbing her neck and closing her eyes. Coffee, she thought. That's what I need! She stood up abruptly, and was filling the kettle just as the phone rang.

'Miss Marsden?' Kate could not immediately place the voice, especially when she was addressed in such a formal way.

'Kate? It's Charles here, Charles Waite.'

'Charles, hello,' replied Kate, perching on the side of the bed.

'I thought I would just contact you, to find out if everything is going smoothly. Are there any arrangements that I can assist you with?'

'How kind of you to offer, Charles, but no, I think we're all organized.'

'I'm afraid I've been rather busy lately, and unfortunately had to delegate the seating arrangements in the church. I am concerned that Jack Diggens is rather new to our church community, and may be— how shall I put it? A wild card, shall we say?'

'Really?' replied Kate. 'We were only saying this morning that he has been so efficient. No, you've no need to worry on that score, Charles. Jack seems to have everything well in hand.'

'Excellent. That's excellent.' Charles paused for a few seconds, before continuing.

'About tickets for the recording?' Charles cleared his throat. 'I was aghast to learn from a very prominent member of our Parish Council, Major James Gregory, that his wife, Mrs Marjorie Gregory, has not been allocated a ticket. This really is unforgivable. Of course, the Major and his wife must have seats for the recording.'

'Oh, I'm afraid I'm not the one to talk to about tickets, Charles. Why don't you talk to Jack, to see if he can sort anything out? Otherwise, I suppose if you feel strongly enough about it, you could give Mrs Gregory *your* ticket...'

Kate held her breath. There was silence at the other end of the phone. Finally, Charles spoke.

'I see, Miss Marsden. I do see. Good afternoon.' And with that, the phone went dead.

Clive looked up in surprise as Helen burst in through the greenhouse door. 'For heaven's sake, Clive, whatever are you thinking of? People have been trying to track you down all afternoon. I feel such a fool, never knowing where you are!'

'Look, darling!' Clive held out a cactus for her inspection. The cactus was drab and nondescript—but somehow it had managed to burst into bud, as two vibrant red blooms dropped like tears from the end of its gangly leaves. 'It's never flowered before. I read somewhere that they only flower once every seven years. How long have we had it, do you think? It must be almost that long, mustn't it?'

'Clive, there's no time for gardening now. That Engineering Manager, Simon, is desperate to talk to you. Jan, the Producer, has rung three times, and left urgent messages for you to contact her. Jack Diggens needs a word. The choir rehearsal starts in just three hours, and you've got no idea what's going on! Where on earth have you been?'

Clive put the cactus down, and lovingly fingered the flowers. 'Oh, I just had a few calls to make. This is beautiful, isn't it? Perfect! Only God could make something as perfectly beautiful as this...'

'Clive!' Helen's voice was unnaturally sharp. 'You must come *now*! This is the most important event ever to take place in this church, and it's *your* responsibility to guide us through it. It's just not fair to leave it to all the rest of us to sort out. We've had enough. I've had enough...'

Clive's eyes widened in surprise, and then concern. He laid his hands on Helen's shoulders, and gently turned her to him. 'Darling, you *are* out of sorts. This is so unlike you. You're so good at coping. I'm always telling people how wonderfully well you cope!'

'Well, I'm up to my ears in coping! I'm fed up with doing so much of your job for you. *You're* the vicar. I'm just your wife. I am not your employee. I don't have to run round after you, covering up for all the things you can't be bothered to do yourself!'

Clive dropped his hands in shock at this outburst.

'And I'm telling you now—either you get yourself out of here, and over to the church where you're needed—or I'll—I'll—I'll think very carefully about my position here!'

And with that, Helen turned on her heel, and ran up the path towards the kitchen door, leaving Clive rooted to the spot, wordless with disbelief.

Pam and Roger arrived back at Grove House from their filming with the fishermen, to find Jan hard at work on the word processor in their makeshift 'office'.

'How did it go? Did it rain on you?'

Roger flopped down in the chair next to her. 'Not quite, although it tried hard. What an afternoon! I have never met three people who are at the same time so exhausting, and so totally disarming!'

Pam had her back to them both, as she put the kettle on, and hunted for some tea bags to put in the pot. 'That Sidney is quite the most bad-tempered bully I've come across in a long time!' she laughed. 'But the odd thing is that Frank and Bo just seem to take his nagging in their stride.'

'All goes in one ear, and out the other, I reckon!' added Roger.

'Does it work as an item, do you think?' asked Jan.

'Honestly, Jan, it's going to go together a treat. Sidney was still insisting that they should sing "Eternal Father"—and so I let him. But then, I asked them if they'd sing "The Old Rugged Cross", just for us—and you know, we only really want the first verse of that from them, because after that we'll cut back to the church to hear the whole congregation singing the rest of the hymn—but there's something so moving about the way that they sing together. And when Sidney read that passage from the Bible—well, it's wonderful!'

'And did you manage to get much of an interview out of them?'

Pam chuckled. 'Not bad—well, not after I'd managed to decipher the accent a bit. It takes a bit of tuning in to! I talked to all three of them, just standing alongside the boat on the shore, and although Sidney probably had the most to say, I have a feeling that we're just as likely to use the pieces from Bo and Frank. They come across as so matter-of-fact about their faith. It's just implicit in every word they say. They don't analyze their relationship with God, or worry about why they believe—they just do!'

'And how are your sea legs?'

'We had another boat, of course,' said Roger, helping himself to a chocolate biscuit, 'so that we could film them from a distance. Then, the cameraman and sound recordist, Keith and Bob, went in their boat with them, to do the close-ups. Keith looked a bit green when he got out! I think you can feel really seasick, when you're rocking up and down yourself, looking through the viewfinder at someone's face that's also rocking up and down!'

Pam handed out cups of tea, and glanced at her watch. 'Ten to six. I'm going up to give the kids a ring at home—and soak in the bath for half an hour. What's happening later?'

'I'm going along to the choir rehearsal at the Village Hall at seven o'clock, and Sue will come to that too, so that she can get some timings on the hymns,' replied Jan. 'Perhaps Ian, Sue and I can meet you in The Bull later, to have a bite to eat?'

Pam glanced at Roger. 'Well, Roger and I thought we might pop over to The Bull quite early, and then I think I'll spend a couple of hours this evening just thinking about the commentary and pieces to camera that we need for the programme. I'd like to come up with something just right for my final piece, after the last hymn. As this programme is the end of "Village Praise" this year, it would be good to tie it all up with a piece that sums up the feel and sentiment of all the villages we've visited throughout the series.'

'Good idea. See you later then!'

Pam made her way up to her room, and rang her home number. It was Max that answered the phone.

'Mum, can you ring back? I'm just watching "Star Trek".'

Nice to be missed, Pam thought wryly. No one could say that her youngsters were pining for her, while she was on the road. It was very reassuring that they were so settled and happy, even though during 'Village Praise', she wasn't there as much as she'd like to be.

'OK,' she said, 'I'll give you a ring before bedtime. Have you got homework to do?'

'Probably,' was the non-committal answer, 'I'm not sure. Got to go, Mum! Here's Bethan...'

When Bethan's voice came on the phone, she sounded unusually tired. 'Mummy, my legs hurt.'

'Do they, darling? Why's that? Did you fall over today?'

'No, they just hurt.'

'Where do they hurt?'

'All over, they hurt all over.'

'And is it an achy sort of pain, or a stinging sort of pain?'

'Umm...' Bethan gave the question serious consideration. Finally, she said, 'It's achy—all over.'

'Have you been running round a lot? Perhaps you've been using your muscles more than usual, and they've got tired.'

'No, that's not it.'

'Oh, what do you think's the matter then?'

'It's because I've grown. When I woke up this morning, my legs were growing. I was watching them grow.'

'Were you? How could you tell they were growing?'

'Well,' said Bethan, 'you know I've got that mole on my leg—well, it *used* to be down at the bottom of my leg.'

'Ummm,' agreed Pam, rather doubtfully.

'Well, it's in the middle now! It's moved. It had to move, you see, because I've grown!'

'Are you sure it's not dirt?' asked Pam, stifling a smile.

'No, Mum!' Bethan's voice rang with indignation at such a stupid question. 'It's my mole—and it's moved because my legs have grown *that* much during the night.'

Pam could only imagine just how much exactly '*that* much' was!

'Well, no wonder your legs are hurting!' Pam's voice was full of sympathy. 'I think it might be a good idea for you to have a long soak and rest in a nice hot bathtub tonight, just before you go to bed. That might make your legs feel a lot better. What do you think?'

'I thought perhaps I should have my tea on a tray on the settee, all cuddled up in my duvet—and watch a video, one I haven't seen from the video shop. I think that would make my legs feel much better.'

'Ooh, I don't know. Sore legs usually feel better, if you give them plenty of exercise. I think you should sit up at the kitchen table to have your tea, so that you don't drop it everywhere—and then have a good run in the garden, before you take that nice warm bath!'

'But Mum, I do think a video would do my legs much *more* good.'

'I don't think videos are a good idea on school days, do you, because you'd be too tired in the morning? Tell you what, though— let's have a video on Saturday, when I'm home with you. We'll all have a Cuddly Night, curled up in front of the telly! Is that a good idea?'

'With popcorn?'

'Is there any other way?'

'OK,' said Bethan, 'I'm going to have my tea now.'

'Love you lots, then,' said Pam, reluctant to let her go. 'Shall we do 1—2—3?'

'OK' said Bethan again. 'And I'll say it, not you!' She took a big breath, and started to count loudly. 'One! Two!' And on 'three', the phone clicked dead.

Jack Diggens was ferrying some chairs from the Village Hall, so that a few more people could be squeezed into corners of the church for the recording, when he saw her. Margaret. Without a doubt. He'd know her anywhere, even if the light was fading fast on this early April evening. She was some distance away, walking along the path on the outside of the church wall, deep in conversation with someone else. Jack put down the chairs he was holding, and strained his eyes to peer closer. It was a man, of that he was sure, but as Margaret herself was shielding a clear view of her companion, Jack was not able to see who she was with. He was taller than Margaret, but not by much. It was impossible to tell his age, because the little Jack was able to glimpse of his features and hair colour, gave little away.

Jack watched them as they walked along to where, he suddenly realized, Margaret had left her little car. At this point, still deep in conversation with her companion, Margaret turned towards Jack's direction. With a stab of pain, he saw happy animation in her face. This man made her happy. Margaret deserved to be happy. I should be glad for her, Jack thought. I should be glad.

He watched as they said goodbye. He watched as she got into her car, and drove off, while her friend looked on. And as the man turned to walk away, Jack might even have been able to put a name to the face, if it wasn't for the tears that had unexpectedly misted his eyes.

Ian planned to get to the hall at half past six, before the choir members arrived, to have a last run through Anna's solo. First thing the next morning, they planned to record, in sound only, the musical track that Anna would then mime to when they went to record the pictures at Haycliffe ruins. The lilting, gentle accompaniment Ian had written for the piece brought out the sweetness of Anna's voice. He had every confidence that 'Just As I Am' would be one of the high spots of what was turning out to be a very promising programme.

He was just about to leave his room in Grove House, knowing he would be late at the church if he didn't leave immediately, when, without thought, he grabbed the telephone, and dialled Sarah's number. Since her cryptic message the previous evening, he hadn't managed to speak to her.

He wasn't even sure what her plans were that day. Was she at home? Was she working this week? He realized with a pang, that he had been so preoccupied with the pressure of his own work, that he hadn't even thought what she might be doing.

He heard the familiar ring of the phone in her flat. It rang—three times, four—please be home, Sarah, please be home—and then, her answerphone clicked in. He closed his eyes in frustration, as he heard her voice. So near, so distant. Oh, Sarah, how I wish you'd been in!

'... please leave your message after the long tone,' her voice said.

He waited, and then spoke. 'I hate leaving messages for you. These things drive me mad! And how can I ask you anything—properly or otherwise—if the only way we ever manage to speak to each other is by leaving messages on blessed answerphones?'

He stopped, wondering what to say next. And then, 'Sarah, I miss you. I miss you so much. Ring me, please. Just ring me when you can!'

He was about to say more, when the answerphone beeped, to say that his time was up.

When Jan and Sue arrived at the church for the rehearsal just on seven, the place was already crowded. There was an excited buzz of conversation. This was the last rehearsal, before they moved into the church the following evening, for the television rehearsal. A sense of occasion and anticipation hung in the air. Nothing quite like this had ever happened in Sandford. Nothing quite like it was ever likely to happen again.

Jan searched the room to find Ian. She saw him at last—pinned into a corner of the hall by the leader of the St Mark's Choir, Mrs Hulme. She was pointing urgently at a sheet of music that she was holding under his nose. Mrs Hulme was not a woman to be ignored.

Jan caught Ian's eye, with a smile. Relieved to see her, Ian spoke apologetically to Mrs Hulme, and extricated himself from her grasp. As he reached Jan, he grimaced. 'No wonder that choir sings so well! They must all be terrified of her. Heaven knows what happens, if you don't do as you're told!'

Jan looked round at the full hall. 'A good turn out! Are you about to get the rehearsal under way?'

Nodding in reply, Ian picked up his pile of arrangements, moved away to the front of the hall, and banged on the table to get attention.

'Settle down, everyone. Can you get into the right places please? Sopranos over to the right, altos down here on the left, tenors and basses on either side at the back!'

It was like Musical Chairs, without the music, as people criss-crossed the room, taking their proper seats. The voice of Rose Smith, the highly organized organizer of the Women's Institute Choir, rose above everyone else's, as she directed Sopranos there, and Basses there. Once they were all settled—and once they'd managed to persuade Mrs Hadlow that Ian had said 'Altos to the left', and that she was actually sitting amongst the Sopranos—Colin took his seat at the electronic keyboard, Ian raised his baton, and the rehearsal began.

Outside the church, in his small beige caravan, Joe, the Security Man, stetched out on his bed, watching his small portable television, eating toast and marmite. Every hour throughout the night, he would patrol the BBC vehicles, and the church which was already full of microphones and cameras, to make sure that everything was secure. He had thought about nipping over to The Bull, to join the rest of the lads for a quick pint. They'd all be here now, the complete team—the outside broadcast camera and sound men, the videotape editor, the floor manager. He smiled as he thought of the floor manager who was working on this whole series of 'Village Praise'. It was a complicated job. The floor manager was in the church throughout the television rehearsal and recording, relaying the instructions of the director, who stayed outside in the scanner, to the congregation as a whole, or to individual people inside the building. If the director looking at the pictures out in the scanner said, 'Tell that idiot woman in the third row to take her hat off!', it was the floor manager's job to pass on the message tactfully—a diplomatic word in the ear suggesting that the hat was so eye-catching, that it might distract the attention of the viewer at home, and so, reluctantly, the director wondered if she would be kind enough to take if off for the remainder of the recording! It was a tremendous skill. It required nerves of steel, a straight face, and an indisputable air of authority.

The floor manager on this series was considered to be one of the best, with the ability to quieten a congregation with nothing more than a look. Most floor managers were men. With her crop of red curly hair, and trim figure, this one most definitely was not! Yes, thought Joe, the smile still on his face. Ros was definitely all woman— and with that thought in mind, Joe lay back against his pillow, and closed his eyes.

31 March

Anna didn't sleep much that night, and long before her alarm was due to go off, she was up and locked herself into the bathroom. When her dad, Don, banged on the door at half past six, wanting to get ready to open the shop, she bluntly told him that she had just got into the bath, and wouldn't be coming out for at least quarter of an hour. While he waited for the kettle to boil, Don rinsed his face in the kitchen sink, and thought that he would forgive his daughter anything this morning. He was so proud of her. To think that today she was going to be recorded for television, so that people all over the country would recognize her talent when they heard her sing on Sunday night. His heart swelled with pride every time he thought of it.

He wondered if she was nervous, as nervous as he was? He knew that she and her Mum had gone all the way to Ipswich yesterday, to choose just the right outfit for her to wear. Funny, she'd never shown much interest in clothes before. Joan always said that Anna seemed to have no opinions of her own when it came to what she wore. She simply wanted to look like every other girl of her age. In other words, she wore black—and if not black, the blackest-looking version of any of the grungy colours that the girls seemed to favour at the moment.

Don had taken the bread delivery, sorted out the papers, and arranged the trays of pot plants for sale outside the shop, before he finally saw her. She came downstairs, and walked through the shop at quarter to nine, on her way to meet Ian and the crew at the church at nine.

Don caught his breath. His daughter looked lovely. She was wearing a jacket and straight skirt in a warm, plum-red shade, a colour that seemed to bring out the red highlights in her hair, and the hazel of her eyes. Her shoes were flat, but elegant. She wore simple gold studs in her ears, and around her neck, the finishing touch was the small yellow cross that her godmother, Helen, had given her when she was confirmed.

Don looked at his little girl, and glimpsed a woman. 'You look smashing, love. Really smashing!'

'Do I, Dad? Really, do I look alright?'

'Anna, you're beautiful...'

She almost smiled, until she thought better of it. She strode towards the door. 'Right! Got to go! See ya!' And the bell on the shop door jangled, as she pulled it shut behind her.

Standing at the door of the hair salon, cup of coffee in hand, Debbie the receptionist watched as Anna made her way from Don's shop towards the church.

'Iris, quick, come and have a look! They must be recording Anna today. Come and have a look at her, quick!'

Iris hurried to the door, just in time to see Anna open the church gate.

'Anna!' she called out across the road. 'You look great! Give it all you've got! We're rooting for you!'

Anna turned and waved, before starting to walk towards the church door.

'Heavens,' said Debbie, taking a gulp of coffee. 'I almost didn't recognize her. I've never seen her look like that before.'

Iris laughed. 'A bit different from school uniform, isn't it? I wonder how much persuasion it took from Joan, to get her to wear something so—normal! It wasn't even black!'

'You're so jammy, getting a ticket, just because you did those grass arrangements,' grumbled Debbie. 'I wish I'd helped you now, then I'd have got a ticket too.'

'Well, it wasn't just because I did the displays for the recording,' said Iris. 'I do the flowers every other week—and I go along to the service most Sundays, you know!'

'So what are you going to wear, then, on the big night? Have you decided?'

'Well,' replied Iris, as she perched herself on the reception desk, 'apparently, the choir have been told that they should all wear something smart, but not patterned—plain material is better. Betty was telling me when I was cutting her hair yesterday, that most people thought they'd wear jackets—but then, she was saying that someone overheard Mrs Hulme—you know, the one who conducts the choir from St Mark's—saying that she wanted all her choir to wear *red* jackets, so that they would stand out from everyone else. And then, when Rose Smith and the Women's Institute lot heard about that, they got in a huddle and decided they'd wear red too!'

Debbie's eyes widened. 'No! What are you going to do about that?'

'Well, if red jackets are good enough for them, I'll do one better! I want my sister in Chelmsford to pick me out in the crowd on the TV, so I have no intention of being a wilting wallflower! Oh, no, those cameras aren't going to miss me, if I have anything to do with it!'

'Oh, Iris, are you going to dye your hair blue, or something?'

'Nothing quite that drastic, but what do you think of the idea of having a notice pinned to my chest—HAIR BY IRIS OF SANDFORD—and the phone number? Do you think it would be good for business?'

'Iris, they'd be turning up in coachloads!'

And they were both giggling like schoolgirls, when Mrs Hadlow's friend, Ivy Murray, arrived for her nine o'clock appointment for a wash and roller set.

'Anna! I hardly recognized you!'

Anna turned as she made her way up the path to the church, to see her companion from the school bus, Matthew, coming from around the corner, where she knew all the BBC vans were parked.

'Look, don't make a big thing of it! They just told me I had to wear something like this, so I did.'

'But you look great. You do look really great, Anna.'

Anna shrugged. 'I heard you were spending a lot of time here. Trying to talk yourself into a job, are you?'

'Well, I wouldn't mind. I didn't know anything about jobs in television until I met this lot, and they've been really nice to me. Yeah, I'd like to work in sound, or something like that, later on. This week has decided me. I know what I want to do now, where I'm heading.'

There was a hint of admiration in Anna's eyes, but just for a second. She turned to look towards the church door. 'Is there anyone in there yet? Have they all arrived?'

'Yes, they've been rigging for about half an hour now.'

'I'd better go on in then,' Anna said, but she didn't move from where she stood.

Matthew gently touched her arm. 'Are you nervous?' He could see that she was.

'Don't be daft!' retorted Anna, brushing off his hand, 'What have I got to be nervous about? Look, don't hold me up. I'll be late!' And with that, she pulled back her shoulders, and opened the church door.

'Clive.'

Helen was carrying a cup of coffee as she walked into the study, where Clive was sitting at the desk. In front of him was his Bible, open, but she suspected, not being read. He was staring out in front of him towards the garden, deep in thought.

'Clive, your coffee.'

At this, he did turn. 'Oh, thank you.'

He looked as if he was about to say more, but didn't. Helen began to move towards the door again, but changed her mind, and clearing a space for herself amid the papers strewn across the battered old armchair, she sat down, and looked at him in silence.

At last, she spoke.

'Well, are we going to talk?'

'Helen, we don't seem to be able to talk any more, without you snapping my head off.'

'That's not fair.'

'Probably not, but that's how I feel.'

'So it's my fault, is it? Don't you ever wonder *why* I'm snapping your head off? What it is about your behaviour that exasperates me so?'

'You've never really understood the nature of my work. You expect me to be an organizer, a cog in the parish wheel. But that's never what I've wanted! I became a priest because I believe I have a real calling to do God's work, to live a life of devotion and prayer.'

'So, you get on with the devotion and prayer, while I'm left with all the work. Is that it?'

Clive wearily ran his fingers through his hair. 'Helen, I don't know what you want any more. I don't think I've changed—but you have. You used to love getting involved in the running of the parish, relish being the hub of everything that goes on round here! I've grown to rely on you. I thought that's what you wanted.'

'I don't think you've thought about what I want at all. I don't think you even notice me, until something goes wrong. I feel about as important to you as that chair you're sitting on—comfy, convenient and perfectly alright as long as it works for you!'

Clive looked at her wordlessly. Helen returned his stare, and then got up abruptly.

'I've tried to make you happy, Helen. Apparently, I'm not very good at it.'

Helen turned in the doorway. 'No, I'm not happy. I know I'm tired. I know that this programme has meant a lot of pressure on us all. But I know that I am unhappy in a way that has nothing to do with what's going on this week.'

'What can I do to help? What do you want from me?'

'I think, Clive,' she said slowly, 'the fact that you have to ask, means that you are probably not able to help at all.' And there was sadness in her face as she walked back downstairs to the kitchen.

Betty Waite timed it just right. She knew the sound of Anna's song was to be recorded in the church that morning, and as she had to pop in to drop off some music some time during the day, she made sure she was sitting at the organ, out of sight, but well in earshot, as the recording began.

She was surprised at how long it took to set up all the technical equipment needed to record Anna. Apparently, they had to get the ambience just right, so that the sound was neither too echoey, nor too muffled. And they had to balance the volume of Anna's voice with the accompaniment Ian was providing on his electronic keyboard. He had already laid down some tracks, so that the sound he produced was, at first, simple and restrained, with Anna's voice ringing out clearly above it—and then, with each verse, the accompaniment built, until at last, it was rich, vibrant and melodic, soaring towards a crescendo for the final line.

Betty peeped out of her hiding place, to look at Anna, the little girl who used to come and stand by her elbow as she played the organ, oh, it seemed only yesterday! Betty remembered how Anna, barely more than six years old, had got her way, and been allowed to join the church choir. Because she'd been far too small for any of the robes they had at St Michael's, Betty had sat up late one night, creating a tiny robe, just for her. And she remembered that Christmas Eve, perhaps three or four years ago, when, amid the candles and eager faces that filled the church at the late night service, Anna had sung unaccompanied, 'Once in Royal David's City'. Her voice had been so pure and sweet, the tune dear and familiar, her words seeming to hang in the air around them, filling the church like a prayer.

And here she was now, little Anna, composed and serene, her voice soaring and tender with emotion as she sang:

Just as I am, poor, wretched, blind;
Sight, riches, healing of the mind,
Yes, all I need, in Thee to find,
O Lamb of God, I come.

And as Betty listened, she found herself with her head in her hands, overcome with the thought of all the moments, the music, the hymns that she and this organ had shared in worship over the years. And now, this minute, with the voice of a young girl echoing round the church, Betty felt for the very first time, she could reach out and touch the Spirit of God that gently enfolded them all.

Helen hadn't meant to go looking for Michael, but somehow, as she walked down the High Street to get a few things from Don and Joan's shop, she wasn't surprised to see him. Without a word, he fell into step beside her, and together they walked past the shop entrance, and on, down the street, turning left towards Jack Diggens' house, past John's old house, now up for sale since his death, and towards the stone bridge.

Neither of them spoke. It wasn't until they'd crossed the bridge, and of one accord, turned right into the area of river bank that was sheltered and hidden, that they finally stopped, and sat down on the driest bit of rock they could find.

Michael's arm went around her shoulders, and Helen slumped against him as, at last, the tears came. Tears of frustration, tears of guilt, of sadness and pain. She cried for Clive. She cried for the past. She cried for herself, and for what lay ahead. She cried in fear and sadness, for her failure—to Clive, to God, to herself. And she cried for Michael—that he was the one, not Clive, that she had turned to. She cried for her faithlessness, for her shame, for the physical longing she felt for the strong, quiet man beside her. And when at last, she could cry no more, she lay her head against his shoulder until the shuddering sobs had subsided, and she was left, numb and drained.

She felt no need to explain her feelings to Michael. Somehow, he seemed to know. From the very start, he had been able to look into her eyes, and see into her soul.

And when he gently tilted her face up towards his, her very self was laid bare before him. She reached out to draw his head towards her, until his lips were on hers.

It was while Mrs Hadlow was walking down towards Iris's hair salon, to pick up her friend Ivy after her appointment, that she had spotted Helen making her way towards the village shop. Mrs Hadlow had quickened her pace to catch up with her, as she had been meaning for some time to have a word with her about the state of the vestry cupboard. And then, she'd seen him, the same BBC man that she had spotted helping Helen up, after she had stumbled in the church the day before.

Mrs Hadlow stopped and watched as the man changed direction to walk alongside Helen. She watched as the two of them walked urgently away, heading off towards the river. And she thought to herself that Helen was behaving in a way that hardly seemed suitable for someone who was, after all, a vicar's wife. Perhaps she was ill? Perhaps the strain of this BBC invasion was taking its toll on her health and judgement? Perhaps, in view of this odd behaviour, a careful eye should be kept on her, in case she was sickening for something. And who better to voice these concerns to than Helen's husband?

When Matthew asked the Sound Supervisor, Frank Harris, if it would be alright for him to go along to Haycliffe ruins when Anna recorded the pictures needed to go with her sound track, Frank said it was OK with him, if it was OK with Bob, the sound man who would be in charge out on location. The plan was to play back the recording that Anna had made in the church that morning, so that Anna could mime the singing of different parts of the hymn, in a variety of moody surroundings within the ruins.

It was a cold, bright morning, perfect for the pictures they hoped to get, but chilly for Anna, shivering in her new lightweight suit. Not that she minded. Nothing, not even the weather, could spoil her enjoyment of this wonderful morning. And nothing could have prepared her for her feelings when she heard the tape they'd made in the church. She could hardly recognize her own voice, perfectly balanced against the beauty of Ian's arrangement. She supposed that you could never hear yourself as others hear you. But that recording, with its strong, emotive singing, took her by surprise. Was that really her? Could she sound like that? And best of all, when Ian spotted the delight and thrill in her face as she listened to the music they'd made together, he came up to put an arm round her shoulders, smiling down at her with warmth and affection. 'Well done,' he said. 'That was wonderful!' And Anna had never felt so wonderful in her whole life.

When they arrived at Haycliffe, the place was alive with preparation. Lights were being moved into place and adjusted.

Speakers were being put up, so that Anna could hear her own voice clearly. Keith, the cameraman, was putting the camera onto tall legs, and discussing intently with Roger, the director, exactly what shots were planned. For a while after Anna arrived, no one seemed to notice her. Until they were ready for her to perform, everyone was just too busy to talk to her. She was content, though, to lean against the wall, and watch, and commit to memory every last detail of what she saw.

She didn't hear Matthew come and stand behind her. She wasn't aware of his presence until he said, almost to himself, 'Can you believe it? That we're really here, part of all this?'

Anna didn't take her eyes off the scene in front of her. 'This is what I want, Matthew. I want to belong to all this. I want to sing. I've got to sing—and be good enough at it, to be asked to work like this again.'

'Oh,' said Matthew softly, 'you're good enough. You're the best, Anna. Today has proved that.'

Anna's eyes were shining back at him. 'Am I? Do you really think I could make it as a singer?'

'I think you could do anything you put your mind to. You'll have to work hard. You'll have to get some good qualifications behind you before you leave school, so that you've got something to fall back on.' He gently pushed back a strand of hair from her face, and this time she didn't look away. 'But yes, Anna, you can do it. I know you can.' His hand rested on her shoulder, and she let her head drop, until her cheek rested against it.

'Thanks, Matthew,' she said. 'You're not bad yourself.'

Jack Diggens had expected this to be a busy day, knowing that in the evening there would be the first technical rehearsal with all the lights, microphones and TV cameras in place. He'd thought there'd be lots of last minute changes and reorganization to be done. In the event, the day was turning out to be a bit of an anticlimax. It seemed that he'd planned the seating, the stewarding and the publicity so well that no one needed to ask him anything!

He had been restless and out of sorts all morning. He put it down to the fact that he had slept fitfully, aware of the chime of the church clock every quarter of an hour throughout the night. His mind was whirling with arrangements, numbers, seating plans and names. At half past five that morning, he'd suddenly woken with a start, to find himself sitting bolt upright in bed, sweating in the certainty that he'd forgotten something absolutely vital—and yet, as his mind and vision cleared, the memory of what it was he'd forgotten, began tantalizingly to fade. He knew that any more sleep would elude him, and so, after twenty minutes of willing himself to doze off again, he gave in, and got up.

And that was why, at six o'clock that morning, he found himself staring dolefully into a cup of tea, wondering how his whole life, and his peace of mind, had been turned upside down in a matter of days.

It was Margaret, of course, who had brought this deep melancholy upon him. Margaret, who'd breezed into his neat and ordered world, with her smiles, and her conversation, and her arm linked through his. She made him laugh, and think, and speak his mind. She had reassured him that it was alright to admit to being lonely, alright to recognize his fear of a future on his own, alright to acknowledge the kindling of the flame of faith that had danced around him for so many years. She'd warmed his cold heart with her easy friendship—and then, she had taken that friendship away, without a word of warning.

Was that true? Had she taken her friendship away? Or had she simply made it clear that she had many friends, and that she wouldn't let him monopolize her? Of course, a lovely woman like Margaret would have friends. Not like him, he mused sadly. Since John had died, he could only think of people he vaguely knew. There was no one to be called a real friend. No one except Margaret. No one he wanted to be friends with, as he longed to be with her.

He still wasn't sure what brought about the change. One moment she was fine. The next, she suddenly became secretive. And then, he'd seen her with that man. If that man was just a 'friend', why on earth had she been so evasive?

He sighed. Women had been a mystery to him all his life. That was why he'd chosen to stay clear of them. And because he still couldn't fathom them, clear of them was exactly how he intended to stay.

❦

Clive had been told to arrive at Haycliffe around twelve noon. In fact, as he drove up at about quarter to twelve, the crew were obviously still busy recording the last of Anna's solo. Kate, the researcher, saw him approach, and beckoned to him to come and stand alongside her, where he could get a good view of the monitor, showing exactly what was being recorded.

Clive stared in admiration. Anna looked lovely, singing as she stood looking out over an expanse of Suffolk countryside, with the atmospheric shape of the old church ruins providing a backdrop.

He'd never imagined that so much concentration and effort would be put into such a short time on television. Roger, the director, asked Anna to sing the last verse seven times, before he was totally satisfied with the perfection of his pictures.

And suddenly, it was over. At an order from Roger, the crew began dismantling lights and sound cables, and piling equipment into the waiting van. It was then that Roger turned his attention to Clive.

'Clive, sorry to keep you waiting. I think I've found the perfect spot for you to record your prayer. We feel it will work very well to see you outside in the countryside while you speak your prayer, although, of course, during the outside broadcast in the church tomorrow night, we'll ask you to record the blessing, so that the whole congregation can feel part of it. How are you getting on with the words? Jan tells me you've come up with a stunning prayer.'

Clive fumbled in his pocket. 'I've got a copy here. I thought perhaps I could keep it in my hand, just in case I lose my way, or anything...'

'Not possible, I'm afraid,' smiled Roger. 'We'll start with a long shot of you, and move in as you speak until you are in close-up as you finish. I think it would look rather odd if you have a bit of paper clutched in your hand. And it would be very distracting if you were looking down all the time. Do you think you could possibly manage it from memory?'

Clive looked down at his notes. 'Well, I should do, I suppose. I wrote it.'

'Quite,' agreed Roger, 'and anyway, you vicars should be good at reciting in public. You do it all the time, don't you!'

At that moment, Roger was hailed by Keith, the cameraman. 'Got to go, Clive. We're setting up over there, down the hill a bit, with the church ruins way in the background. Come over in a minute or two, when we're a bit more organized!'

Clive sat down heavily on a low, crumbling wall, as he watched Roger move away. He looked down at the prayer he'd written in the greenhouse, the one that Jan had been so enthusiastic about, when he read it to her. Could he remember it? He closed his eyes, and tried to think of the first line. 'Lord of the... Lord of the... Lord of the Heavens, that was it!' Or was it? Didn't that bit come later on? He frowned, and looked again at the paper in his hand. It was no good, he just didn't seem to be able to concentrate today.

The truth was that he was shaken to the marrow by Helen's behaviour this morning. Never, in all the years he'd known her, had he seen such an outburst from her. Whatever was the matter with this woman he knew so well? She was tired most probably, and why not, with all this excitement going on? But it was unlike Helen to be so critical, so openly hostile. She'd always supported and understood him, at least, he'd thought she understood. Perhaps, just perhaps, she'd never understood at all, never really appreciated his needs, and the demands of his role as a man of God.

Most likely she was tired. That was the answer. That had to be the answer, and he would have to make sure that she got a good rest after all these television people had gone. Perhaps they could get away from Sandford for a few days. Go up and see Jane, their daughter who was a nurse in Leeds, perhaps? Or go down to Wisley, the beautiful Royal Horticultural Society gardens just south of London. He always enjoyed an outing to look and learn from the experts at a garden like Wisley. It was one of his favourite places to visit. And Helen knew how much he liked to visit gardens. A trip like that would be nice for her.

He felt happier to have worked out the problem, and decided on a course of action. He'd tell her this afternoon what he'd decided, and then she could get on with organizing an hotel for them. What a splendid treat it would be!

He was aware of Roger calling to him. His pace lightened as he made his way over to where the crew were waiting. As Roger gave him precise instructions about exactly where and how to stand, so that the picture would frame up just right, Clive was barely listening. He was already thinking himself into prayer, drawing his world down to simple thoughts—that God was here, that God was listening, that God would fill his mind and mouth with the right words. He stood with his eyes closed, perfectly composed, as Roger directed the cameraman to start recording. When he heard Roger softly ask him to begin, Clive's mind was clear. Slowly, he opened his eyes, and let the words flow out of him.

Lord of our World—you lived on earth, and know its beauty
Lord of our Homes—you know our hearts, our hopes, our fears
Lord of Forgiveness—you heard their cheers turn to derision
Lord of the Heavens—you died on the cross, that we might live

Open our eyes to your wonder around us,
Open our minds to the beauty within,
Be there, in our homes, in our thoughts, in our loved ones,
Lord of all love—our praises we bring.

His words echoed around the ancient old building, and across the fields around them. And as they faded away, the only sound to break the silence was the gentle wind that rustled through the hedgerow. God is here, Clive thought, God is here!

'Cut!' yelled Roger. 'That's a wrap! Thank you, everyone! Back in the church at two-thirty, for the technical run-through! Thanks, Clive. That was great. Are you coming to join us at The Bull for a spot of lunch? No? We'll see you later then, at six o'clock in the church, for the Stewards' Meeting? Sue, did you pick up my clipboard? Who's got it then? Kate, have you seen my clipboard?' And with that, Roger walked away, leaving Clive still euphoric and dazed by the spiritual experience he'd just had.

When Anna arrived back at the shop about an hour later, Pam, the presenter, was with her.

'Well?' asked Don and Joan almost in unison. 'How did it go?'

Anna shrugged non-committally, although she broke into a smile.

'She was great!' said Pam. 'Really, she was wonderful. I'm sure you'll all be very pleased with it, when you see finished piece. Anyway, you'll be able to hear the recording in the church tomorrow night, because in the final programme we'll start by seeing Anna singing in the church, and then we'll go on to see what we recorded at Haycliffe this morning.'

'And were *you* pleased, Anna?' Don asked.

'Yeah,' replied Anna, trying not to look as happy as she felt, 'it was alright.'

'Never one for overstatement, our daughter,' laughed Joan. 'Come on, love. Let's go upstairs for a cup of tea, then you can tell me all about it!'

Minutes later, Bunty burst in. 'Oh, Don, just popped in for a loaf of bread—and have you got any of those packs of currant buns? I just fancy one of them toasted for lunch...'

She stopped mid-sentence as she noticed that Pam was browsing amongst the children's toys on the bottom shelf at the other end of the shop.

Her voice became an excited whisper. 'Is that...? Isn't that...?'

'Yes, it is,' laughed Don, 'and I should just go and say hello. Go on!'

Bunty drew a deep breath, and sidled up alongside Pam. 'Miss Rhodes,' she began, 'may I just say how delighted we all are to see you here in Sandford.'

Pam smiled up at her from where she sat crouching in front of the shelf. 'The name is Pam—and believe me, I'm delighted to be here. We all are. I know that having a hoard of television people and vehicles in the middle of your village must be quite an imposition.'

'Not at all, not at all,' enthused Bunty. 'Really, we're all thrilled. How's it going? Is the programme coming along alright?'

'Well, we've just recorded Anna's solo this morning, which worked a treat, and we've some very interesting interviews already completed. I suppose we could do with a bit of sunshine, so that we can show the countryside off to its best advantage—but, really, it's all going fine!'

'Have you been in the church yet? Oh, how silly of me, of course you'll have been in the church!'

'Yes, I have, but it was full of cables and riggers when I was there,' answered Pam.

Bunty's voice was carefully casual. 'Did you notice the grass arrangements, by any chance?'

'How could I miss them? They're superb, quite lovely, and so appropriate for this time in the Christian calendar. Most impressive.'

Bunty flushed scarlet with pride. 'Well, we're a small team, you know, but we try our best.'

It suddenly struck Pam that she must look quite comical squatting on the floor of the shop. She stood up, and before Bunty could stop herself, she exclaimed, 'Oh! You're tall, aren't you? I never realized you were so tall!'

Pam laughed. 'Yes, I am, and that often takes people by surprise.' Bunty looked aghast that she had made such a personal—and possibly offensive—comment. 'Don't worry,' said Pam, 'at least you didn't say that I look much older than I do on telly! That's the one that really hurts!' She looked down at the toy shelf again. 'I'm looking for something imaginative to take home to my youngsters. My son gets through fountain pens at the rate of one a week, or perhaps it just feels like that! Anyway, I thought perhaps one of these neon-coloured jobs might suit him. And Bethan—she's five—she loves writing and drawing. She might like one of these little notebooks, or maybe this pack of sewing cards? She spends ages playing with them, too.'

'You must miss them, being away so much.'

'Yes, I do, although usually I'm not away for more than a couple of days at a time. It is hard though, when I'm working on something like "Village Praise", with such a relentless schedule for six weeks. As much as I like Sandford, it will be good to be home, I can tell you!'

'Well, if you want to get away from work for a bit, perhaps just put your feet up, you're very welcome to pop in for a cup of tea, any time—just come when you feel like it! We're only across the road, and down to the right a bit—the pink cottage. Number 29 High Street.'

'That's really kind, and I promise I will pop in, if I can. They are inclined to keep me rather busy, though.'

'Any time, any time at all, just come!' repeated Bunty. 'Well, I'll see you tonight then, at the rehearsal.'

'We'll make sure that we light your displays so that they look their very best!' smiled Pam, as Bunty backed away towards the counter, where her bread and currant buns were waiting.

❧

Jack Diggens had his lunch at The Bull—an extravagance, but he felt that he needed something to raise his spirits. Talk in the Public Bar was all about the programme, and the impact that the television team had made on every aspect of life in the village.

'What I don't understand,' said Stanley, who was rooted onto his favourite stool at the end of the bar, 'is why it takes so flipping many of them, just to make thirty-five minutes on the telly!'

'How many are there altogether then?' asked Bill, as he pulled a pint of bitter for Jack.

'Well,' said Brian, 'we've got seven of them staying with us at Grove House. And there must be about ten here, aren't there, Bill?'

Bill nodded. 'And there are a couple of them staying over at Mrs Baker's, and another chap at that farm near Dinton where they do B & B.'

'And the rest are staying at the Angel Inn over near the coast, so I heard,' said Dave. 'I don't know, how many does that make? About thirty, or so, I reckon.'

'It takes a long time, doesn't it?' mused Stanley into his pint, 'just to make a little television programme. Hardly seems worth all the effort, really. People don't watch "Songs of Praise", do they?'

'Maureen does,' said Bill. 'She refuses to do anything in this place while "Songs of Praise" is on.'

'Ellen's the same,' agreed Brian. 'She won't miss it.'

Bill nodded in understanding. 'Perhaps it's a woman's programme. They like the singing, especially now they've put the words up on the screen.'

'Oh, I don't know,' grinned Brian, 'I'm not against a spot of hymn singing myself. A bit like karaoke, really!'

'What do you think they're going to say about Sandford, then?' Stanley scanned the group. 'Will they put us across right?'

'Well, who are they going to put in the programme? Does anyone know?'

'Well, our Natalie, for a start,' said Brian. 'Apparently, they're going to film at her school tomorrow morning—something about choosing a donkey for the Palm Sunday parade. Ellen's insisted on buying her a new gaberdine raincoat, just in case she gets in shot!'

'And you know who else?' Stanley's face was very solemn. 'Can you believe it? That cantankerous old devil, Sidney West! You know, the bad-tempered old codger who goes out fishing, and never catches anything. Bo's friend, you know him!'

'What on earth are they talking to him about?' asked Bill.

'Heaven knows,' replied Stanley, 'but he's in it, I'm sure of it!'

'Well, fancy!' said Bill, as he mopped a dishcloth across the surface of the bar.

'And then, there's Charles Waite, of course,' added Brian.

'Oh yes,' said Bill, 'I bumped into him the other morning, when he was just going off to be interviewed in the church. He was full of it!'

'But Charles Waite is so—so—*boring!*' said Stanley, who was never normally lost for words.

The others digested this information in silence.

'Can't see it'll be much of a programme, then,' said Stanley finally.

'Oh, I don't know,' said Brian, 'Anna's singing in it. She's good.'

'Well, it will have its moments then, won't it?' Bill stopped wiping and leant on the bar. 'I suppose we'll just have to wait until Sunday, and see.'

'Umm,' agreed the others.

'I thought I might have a Bangers and Mash night, and have the programme on the TV in the Lounge Bar. What do you think?'

'You've just got yourself one customer,' said Stanley. 'Sounds like a great idea to me!'

❧

As soon as Clive arrived back home from Haycliffe ruins, he put on his wellies, and headed for the greenhouse. His mind was still full of the experience he'd had there, the way God had given him just the right words that echoed and filled the air around them all. He knew they were words that would touch the hearts of millions of people as they watched the programme on Sunday. God's words.

It was minutes later, while he was still deep in thought, that he was aware of someone coming down the garden path towards him. Helen probably, coming to find out how he'd got on. Coming to apologize for this morning perhaps? He was glad. He couldn't bear the thought that she might be unhappy or angry with him. Heaven alone knew what had thrown her into this difficult mood. When things had settled down again next week, she'd be right as rain.

But it wasn't Helen who knocked tentatively on the greenhouse door. It was Mrs Hadlow.

'I'm sorry to disturb you, vicar, when you're busy out here. I wondered if I might have a quiet word.'

'Well...' mumbled Clive, looking helplessly at the dirt on his hands, 'I'm sort of in the middle of things here.'

'This won't take long, vicar. I just wanted to have a little word with you about—about Mrs Linton—Helen.'

'Helen?' Clive's eyebrows shot up in surprise. 'Why? Is she alright?'

'Well, that was what I wanted to ask you. It's just that I wondered if she was sickening for something?'

'Sickening for something?' repeated Clive. 'Unwell, do you mean?'

'Is she? Not well?' Mrs Hadlow took a step inside the greenhouse, and lowered her voice. 'I was wondering if perhaps she's not as well as she should be, you see. And I thought I'd pop by to see if there's anything I can do to help.'

Clive sat down heavily on the old stool he kept for gardening, and stared at Mrs Hadlow.

'Not as well as she should be?' he said at last. 'What makes you think that?'

'Well, I—I just thought she didn't seem to be quite herself.'

Clive sighed. 'So, you've noticed it too. And I wonder who else in the village is thinking the same thing?' He looked down at his hands, and thought for a moment. 'This whole episode, this television thing, it's put a strain on us all. I know Helen has found it a bit of a worry. She's always been busy, but perhaps this recording is just the straw that broke the camel's back.'

'Oh, I don't know,' said Mrs Hadlow carefully, 'she seems to get on very well with the television team.'

'Helen gets on well with everyone.'

'Perhaps too well.'

'Is it possible to get on too well with people? That's always been Helen's strong point. Everyone gets on with her. That's why she's such a wonderful and caring person when it comes to sorting out problems in the parish. Everyone loves her. They always have.'

Mrs Hadlow said nothing.

'I rely on her entirely,' Clive went on. 'Entirely.'

'Perhaps,' Mrs Hadlow said at last, 'I should have a word with her, to see if there's anything on her mind, anything that I can help with.'

'Well, yes, of course,' agreed Clive, 'if she's feeling the strain at present, we must all rally round and help.'

'And you, vicar, how are you?'

Clive looked at her gratefully. 'How kind of you to ask. I'm fine, thank you. Fine. And of course, we're all looking forward to the recording this week. You're in the choir, I hear. Jolly good. That's excellent!'

There was an awkward gap in the conversation. At last, Mrs Hadlow turned, and started to leave the greenhouse. 'Well, goodbye then, vicar. I know you'll look after your own wife. You always do. But if there's anything at all I can do to help, dear, you have only to ask.'

'Mrs Hadlow, that's most kind. Thank you.'

Clive watched as Mrs Hadlow picked her slow way down the garden path. She knew his eyes were on her, and was glad that he could not read her thoughts. Poor trusting man, she was thinking. Why on earth didn't I tell him exactly what his wife is up to?

Clive was too engrossed with his gardening all that afternoon, to notice that Helen was not at home. At five o'clock, when the sky darkened, and it began to rain, he could no longer see clearly what he was doing in the greenhouse, and it was when he went inside a little later that he found her, in the failing light of the evening, sitting at the kitchen table, her coat still on.

'Oh, Helen. I'm glad you're back. I was wondering what you'd planned for tea?' Clive had his back to her, as he washed his hands in the sink. When she didn't reply, he turned to face her, as he dried off on the tea towel. 'Helen? Darling, are you alright?'

Helen looked at him then, an uncomfortable, searching look.

'No, I don't think I am alright,' she said at last, 'I don't think anything is alright at all.'

Clive came across to sit in the seat beside her, and placed his large damp hand on top of hers. 'Of course it is, my love. You're just a bit tired, that's all. Everything's fine.'

To his horror, her eyes filled with tears. 'Oh Clive,' she said, her voice hardly more than a whisper, 'Clive, you don't understand at all.'

'I do, I do, darling. Let's just get this wretched television business out the way, and then we can take a bit of a break. Go and see Jane, perhaps. Or I thought you might like a couple of days at Wisley. You'd like that, darling. You like gardens.'

She didn't answer.

'Helen, you'd like that, wouldn't you? A complete change of scenery. That's what we need.'

She turned her face towards him, tears coursing down her cheeks. Gently, she reached out to touch his face. 'I do love you, you know. You'll always remember that, won't you?'

'Heavens, I never doubt that for a moment.'

'Don't you? Shouldn't you? Is it fair to rely on people we love never changing—take it for granted that they'll always be the same?'

Her question surprised him. 'Yes, of course it is. We're married. We're Christians. We love each other. We always have. We always will.'

Her shoulders sagged, as she looked down at her hands. 'It's... it's just that I feel... so... lost.'

Suddenly, Clive was beside her, his arms cradling her head. 'No, you're not lost, my darling. You're just tired and overwrought. Don't you worry about anything. I'll take care of everything. Just leave everything to me.'

She lifted her tear-stained face up towards him.

'Now!' he said, with businesslike firmness. 'What are you going to cook for tea?'

❧

At Grove House, Pam and Ian were in rooms that were next door to each other on the first landing. Both of them were on the phone.

Ian was ringing Sarah. His heart fell when he heard her answerphone click into life, again!

He wondered whether or not to leave a message. He wasn't sure what to say. Where on earth was she? Why hadn't she rung back?

He hesitated after the long bleep, still undecided what to do. In the end, he made the decision to ring her later, and put the phone down.

Next door, the phone at Pam's home had been picked up by Bethan.

'Oh, Mum, something really *horrible* has happened!'

An accident? A break-in? Pam's mind raced with 'horrible' possibilities.

'It's Samantha! She's dumped me!'

Trying not to sound relieved, Pam's voice was full of sympathy. 'Oh no! Why?'

'She says that she's really fed up that I'm not going to go to ballet any more, and she says I can't be her friend now. So she *dumped* me!'

'But you've got lots of friends. If Samantha doesn't want to be your friend for a while, just play with other people that you like.'

'But I don't like anyone as much as I like Samantha.'

'But what about Debbie? And Eleanor? You like them a lot, don't you?'

'Yes, but they like Samantha more than they like me, and if she's not friends with me, they won't be my friends either.'

'Oh, I see,' said Pam. 'Tell you what, why don't you try and patch things up with Samantha? Ask her round for tea, so that she can play with your rabbit. I bet she'd come if you told her you'd let her hold the rabbit, and give him a lettuce leaf!'

'Yes!' There was triumph in Bethan's voice. 'That's it! She loves my rabbit. So I'm going to tell that Samantha that she can never *never* come round to my house and see my rabbit *ever* again!!'

Although the television rehearsal didn't begin in the church until seven o'clock, people started arriving well before half past six. Jack was one of the first to arrive, and he was hard at work rearranging chairs yet again, so that they wouldn't get in the way of the camera cables, when Margaret touched his arm. He stiffened, although in spite of himself, he was pleased to see her.

'Jack, have you a minute? Could you just give me a hand bringing the harp in? It's been in the vicarage overnight, but I've got it sort of wedged in the side door!'

'You wait here!' he said, and minutes later, he reappeared in the church, his arms round the bulky covered harp.

Margaret laughed as he staggered in behind the ungainly shape, and he found himself grinning too. 'Where do you want it? Up at the front there?'

'Well, we're not doing "O Sacred Head" this evening, because we're recording that at Dinton Church tomorrow. But Ian's written a special instrumental section for me in "For the Beauty of the Earth", so the harp won't be needed until we practise that one tonight.'

'Right!' said Jack, as he started to move off.

Margaret followed him into the vestry, and watched as he manoeuvred the harp into a corner.

'Thanks, Jack,' she smiled at him. 'How are you? I don't seem to have seen much of you for a few days.'

'No, well, it's a busy week for me.' To his acute discomfort, Jack felt colour rise up his neck. She was talking to him as if nothing at all had happened! She'd been the one to snub *him*! And now, she was chatting away as if nothing had happened!

'Mr Diggens!' The unmistakeable voice of Charles Waite summoned Jack from outside the vestry.

It was almost a relief to be called away. Jack looked back at Margaret. 'Duty calls, I'm afraid. Must go, sorry!'

Margaret's smile was disarming. 'Of course you must. But don't be a stranger, will you?'

'Mr Diggens!' Charles Waite was becoming impatient. 'You're needed here, immediately!'

Jack shrugged his shoulders, and began to turn away from Margaret, when suddenly, to his astonishment, she leant forward, and kissed his cheek. He looked at her in amazement, just as Charles marched into the vestry.

'Mr Diggens! It's chaos out here. Nobody knows where they should be sitting. As you've insisted on being charge of the seating arrangements, come here immediately, and sort it out!'

'Mr Waite,' said Jack, visibly controlling his temper. 'You are quite the rudest, and most impatient man, I have ever had the misfortune to meet!' And with that, he walked out of the vestry, leaving Margaret to hide her smile, and Charles fuming with indignation.

By seven o'clock, the church was full, except for one row of seats at the back. Everyone was buzzing with anticipation and excitement. Bunty Maddocks was probably the most excited of all. She sat among her flower ladies, pointing out her displays to anyone she felt may not have noticed them, basking in comments about how the television lights brought out the best in them, and how very appropriate and imaginative the designs were.

Because she was kept late at the hair salon, Iris was one of the last to arrive. She looked striking and splendid in a bright daffodil-yellow jacket, teamed with a black pleated skirt, and a silky patterned blouse. She waved and nodded to people she knew as she made her way down the aisle, and then stopped and burst out laughing, as she took in the view in front of her. The front block of the church was completely filled by members of the choir, with Sopranos on the right, and Altos on the left. And just about every lady member of the choir was wearing a red jacket—dozens of them, in a dozen different shades of red that hurt the eyes and jarred against each other! The only exception that Iris could see was Mrs Hadlow, who sat stoutly at the far end of the Altos, in her sensible grey jacket and blouse.

Mrs Hadlow's attention was elsewhere though. She'd been watching the door to see Helen arrive, late, her face pale and unsmiling. She looked as if she might have been crying. Mrs Hadlow noticed how her eyes darted immediately to the tall, grey-haired rigger that she had seen her with earlier. He was adjusting the base pedestal of a camera that stood in the aisle at the back of the church, and as if he was watching for her too, he looked up as she entered. Their gaze held for just a second, before Helen moved away, to take her place towards the front of the church.

Clive was already sitting in his usual seat at the end of the choir stalls, deep in conversation with Jan, the Producer of the programme. Jan looked at her watch, and went over to talk to Ian, who was adjusting his earpiece so that he could hear what Roger, who was directing from the scanner vehicle outside the church, wanted to say to him throughout the evening.

Suddenly, the Floor Manager, Ros, stepped in front of the aisle, and held up her hand in an authoritative way that brought silence to the church.

'Good evening, everybody!' she said. 'Thank you so much for turning out on such a wet and dreadful night, but welcome nevertheless to this rehearsal for "Village Praise". This evening, we will all have a chance to practise for tomorrow. You will have time to become familiar with the hymns, so that you're all absolutely sure of them by tomorrow evening—and we will be able to practise our camera moves and shots, to make sure that we can see and hear everything in the best possible way. Now, before we begin, I'd just like to point out that we do have some St John's Ambulance people here this evening, so if anyone feels at all unwell, please let us know. And just in case, for any unlikely reason, we have to evacuate the building, I'd like to go through the procedure for leaving, and where the exits are...'

'Right,' said Jan in Ian's ear, 'I'm going out to the scanner to keep an eye on the monitors. Good luck!'

'... and finally,' said Ros, 'I'd like to introduce you to our Musical Director for the programme, *Ian Spence*!'

This announcement was greeted with a round of applause, because Ian had already become a familiar and popular face in Sandford.

'Hello!' said Ian. 'We're going to start with the hymn right at the top of the programme, "Ride On, Ride On in Majesty". Now, the first verse of this hymn will be sung over shots of the Palm Sunday procession, led by a donkey, that we'll record walking from the green towards the church at six o'clock tomorrow evening. That will involve the children from the school, the choir and the clergy. Then, tomorrow night, here in the church, we'll see that same procession arriving at the door, and coming down the aisle to join us. Can you turn to Page 4 in your hymn books, and let's just try the first verse!'

Ian spent about ten minutes rehearsing the hymn, pointing out where breaths should be taken, and how the first words or the last consonants of particular lines were getting lost, as they were sung. At last, they were ready for a run-through.

Ros held up her hand to cue Ian to start, and silence fell over the church. At least, no one spoke—but you could hardly describe the church as silent.

'What on earth is that terrible din?' yelled Frank, the Sound Supervisor, from his cubicle in the scanner. All the people who were wearing headphones, the cameramen, the riggers, the sound men and the Floor Manager, looked around them, and eventually every pair of eyes stared up towards the roof.

'It's the roof,' said Ros into her walkie-talkie, 'the rain is hammering down on it, and making a devil of a noise!'

Gradually, the congregation began to look above them too, speaking in whispers to each other, and pointing towards the ceiling.

'Ros!' It was Frank speaking in her ear again. 'Is there anything at all we can do, or do we just have to go with it?'

'Well, it's probably only a shower. Can we just carry on and ignore the noise for the time being?'

Roger's voice broke in. 'We'll go with it. Places everyone! OK, Ian, the whole hymn, when you're ready!'

Ian managed to settle everyone down, and cued the organist, Colin, with Betty at his side, for the introduction. They sang right through the hymn, and immediately they'd finished, the sound of a telephone ringing filled the church. The congregation at first stared in amazement, and then in laughter as Ian stooped to pick up the receiver on the phone that was placed by his feet on the rostrum. It was the 'Songs of Praise' Music Adviser, Richard, ringing from the scanner. He was sitting in the sound booth, listening to the mix of musicians and voices, so that he could arrange for the balance to be just right.

'Well, that was terrible, to be frank,' said Richard's voice in Ian's ear. 'Mind you, I could hardly hear a thing, for all that thundering on the roof!'

'It seemed to me that we have rather a shrill soprano that stands out above all the others somewhere,' said Ian.

'I noticed that too. Don't know who it was, but it came from right down at the front, so Frank thinks.'

'I know exactly who it is,' replied Ian, as he glanced up in the direction of Mrs Hulme, the formidable leader of the St Mark's Church choir.' I'll just have to say something general to everyone, and hope she gets the message, he thought. Richard's voice continued in his earpiece. '... And the tenors are overpowering the basses. Can you ask them just to hold back on the volume a bit?'

'Right. We'll go again.'

And so, while Ian tactfully relayed this information to the congregation, the director, Roger's, voice was booming into the earpieces of all the technicians, talking to each individual cameraman, suggesting shots, trying to work out how they could get Camera 3 to avoid taking a picture of Camera 1 as it retreated down the aisle during verse two.

Rehearsing the next hymn was the high spot of the evening. The youngsters from Sandford Junior Mixed and Infants School, who had been allowed to stay up specially late for the occasion, were brought out to the front of the church to practise 'There Is a Green Hill Far Away'. There were twenty children in all, from the tiny four and a half-year-olds in the front row, to the seven-year-olds at the back, who barely seemed to have a front tooth between them. When people at the back of the church stood up, so they could see them better, Ros had to ask them, politely but firmly, to sit down, so that the cameras could get a clear view.

And then, when the little ones had been applauded, tucked into their coats, and taken home, Ros began to rearrange the front of the church to fit in the small ensemble of musicians that Ian had gathered together, with Margaret and her harp amongst them.

'Right!' Ian announced. 'We're going to sing "For the Beauty of the Earth" just as soon as we've got the musicians organized. Now, can you just mark up your books—I'd like ladies only for the first four lines of verse one, but everyone joins in for the last two lines. Verse two is in harmony—Altos, keep the volume up on that! Everyone in unison for verse three—and watch out for a musical interlude between verses three and four. Keep your eye on me, so you know when to start verse four, and remember, verse four is in unison up until the last two lines, which are in harmony.'

There was a rummaging of pencils and comparing of notes while everyone caught up with the instructions.

'Got that?' asked Ian. 'Let's give it a go, shall we?'

All went well, until verse three. It was then that Ian became aware that the music was going awry, and when he looked towards the cellist, he saw the musician had stopped playing. Then the trumpeter suddenly leapt to his feet, dragging his music stand several yards backwards. Margaret was still sitting at her harp, but she was reaching for her hankie from the sleeve of her dress.

Everything stopped in confusion. Ian looked up to see that in several places exactly above where the musicians were sitting, rainwater was seeping through the roof, and falling in steady streams on to heads, sheets of music, and electric cables.

'What the devil's going on?' demanded the irate voice of Roger in everyone's earpieces.

'Give us a minute, will you?' replied Ros. 'We're going to have to move the musicians before they go up in smoke. Frank, we might need help from some of your sound boys to sort the mikes and all the cabling out!'

While the technicians hurried to rearrange the musicians, general conversation broke out in the church. No one had imagined that a rehearsal night could be so entertaining! Bunty, who was making notes on everything so she could write a really detailed article on the making of the programme in next's month's Parish Magazine, stood up so that she could get a better view, just to make sure she didn't miss anything important.

And as everyone around her relaxed and gossiped, Helen allowed herself a small glance in Michael's direction. He was on the other side of the church, with his back towards her. Such a strong back, with wide shoulders. She looked at his tall frame, the back of his head. She remembered the feel of his hair, as she ran her fingers through it. And almost as if he knew she was looking at him, he slowly turned towards her. Their eyes met for just a moment, before she looked down, her face red and her palms wet with perspiration.

At last, the musicians were set into their new positions.

'This is no good for the cameras at all,' moaned Roger. 'Those musicians aren't lit in that position. Just busk it, will you, everyone? Right, we've lost enough time already. Let's go, as quick as you can!'

And the evening did go quickly after that—too quickly for the director, Roger, who would have liked to have had another run through all the hymns. 'Never mind,' he said philosophically to Jan, who was sitting beside him in the scanner, when they'd finished practising the last hymn, 'When I Survey the Wondrous Cross'. 'You know what they say about a bad rehearsal. I'll get it right by tomorrow evening!' He spoke into the mike that allowed him to talk directly into the earpieces of all the technical crew in the church. 'That's a wrap, everyone. Thanks very much. I'll stand a drink to anyone who happens to be in the bar of The Bull in twenty minutes' time! Jan's just coming out to say goodnight to the congregation, and remind them to get here in good time for a seven-thirty start tomorrow!'

By this time, Jan had arrived at the church door, and was making her way towards the front of the church.

'I just wanted to say a huge thank you to all you who've turned out this evening in such foul weather. I can't say that I can ever remember the rain having quite such a disastrous effect on a rehearsal, but let's just hope, and pray, that we'll be luckier with the sound effects tomorrow night. We plan to start recording at half past seven tomorrow, and we would be very glad if you could all be in your seats by seven-fifteen. And...' Jan paused for a moment, choosing her words carefully. 'I've been watching the pictures outside in the van, and you are all looking absolutely splendid. I might just suggest, though, that red is not a very good colour for television cameras. It tends to saturate the screen with colour, and can only be used with great care. I wonder if those of you who have worn red jackets tonight might like to consider wearing some other colour tomorrow? Something plain in a pastel shade, perhaps? That always seems to look best.'

Mrs Hulme turned beetroot-coloured with indignation, Rose Smith's jaw dropped, and Iris smothered a giggle behind her hankie.

'Safe journey home, everyone. Look forward to seeing you tomorrow evening! And don't forget, if you're involved in the Palm Sunday procession—meet on the green at six o'clock! Good night!'

It takes a long time to clear a full church. By the time all the goodbyes had been said, groups gathered, and belongings collected, the technical crew had practically finished bedding everything down for the night, and were thinking of heading for The Bull for a nightcap.

Margaret was pulling her coat on, watching Jack as he made last-minute arrangements for the following evening. He didn't notice her, until she'd finished putting her scarf around her shoulders, and came close to him, as she moved towards the door.

'Night!' she called, with a cheery wave. 'See you tomorrow, Jack!'

Jack stared after her. Women! He just couldn't fathom them!

Clive was deep in conversation with Norman Oates, the Methodist minister. Helen kept herself busy in the vestry as long as she could, so that she could be among the last to leave. Then she slipped out of the church, and walked alongside the television vans in the darkness.

Suddenly, Michael was there. She knew he would be.

'Tomorrow?' he whispered urgently.

'Where?'

'Down by the river, where we were this morning?'

'I don't know—it's so difficult...'

'Helen, please?'

'What time?'

'You say.'

Helen sifted through her muddled thoughts trying to think what the timetable for the next day was likely to be.

'At eleven o'clock, Clive has to be at the Crematorium, to take a service. He'll be leaving about ten-thirty. How about fifteen minutes after that?'

'Quarter to eleven. Right.'

Helen rubbed a weary hand across her forehead. 'I can't believe I'm doing this. This isn't me. I don't know what I'm doing.'

Michael reached for her hand in the darkness, and gently put it to his lips. 'Sshh. Don't! Don't try to think too much. Just feel. Just for now.'

She looked at him with tear-filled eyes.

'I must go.'

'Until tomorrow.'

Reluctantly, she drew away from him, and turned towards the vicarage.

Before Ian went to The Bull, he checked his mobile phone for messages. There was just one—the one he had been waiting for—a message from Sarah. It was short, and cryptic.

'We can't go on like this, you know, Ian. We just never seem to see each other. This needs sorting out, and that's just what I plan to do. Speak to you soon.'

And she was gone. Sorting out? Can't go on? Ian felt a chill drain through his body as, with shaking hands, he switched off the phone, and went to join the others in the bar.

1 April

The phone rang in Pam's room at seven o'clock, just before her alarm was about to go off anyway. It was her eleven-year-old son, Max.

'Mum, I feel sick.'

Pam was suddenly wide awake.

'What sort of sick?'

'Sick sick. My stomach hurts, and I feel really dizzy.'

'What's brought that on? Do you think you ate something that disagreed with you?'

'I don't know.'

'What does Dad say?'

'He says I don't look sick.'

'Oh, I see.'

'He says I've got to school—but I'll be sick, Mum, I know I will. Probably on the bus!'

'What time did you get to bed last night?'

'Oh, Mum, it's not that!'

'Were you in bed by half past eight?'

'Ben was here. He didn't go home till late.'

'And you had a late night.'

'Only a bit. But I couldn't get to sleep. I was awake *all* night, because I felt so sick.'

'And have you done your homework?'

'Yes. Most of it.'

'What happened to the rest?'

'I'll do it on the bus.'

'What have you got left to do?'

'Only some reading.'

'How much?'

'One chapter of my history book.'

Pam thought for a moment. It was difficult enough when she was at home, to decide whether the 'I'm too sick to go to school today' syndrome was genuine or not—it was nigh on impossible to make the right decision long-distance!

'Well, if Dad thinks you're well enough to go to school, I think so too...'

'Oh, Mum!'

'... *but* have a spoonful of Calpol before you go this morning, and if you do feel ill, take yourself over to the nurse at school, and she'll decide what's best.'

There was silence from Max's end of the phone.

'OK?' prompted Pam.

'No, it's not OK! None of the other Mums would send my friends to school, if they were feeling sick! Oh, never mind!' And Max slammed the phone down. Pam laid her head back on the pillow, and covered her face with her hands. How can I, a grown woman, have an argument with an eleven-year-old—and lose?!

Breakfast at the vicarage was a subdued affair. After a night of lying stiffly alongside Clive, when sleep was impossible, Helen felt drained and washed out. She didn't trust herself to speak to Clive. She had no idea what to say. Perhaps to say anything would betray the deceit she feared was written all over her.

Her distant silence did more than just puzzle Clive. It irritated him. Didn't she know that this was the most important week of all, for St Michael's, for him? How could she be so disloyal? To play prima donna, and let him down so badly, exactly when he needed her most! Couldn't she have waited a week, if she felt she had a point to make? Her behaviour was unforgivable. Out of character, unexpected—and totally unforgivable.

Clive ate his toast with his head buried into some church papers. Helen stood at the sink, sipping absent-mindedly at her cup of tea, until she was jolted from her thoughts by the shrill ringing of the phone.

It was Bunty. 'Helen! I'm so glad I caught you! What did you think about last night? It was great, wasn't it! I had no idea that so much work was involved. That Ian is nice, isn't he? I think he got us all to sound like a professional choir. And did you see Mrs Hulme's face when that producer lady mentioned about not wearing red jackets? I nearly died!'

Helen smiled to herself. When Bunty was in full flow like this, there was really no need to contribute anything to the conversation.

'I saw Iris this morning. She thought it was a great night too. And what about when the roof nearly caved in on us, with all that rain! Honestly, I've heard about singing to raise the roof, but that was ridiculous! We're going to have to do something about that roof, aren't we? What did Clive say?'

Helen glanced at Clive, who was showing no interest whatsoever in the phone call.

'Well, I've not had much chance to talk to him about it yet.'

'Of course not, you must both be so busy. And today will be even busier, I expect, with the recording this evening.'

'I don't know really. I'm not sure.'

'Do you need a hand with anything? Anything I can do to help? I'm around today, if you need me. If there's anything I can do at the church, anything the television people need, do call me. You will, won't you?'

'Bunty, you know me! Never slow to ask for help!'

'Actually, Helen, there is something special I want to ask—well, a suggestion really. I just thought it would be nice to organize a get-together on Sunday evening when the programme goes out, for all of us who've been closely involved in the production. You know, a bit of a "thank you"—perhaps at the vicarage? What do you think?'

Helen slumped against the work surface, her hand cradling her forehead, as she clung on to the receiver. In the moment's pause that followed, Bunty sensed reluctance, and moved in for the kill.

'Now look, you don't need to worry about a thing! I'll organize everything. I know how you hate having to cater for crowds, and I— well, I love it, so I won't mind at all. You could just leave the whole lot to me!'

'Who would come?' Helen found her voice at last.

'That's for you to decide, of course, you and Clive. But I have drawn up a provisional list of suggestions, just about twenty people or so. And Iris says she'll happily come and help with the arrangements. And Joan in the shop says that Don is doing a Cash and Carry run today, so he could get us in some wine.' Bunty drew breath, but only for a moment. 'Well, that is, of course, if Clive approves of wine. He might prefer tea and sandwiches.'

'Well...' started Helen.

'Oh, come on, Helen! It will be fun! And so much nicer if we can share the experience of watching the programme together.'

After another pause, Bunty played her trump card. 'And naturally, we'll start with a prayer, so it's a real act of fellowship—Clive would like that, wouldn't he?'

In spite of the weight of weariness that steamrollered over her, Helen knew when she was beaten.

'Tell you what, let me talk it over with Clive. It's rather a difficult— well, awkward, time for us at the moment. I'll see how he feels.'

'But you think it's a good idea.' Bunty was gently persistent.

'Yes, I do, and it's kind of you to offer. Leave it to me. I'll ring you in an hour or so.'

'It will take a bit of organizing, you know, so we need all the time we can get.'

'Yes, I understand.'

'And you'll ring me in an hour.'

'I will, I promise.'

'I'll stay by the phone.'

'Bye then, Bunty...'

'Oh, Helen, I nearly forgot. What did you think about the grass arrangements last night? Didn't you think they looked great under the lights? I had so many comments on them. What did Clive think? Did he say anything? Do you think he's forgiven us, for going against his wishes?'

Helen looked again towards Clive, still engrossed in his papers. He hadn't said another word about it all. His mind was on much too high a plane to consider trivial niceties like that, Helen thought wryly.

'He said that he thought they were brilliant, and that you had all managed to keep very much in the spirit of Lent, in a way that was inspiring and tasteful. You did a marvellous job, Bunty. You always do.'

Bunty's voice practically purred with relief. 'Thanks, Helen—and thank Clive too. Speak to you shortly then. Love to you both. Bye!'

Helen replaced the receiver, and turned to Clive. She had no inclination to sit beside him at the table, as she had every other morning of their married life. She stood by the sink, separate from him.

'Bunty's planning a "do" on Sunday night, as "Village Praise" goes out. She thinks it should be here. What do you think?'

Clive's eyes flicked towards her, and back to what he was reading. 'Alright.'

'There'll be about twenty people here, she says. She's drawn up a list. Do you want to see it?'

'Bunty is an admirable organizer. I am sure she will have everything under control. Whoever else may let me down, she's someone I know I can always rely on...'

Helen stiffened. 'Meaning what? That you can't rely on me?'

Clive said nothing, apparently absorbed in his paper.

'Is that what you mean, Clive? After all these years, when I have organized the world and his brother around you, protected you, cushioned you, unburdened you—after all that, *you* can't rely on *me*.'

'You're ill, Helen—you're not yourself. It seems to me that everything you do and say is designed to make this week, this difficult, important week, even more difficult for me. I will not allow your sulking to get me down. I have too much on my mind to let you do that.'

'Sulking? Is that how you see it? Sulking? Don't you ask yourself why? Aren't you interested enough to want to know? Don't you love me enough to find out?'

Clive stared at her, deliberately putting down the paper. 'OK, then, Helen, why? Why are you doing this?'

His directness took her by surprise. To her dismay, her eyes filled, as her head emptied of every coherent thought. Her shoulders slumped as she wept. Tears rolled down her face, but she made no attempt to wipe them away. She was empty, spent of feeling or action.

She was bleakly aware that Clive was at her side. She felt his arms go round her, the touch of his jacket, the smell of his hair, dear and familiar to her. She curled her head downwards, her hands clasped tightly in front of her, and he rocked her as if she were a child. He spoke, but she heard his words only as soothing, comforting sounds. She gave herself up to the security, the rightness of him. Clive, dear Clive. Her husband. Her friend. Her companion of so many years. This was where she belonged. This was where she should be.

It was some minutes before she realized that she was sitting at the table, Clive beside her, his huge hands covering hers.

'I think you should go and see the doctor, Helen. That should sort you out. Mrs Hadlow thinks you should go too.'

'Mrs Hadlow? What's she got to do with this?'

'She's very concerned about you, as we all are. She must have noticed you at some time yesterday, and wondered whether you were quite well.'

The colour drained from Helen's face.

'And she popped in to see me yesterday afternoon,' continued Clive, 'to ask if there was anything wrong, any way that she could help.'

'I bet she did,' murmured Helen.

'You will go then, darling. You will ring the doctor today, and make an appointment?'

'Today's such a busy day, what with everything that's going on...'

'Well, tomorrow then. Make an appointment for tomorrow.'

Helen nodded without enthusiasm. 'I'm not ill, Clive. I'm just a bit mixed up, that's all.'

'And the doctor will put you right, I'm sure of that. You probably just need a tonic. It will all be alright, Helen, you'll see.'

She was too tired to argue. She knew he was relieved that her tearful outburst was over. In spite of his job, he'd never found it easy to handle emotion. It was too messy and embarrassing.

He stood up suddenly. 'Well, I must get on. I thought I should say a few words at the start of the recording tonight—you know, something about the build-up to this programme, and what it means to us, that sort of thing. What do you think, darling? Would that be a good idea?'

He can't cope with me like this, thought Helen bleakly. He needs it to be business as usual, comfy old Helen behaving as she always has, and always must. But why must I be strong for him, if he collapses in a heap when I need help?

Her voice hardly shook as she replied. 'Fine. Yes, that sounds a good idea.'

'Well, I'll take myself off to the greenhouse then. You know how I always get my best ideas in there. That's where I'll be if you need me.'

It was as he reached the back door, that he turned again to her. 'Oh, by the way, have you booked up for us to visit Wisley? It's a good time to go, this—rather early for the rhododendrons, but good for the rest of the spring flowers. I'd really enjoy it.'

'I thought, Clive,' she said slowly, 'that seeing as I was a bit under the weather, you might have made the arrangements yourself, just this once.'

'Heavens, darling, you know how hopeless I am at that sort of thing. I'm not even sure where the chequebook is! Oh no, I'll leave it to you. I know my place!'

He turned the handle, and was almost through the door when he added, 'And if you're making a cup of coffee, I'd love one!' And he was gone, before he ever saw the gleam of raw anger in Helen's eyes.

Pam and the crew arrived at David Hughes' farmhouse shortly after nine, and by half past, with the sun half-heartedly peering through a break in the grey clouds, they were all heading for the far corner of one of David's fields. From here, they could look back across the farm, towards Dinton Hill, with its drab grey church standing solidly to one side, guarding its domain as it had for nine centuries.

David had been surprised, if not taken aback, when Kate had rung him to ask if he would consider being an interviewee on the programme. When she'd visited him before, it had been—he'd thought—to inspect his donkeys, Doreen and Denis, with a view to them taking a starring role in the Palm Sunday procession. But as they'd talked, his love of the land, his sense of guardianship for this little patch that his family had farmed for centuries, had moved Kate, and she knew it would move others too. David was essentially a shy man, probably because of the long hours he spent at work on his own. Having a friendly conversation over a cup of coffee in the kitchen was one thing. Gathering his thoughts for a television interview was quite another.

When Pam looked back on the interview later, she decided that it was her favourite piece in the whole programme from Sandford. There was something solid and down-to-earth about David that was thoughtful, reassuring and confident. He leant against the gate in his field, with the small church behind him, and talked about the generations of his family that had farmed there before him. He looked towards the small graveyard around Dinton Church, and remarked that almost half of the tombstones there carried his family name. 'Whenever things get me down, whenever I feel I've had enough—of the bureaucracy we farmers have to deal with nowadays, the paperwork, the limits on how much we're allowed to produce—when there's too much rain, or not enough; when the crops won't grow, or the lambs are down—I like to just sit in that graveyard. I think about myself as part of a long line of caretakers, picking a life out for ourselves from this land that is so full of God's gifts. And somehow just sitting there, in that holy place where people have worshipped for so long, a calmness comes over me. A peace. The peace of God. I know the peace of God.'

And as Pam listened, she envied him. He was a practical, matter-of-fact man with a simple, solid faith. No frills. No confusion. And no doubt that in every area of his life, throughout every minute of his day, God walked with him.

Iris had arrived at the hair salon before seven that morning. Her first customer followed her in at quarter past, and by half past ten, when Bunty popped in, she'd already done four cut-and-blow-dries, one perm, one rinse and three curler-set and brush-outs.

'Not now, Bunty. Whatever it is, not now. I'm up to my eyes!'

Bunty glanced along the row of customers, and recognized that every one of them had been in the church the night before. Today was the big day. Each lady in the salon had hopes that her face would fill the screen for a few delicious seconds, and be watched by everyone they knew, the length and breadth of the country!

'Right, will you give me a ring then? It's about Sunday.'

'Bunty, I can't think about Sunday. I can't even think about tomorrow. I'm never going to live through today, the rate I'm going!'

'OK, I get the message. But it's *on*! You know, the "do" at the vicarage as the programme goes out! Clive has agreed, and I'm Head of Catering! I just wanted your input, really. You're so imaginative, so full of ideas.'

'My salon's full of customers, I'm running twenty minutes late already, I've been dying to go to the loo for the past hour—and my feet are killing me! Goodbye, Bunty—probably for ever!'

Bunty grinned, and on her way out, stopped to speak in a low voice to the receptionist, Debbie.

'Make Iris a cup of coffee, Debbie, there's a dear! I think she needs one! And tell her I'll pop back later!'

In the end, because Helen didn't remind Clive about the funeral service he was booked to take that morning, he didn't leave until the Crematorium rang to ask where he was. He flew out of the house, shouting goodbye to Helen over his shoulder, his look plainly saying that he couldn't believe she hadn't made sure he was ready on time, the way she always did.

Helen heard the front door bang, as she sat at her dressing table, slowly brushing her hair. She had been sitting there for a long time, thoughtlessly, without real purpose, just brushing her hair.

When she heard the wheels of the car scrunch their way out of the drive, she stood up, smoothed down her skirt, pulled on her jacket, and left the house too.

She kept her head down as she walked, not wishing to meet or speak to anyone. She wanted to be invisible, to be nobody that mattered. She wanted to be alone—except for him, of course.

He was there before she was. As she turned off the path towards the river bank, she saw him, almost hidden in the hedgerow. He turned as she approached, and stood to greet her—and then, they were together, clinging wordlessly to each other.

Michael became aware that they could be visible from the road, and drew her down to sit on the bank beside him. The roughness of his woollen jacket scratched her face, as she leant against him.

'Are you alright?' he said at last.

'Now I'm here, with you, yes I am. But it's been awful at home. I can't believe how much has changed in just a few short hours. I've been a loyal, loving, totally devoted vicar's wife all these years, and I've never questioned it. I just don't recognize myself now. Look at me! Huddled up in the bushes with a man who is almost a stranger. Whatever am I doing?'

'Perhaps, for a change, you're not just being a vicar's wife. You're being yourself.'

'Selfish, disloyal, deceitful...'

'Questioning, feeling, free.' She looked up to find his eyes, his warm, knowing grey eyes, looking down at her.

'Free? How can I be free?'

'By leaving.'

'I can't do that.'

'You feel you can't, but perhaps you should. Perhaps not straight away. Perhaps not because of me—but because you need to have some time to yourself, to find out who you really are, when you stop thinking of yourself as nothing more than a "vicar's wife".'

'Michael, I've been a wife and mother for so many years. I can't remember being anything but a wife and mother. And I can only ever remember being at Clive's side, supporting him, loving him. That is me.'

'That's the you you've become. But is it enough? If it is, why are you here now?'

'Because I'm a foolish middle-aged woman, whose head has been turned by the equivalent of a travelling gypsy.'

He laughed then, a warm, delighted laugh, and as he hugged her close, she found herself smiling too.

'It's true though, isn't it? How long are you here? Five days? Six? Last week, you were somewhere else, just as you were the week before that. And next week? And the next? Do you leave a confused, infatuated woman behind in every place?'

He stopped smiling then, and took her face between his hands.

'No, I don't. And I won't be doing that here, either. Other people may think that of me, but you must know that's not true. What's happened between us, this—whatever it is—it's taken me as much by surprise as it has you.'

'But you'll move on. You'll forget. And I'll still be here, still the vicar's wife, pretending that life goes on just the same. But it isn't, not for me. It can never be the same again, because you've turned it upsidedown. I thought I was immune. I thought that emotion, attraction, physical longing was for the young, that I was too grown-up for it. And here I am, in your arms, wishing with all my heart that we could find somewhere dark and safe and secret, and...'

He kissed her then, with a tenderness that took her breath away, gentle and comforting at first, then drawing her closer, nearer, deeper into him.

At last, she drew back, and they sat looking at one another for a while, saying nothing.

'When do you leave?' she asked at last.

'On Saturday. I drive the scanner van—the last vehicle to leave, because the editing will be going on in there until the wee small hours on Friday night.'

'And then? Where do you go next?'

'Home. Back to London. With a bit of luck, unless the schedules have changed, I should have five days at home, before I head off to cover football next weekend.'

'Will we ever see each other again, Michael?'

'If you want to, yes, I'd like that very much.'

'Would you? Would you really? How? I mean, what would we be to each other? Friends? Lovers?'

'I am your friend, Helen. I will always be your friend. I feel we've started something that could develop beyond friendship—but who knows, when our friendship is so new?' He reached for her hand, staring down at it as he spoke. 'But what's more important, surely, is not what *we* are going to do, but what *you* decide. You're unhappy, I know, but why? Is that just because of me, or have you been unhappy for a long time?'

'I think,' said Helen carefully, 'that for some years, I've been living on a plateau, where I felt little real emotion, questioned nothing, and accepted that all I have is all there is. I can't remember feeling genuine enthusiasm for anything. Nothing touches me. I see and feel in black and white. But I've played the part, with the proficiency of years of practice. I've cleaned the church, organized the meetings, run the

Sunday school, sat on committees. I've listened as Clive tries out his sermons on me, I've brushed up confetti behind bride after bride. I've stepped in to smooth over parish squabbles, and sat up throughout countless nights providing tea and a shoulder to this bereaved husband, or that despairing wife. I've done it all with a smile pinned on my face, and a yawning, aching void inside me.'

'And Clive? Did he know?'

'I realize now, with a clarity that hits me between the eyes, that he doesn't know me at all. How could he, when I hardly know myself? He doesn't know me, and doesn't want to know—not if it undermines his security, or his freedom to get on with living as he always has, without responsibility, with me playing Mum to him, wiping his nose and tucking his vest in...'

'Do you love him?'

'Yes, yes, I do, very much.' She caught sight of Michael's expression. 'Does that surprise you? Yes, I love him. We've been through so many years together, some very happy times. And yes, I will always love him.'

'But...' Michael prompted gently.

'But,' Helen went, 'I'm not sure I want to live with him any more.'

'Then you must leave.'

'And do what? Go where? I have no money of my own. I haven't had a proper job for more than twenty years. I'm a vicar's wife. That's what I am.'

'You're practical, resourceful, and more capable than you know. You'd manage. You would.'

Helen sighed, her shoulders slumping with melancholy and defeat.

'I'd help you, you know.'

'I can't leave him for you. I can't leave one man for another. I couldn't.'

'But if you need me, if you want me—I will be there.'

Her eyes shone with tears. 'I know,' she whispered. 'I know.'

When the film crew's vehicle turned into the playground at Sandford School, the windows of the low brick building were lined with faces pressed against the panes, straining to see more. Minutes after the crew arrived, another vehicle manoeuvred itself carefully through the gate. David Hughes had attached a horsebox to the back of his Landrover, so that Denis and Doreen could arrive in style!

While Roger and the cameraman stayed out in the playground, setting up the gear, and discussing the shots, Pam and Jan, the Producer, headed into the school building.

'Do me a favour,' Jan whispered confidentially on the way in, 'I'll talk to Mrs Gearing, the headmistress, but would you talk to the children? I don't feel comfortable with anyone under the age of ten. I never know what to say to them!'

The youngsters had all been assembled in the main hall, as there were scarcely fifty children in the whole school, the hall was small, homely, and doubled in duty as a classroom for the most senior pupils.

Pam gathered, with a chuckle, that they were under strict instructions to behave themselves. She walked in to find them all sitting in rows, cross-legged, with backs ramrod straight, and arms folded.

'Hello!' she said, looking around at the serious, excited faces. 'I know some of you already, don't I?'

'Yes, Miss Rhodes!' they all chanted in unison.

'Well, I thought when I saw you all singing in the church last night, that your hymn was the best bit of the whole evening!'

'Yes, Miss Rhodes!'

'I'll tell you what, let's make a deal,' Pam smiled. 'You stop calling me Miss Rhodes, and start calling me Pam, and I'll take you out in a few minutes to meet the two special friends we've brought along with us—Denis and Doreen!'

That took a second or two to sink in before a grinning reply came from every scrubbed face in the hall. 'Yes, Pam!'

'Now, how many of you have met Denis and Doreen before?'

'I have, Miss! I have!' The lad whose hand shot up first looked about seven years old, with gappy front teeth, an over-generous helping of freckles, and a mop of straight ginger hair. 'I live next door to them—well, our field runs down to their field, and quite often, they end up in our field when they're not supposed to, and my Dad sends me down to put them back again.' The words tumbled out so fast, that he had to gasp for breath at the end.

'And, Miss!' he went on. 'Doreen is alright, but Denis has got a really bad temper. He bit me once!'

'Why? What did you do to him?'

'Nothing, Miss! I'd taken two carrots down, one for each of them. I gave Denis his, and he liked it so much, he bit me so that I dropped Doreen's, and he ate that too!'

'Oh, dear,' said Pam. 'He'd better not try anything like that today, if he wants to lead the Palm Sunday procession. That's why we've come along this afternoon, of course, so that we can put Denis and Doreen through their paces, and you can all decide which of them should get the starring role.'

'Miss! Miss!' The same young man's hand was high in the air. 'Who's going to be Jesus, Miss?'

'That's enough, Gregory. Put your hand down now.' Mrs Gearing, the headmistress, had arrived in the hall, with Jan at her side.

'But Miss, there's got to be a Jesus? Are you going to choose a Jesus, Miss?' Gregory was not going to be deflected from his need to know!

'We need someone to play the part who's familiar with donkeys, and who will be able to cope if it starts playing up,' replied Mrs Gearing calmly. 'The most obvious pupil is one who has, in the past at least, had a donkey of their own.'

Gregory looked around him, first with curiosity, then disbelief. 'Not Jessica, Miss! You can't mean Jessica!'

A tall dark girl, with a pudding basin haircut, sitting at the other side of the hall, suddenly turned scarlet and studied her shoes.

'Jessica has had the right sort of experience to play the part, and so she has been chosen, yes,' said Mrs Gearing.

Gregory's eyes were wide with indignation. 'But—Jessica's a *girl*, Miss!'

'That's right, Gregory, but that really doesn't matter at all...'

'But Jesus was a *boy*, Miss...'

'And Jessica will look just like a boy—I mean, man—when we've dressed her up in the right clothes, and sorted her out a bit.'

'But I know all about donkeys—and I'm much more of a man than *she* is! I'd make a better Jesus than a girl would, Miss, please!'

'Gregory!' Mrs Gearing's voice was firm. 'The decision is made. Please put your hand down. Right, everyone...'

'But does she know how to make it go, if it doesn't want to—does she?' Gregory's face was redder than ever. 'And what happens if it won't stop when she wants it to?'

Jessica looked uncomfortable, but said nothing.

'Gregory!' said Mrs Gearing sternly. 'We are not going to discuss this further. If you have any objection, you can stay inside, while all the rest of us go out to meet the donkeys!'

Just the threat of being left out completely was enough to silence Gregory, who looked suspiciously near to tears.

'Right!' continued the headmistress. 'Two things are going to happen now. All of you who have brought costumes to wear this afternoon—you can go and get your bags, and get dressed—*quietly*— at the back of the hall. And while you're doing that, Miss Rhodes will be taking a look at all the eggs you've been painting and decorating, which are on display at the front here. When you come back, we should be able to tell you who the winners are. Remember, there'll be one winner from the Infants, and one from the Juniors, and they'll each be getting an enormous Easter egg to take home!'

Choosing the two winners turned out to be a very difficult job. Pam looked at each egg in turn, every one of them a real egg that had been pricked, blown out, and then decorated to look like anything from a spaceship to Barbie Doll! Finally, she chose a comical, brightly coloured effort from a six-year-old, that reminded her faintly of Captain Pugwash—and for the Juniors, a beautifully painted scene of Calvary, complete with three crosses, that seemed totally appropriate for this time of year.

By the time the children had returned, dressed in their Mum's best nightshirts, with tea towels tied around their heads, they were anxious to know who'd won. A tiny, golden-haired youngster from the Infants came up to claim her Easter egg prize, followed by the winner from the Juniors, who was a studious-looking nine-year-old, with enormous glasses, and a lopsided grin of delight.

'Jesus' was the last to appear in the hall. Jessica had been completely transformed, with a long striped shirt that scraped the floor around her school shoes, and a fluffy black beard plastered on to her chin, that looked as if it had done the honours at many a school play in the past! She was plainly uncomfortable.

'Mrs Gearing,' she whispered urgently, 'I don't mind if I don't do this. I never liked our donkey much. It was my brother's really...'

'It's too late to change your mind now. Come on everyone, let's go out to the playground, and meet the donkeys. *Quietly* now!'

Doreen and Denis had been munching contentedly on the school playing field, when their peace was disturbed by the arrival of fifty strangely dressed youngsters, pointing at them, and shrieking with excitement.

'Hold it, everyone!' yelled Roger. 'Don't move until I tell you! Then all of you, gather round the donkeys and say hello to them! OK, Pam? Know what you're going to say?'

'Sort of,' replied Pam. 'Let's give it a go!'

Pam moved out in front of the group, so that, on cue, the children crossed behind her to where the donkeys, now deeply suspicious, were standing.

She began speaking to the camera. 'Every Palm Sunday, the locals here in Sandford organize a procession, to recall how Jesus rode into Jerusalem on a humble donkey, to be met by crowds cheering with enthusiasm to see him, and covering the road before him with palm leaves. But he knew that within days, the people of that same city would condemn him to death on the cross.

'Today, the children here at Sandford School are all dressed up to take part in their procession—but the starring role has not yet been cast. Which donkey will be chosen to do the honours? The choice has been whittled down to two—Doreen, who's a relative youngster, only six years old, and rather shy—or Denis, who's a showbusiness veteran, having played a similarly key role in the playschool nativity play last Christmas! Well, the children have to decide. Let's see what they think!'

Pam moved over with the microphone, to gather a few comments from the children, as they huddled around the donkeys. Denis, frankly, looked terrified, with the whites of his eyes staring out from beneath his rather untidy fringe. As his nose was patted, and his mane stroked, he began to move very slowly backwards, almost as if he was hoping that no one would notice. Doreen, on the other hand, took it all in her stride. In fact, she never stopped munching, and seemed hardly to notice that she was being prodded and hugged.

'Well?' Pam asked a group of three children nearest to her. 'What do you think?'

'Oh,' said the first, a girl with a mass of brown curls and a pronounced lisp, 'I like Denith beth. I think he'th got lovely eyeth.'

'No, Denis won last Christmas!' said the boy beside her. 'It's Doreen's turn this time!'

'I think Doreen should win, because she's a girl, and I like girls best...' said the last, a dark little girl, with a voice that could hardly be heard above the chatter of all the other children.

'Well,' said Pam to them all, 'do you think it would be a good idea to see how well each of them walks, when they have a passenger on their back? Where's Jesus? Can we have Jesus up here, to try out the donkeys for size?'

Jessica had apparently been making herself scarce at the back of the crowd. Reluctantly, she allowed herself to be pushed forward by her schoolfriends. She eyed Doreen with trepidation.

'Do you need a hand up?' Pam asked.

'I don't know...' mumbled Jessica, as she edged nearer.

'I'll do it, if she's scared!' Gregory's unmistakeable voice piped up from the middle of the crowd.

'Come here, Jessica,' urged Pam. 'Let me lift you on.'

Now Jessica was no lightweight, and the nightshirt she was wearing had seams that ran right down to her ankles. After a bit of rearranging of clothing, while the shirt was yanked up above her knees, she very gingerly allowed herself to be lowered on to Doreen's back.

'Right!' encouraged Pam. 'Giddyup then! Take her for a bit of a stroll...!'

Jessica dug her heels into the donkey's sides. Doreen didn't react.

Jessica kicked again. Doreen lowered her head to chew off another mouthful of the school playing field, and totally ignored them all.

'She's doing it wrong! I'll do it!' Gregory volunteered again.

'How about if someone leads her on the rein?' suggested Pam, who didn't know a thing about donkeys, except never to stand behind them!

'I'll do that, Miss! I know how to get her started!' And like a shot, Gregory emerged from the crowd, grabbed the rein, and started to tug, as he stroked Doreen's nose encouragingly.

Doreen was unimpressed. She glared at Gregory, lowered her head with unexpected suddenness—and Jesus was tipped unceremoniously over her ears!

Jessica burst into tears, as willing hands gathered round to pick her up. 'I knew I'd be no good at this!' she sobbed. 'I told Miss I didn't want to do it! My brother's donkey hated me too. Donkeys always hate me!'

'Well,' said Pam to the camera, trying desperately to save the situation, 'let's give Denis a try, shall we? Perhaps he'll have more sense of occasion. Now, we seem to have lost Jesus, just for the moment...'

She needn't have worried. Gregory was already strides ahead of her, reaching Denis, who had successfully managed to back several yards away from the crowd surrounding Doreen.

'I'll do it, Miss! I can do it!'

Denis' eyes flashed dangerously. 'Now, you behave yourself!' said Gregory sternly, pointing a finger directly at the donkey's nose. 'You know you want to be on telly, so you *behave*!'

Impressive, thought Pam, stifling a grin.

Like a practised cowboy, Gregory swung himself up onto the donkey's back. 'Right!' shouted Gregory, clicking his heels, 'Let's go!'

Denis didn't need telling twice. Go he did! Like lightning! He set off at a canter, and had hit gallop speed by the time he had reached the other side of the field. Pam, the camera crew, fifty children wearing tea towels, and a very agitated Mrs Gearing, were hotfoot behind him.

When Denis turned, and began to head in their direction, the following crowd screamed and scattered. And the last shot the cameraman managed to capture was of a small, red-haired, freckled-faced Gregory, whooping triumphantly as he sped past, looking every inch the Lone Ranger!

Jack was pulling the front door shut, when he heard the phone ring. He hesitated. He was just nipping over to The Bull for lunch—and to get away from the phone, which seemed to have rung non-stop all morning. Mostly, the calls were from people who were ringing up on the off chance that there may be some tickets left for the recording that evening. The answer to them was easy. There were no seats left at all, not for love, money nor sweet talk! As it was, Jack had the sneaking suspicion that there were more people sitting in the pews the previous night than there were tickets issued! Charles Waite seemed to have thought that too! Two of the calls that morning had been from him—the first one to complain about overcrowding; the second to demand that space must be made for a local JP and his wife, who'd made a last-minute decision that they would like to attend. Jack had enjoyed saying 'no' to Charles. He would have liked to have said a lot more than 'no', but he had held his tongue and his temper, and simply told Charles, politely and firmly, that no exceptions could be made.

Should he answer that phone? It was true that the calls had been incessant this morning, but before the build-up to this recording, Jack's phone had often remained silent for days! He turned the key in the door, and reached for the receiver.

'Oh!' said Margaret's voice. 'I was just about to give up. I thought I must have missed you!'

'Margaret...' Jack was at a loss for what to say. She was the last person he expected to hear, and the one he longed to hear from most.

'Your line has been so busy!' she continued. 'I've rung several times. My, you're a popular fella this morning!'

He found himself fiddling with the coiled telephone wire. Why on earth was he so nervous?

'Well, it's the seating for tonight. It's quite difficult to fit everybody in.'

'It all seemed to work well last night, didn't you think so?' He'd almost forgotten how warm she could be, the lilt of laughter that caught in her voice, and shone in her eyes. He remembered her eyes.

'It was a good atmosphere,' he agreed, 'although I think the television people were a bit frustrated, especially with the din on the roof from all that rain.'

'We should be alright tonight, though,' laughed Margaret, 'the weather forecast is for cold, *dry* weather—so wrap up warm!'

Why was she ringing? To talk about the weather?

Jack cleared his throat. 'Well, I ought to...'

'Of course, you must be busy. I just wanted to ask you if you plan to be at home tomorrow afternoon?'

Jack's mind raced. He hadn't really thought of anything beyond the TV recording for days on end!

'Yes, I should think so.'

'Good!' she said immediately. 'Then, would you mind if I pop in to see you? There's something I'd like to show you—if you don't mind, that is...'

'No, of course not. What is it?'

'Let me surprise you! It's all been quite a surprise to me, you see! I've been completely bowled over! I just can't believe what's happening to me, all so quickly too!'

Jack's mouth went dry. She was in love. It was so obvious. That man he'd seen her with. They were in love! Did he really want to hear all about it? See her face light up as she talked about her feelings for someone else? Wouldn't he rather keep his distance? Wouldn't it be better not to see her at all?

'That will be alright then,' he heard himself saying. 'What time?'

'About four? Teatime?'

'I'll have the kettle on.'

'Oh, Jack, I will look forward to that.'

How could she say that? How could she?

'Goodbye then, Margaret,' he said stiffly, and as he replaced the receiver, he wished he'd let the phone ring, and gone to The Bull without stopping.

❧

Ian put the finishing touches to his musical score for that evening, and thought lunch at The Bull would go down a treat. He pulled on his jacket, and went to put the mobile phone in his pocket, when he decided to try Sarah one more time.

It was no surprise to hear her answerphone click into action again. The answerphone was all he ever seemed to get these days! Where on earth was she? Why was she being so elusive? Was she trying to tell him something? That it was over? That she'd changed her mind? Met someone else?

That thought brought a kick of pain to the pit of his stomach. Suddenly, the idea of lunch was not so appealing. With his jacket still on, he lay down on the bed, grabbed a pillow, and curled his body round it in a small tight ball.

'Sarah,' he whispered, 'don't do this. Please! Don't do this!'

Clive didn't return to the vicarage after his service at the Crematorium. Helen had no idea where he was, but she was glad of his absence. It was hard to believe the turnaround in her feelings in just a few short days. For years and years, her loyalty, love and commitment to Clive had been without question. She was his wife. That was all there was to it. And now? Now, she realized that she'd been lonely within her marriage for a very long time, a loneliness she'd never allowed herself to recognize—until Michael. A stranger had seen what she was blind to—the deep well of sadness, frustration and resentment that had been festering away within her.

Was he right that she should leave? How could she? Her life was here, her life as Clive's partner, a vicar's wife. Clive would never understand, of course he wouldn't. He would only see her wish for time to herself, for space to sort out her muddled thoughts and feelings, as a simple desire to desert him. She knew he would be lost without her, and if she went, even for a few days, there would be no question in Clive's mind that his fear of coping alone would be her fault. He couldn't bear for her to be less than she had always been—his rock, his champion. She was like a trampoline to him. Because she was there, he could soar higher and higher, knowing that whatever happened, he would be safe.

Clive. Dear, dear Clive. How could she even think of leaving him? He'd be lost on his own. She'd promised before God, in church, that she would always be there for him. In her whole life, she'd never made a promise that she didn't mean to keep. That promise, made so solemnly, was the most precious and important one of all. And yet, could she ever have imagined that Clive's needs, his insecurities, the demands of his job, would completely overshadow their lives, in the way they do now? Wasn't marriage intended to be about give and take on *both* sides? Where was Clive's understanding and support for her? When she called out to him, hoping that he would draw her in with love and strength enough for them both, she saw only panic in his eyes. His strength relied on her. If she collapsed, he would prefer to ignore the problem, in the hope that she would pull herself together, so that the problem would go away.

Words kept echoing round her head. There'd been a wedding service at the church some months before, when the couple had requested a reading by Kahlil Gibran. Because it was not one of the usual readings for a wedding, the Prophet's thoughts on marriage had stayed with her.

Let there be spaces in your togetherness, let each one of you be alone,
Even as the strings of a lute are alone, though they quiver with the same
music.

Alone. Of course she was alone, as everyone truly is. Married, but separate and alone.

Helen sat down heavily on the stairs. And Michael? What did she really feel about him? Was this love? How could it be, when they'd only known each other for a few short days? And if it wasn't love, what was it? Lust? She shuddered at the thought. Lust, at her age? How ridiculous! How juvenile! How utterly overpowering and potent it was! How wonderful that her feelings could soar to such heights, however immature those feelings might be!

Michael wasn't married. Why not? Not, she was sure, because of lack of opportunity. He was too special, too sensitive and caring to have escaped the attention of women in the past. So, why wasn't he married? Because he was a rolling stone, constantly on the road, not able to commit himself in a practical sense, let alone emotionally. Perhaps he was playing with her then? Toying with the insecurities of a pathetic, forty-something woman, who'd been bowled over by his attention. Was that all it was?

And then she remembered his eyes, the sincerity and depth she'd seen there. She remembered his promise that if she needed him, he would be there for her. Did she want that? Did she want him? Or did she want to be herself, on her own, to get her feelings straight, to come to terms with the new person she was emerging to be? Would she leave? Could she stay? Was there really any alternative?

Helen buried her head in her hands, her whole being shaking with racking, despairing sobs.

❧

By the time the Egg Rolling Race had been set up on Dinton Hill, the sky had grown heavy and grey. Some of the Mums waiting at the foot of the hill for the youngsters from Sandford School remarked that a fall of snow wouldn't surprise them, especially as there was an ice-cold nip in the air. Their offspring didn't seem to notice the cold, though. They raced to the top of the hill, clutching the second version of their painted eggs. Their *best* eggs, of course, were the ones entered for the School Competition that Pam had judged that morning, covered in sequins, material and carefully applied appendages. *These* eggs were designed for speed, not beauty. They were hard-boiled, to give them weight, and covered with go-faster stripes in shiny paint designed to slide over the grass, and confound their rivals.

Headmistress, Mrs Gearing, wore the expression of a woman who'd had a long day. The events of the morning—the competition, the dressing-up, the recording, not to mention Denis' stampede, and Gregory's sudden elevation to star status amongst his schoolmates, had taken its toll on her. Her head ached, she had a ladder in her tights, and she found herself dreaming of retirement, soon, very soon.

'Right! Here's the plan!' Roger had his arm draped round Pam's shoulders, as they walked towards the point where the crew were set up, about one-third of the way up the hill. 'I'll give the first cue to the children, to get the race under way. They'll set off, rolling their eggs down the hill. The camera will capture all that from here, although we'll go in for closer cutaway shots as soon as we can. Then, keep your eye on me, and I'll give a second cue. That will be for you to walk into shot, and start talking, with the race going on behind you. It should work. OK! Places, everyone! Are you ready?' His voice bellowed up the hill, to where Mrs Gearing was having a spot of trouble getting all the enthusiastic, determined young competitors into the semblance of a starting line.

'Let me know when you're recording, Keith,' Roger said over his shoulder to the cameraman. 'Running!' confirmed Keith.

Roger's voice echoed up the hill again. 'OK, Mrs Gearing, ready when you are!'

Mrs Gearing puckered up, to give a mighty blast on her whistle. They were off! At least, some of them were! The problem seemed to be the length of the grass, the dampness underfoot from the downpour of rain the night before, and the nooks and crannies that lay hidden across the hill. They all conspired to make it almost impossible to get the eggs rolling, even with the help of gravity! The children had been told that on no account were they to do anything other than *roll* their eggs—no throwing, kicking, interfering with anyone else's egg, or arguing with the judge, by order of Mrs Gearing! She was too close to them to think about disobeying, but it was clear that frustration soon set in when the most cut-throat of competitors found that their eggs were more inclined to roll *round* the hill, than *down* it.

The camera stayed on the scene for several minutes, as the event fell apart. Roger spent those minutes with his hand in the air, waiting for the right moment to cue Pam to walk into shot and start talking. That moment never came—and it was at the point when one bruiser of an eight-year-old picked up the egg of his arch rival, and stamped on it, that Mrs Gearing's whistle pierced the air again.

'Hold it! Hold it!' shouted Roger, and Pam and the crew looked on in amusement as he began to run up the hill towards the racers. 'I've never seem him move so fast!' chuckled Keith.

'Good job I've brought the hip flask—for medicinal purposes, you understand!' giggled Sue, the Production Assistant.

There followed several minutes of heated discussion at the top of the hill, followed by orders snapped out to the children by Mrs Gearing, and some very extravagant arm signals from Roger to the crew waiting below. The gaggle of children slowly began to move across the hill, above the crew.

Keith was leaning lazily on his camera, watching Roger's arm antics with quiet amusement. 'I think he wants us to move round, and try again,' he said at last.

'You don't suppose he thinks the hill is any less bumpy over there, do you?' asked Sue doubtfully.

'Probably, but he's wrong!' said Keith, as he picked up the camera and tripod. 'And if the sun comes out, it will be squinting right down my lens too!'

'Chance would be a fine thing,' muttered Bob, the sound recordist, as he glanced up towards the sky, which was getting darker by the minute.

As they reached the obvious spot to pitch the camera, Roger was hurtling down the hill towards them. He was breathless and red-faced by the time he reached them.

'Let's give it another go. I'll stay up the top with the kids, to make sure they get it right this time. Keith, can you give me a signal to let me know when you're recording, then my cue will be for the children. Can you anticipate your own cue, Pam, when you think the first eggs and youngsters are about to appear in shot behind you. Right? Right!'

And he was off again, slower this time, dragging his rather rotund frame up to the top of the hill, where fifty young competitors were eager to restart the race.

'I'm running,' said Keith quietly. 'Give him a sign, will you, Bob? A polite one?'

Bob waved his arm in the air, and Mrs Gearing's whistle went into action. With squeals of delight, the youngsters tried again to get their eggs to roll down the hill. It was a slow business. It wasn't long before the more ambitious racers decided that rolling was out, and throwing worked better, tiny throws at first, that hopefully Mrs Gearing wouldn't notice, turning into overarmers a professional cricket team would be proud of, as the competition hotted up. By the time Pam stepped into the shot, to deliver her piece to camera explaining that on this green hill, so reminiscent of the hill at Calvary, the children were rolling eggs to remind them how the huge stone was rolled away from Christ's tomb—it was a free-for-all! The bigger boys were alternately kicking their own eggs, and each other's shins—and the girl who reached the line first had simply picked up her egg, shut her eyes tight, and belted for the finishing line for all she was worth!

Mrs Gearing was waddling down the hill behind them, yelling to any of them that would listen, that cheats would be disqualified. Roger was standing at the top of the hill, with his hands on his hips, his mouth open but speechless. And as Pam finished her piece to camera, the small girl with brown curls that she had spoken to earlier about the donkeys, came up and tugged at her sleeve.

'Mith! Mith!' she said mournfully, her huge blue eyes swimming with tears. She held out a totally flattened, scarlet and green egg, its hard-boiled yolk squeezing through the shattered shell. 'Juth look at thith! It was Thimon! He thmashed it! And I'm going to go and thmash him! I am!'

'He's bigger than you,' said Pam, rummaging in her coat pocket. 'How about a fruit gum instead?' It took no more than a moment's thought before the little girl helped herself to a sweet, linked her hand into Pam's, and together they headed down towards the finishing line.

Ever since the television crew had recorded her singing the morning before, Anna had been unable to settle. The sheer elation of the experience—the sound, the pictures she'd seen, the praise, especially from Ian—she was beside herself with excitement about it all. She was not a girl who, nowadays, was known for her enthusiasm for anything, but on this occasion, she couldn't stop talking about all that had happened to her, and all that she hoped would happen once her performance was seen throughout the country. This could be it! Who knows who would see her, and like her, and book her for other things! She might need to get a manager! She'd certainly have to be careful that she wasn't exploited, that she was selective about what offer to take first.

She rang her friend, Karen, and spent an hour on the phone telling her all about it. Then she rang her cousin in Newcastle, and was half an hour into that conversation before her Mum came and told her off about the phone bill. She called in at Iris's hair salon, for a chat with Debbie, the receptionist—and she'd stayed in there for ages because every customer that day was someone who had been at the rehearsal the night before, and no one wanted to talk about anything except that night's recording! When, finally, she knocked on Betty Waite's door, and got no reply, she decided that Betty was probably over sorting out music in the church, and perhaps she should nip over there to see her. It would be good to see the television crew again. They all felt like friends to her now. And perhaps Matthew would be there too? She'd like to see him. Funny really, considering what a twerp she'd always thought he was! Well, it was so embarrassing, because *everyone* knew what a crush he had on her! But he was improving. Yesterday, she had been so glad to have his company, when the television recording had seemed strange and confusing, and she'd been really nervous. Yes, he was definitely growing on her...

The door of the church was open, as she slipped silently inside. The place was alive with bustling activity. Bunty and Grace were up at the altar, refreshing the grass displays, and pummelling them into perfect formation. The camera crew were all huddled together in the front couple of pews, each with scripts open in front of them. There was obvious a detailed discussion going on about possibilities and problems of the shots they'd tried the night before, and she shrank into the shadows so that she could watch them without being noticed.

Matthew was there. He was sitting on the edge of the group, listening intently. He looked older. Perhaps because she was used to seeing him in school uniform, he seemed relaxed and more mature in his jeans and big, warm, cableknit jersey. Some people might have thought he was goodlooking. She didn't, of course, but she could see his attraction, to other people, if not to her. He was tallish, and his hair just kind of fell into place. He didn't have spots, not that she'd ever been near enough to look closely—and he could be quite a laugh, when he put his mind to it. I suppose he's not bad, she thought to herself, if you like that sort of thing. Not that she did, not at all.

She sat there for about ten minutes before Matthew spotted her. The meeting was over, with the group breaking up into twos and threes as they set about their separate tasks. Matthew was walking behind Frank, the Sound Supervisor who had been so kind to her the day before.

'Hello Anna!' called Frank. 'Have you recovered from being frozen to the marrow at the ruins yesterday?'

'Oh, I was fine! I didn't mind a bit!'

Frank moved over to where she was sitting. 'You know we're recording the first verse of your solo again, here in the church tonight.

I gather we'll be doing that about halfway through the evening, but if you just sit in with the choir, as usual, we'll come and get you, to sort out mikes just before we record, OK?'

'Yep, fine!' replied Anna, hoping she sounded cool, able to take everything in her stride.

'We'll look after you, Anna!' said Matthew, when he finally spoke.

'What do you mean? What are you doing this evening? Have you got a proper job to do?' she asked.

'Well,' was the nonchalent reply, 'the riggers say I could learn a lot from watching them cable-bashing—you know, keeping the camera cables out of shot—and then, Frank says I can trail the sound recordists, to give them a hand with the mikes, if they need it.'

'Sounds great!' Anna smiled. 'It is!' he grinned back, and the two of them stood there, their faces aglow like children, savouring the specialness of the experiences each of them was enjoying.

'Got to go,' said Matthew at last, 'I said I'd do a sweet run to your Dad's shop before it closes.'

'I'll walk back with you then.'

'Don't worry about that. I've got to sort out the list of what everyone wants yet, and that can take ages. I'll see you tonight then!'

And he was gone, leaving Anna to think that she had never experienced Matthew being offhand towards her before. That was a new one on her. And she didn't like it one little bit!

Bearing in mind how icily cold it was by six o'clock that evening, it was a surprise that anyone turned up on the village green, for the Palm Sunday procession into the church. Because the cameras had to be cabled up and positioned inside the church for the main recording at half past seven, it had been decided that the exterior part of the procession should be recorded earlier on, to give the television people time to reset.

Denis was there, of course, but he was not happy. Being an elderly donkey, Denis liked his routine. He hated being the centre of attention. He hated very small people who kept patting him, and wanting to climb on his back. He hated the fact that it was dark, and he wasn't tucked up in his shed, snoozing quietly. No, Denis was definitely not a happy donkey!

Most of all, he had his suspicions about the small, red-haired person who'd climbed on his back without as much as a 'by your leave' earlier that morning, and galloped away with him! That same small person was at his side again, dressed in a most peculiar outfit that looked like a frock, with some funny-looking curtains draped around his head. Most ridiculous of all was the fluffy black growth of hair that had been stuck on the small person's chin, looking so out of place against the carrot-coloured fringe that practically covered his eyes.

There was a mass of people crowding round the two of them, some holding huge branches and leaves. If they thought a sensible donkey like him was going anywhere near those things, they had another think coming!

Suddenly, Denis realized in amazement that Carrot-Hair was in front of him, pointing a grubby finger at his nose, and looking directly into his eyes. The small person was talking very urgently and deliberately at him, so Denis concentrated on looking suitably bored, just to let him know who was boss! Suddenly, though, his nostrils flared. He picked up a *very* interesting smell. Peppermint! His favourite smell of all smells!

He peered at Carrot-Hair, and at the round, white mint being dangled in front of his eyes. Denis went to snatch it—but it disappeared! Quick as a flash, Carrot-Hair had hidden it—and Denis got the message, loud and clear. If you want the mints, play the game!

He glared indignantly at Carrot-Hair, and snorted with resignation. With a gleam of triumph in his eyes, the small person swung himself easily up on to Denis' back, and propelled the reluctant donkey forward. Suddenly, the crowd around them started singing, and waving the branches and leaves in their direction. Denis sighed heavily. He'd need a lot of mints to make up for this, and with nothing but that in mind, he put his head down, and plodded on.

By ten past seven that evening, there was standing room only in St Michael's Church. All the locals of Sandford were there in the

Very Best of their Sunday Best. Not a hair was out of place, shoes were shiny, shirt collars stiff with newness, and the ladies had excelled themselves in their smart, plain jackets in every possible pastel hue.

'Who'd have thought!' said Ivy to her friend, Mrs Hadlow, in a stage whisper that carried across two rows of pews, 'that "Songs of Praise" would ever come to a small place like Sandford!'

'Oh, I don't know, dear,' replied Mrs Hadlow, as she straightened her jacket for the umpteenth time, 'there's a lot of talent here, you know. Some very good voices, for a start!'

'Um, I suppose you're right,' mused Ivy, as she peered around her to see who'd arrived.

At that moment, Bunty came out of the vestry, deep in conversation with Betty Waite. 'He's driving me round the bend!' wailed Betty, in the way you only can to a very trusted friend. 'He's beside himself that Jack Diggens has organized this whole event so well. Charles is vitriolic about the poor man, and can't wait for him to make the slightest little mistake, so that he can pounce on him!'

'But Jack is such a nice chap,' said Bunty. 'I never really knew him before, because he kept himself very much to himself—but he's worked so hard for this, he really has!'

'And he's had nothing but backstabbing from Charles. Honestly, I'm ashamed of my own husband. He's such a dog in a manger. He did everything he could to prevent this programme being made—and then, when he changed his mind, he thought he could just waltz in and take over, as usual.' Betty's face was flushed with anger.

'He's met his match in Jack though, obviously!' chuckled Bunty.

'I sincerely hope so!' said Betty. 'It would do him the world of good to be taken down a peg or two. It would be the making of him!'

Michael spotted Helen as she arrived in the porch, pushing a neighbour in a wheelchair. He left the camera cabling he was sorting out, and went over to give her a hand. Helen kept her eyes on the wheels of the chair, careful not to look at him.

'Thanks,' she mumbled, 'I think we can manage now.'

'You're alright then?'

'Yes, I'm fine, we're fine,' she said, but the glassiness of her eyes told a different story.

His hand brushed hers on the handle of the wheelchair. 'See you later then.'

'Perhaps. I hope so...'

Their eyes met—and then she was gone, disappearing up the aisle as she pushed the cumbersome chair before her.

'Ladies and gentlemen!' The voice of Ros Denham, the Floor Manager, rang out over the chatter. 'Would you mind taking your seats please, so that we can see if there are spaces that need filling. And if there are any members of the St John's Ambulance Brigade here, please could they make themselves known to me? Thank you!'

A buzz of excitement ricocheted around the building, as people hurried to secure their place, just in case anyone else was quicker than them, and pinched it! Last to arrive, looking harassed and unprepared, quite unlike her usual self, was Iris, who'd rushed hotfoot from the salon, after the busiest day she'd ever had in the whole of her hairdressing career. She slid into the seat saved for her by her friend, Grace, sighed heavily—and slipped her shoes off.

Jan Harding, the Producer lady that most of them had seen often in the village, was the first to speak. She explained that before they recorded each hymn, they would rehearse it, partly so that everyone singing was absolutely sure of the tune, the words and the pitfalls, but mostly because the BBC people were anxious to get the pictures right!

'I hope you'll be patient with us, because sometimes we'll have to ask you to sing a verse, or even a complete hymn, over again, just so that we can get the range of shots we need. You can see how big the cameras are, and the last thing we want is let them appear in any of the pictures we record. That means that if we want to get a great big view of everyone in the church singing together, we have to hide the cameras in the corners, and behind pillars, wherever we can! That takes a bit of time to organize, and so we may ask you to repeat some bits of your singing, so that we can get the shots we need.

'One thing I would ask you to remember is that this programme will be watched by as many as six million people in their homes all over the country, and for many of them, "Songs of Praise" is an important act of worship, often the only Christian fellowship they have all week. Now, if we want the lovely warm, friendly atmosphere that we can all feel here tonight, to come across to them wherever they are, then you have to show it on your faces! Welcome them in! Think about the words you're singing, keep your heads up, and sparkle for us! For them! OK?' There were enthusiastic nods of agreement all round.

'Fine! Well, as this is an act of worship, I think we should start by asking the Reverend Clive Linton to lead us in prayer...'

'Miss! Miss!' A small girl in the front row, with long red plaits, and the words 'Sandford Junior Mixed Infants' emblazoned across her sweatshirt, shot up her hand with great urgency. 'I need a wee, Miss!'

Mrs Gearing was at her side within seconds, clucking apologetically as she steered the youngster in the direction of the vestry, followed by two giggling boys who decided they couldn't wait either!

Clive, looking splendid in his clerical robes, moved up to the pulpit.

'Oh, heck!' the director, Roger, grumbled into the earpieces of all the television crew, 'I told him we wanted a quick prayer. It looks to me as if he's puckering up for a sermon!'

Clive settled himself comfortably in the pulpit, and laid out in front of him several sheets of notes. He looked up at his church, overwhelmed with the satisfaction of knowing that it was full to bursting point, and that their worship that evening in St Michael's would make its mark on the lives of millions of people around the country. This was why he had wanted to become a minister. This was his moment!

'I can't tell you how wonderful it is to see you all here tonight!' he began. 'And I thought I'd take this opportunity to explain to you something of the events that have led up to this very special evening...'

'Stop him, Ros!' Roger hissed urgently in the Floor Manager's ear. 'We haven't got time for an explanation, just a prayer! Tell him—*just a prayer!*'

With an air of authority that would have befitted a Sergeant Major, Ros marched across the front of the church, sharply tugged at Clive's robes, and stopped him as he was just getting into full flow. He bent down so that she could whisper in his ear. 'That was wonderful, Vicar!

Thank you so much! Do you think you could go straight on to the prayer now? We'd be very grateful.'

'Oh, but I've not quite finished...'

'What you said was terrific! Just the prayer next, so that we can get going!'

To be fair, Clive hid his disappointment well. No one, except Helen, would have guessed that he'd been preparing that speech practically all day. He pinned a smile on his face. 'Let us pray!' he said. 'Lord, we ask for your blessing on all we do here in St Michael's this evening. Guide us, and be with us, as we sing to your glory, that our worship may inspire and include all the other people who will be watching, and worshipping with us, in their own homes. We ask this in the name of your Son, Jesus Christ our Lord.'

'Amen!' came the response.

Ros was waiting at the bottom of the pulpit, to usher Clive back to his seat, so that Ian, the Musical Director, could take over.

'How are you all then?' Ian beamed at the now familiar faces. 'Have you got any voice left after last night?'

A burble of answers from the congregation brought smiles all round. 'Right!' continued Ian. 'We're going to start with the first hymn in the programme, "Ride On, Ride On in Majesty". Now, during the first verse of this, we'll be showing the pictures we recorded earlier this evening, of the Palm Sunday procession making its way towards the church. That means that during the second verse, we'll see the procession apparently just arriving at the door of the church, and making its way down the aisle to the front here. Anyone who should be in that procession—in other words, anyone who was in the procession earlier this evening—can they make their way to the back of the church now please?'

The children in the front two rows were the first to reach the church porch, pulling on their headdresses as they went. Gregory was already dressed up and in position just outside the church, clutching tightly at Denis the Donkey's rein. Denis was not amused. He was tired. He was hungry, and he'd seen precious little of the promised peppermints. He was not in the mood to do any favours, as he eyed with suspicion the crowd of people who were making their way to join him and Carrot-Hair outside the church.

Ros, the Floor Manager, was in charge, organizing everyone into more or less the order they'd walked in previously.

'OK, Gregory! Up you go!' she said. Giving Denis one last mouthwatering look at the mint he held in his hand, Gregory swung his leg over Denis' back, and waited for the order to move.

Inside the church, as the videotape machines whirred in the scanner, the congregation had reached the end of the first verse. Standing in the porch, Ros brought her arm down to give the procession the cue to start, and Gregory dug his heels deliberately into Denis' flank. More out of surprise than purpose, Denis shot forward, and got himself just inside the door of the church, when he stopped dead.

He was faced with bright lights, hundreds of people, loud singing and an orchestra. His ears went back, his nostrils flared, his hooves dug into the paving stones—and he refused to go a step further.

'Cut! Cut!' screeched Roger's voice over talkback.

'Hold on, Roger—problem with the donkey—give us a second!' said Ros.

'Gregory! Gregory Williams! What did you do to make him stop? You *promised* you knew how to ride a donkey! You promised!' Mrs Gearing's voice hit an hysterical high.

'OK, everyone,' said Ian calmly to the congregation, who were straining their necks to see what was, or rather, *wasn't* happening. 'We need to practise the singing of that verse again anyway. Now, don't forget, you must concentrate on pronouncing all the consonants clearly. We want to make sure that everyone at home can understand what you're saying...'

Meanwhile, Gregory had slipped off Denis' back, and gone round to look him straight in the eye. Denis glared back meanly. To his surprise, Gregory didn't point a finger at him, as he'd done before. Instead, three smooth round mints were slipped into the donkey's grateful mouth, as the boy placed sympathetic, small arms around his neck.

Gregory turned his head away for just a moment. 'Psst!' he hissed to another boy standing nearby. 'Psst! Sam! Over here!'

The two boys whispered together in a conspirators' huddle. A small white bag was handed over, which Sam stuffed into his pocket.

Minutes later, when Ros gave the cue that they were going to try recording again, it was hard to believe the transformation. The procession was dignified and colourful, as it made its solemn way down the aisle to the front of the church, with the children at the front, and the clergy and choir bringing up the rear. Gregory was splendid as Jesus. Everyone said so, even Mrs Gearing. Denis the Donkey excelled himself, as he marched smartly through the church with what seemed like a smile on his face.

But it wasn't a smile. It was a grimace. Walking three paces in front of him was Sam, his hands apparently clasped behind his back in respectful reverence. What no one, not even the cameras, could see, were the Mint Imperials he held out between his fingers, which he carefully wafted in range of Denis' nose—but out of reach of his teeth!

Two hours later, having sung, sung and sung again, the congregation was beginning to flag. They were grateful for the chance to sit quietly to hear Anna sing her solo, 'Just As I Am', which everyone said was as professional a sound as they had ever heard anywhere—and then they were off singing again! They sang completely through the last hymn in the programme 'When I Survey the Wondrous Cross', four times, before at last, exhausted and exhilarated, they watched as a recording was made of Clive giving the blessing. He seemed nervous, which was quite unlike him. Still, it must be nerve-racking to have to perform on his own in front of cameras, knowing that millions of people would be watching

And then, all too soon it was over! The last hymn sung, the last word said, the last shot safely on tape—and Ian was announcing that Jan, the Producer, was on her way in from the scanner, to come and say goodbye and thank you to them all.

As Jan began to speak, Ian started to pack up his music, and walk down from the pulpit to stand at the top of the aisle. Something at the back of the church caught his eye. Someone silhouetted in the open doorway. He strained his eyes to see clearer. A woman was there, wearing a long camel coat that looked familiar. As his gaze moved up to her face, he gasped. Surely, it couldn't be! But it was! Sarah! She was here!

Without thinking, or taking any notice of the speeches that were being made around him, let alone the interested glances he was drawing from the congregation, he sped down the aisle towards her. She held out her arms to him, and he walked straight into them, clasping her in a bearhug as if he would never let her go.

'Whatever are you doing here? Where've you been? I've been so worried about...'

She put her finger to his lips to hush him, because he seemed to be the only one not aware of a spectacle they were providing for hundred of pairs of eyes in the church.

She put her mouth up to his ear, and said, so that only he could hear, 'Haven't you got something you want to ask me?'

He pulled back from her in surprise, looking at her intently. 'Well, yes—yes, I suppose I have—but not here...'

'Why not here?'

'Because—oh, you know why! I need somewhere more private.'

'He who hesitates is lost!'

'Sarah, you can't be serious!'

'Never more so. Now is the moment, Ian.'

Two rows away from them, Bunty was the first in the congregation to stand up, to get a better view of the fascinating drama unfolding at the back of the church.

There was one last look of pleading from Ian, as Sarah said, with a teasing, affectionate grin, 'You will do it properly, won't you? You know what I mean.' And her gaze lowered to the level of his knees.

'Sarah...' Ian groaned, but he knew when he was beaten.

He clasped her hands in his, and dropped to one knee. At that moment, the children in the front pews clambered up to stand on their seats.

Ian looked up, to see nothing and no one but his own dear Sarah. He loved her. He needed her. His life was nothing without her.

'I love you, Sarah. I always will. Please, marry me? I don't want to live another day without you .'

She drew him up towards her then. She didn't answer. She didn't need to. The expression in her eyes, and the warmth of her kiss, gave him the reply he longed for.

Spontaneous and delighted applause exploded around them.

'Oh, that was *lovely*!' wailed Bunty, as she reached into her bag for a hankie to wipe her eyes. 'Just *lovely*!'

FRIDAY

2 April

B y nine o'clock the next morning, all the television paraphernalia had been removed from St Michael's. The locals looked on with mixed feelings as cables were rolled up, and piled back into vans, and lights trundled out to be packed away in huge boxes.

Mrs Hadlow and Ivy watched from the bench just outside the church gate, where they often sat on a Friday morning, for a breather between shopping at the village store, and coffee at Ivy's house.

'Don't take long, do they?' said Ivy, as she watched. 'It'll seem odd them not being around, won't it?'

'Oh, they know what they're doing, dear,' agreed Mrs Hadlow. 'They're professionals.'

'They've finished all their work now, have they?' Ivy had no doubt that if anyone had inside knowledge of the TV people's timetable, it would be Mrs Hadlow.

'Not quite. They're recording the St Mark's Choir up at Dinton Church this morning. They've been given a solo spot. Can't think why! I never thought they were as good as that Mrs Hulme says they are.'

'And you? Did you enjoy all those rehearsals to get ready for the singing last night?'

'Well,' said Mrs Hadlow, picking an imaginary bit of fluff off her coat sleeve, 'it comes back, you know, dear. When you've done as much singing as I have in the past, it never really leaves you. All that training, I suppose...'

'Umm!' commented Ivy, clearly impressed, and the two women fell silent again, gazing at the activity going on in front of them.

316

Some minutes later, Helen came out of the church. They watched without comment, as she walked nonchalantly up and down the television vehicles, as though looking for something. Whatever it was, she apparently had no luck, and it was as she was heading down the path towards them, that Mrs Hadlow suddenly said, 'Tell you what, Ivy, you go ahead and put the kettle on. I'll be along directly. I just need a word with the vicar's wife.'

This was a departure from routine, which surprised Ivy. Still, she stood up, and walking carefully to compensate for her painful leg, she hobbled down the road towards her home.

Helen didn't spot Mrs Hadlow on the bench, until she had come through and shut the church gate—and even then, she heard her voice before anything else.

'I saw you, you know!'

Helen stopped abruptly, as the blood turned cold in her veins. Slowly, she turned round to look Mrs Hadlow full in the face.

'I saw you and him—when you went down to the river—and when you came back again.'

Helen stood rooted to the spot, unable to speak.

'I know what you're up to!' Mrs Hadlow's face was a dispassionate mask. Helen felt her world drop away from her. If Mrs Hadlow knew, it was only a matter of time before the rest of the village knew as well.

'I think we should talk,' Mrs Hadlow's calm voice continued. 'I'll pop in for a cup of tea at the vicarage this afternoon. Four o'clock would suit me.'

Helen nodded dumbly, before turning abruptly on her heel, and breaking into a run as she headed home. She slammed the front door behind her, and slid down until she was sitting on the hall carpet, her whole body cold with dread.

'The thing is,' Mrs Hulme's shrill voice piped into Ian's ear, 'that's the way we've rehearsed it, and that's the way we prefer to sing it.'

'Yes, Mrs Hulme,' said Ian patiently, 'but if you sing those lines so loudly, it will be completely at odds with the very gentle harp accompaniment at that point.'

'Then change the accompaniment!' Mrs Hulme folded her arms and stared with icy coolness at the young man in front of her. He might be the BBC Music Director, but there was nothing *he* could tell her about how hymns should be sung!

'But think about the words, Mrs Hulme!

'In this thy bitter passion,
Good shepherd, think of me
With thy most sweet compassion,
Unworthy though I be.

'My instinct is that these words should be almost whispered, with great feeling. It will add pathos and meaning. After all, "O Sacred Head" is a very emotive hymn.'

'Passion should be expressed with strength and enthusiasm!' Mrs Hulme retorted. 'Whoever heard of someone feeling passionate who wanted to whisper about it?'

Ian almost smiled, as he remembered his elation at the events of last night—Sarah's unexpected arrival, his proposal, her acceptance, the congratulations and delight of everyone in the church—and then, at last, the moment when they were able to be alone, the rightness of it, the knowledge that from now on, the future would be shared by the two of them, together. Yes, he did feel like shouting his feelings from the rooftops, so that the whole world could share their happiness, and the thought of that almost made him soften as he looked into Mrs Hulme's determined face. Almost, but not quite. He could take anything life threw at him today! Just this last item to record, and that was *it*! No more 'Village Praise' for this year! The chance to head home, with Sarah, to plan the rest of their lives together! Even Mrs Hulme, champion of the St Mark's Choir, couldn't spoil that!

His face broke into a beaming smile, as he swept the astonished Mrs Hulme up in a hug. 'I understand exactly what you mean,' he grinned, releasing her suddenly, 'but I don't agree with you in this instance. Your choir are so well trained, it will be no problem to change what they've practised! Leave it to me! I'll sort it out!' And he turned, and marched away to talk to the choir, before the disconcerted woman had time to open her mouth to object.

Dinton Church was transformed. Simon Martin, the Engineering Manager, had designed a lighting rig that created atmosphere rather than illumination. For a couple of hours, the sparks, Jim and Terry, had been chasing up and down ladders, carrying lights, and fixing them to scaffolding attached to the roof of the small church. For both of them, it had been a hard six weeks on the road, without the opportunity to get home at all. For Terry, that didn't matter so much, as he was a young, single man, who'd made the most of getting to know local people in every village he'd visited—especially the female members of the community, many of whose phone numbers were now scribbled on scraps of paper stuffed into his wallet. Jim, on the other hand, was a family man—a good-humoured hard worker, who disregarded protocol in favour of being practical, by insisting on wearing very short shorts while he was working, even in the most high of High Churches! Rose Hulme had clucked loudly in disgust when she had first glimpsed his bare legs in the church that morning. To make matters worse, Mrs Hulme noted with chagrin that the more flighty lady members of her choir couldn't take their eyes off him!

The choir members were not in a biddable mood that morning. Those who weren't distracted by Jim's legs, had their eyes drawn to the other small drama that was keeping a huddle of technicians busy in the far corner of the church. The problem was the smoke machine. It had been brought in to puff out a gentle mist, that would create a haunting, atmospheric softness to the pictures. However, instead of 'puffing', the machine was billowing. Where there should have been softness and light, there was thick, wet cloud, and pitch darkness.

It was a small, thin, elderly gentleman in the choir who started coughing first, closely followed by a younger, red-faced lady who melodramatically dabbed her eyes with a neatly ironed hankie. 'It's no use, Mrs Hulme!' she sobbed. 'I can't go on! My voice will be ruined if I try to sing in this smoke!'

'Oh, it's not smoke! Just steam, with a little bit of oil in!' The disembodied voice of the technician kneeling next to the machine, floated out of the dark cloud. 'Can't do you any harm, and we'll have it fixed in just a jiffy!'

'Mr Spence!' Mrs Hulme peered into the gloom to find Ian, and marched over to poke a finger in his chest as she spoke. 'This is unacceptable. My choir simply aren't used to such treatment! Either you sort out this ridiculous situation, or they won't sing, and that's that!'

The choir members looked at each other in alarm. What was she talking about? Not sing! They were about to go on televison, to be seen by millions of people around the country! Not sing! Whatever was she talking about?

A comfortably rounded, middle-aged lady bustled into action. 'Come on, Brenda! You too, Harry! Let's pop outside for a breath of fresh air, and I reckon by the time we're back, they'll have sorted the problem with the machine!'

'Too right!' said the technician's bodyless voice from the direction of the cloud. 'Give us five minutes, and we'll be on top of this!'

In fact, it took less than that. With the help of plenty of arm and door flapping to disperse the steam, the church cleared so that the cameras could actually see the choir through the gloom. They were dressed in deep scarlet robes, with starched white collars that sparkled with brightness. They, and Margaret, who was playing the harp to accompany them, had been placed within a circle of large, brightly lit candles, that threw warm, golden light on to their faces. St Mark's Choir were good, there was no doubt about that. Their disciplined, rich voices drew every ounce of meaning and emotion from the words. And as they sang, in the still, glowing warmth of Dinton Church, Ian thought that he had never heard anything lovelier.

Lunchtime in the bar of The Bull Hotel was a noisy affair. Most of the BBC technical crew dropped in for a drink and a sandwich, once the de-rigging in both St Michael's and Dinton Church was complete. The crew were demob happy, heading for home at the end of a long, but mostly enjoyable, six-week stint on the road with 'Village Praise'.

'So, where will you lads be next week, then?' asked the landlord, Bill, as he pulled a pint of the local brew for Des and Charlie, the riggers.

'Going to put me feet up for a couple of days,' mused Charlie into his beer. 'Get to know the wife again—remind her how nice it is to have me around!'

'It's a funny thing,' said Des, 'but I always get the impression that my missus thinks I'm in her way, whenever I get home. She spends every phone call while I'm on the road nagging at me because I'm away so much, and never around when she needs me—and all the time when I'm home, asking when I'm going off again!'

'Ah, well, she won't have to wait long, will she?' said Charlie. 'You're off to Scotland for the golf next weekend, aren't you?'

'Yep, another week away. She'll like that!'

The two men made their way over to the window seat, to wait for the arrival of the sandwiches they'd ordered.

'Blimey, look, there's Michael! Going over to the phone box, there, can you see him?'

'I thought he was coming over here to join us, for a quick one before we leave him to it,' said Des. He watched as Michael stepped into the box on the green, shutting the door behind him. 'He's a dark horse, that one. Never really know what he's thinking.'

'Worse than ever this week. He's just not had his mind on the job, has he?'

'What is it with him, do you think? Homesick? Or just sick of being on the road all the time?'

'Honestly, Des, I can't make him out. I had a drink with him the other night, and he just let me do all the talking. Just sat here, he did, hardly saying a word.'

Des looked out towards the phone box. 'He must have something on his mind, I reckon, something that's worrying him.'

'Do you think I ought to try and talk to him about it? You know, maybe he's ill, or something.'

'No,' said Des, taking a gulp from the top of his beer. 'He's a big boy. He'll talk when he's ready. And when he needs friends, we'll be here for him. He knows that.'

The phone rang several times, before Helen picked it up.

'Helen! It's me! Are you alright?' Michael put his mouth nearer to the receiver, although he knew the phone box was too far away from anyone to overhear.

'Michael, oh Michael, it's so good to hear your voice. Where are you?'

'On the green, in the phone box. I couldn't think how else to contact you.'

'I looked for you too, this morning. You weren't in the van, or the church...'

'I must see you!'

'When?'

'Well, we've finished de-rigging. In fact, most of the lads are on their way this afternoon, so I've not got much to do now, until the editing is finished, probably late tonight, or tomorrow morning. Then, I'll take the scanner back to base in the afternoon.'

'This evening then? Could we manage this evening?'

'Will your husband be at home?'

'Honestly, I don't know. I'm coming to see you anyway. I'll think of something, if he asks, which he probably won't.'

'Where shall we meet?' He chuckled. 'It'll be a bit cold down by the river...'

Helen's mind was racing. 'You haven't got a car, have you? Suppose I pick you up at the end of the lane leading down to the river? That's far enough away from the main street to be discreet. Then we can drive on somewhere, and have a talk.'

'When can you get away?'

'I don't know. Let me think—about quarter to eight?'

'I'll be there.'

'It's good to hear you...' There was a catch in Helen's voice.

'Helen, don't, please don't!'

She couldn't answer.

'I'll see you tonight. I'll be there early. Come when you can. I'll wait.'

'Yes,' she said flatly. 'Till then.' And the phone went dead in Michael's hand.

When the time came for Ian and Sarah to leave Grove House, the owners, Brian and Ellen hugged them both. Over the past few weeks, Ian had been a regular visitor to their guest house, and Brian and Ellen had to admit that the presence of the BBC production team had turned their lives upside down in the most enjoyable and unpredictable way. They stayed up writing and planning well into the night. They got up early, and needed breakfast long before most of their usual guests surfaced. They seemed to have a capacity for tea and coffee drinking that plumbed new depths, and they could demolish the whole of Ellen's homemade cakes in one sitting! And now, the first of them was leaving! With the music recording all complete, Ian's job was done.

Ellen had been in the church the night before, to see Sarah's arrival. Like the rest of the congregation, she'd looked on with interest and delight, to see him propose, and her accept. She had reached that 'certain age', when like most women, she felt romance was probably a dim distant memory! These two young people, and the obvious love between them had warmed and mellowed her—and as they packed the car now, ready to leave, she was glad to hear Ian was already talking about a return visit.

'Perhaps we'll be married by then,' he said, with his arm around Sarah. 'When are you planning to make an honest man of me?'

Sarah kissed him then, an affectionate, smiling kiss. 'As soon as possible would suit me fine!'

'Hello.' A quiet voice interrupted them. Anna had walked into the driveway, and now stood waiting rather shyly just inside the gate. 'I thought I'd come to say goodbye.'

'Anna!' enthused Ian. 'How great to see you!' He walked over to draw her closer. 'Did you two meet last night? Anna, this is Sarah...' He broke off to smile with pride at Sarah, '... my fiancée.'

'Congratulations,' said Anna, who was clearly ill at ease. 'You're leaving! Don't let me stop you. I just wanted to say thank you. You've been—it's been wonderful!'

'Anna, I should be thanking you,' said Ian warmly. 'You have great talent, and I hope it takes you far!'

Anna grinned. 'You don't reckon I should aim for the pop charts then?'

'I think you should consider studying music properly, perhaps get yourself a place to study singing at Music School. And then, well, the world's your oyster, isn't it! Maybe you'll be the next Madonna! Or maybe, you'll find you really enjoy singing the kind of piece you did for us!'

'Will you help me?' She spoke suddenly, as if she was afraid to ask.

'Of course I will! We'll keep in touch, and when you're a star, I'll come along to your first big concert and sit in the audience and tell everyone I always knew you'd make it!'

She seemed uncertain what to say, when suddenly she stepped towards him, and kissed him on the cheek. And then, with mumbled thanks, she was gone, scuttling away as she had come, through the drive gate.

'That girl has a crush on you,' Sarah said shrewdly.

'Don't be daft!' replied Ian, pulling her to him. 'And don't tell me you're starting to nag me already!'

Ivy opened the door of the salon just in time to see two large television vans, the one carrying camera equipment, and the lighting truck, trundle past her on their way out of Sandford. Charlie hung out of the cab to return her wave, as he steered the camera van past the phone box on the green, and headed round the corner. She was just about to close the door on the chill April air, when she spotted Ian's car pulling out of Grove House. She smiled to see the girl who'd arrived so unexpectedly in the church the night before sitting beside him in the passenger seat.

'Ian!' she shouted. 'Ian! Good luck! Come and see us again soon!'

Ian rolled down the window, and leant out to call goodbye to her. And then he was gone, following the trucks round the bend, and out of sight.

Ivy closed the door then, and sat down on the settee at the front of the salon. 'Aah!' she said. 'I'll miss that lot!'

'Yeah,' replied the receptionist, Debbie, wistfully, as she thought again about that cute electrician, Terry, she'd had a drink with in The Bull, after the rehearsal a couple of nights ago. 'So will I!'

Jack went to the gate rather warily when he saw Margaret's car draw up outside his house. He was still not totally comfortable with her.

Over the past few days, he'd run the gauntlet of feelings about her behaviour towards him. He didn't know why she wanted to visit him this afternoon. He only knew that he was glad that she had.

'Jack!' Her face lit up to see him, and she hugged him warmly. 'It's good to see you!'

'The kettle's on,' said Jack, his face flushed at her embrace, his emotions in a turmoil.

'Well, let's leave the kettle to bubble for a bit,' she said, slipping her arm through his. 'Before we go in, I'd like us to take a little walk. Not far, but there's something I need to show you.'

This surprised him. A walk? So that she could tell him about the new man in her life? 'Oh, well, let me just get the key,' he managed to say, and seconds later, he pulled the door shut, and opened the garden gate for her.

'This way!' she said, her face full of excitement. 'Just down here!'

Puzzled, he allowed himself to be led down the pathway, towards the river. And then, just before the bridge, she turned right, until they stood in front of a little cottage, with its garden that ran down to the river bank—the little cottage that his friend, John, had lived in, until his death two months before.

'There!' she said triumphantly. 'What do you think?'

'Think?' His face was blank.

'Look at the sign! Just look!'

And he did. He looked to see that the For Sale sign had been changed, and replaced by a new notice.

'Under Offer,' he read. 'They've sold it.'

'To me! I've made the offer! This wonderful cottage is going to be mine!'

'What do you mean? How can it be?'

'I loved it the moment I saw it, you remember, when you brought me here, a few weeks back? It just kept playing on my mind. It was the place I'd always dreamed of. I just loved it.'

'But you never said anything!'

'Well, I wasn't really serious about it, not at that stage anyway. But you remember when Jan came to see me at home, to hear me play the harp that first day? Well, she brought the organist, Colin Brown, with her—and he's an estate agent, but I didn't know that until then.

Somehow in the conversation he mentioned what his job was, and I just found myself telling him how I'd seen that cottage, and loved it! The amazing thing was that it turned out to be one of the properties on his books! So he had a proper look around my house while he was there, so that he could draw up details if I decided to put it on the market. Then, he arranged to meet with me here at the cottage the next day, so that I could take a look inside. And I loved it, Jack! I loved it even more, but I was so scared to be thinking about a major upheaval like this, at my age!'

The relief that Jack felt was immense and immediate. An estate agent! Not a lover at all!

'But why on earth didn't you tell me about it? I'd have been thrilled for you!'

'Just superstitious, I suppose. I thought if I told anyone, it might disappear! And I still had the problem of whether I could sell my own house. But Colin had an answer for that too. He already had a young couple in mind, who were looking for a small house near to the school, which of course mine is! He arranged for them to come and take a look very quickly. And it turned out to be just what they were after! I've been biting my nails ever since, what with surveys, and their mortgage to sort out—but it's done! The papers are signed, we've exchanged contracts—and at the beginning of May, I hope you'll be helping me to move in!'

'So you're going to be my neighbour!'

'I'll be popping in for a cup of tea every day!'

'Margaret, that's wonderful!' And without a moment's thought, he scooped her up in his arms, and danced round with her. Later, it occurred to him that, for a crusty old bachelor, that was very out of character. At the time, he felt nothing but delight that she was still his friend, and once she was nearer to him, there would be chance for that friendship to grow—and who knew where that would take them?

Words tumbled out, then. 'I couldn't understand why you were being so secretive. I thought—well, you'll laugh if I tell you what I thought! I saw you with Colin, you see, only I didn't recognize him. I saw you together by your car, and you seemed so close, so huddled in conversation—I thought... I thought...'

Realization dawned on Margaret's face. 'You thought,' she said slowly, 'that I was getting involved with someone else. And, I suppose, I *was*, only not in the way you meant!' She reached up to take his face gently in her hands, her eyes full of warmth and care. 'Jack Diggens, getting to know you has been a special pleasure for me. Getting to know you even better is something I look forward to very much.' And she leant up to kiss him softly on the cheek, a kiss of affection and promise. The two of them stood quite still, their gaze holding, and then, without a word, he took her hand, and led her towards the cottage that was to be her home.

After the recording of St Mark's Choir at Dinton Church that morning, Pam and the crew had spent a couple of hours visiting locations that had been selected because they had good views of the area. Roger wanted to get some general shots, that could be dropped in throughout the programme, and there was the odd linking piece that Pam needed to do to the camera. She always preferred to record these pieces late on during the recording, so that her impression of the place and the people was well formed in her mind, and she had a clear idea of what she wanted to say.

Most important of all was the final summing-up piece which would come at the end of this programme in Sandford, but which would actually draw to a close the series, in a way that would include all the places around the country that had been featured during its six-week run. In the end, Roger chose a small alleyway down near the river, at the back of St Michael's, where it was possible for Pam to start walking and talking with just a pretty rural background at first, and where, at just the right moment, the church itself would come into view. While the cameraman set up for the shot, and the sound recordist fixed on her microphone, Pam muttered to herself the words she was planning to say. She didn't have them exactly fixed in her mind, because she found that the result was more conversational if she remembered what she wanted to say under headings, and then just busked her way through.

At just the right moment, the sun broke through the layered clouds. Pam stood beside a cherry tree in full blossom at the top of the lane.

'Running!' called the cameraman, and Pam began to walk.

'So, here we are, at the end of another series where we've travelled the length and breadth of the country, finding villages that have all been so different in surroundings, livelihood, even language. But what they all have in common is a very high quality of village life—perhaps because of their size, small enough to be comfortable and caring, and yet capable of standing together in the face of unwelcome change or pressure.

'We've met people who can trace their families back in the area for generations, others who are newcomers bringing in different skills and enthusiasms; older people whose age is also recognized as experience, and who often now have time to contribute in a very full way to the life of the village; and younger families, with children who go to the village school, and who hold the key to the future.

'And always, there's the church, sharing their joys and their grief, and the age-old festivals of the Christian calendar through countless generations past, and many more to come.'

'That's a wrap!' yelled Roger. 'Pam, have you written all the commentary we're likely to need now?'

'Nearly,' she replied, as she unclipped her microphone, 'I just need to ring the office to make sure I know what to say about next week's programme.'

'Can we see you back at the scanner in about quarter of an hour then? We can record your voice-overs in there—and that will be that!'

Pam and he looked at each other, with a mixture of sadness that the series was over, but with the longing to get home that everyone on the crew felt.

'It will be good not to have you nagging at me next week!' she grinned.

'I won't miss you either!'

And with arms around each other, they wandered back in the direction of the car.

Mrs Hadlow knocked on the vicarage door at exactly four o'clock. Helen was filled with relief that Clive was out hospital visiting, as usual on a Friday afternoon, but the sense of dread that drained through her when she heard the knock at the door made her hesitate for several seconds before making her way slowly to answer it.

The two women didn't greet each other. Helen gestured that they should go through to the front room. She wanted to keep a formality to this conversation. To chat over the kitchen table would be too friendly, too intimate, too difficult.

Neither of them seemed willing to start. They sat, perched on the edge of their chairs, avoiding conversation, and each other's eyes. At last, it was Mrs Hadlow who spoke.

'You're having an affair, aren't you?'

'Mrs Hadlow, that is a ridiculous suggestion! And even if it were true, it would be none of your business!' Two bright scarlet splashes of anger lit up Helen's cheeks.

'I've seen the way you look at him. I've watched him too. He can't take his eyes off you.'

'I don't know what you're talking about...'

'You do. You just don't know what you should do about it. That's why I'm here.'

'Why? To gloat? To lecture? To gossip? Just why are you here, Mrs Hadlow?'

'To help. To talk, if you'd like to.'

'To you?' Helen's eyes dropped to her hands, clasped tightly together in her lap. 'I don't think so.'

Silence fell again. Mrs Hadlow smoothed down her skirt, and waited.

Finally, she said, 'And him? He'll be leaving soon. Do you plan to follow him?'

Helen didn't answer.

'Does he want you to?'

Helen looked up, as if to speak, but changed her mind.

'Your Clive, he's a good vicar, a man of God. I don't suppose he's a perfect husband, but do you think any man really is?'

Helen stared at Mrs Hadlow.

'You've had a good few years together. You've got along. Are you going to throw that all away? For what? For a man you hardly know? For a rolling stone, on the road all the time? Can you see a life for yourself with a man like that?'

Still, Helen did not answer.

'He'll have played the same trick on women everywhere he's been. You're not that special. You don't really think he *cares* about you, do you? A man like him?'

Helen stood up then, her hands clenched in fists at her side, her body quivering with anger.

'Mrs Hadlow, I have always thought you were a nosey, insensitive, busybody, but I never knew till now that your interference could be so evil, so cruel! How could you possibly understand love and emotion in other people when, in all your mean-minded, selfish life, I don't suppose you've ever been faced with having to choose between duty—and love!'

Before Helen could say more, she stopped abruptly. Mrs Hadlow had turned suddenly pale, her eyes staring and unfocused. With horror, Helen watched the older woman begin to sway, as if she might faint. Helen reached out a hand towards her, but Mrs Hadlow quickly gathered herself, and her things together, to make her escape. 'I'm sorry, I shouldn't have come...' she mumbled, as she brushed past—and as she spoke, Helen glimpsed in her eyes dark, raw, lonely pain.

And then, she was gone. The door banged shut behind her, and Helen sank back on to her chair, wondering whatever it was she'd said, to cause such hurt?

❧

Pam pulled up her car outside the village shop, as she headed out of the village. She'd spotted Joan just outside the doorway, and wound down her window to shout goodbye.

'Come back again soon!' called Joan, as Don joined her from inside the shop. 'And bring the family next time!'

'Thanks, I will! Say goodbye to Anna for me, will you? Tell her to keep in touch!'

At the very moment that Pam drove out of Sandford for the last time, Anna was upstairs above the shop, on the phone. It was Major Gregory that answered the call.

'Oh, hello, is Matthew there please?'

'Shouldn't think so for one minute!' was the gruff reply. 'Marjorie, is Matthew in?' There was silence for a while, and Anna nearly put down the phone in exasperation, when finally, Matthew was there, on the end of the line.

'Matthew, it's Anna.'

'Oh, hi! You only just caught me. I've been over in The Bull, talking to Frank Harris, the Sound Supervisor, about doing some work experience with them next summer. He seems quite keen to help me. He's told me who to write to, and everything, so I'm just working out the letter now, while it's fresh in my mind.'

'You'll be too busy to come round for a coffee tonight, then?' said Anna casually.

'Afraid so. They're letting me sit in on some of the editing in the scanner this evening. Sorry, Anna.'

'No sweat,' she replied, too quickly. 'It doesn't matter. Bye then!' And she slammed down the phone, cursing herself for letting him bug her! It was him that had always been chasing her! If he was too busy with new friends to bother with her now, stuff him! He could just get lost!

She picked up the cushion on the settee beside her, and clenching her fists, thumped it with all her might.

Clive returned to the vicarage in high spirits. Several of the staff at the local hospital had been at the recording the night before, and there seemed to be talk of little else, except what a success the whole thing had been. Clive basked in the glory of their comments, glad that he'd had the foresight to encourage the BBC to make the programme, relieved beyond words that everyone locally seemed to feel the experience was a pleasant one.

As he opened the front door, his nose twitched with the smell of cooking. He walked through to the kitchen, to find Helen washing up, having obviously prepared the casserole he could see bubbling away in the oven.

Thank God, he thought. She's back. Helen is back to normal, at last!

'Darling, that smells great. When will it be ready?'

Helen glanced at the kitchen clock. 'About forty-five minutes. You'll need to eat then, won't you? You've got that meeting at Norman and Marion's at half past seven tonight.' Clive racked his brain, trying to remember what meeting that was. The Reverend Norman Oates was an enthusiastic caller of meetings—although, whatever the subject, the evenings usually degenerated into a social affair where whisky glasses replaced teacups, and any women were banished to the other room. Yes, he enjoyed going to meetings at Norman's house!

Clive looked at his wife, as she wiped her hands, and busied herself in the kitchen. He wondered what she was thinking. She seemed normal enough. A bit pale, perhaps, but no sign of the tantrums he'd grown to expect lately. Should he ask her how she's feeling? He thought for a few moments, and decided that it was better to leave well alone. Least said, soonest mended.

'Give me a yell when it's ready, then,' he said. 'I'll pop up and have a bath.'

Bunty knocked on Betty Waite's door, not really expecting her to be in. Betty took so long to answer, that Bunty was about to walk away, when the door opened.

'Betty! Sorry to disturb you! Just wanted to make sure that you and Charles are OK for Sunday night!'

'Come in, Bunty, it's cold on the doorstep! Yes, I'll definitely be there, and I'll lend a hand if you need me to. I'm not sure what Charles is planning to do, though.' She grimaced at Bunty, as the two women walked along the hall into the light of the living room.

Charles was sitting at the table, surrounded by parish papers. He didn't look up as they entered.

'Charles,' said Betty quietly, 'Bunty is just checking on numbers for the get-together at the vicarage to watch the programme go out on Sunday night. Have you decided yet whether you're going?'

Charles continued writing until he reached the end of what was obviously a long sentence, before he looked up at Bunty.

'Will Jack Diggens be going?'

'I jolly well hope so. He's been marvellous in organizing everything, absolutely marvellous!'

'Then I shan't.'

'Why ever not?' asked Bunty, her eyes opening wide with disbelief. 'Everyone will be there, everyone in the village that's been involved with making the programme such a success. It would be unthinkable that you're not there too!'

Charles continued to write. Bunty looked at Betty, who shrugged her shoulders indifferently.

'But you're an interviewee! You must come! Everyone expects it!'

'I don't, and I shan't! I will not be in the same room as that man!'

Bunty wasn't a woman who was often lost for words, but on this occasion, she was speechless. Finally, she turned in disbelief to Betty. 'You talk to him, Betty. He *must* come. Whatever will people think if Charles isn't there?'

'They can work out my reasons for themselves, and then, they can think what they like!' said Charles emphatically, and he opened a book to start reading, in a way that defied any further conversation.

❀

Clive left in good time for his meeting at Norman Oates' house, which gave Helen half an hour to sort out the kitchen, and get changed, before meeting Michael. She climbed into her old orange Mini dreading that someone might see, and stop her. Her heart thumped against her ribs as she drove down and through the main street, until at last the lane leading to the river came into sight. She slowed down carefully, scouring the darkness to see him. The passenger door opened, he climbed in, and they drove away without a word.

She hadn't really worked out where they were going. She drove, until he pointed out a small road that led towards an old house that had long been derelict. Avoiding the deep pits in the bumpy road, she drove for a few hundred yards, and then pulled over under some trees. When she turned off the engine, and the lights went out, they were plummeted into pitch darkness.

She turned to Michael, who held out his arms to draw her close. There was no need to speak for a while, as they both savoured the moment.

'How did you get away?' he asked at last.

'Clive's out at a meeting tonight. He'll be gone for quite a while, I should think.'

'Have you thought any more about what you want to do?'

She smiled weakly at him. 'Only all the time. I can think of nothing else.'

'And?' he prompted gently.

'And I don't know. I'm frightened at risking everything that's dear and familiar to me, but I honestly think I'm more frightened at the thought of staying, of doing nothing at all.'

'What you probably need is time. Time for yourself, to think things through.'

'With you?'

'If you like—or perhaps on your own.'

'Clive would never understand. Well, let's face it, nobody would understand! Could I bear the thought of what people would say about me, for abandoning my duty, my promises, to my husband?'

'Does it really matter what people think?'

She looked at him through the darkness. 'I've been used to being at the centre of a warm, caring, Christian community. To strike out on my own, without their support and approval, will be very lonely. Perhaps too lonely to bear...'

'Lonely, yes—but free.'

'What about you, Michael? You're on your own so much. You have no wife at home, to share your life with? Do you get lonely?'

He reached for her hand, and linked her fingers through his. 'There's a difference, isn't there, between being 'lonely', and 'alone'. I enjoy my own company. I don't seem to need people around me, to feel complete.'

'And you don't need me. How could you? We hardly know each other.'

'Don't, Helen. I can't pretend I'm something I'm not. I'm not asking you to give up anything for me. I don't have the sort of lifestyle where I would dare to suggest it! But I'll be there for you, if you need me. I'm your friend. I'd like to have the chance to get closer to you, to have time together. But I can't make any promises. I'm not saying I love you. I don't need love or approval, the way I think you do. I can't make up your mind for you. It's just that...'

He stroked a piece of stray hair out of her eyes.

'It's just that—there's something about your unhappiness that touches me very deeply. I want to take the pain away...'

And they melted together then, into the darkness, into each other.

❧

'The thing is,' said Stanley, warming to his subject, 'television people aren't *normal* people, are they? They arrive out of the blue, spend a couple of days here, and think they're experts! How can they possibly know enough about Sandford to make a decent programme about it? They weren't here long enough!'

The public bar of The Bull seemed rather empty, now that the BBC crew had mostly gone. Stanley was perched on his usual stool at the bar, voicing his opinion to anyone who'd listen. Most chose not to. They'd heard it before. Only old Eric, propped up at the other end of the bar, seemed to be paying attention to him—and it was well known that he was as deaf as a post!

Bill's wife, Maureen, walked into the bar, dishcloth in hand, ready to wipe the tables. 'You're only put out, Stanley, because they didn't ask to interview you!'

'Well, why didn't they?' asked Stanley indignantly. 'They might have learnt a thing or two! I am one of the senior residents of Sandford. There's not much about this place I don't know!'

'You know where to get a good pint of ale anyway!' laughed Bill. 'The trouble is, you don't go to church!'

'Well, this business isn't going to make me! All those hypocrites filling up the church for the television cameras. Where are they all on Sunday mornings, that's what I'd like to know!'

'In their own churches, Stanley,' said Maureen. 'It wasn't just the Church of England people who got tickets, you know. There were people there from all the other denominations as well. They *are* all churchgoers, but they usually go to their own churches.'

'Poppycock!' snorted Stanley. 'Hypocrites, the lot of 'em!'

335

'Does this mean that you won't be coming here for our Bangers and Mash night on Sunday, with the telly on so that we can all watch the programme together?'

'Ooh, I'll be here alright,' said Stanley, taking a gulp of his pint. 'It's my bounden duty to watch, just to see how much they've got wrong!'

❧

Clive was in high spirits when he arrived home. It was past midnight, and the whisky had combined with Norman's warm welcome to leave him feeling mellow and pleased with life. Perhaps because he didn't realize quite how late it was, or perhaps because it didn't matter to him anyway, he thumped his way up the stairs, and switched on the bedroom light as he walked in the door.

Helen was in bed, not asleep, but she had been in bed for at least an hour. I won't move, she thought. If he thinks I'm asleep, that's fine. I just don't want to talk to him, not tonight.

'Helen, Helen, you're awake, aren't you?' She didn't move. 'Helen!' he shook her shoulder gently. 'Have you seen my glasses? I forgot to take them with me this evening. I thought I ought to read these notes Norman's given me, before I go to sleep. Helen! Are you listening?'

She gritted her teeth, but said nothing.

He stumbled off to the bathroom then. She heard the toilet flush, and the sound of water running, and then he was back. 'I'm too tired for reading anyway. You can tell me where I left my glasses in the morning.'

He climbed into bed, and snuggled up beside her, although she lay with her back towards him, curled up in a tight ball. She felt him nuzzling her neck. 'Helen,' he whispered, close enough for her to smell the whisky on his breath. 'Come on, darling, how about it?'

No, she thought, please no.

His hand began to wander over her body, touching, stroking, caressing.

Please, Clive, don't do this. Not tonight. She remained silent, her nerves jangling at his touch, her body taut and unresponding. He was pressing himself against her now, demanding, insistent, impatient. 'Helen, come on. I know you're awake.'

He tried to turn her to face him then, but she kept herself rigid and still. 'Oh, for heaven's sake, Helen...' and he twisted her head towards him, so that her eyes shot open and blazed at him.

'*No!*'

'Why not? Are you still in a mood?'

'Clive, I want to go to sleep, and from the look and smell of you, sleep is what you need too.'

'I know what I need,' he replied, burying his head in her hair. 'Come on, darling, please!'

'Clive, no! I can't. Not now!'

'Not now—not ever! What's wrong with you? You're my wife. I have a right...'

Helen sat up abruptly, and moved away from him, her eyes fired with alarm and anger. 'Don't you dare mention "rights"! I understand my duties towards you. I always have! But right now, you're tipsy, and I'm tired, and we're both in danger of saying things we'll regret.'

His face crumbled, angry for a split second, and then, forlorn and distressed. 'Helen, what's happening to us? Why are you so angry all the time? What's changed? Is it me? Have I done something to bring about this change in you?'

Compassion overwhelmed her. Her eyes clouded with tears as she reached for him, to draw him to her, as a mother would a child.

'It's not you, believe me. It's nothing you've done. It's just me. I have a lot of thinking to do.'

He clung to her tightly, his head hard against her shoulder.

'You're going to leave me, aren't you.'

She didn't reply.

'I know you are. And I don't know how to stop you.'

And he started to shake. Slowly at first, his whole body began to move, until he was convulsed with violent shivering. The sight of him in such distress shocked and frightened her. She held him tightly, rocking him to and fro, until the shaking stopped, and he fell into a deep, uneasy sleep.

SATURDAY

3 April

It was no surprise to Brian and Ellen at Grove House when their last remaining BBC guests didn't surface for breakfast on Saturday morning. Ellen had heard them come in about three o'clock that night, having been locked in the scanner editing from early afternoon the day before.

There were only three of them left now—Jan Harding, the Producer, Roger, the Director, and Sue, the Production Assistant. They had told her that they hoped to be back on the road and heading for base later that afternoon, and that would be the end of the BBC's visit to Sandford.

Ellen was perched on the corner of the kitchen table, munching a piece of toast, as Brian came in from the garage, carrying a paintpot and brushes. They had no more guests booked in that week, so he planned to carry on with a bit of touching up on the paintwork, to get the guest house spick and span for the summer trade. It was odd to think that summer was finally just around the corner. It had been a long, dismal winter, which made the promise of spring all the sweeter, as gardens burst into life once again, with splashes of yellow daffodils and delicate, fragrant blossom.

The phone rang. It was Bunty.

'I'm just ringing up to confirm what you'll be bringing along with you to the vicarage "do" tomorrow night. Sausage rolls, four quiches (various), and salad? Will you be able to do a couple of salads as well?'

'No trouble,' said Ellen, scribbling down a list. 'How about puds? I could knock up a pavlova or two?'

'Great! Grace is concentrating on puds too, so there should be enough.'

'How many will be going?'

'About twenty, I should think. Most people have said yes—well, except Charles, of course, who seems to be in a most peculiar mood.'

'I don't know how Betty puts up with him.'

'He can be such a grumpy old devil!'

Ellen laughed. 'So can my Brian, but I still love him!'

'Helen seems in an odd mood at the moment too. I'm not quite sure what that's all about, but she's very edgy.'

'Tired, I expect. All the organizing for this programme must have meant a lot of extra work. And let's face it, Clive's a lovely man, but he's not much good when it comes to organizing anything, is he!'

'And that's why,' said Bunty, 'I want to make sure this get-together doesn't mean dumping any more on Helen. We can sort it all out. She'd be the first to admit that she's not much of a cook anyway...'

'Funny that, for a vicar's wife.'

'Umm,' Bunty agreed. 'I must dash. Can you get your bits to the house by, say, five o'clock tomorrow? People should be arriving from about half past.'

'See you then. Bye!'

❧

If Clive remembered anything about the events of the night before, he didn't show it. He wasn't very talkative anyway. Breakfast was a silent affair, and Helen quickly excused herself to run the vacuum over the carpet. With the houseful that Bunty was planning for them the following evening, she needed to start cleaning early!

Half an hour later, she looked out of the back bedroom window, to see Clive heading down to his greenhouse. Good, she thought, he'll enjoy a few hours in there. She put the cleaner away, and went in to the bathroom, to change the towels, and polish the sink. Then she moved on to their bedroom, duster and spraycan in hand, keeping busy in a way that didn't require much thought, until she found herself dusting the photo, their photo, taken on their wedding day so many years ago.

She sat down on the dressing table stool, and stared at the two young, smiling faces. They'd been so in love, with such a lot in common. They were starting out then, on a life together that had become a rich and productive partnership. They'd been posted to a variety of parishes—from the central town church in Chelmsford that they first took up, right through to the quiet, rural patch of Sandford. Children had come along—Jane first, and then Richard, both now away from home, making lives of their own. Over the years, they'd settled down to a routine of married life that was comfortable and reassuring. Theirs wasn't a passionate relationship, but it worked—at least, it *had* worked in a way that neither of them questioned.

Helen sighed. That was the difficulty really. She had never questioned her marriage, nor whether she was really happy within it. She looked again at the photo, at herself in the satin wedding dress that looked quaintly old-fashioned now. She remembered the vows she'd taken, and meant with all her heart on that day. 'From this day forward... for better for worse... in sickness and in health... forsaking all others...' She remembered, oh so clearly even all these years later, the love in Clive's eyes as he had looked at her, and she remembered clasping her hands together tightly as she prayed with him at the altar rail. She had prayed with every fibre and thought in her body that this marriage would work, that she would be worthy of it, that she would make a good and loving wife to the wonderful man who'd chosen her. She had spoken her vows to Clive, but she'd made her promises to God.

How, then, could she even think about abandoning that promise—to God, who had been so constant and loving throughout the whole of her life? Her faith had never been anything but solid. She'd grown up in a Christian family. She'd always gone to church. Her belief was not based on any flighty emotional experience, nor great grief in her life. It was a slow, steady growth of certain knowledge. She spoke to God, and he listened. She laid her thoughts and problems before him, and in his own way and time, he answered her prayer.

It occurred to her that she'd not felt able to pray for the past few days, since her friendship with Michael began. Prayer was a regular part of her daily life. Each morning started with prayer, and at night, her last thoughts were with God. How could she have moved away so far, acted so out of character, that she had forgotten to share her day with God? But, of course, it wasn't forgetfulness. It was shame, deep, guilty shame—the awful knowledge that she should come to him, and admit her failings, even though at the moment, she wasn't able to repent. How could she say—I'm doing wrong, I am drawn to a man that I am not married to, my feelings towards my husband have changed so dramatically, that although I love him, I am not sure that I *like* him any more? How could she admit all that, and ask for forgiveness, when she didn't regret a minute, when every instinct in her was to run away—from Clive, from the village, from God himself? How could God forgive her, when her thoughts were unforgivable?

She glanced at her watch. It was ten o'clock. In an hour or so, Michael would be gone. She would see him just one last time here in Sandford, her home. And then? Would she meet him again? At *his* home? Was he to be part of her future—or just a turning point, a catalyst that exposed bare her weakness, and urged her to change, to move on—or perhaps just to accept the life she knew?

She looked down again at the wedding photograph in her hand, and then closed her eyes tightly as she wrapped her arms around it, and hugged it to her. 'Clive,' she whispered, 'I'm lost and floundering. There has always been so much love between us. Dear God, let there be enough love for you to draw me back home. Oh, Clive, please—help me home!'

Jack had never liked throwing away anything that might possibly be useful at some time in the future. It was a habit that he had learned from his Mum, and over the years, it had stood him in good stead. It had also filled up his cellar, his garden shed and his garage with stacks of papers, trays of electrical bits and pieces, odd strips of wood in a variety of shapes and thicknesses, crates of washed jam jars, and dozens of empty cardboard boxes. It was the cardboard boxes that came into their own that Saturday morning. The prospect of sorting out, and packing up her home after so many years of living there, was a very daunting one for Margaret. It was certainly a relief when Jack not only offered to come along and help her, especially with the dismantling of shelves and electrics, but that he would be able to supply her with all the boxes she could possibly need.

Jack found himself whistling as he loaded up his car that morning. He had every reason to feel happy. His life had changed so much in just a matter of weeks. He'd always been a good organizer, and his organizing skills had not only come in useful in planning the television visit, but it had brought him into contact with people in the village who'd previously hardly been acquaintances, and now were friends. He had rediscovered the pleasure of going to church. He was still not completely sure of his commitment to it, or whether his faith was all it should be, but after so many years of absence, he was beginning to feel comfortable at last in a church service. And he'd met Margaret, who'd turned his life upside down with her warmth and presence. The thought that he'd lost her, made him realize just much he looked forward to seeing her, and being in her company. And now she was moving in just a few doors away. Yes, life was very good indeed!

Knowing that this was Michael's last morning, and not being sure what time he would leave, Helen couldn't stay in the house a moment longer. She pulled on her jacket, threw the front door key in the flowerpot, and walked up the path, towards the lane where all the BBC vans had been. There was only the scanner left now, and as she walked past to peer in the cab, he was there. Quickly looking around her, she opened the heavy door, and climbed in.

'I was hoping you'd come,' he said. 'I'm all packed up and ready to go, but I wasn't sure how to make contact with you, in case Clive was around.'

'He is, but he's in the greenhouse, so he's unlikely to surface for a while yet.'

She stretched out her hand to meet his, and their fingers twined around each other.

'Meeting you,' she said quietly, 'has been wonderful. You are a very unusual, sensitive, caring man. You will probably never know just how special this has been for me.'

'That sounds as if you're saying goodbye—as if we'll never meet again.' He lifted his hand to tilt up her chin, so that her eyes looked directly into his. 'Is that what you want?'

'No.'

He picked up a small card, that he'd left on the dashboard. 'I've written out my address, and there are all the contact numbers on there. You only have to call... or just arrive...'

'Michael, I'm still not sure. What I feel like doing, and what I should do, are quite at odds with each other. I'm stuck somewhere in the middle, knowing that whatever I do, even if I choose to do nothing at all, there'll be unhappiness.'

His fingers gently stroked her cheek. 'Then I'll wait. I'll just wait.'

Mrs Hadlow was spending some time in the church that morning, with relief that at last, everything could go back in its usual position. She found great comfort in routine. A place for everything, and everything in its place—that was her motto. The television people had brought disruption and upheaval, and although it was a very pleasant experience in many ways, all things considered, she was happy to know that life could return to normal. Better not to dwell on certain events of the past few days, unexpected and painful conversations. Much neater to forget, keep things straight and tidy.

She hadn't meant to be standing in the church porch as the scanner left. She didn't intend to watch as Helen climbed out of the cab, her face drawn and pale. She hadn't planned to see the forlorn unhappiness in the younger woman's eyes, as she waved goodbye to the driver, looking on as he negotiated the tricky procedure of backing out of the lane, and then driving off, past the telephone box, down the High Street, and out of sight. She hadn't wanted Helen to turn at that moment, and see her standing in the porch, looking for all the world as if she was spying. Mrs Hadlow was appalled to see Helen's expression darken with anger, before she turned and ran back towards the vicarage.

And as she ran, Helen's anger cooled, as she wondered again, as she had the previous day, at the depth of pain she'd seen that moment in Mrs Hadlow's eyes—a pain that mirrored her own.

4 April

The news about the Bangers and Mash evening at The Bull went round the village like wildfire. Bill and Maureen originally reckoned about forty people might want to eat in the Public Bar, as 'Village Praise' went out. In the end, Maureen had to take another huge pack of sausages out of the chest freezer, because more than sixty people had squeezed themselves inside the door by half past five that evening.

The level of chatter was so high, it was hard for Bill to catch the orders for drinks as people yelled at him across the counter. The situation wasn't helped by the fact that Stanley was in full flow, holding court from his stool at one end of the bar. A chuckling crowd had gathered around him, especially when a rather heated discussion developed between Stanley, and Sidney West, who was basking in the limelight of being one of the few people who'd been interviewed on the programme.

'What would they want to film you, out in a boat, for?' sniffed Stanley contemptuously. 'It's not even as if you're a fisherman, and there are plenty around here as are!'

'Listen here, you green-eyed old fool, they weren't interested in me and Frank and Bo because of our fishing! We didn't do much fishing that night! No, it was all the other things we do, that really interested them!'

'Like taking the boat just far enough out to have a quick snifter where the wife can't get you!'

Sidney drew himself up until he was peering down on Stanley, whose stool, to be fair, was not very high. 'We were in the presence of God. I hope you are not suggesting that we were drinking in the presence of God!'

Stanley shrank a little. 'Well, maybe not while the filming people were there—but I bet you do normally. I bet you do!'

'You,' snapped Sidney, stabbing at Stanley with his finger, 'are beneath contempt. You were a horrible little boy, and you're a horrible little man! We will just let everyone here...' he waved his arm expansively round the bar, '... decide for themselves, when they see what they see on the telly. Now, if you'll excuse me, my colleagues are waiting for me!' And with haughty dignity, he picked up three pints from the bar, and turned to make his way over to where Frank and Bo were waiting for him.

'Honestly,' Ellen was saying to Maureen, as the pair of them bustled in, bearing steaming plates of bangers and mash, swimming in spicy onion gravy, 'it's so quiet at Grove House now they've all gone! They took the place over really, what with their production office there, and everything. And they looked shattered yesterday when they left—it must have been about midday before they finally got the cars all packed up, and managed to leave.'

'Are they pleased with the programme, do you think?' Maureen asked over her shoulder, as she placed a couple of plates on one of the tables.

'They seem to be! But who knows? It's whether we're pleased with it, that really counts! Blimey, it's manic here tonight. I've never seen this bar so busy, not even at Christmas!'

'Well, you're a good pal, to come and help out like this, especially as I know you're going on to the vicarage later!'

'Actually, I have a feeling it might be more fun here! I imagine the vicarage "do" might be a bit stuffy. They've got all the bigwigs going— you know, Major Gregory, Norman Oates, and all the local worthies. I'd better put in an appearance though, especially seeing as I provided quite a bit of the food, and Bunty will be sure to take umbrage if I don't show up!'

'And it would never do to get on the wrong side of Bunty Maddocks!' Maureen grinned. 'Aah, well, we've not got many left to serve now. Just as long as we can get everyone fed before twenty-five past six, so that I can sit down and watch too, I'll be happy!'

❦

By half past five, the vicarage was humming with people. The kitchen had been completely taken over by the Ladies' Prayer Group, who were quite indistinguishable from the St Michael's Flower Arranging Circle, as most of the members were the same. Bunty was in charge, briskly efficient in yet another lilac twinset, smiling broadly, absolutely in her element. Mrs Hadlow had laid out the table in symmetrical perfection—knives and forks on one side, napkins on the other, serving spoons evenly spaced out in the middle, between the bowls of salad and pasta. Iris and Grace were fetching and carrying, serving piping hot pieces of quiche fresh from the oven, and sausages rolled up in rashers of streaky bacon.

Clive was delegated to the drinks, but because he found it impossible to pour wine without stopping for a ten-minute chat with whoever was holding the glass, it was a slow business. Finally, Major Gregory could bear the wait no longer, and dispatched his son, Matthew, firstly in search of a decent spot of whisky, and secondly, to wrestle the wine bottle from Clive, so that he take over as waiter.

From one corner of the room, Anna watched Matthew as he moved from one guest to another, chatting to one, being warmly greeted by another. He looked nice—well, in a straight sort of way. He was wearing jeans, and a thick dark jumper, that made him seem older and taller. But he looked alright, considering that it was just Matthew. Someone, perhaps some girl or another, might even think he was fanciable—if they didn't know him as well as she did, of course!

Much against his better judgment, Charles Waite did put in an appearance. Bunty peered around the kitchen door to see him arrive, and exchanged meaningful glances with Iris. 'I wonder what Betty said to get him here!' she whispered under her breath. 'Told him she was going anyway, and that he could stay at home, and sulk by himself, I reckon!' giggled Iris. 'Is there any more garlic bread yet, Bunty? We're nearly running out!'

Charles kept himself aloof, as he made his way through the crowd, towards Clive. 'Charles!' Clive greeted him warmly. 'Good to see you! Have you got a drink yet? What a splendid occasion this is turning out to be!'

'That remains to be seen,' replied Charles. 'It depends entirely what the finished programme looks like. Obviously, I made sure that the history of Sandford, and its importance in the context of the development of East Anglia over the centuries, is clearly explained during my interview in the programme...'

Clive's eyes had wandered over Charles' shoulder, and were fixed on the couple who were just entering the room.

'Jack! Margaret! Over here! Come and join us!' Charles stiffened as Jack Diggens, his arm protectively around his lady companion's shoulder, made his way over to where they stood. This was more than Charles could bear. Without a word to Jack and Margaret, he turned his back very pointedly on them, and bent his head so that he could speak quietly in Clive's ear.

'It seems to me, Vicar, that certain things must be said this evening. It is important that this occasion is marked properly. As the Chairman of the Parish Council, I will, if you insist, say a few appropriate words, once the programme is over.'

'Great idea!' beamed Clive. 'So good that I thought of it myself! Very kind of you to offer, but I couldn't possibly ask you to undertake what is clearly *my* job! I've been preparing what I'd like to say all day! Excuse me a moment, would you, Charles? I'm sure you and Jack must have a lot to chat about, and I see that Norman Oates has just arrived!'

If anyone had noticed that Helen was not in the thick of things, it wasn't mentioned. Earlier on, she'd pleaded a headache, and it was true that her head was thumping. She stayed upstairs in the bedroom as long as she possibly could, listening to the gathering level of chatter downstairs, recognizing individual voices, dreading the moment when she would have to make an appearance. Not to watch the programme, after everything that had happened, would be unthinkable. She'd spent the day in a daze of indecision and confusion. Her mind was no clearer now. Her conscience still shrieked at her. Her emotions betrayed her. Just a few hours on, her longing for Michael was a dull ache within her. And then, she found her eyes straying to the wedding photo. She picked up Clive's dressing gown, and breathed in the feel, and the smell of it, of him. Dear, dear Clive. Clive, who saw so much, and understood so little. Why couldn't he recognize her confusion? Why didn't he reach out, and draw her in? Clive, I'm begging you to stop me. Notice—and stop me!

It was quarter past six. She had to go down. She could put it off no longer. She stepped out of the bedroom into the darkness of the landing, just as someone emerged from the bathroom along the hall. Her heart fell when she saw that it was Mrs Hadlow.

Both women stopped, unsure of what to say, how to react. And then, to Helen's surprise, it was Mrs Hadlow who stepped forward, as if to walk past her—but as she did, she softly clasped Helen's hand. 'God bless you, dear,' she said, so quietly that Helen could barely hear her. 'Listen to your heart, follow your instincts, or you will never be at peace again.' And before Helen had time to react, she was gone, down the stairs and into the crowd.

Scattered throughout the vicarage were plenty of chairs and stools, in various shapes and conditions—but that evening, there were simply not enough to go around. With much chatter and laughter, people squeezed up on the settee, perched on chair arms, and balanced on the edge of windowsills. Jack came in the door, with two stools stacked in his arms, except because of the crowd, it was almost impossible to pass them over to the other side of the room, where they were needed. As he stretched over to hand one of the stools to Stephen Yearling, the young minister who'd been interviewed for the programme, the wooden leg collided with the head of someone who was already comfortably settled. Unfortunately, the head belonged to Charles Waite.

'Mr Diggens!' Charles snapped, rubbing his forehead dramatically. 'You made a mess of the seating arrangements in the church, and you are making a mess of the seating arrangements *now*! Will you kindly leave things to people who know what they're doing!!!'

In the stunned silence that followed, no one dared speak. Bunty's hand flew to her mouth. Major Gregory's half-empty whisky glass stopped in mid-air. Suddenly, it was Betty Waite's voice that cut clearly across the room.

'Charles Waite, you are being unbelievably rude and pompous! I am absolutely ashamed of you. Please, will you do us all a favour, and *shut up!*'

And then, someone started to giggle. It might have been Iris. It might have been Margaret—but it was infectious. One by one, people around the room began to join in, until the place was filled with laughter. 'Come on, Charles,' said Jack, his face beaming, 'pass this stool over for me, will you?'

Charles had no choice but to oblige, but his face was poker straight, and a tight, throbbing nerve twitched just beneath his eye. He said nothing. For once, he had nothing to say.

'Here it comes!' shouted Clive. 'Turn it up a bit someone, would you!'

Thirty-five minutes later, a cheer went up around the Public Bar of The Bull, as the closing credits of the programme scanned up across the screen.

'Well, Stanley? What did you think?'

'They didn't make the weather look very nice.'

'But the weather *wasn't* very nice this week, was it?'

'Why didn't they make it in the summer? Everything would have looked much better then!'

'But this is a *Lent* series—that will always be in the springtime.'

'That Sidney, and his Bible reading out in the boat—couldn't understand a word he said, what with his Suffolk accent, and all...'

'Do we care if no one else can understand our accent? *We* can, and that's what counts.'

'And I thought you said Charles Waite was going to be in it! I looked, but I didn't see him!'

'No,' said Bill thoughtfully, wiping a pint glass, 'neither did I!'

'Brilliant!' enthused Bunty. 'Absolutely brilliant!'

'Sandford looked great, didn't it? Everyone will want to come and live here!'

'As long as they come and visit, and spend all their money here next summer, that will do nicely!' said Major Gregory, whose complexion was taking on a reddish glow, thanks to the bottle of whisky that now stood almost empty at the side of his chair.

'I thought the music was wonderful!' said Jack, looking affectionately at Margaret. 'Especially the harp music!'

'And I think,' said Don, 'that my daughter, Anna, has a great future ahead of her, if she continues to sing as beautifully as she did then!'

'So do I!' said Matthew softly, from his position just behind Anna's chair. She felt him put his hand gently on her shoulder, and when he made to move to take it away again, she turned to look at him. 'Well done, Anna,' he said, his eyes smiling into hers, 'I am so proud of you.'

It may have been the glow of watching the programme. It may have been the excitement of everyone around her—but at that moment, Anna would have liked to have leant forward, and kissed Matthew. She didn't. She wouldn't. But sometime soon, if he was very lucky, she knew she'd like to!

'Charles!' Bunty's voice had always been able to carry across a crowd. 'Whatever happened to your interview? Did I miss it?'

Every eye in the room turned on Charles. And then, Betty was beside him, moving to stand behind him, her arm lovingly placed around his shoulders. 'Not enough time, I expect. And they did explain, didn't they, Charles, that they usually collect more material than they need, and they don't always manage to use all the interviews they record? The thing is, did you notice how much of the information Charles gave them has been incorporated into the commentary? They could never have made the programme without him!'

'Here's to you, Charles, with our thanks for everything you do for the church, and the parish, throughout the year!' Surprisingly, it was Jack who spoke, raising his glass, in a gesture that everyone followed. 'Cheers, everybody! Didn't we do well?!'

As the cheers rang in her ears, Helen quietly left the room, and tiptoed towards the front door. Her Mini was already packed, her small suitcase and coat hidden safely in the boot. Silently, she turned the latch, pulled the door to, and began to walk down the path. Suddenly, the dark garden was bathed in light, as the door opened again. Clive was there. She stood motionless, her eyes closed, as she felt him come towards her.

'Please, Helen,' he said at last, his voice broken with emotion, 'please, don't go!'

She didn't turn round. She couldn't. 'I've got to.'

'I love you.'

She looked at him then, her eyes clouded with tears. 'I know.' She held out her hand to him, which he clutched gratefully. 'I love you too. I always will. I just need time, Clive—and so do you. Just let me get away for a while, to think things through...'

'Are you leaving because there's nothing worth staying for?'

'I'm leaving because I'm too close to recognize how lucky I am.' She reached out softly to touch his face. 'Let me go, Clive. Forgive me, and love me in spite of it. Let me go—so that I can come back.'

He pulled her close then, her head on his shoulder. She sank against him, breathing him in, so dear, so familiar and right.

He spoke quietly, and yet there was strength in his words. 'We'll get through this, Helen, and we'll be stronger for it.' He looked down into her face. 'God bless you, and keep you safe. And when you want to come home, I'll be here.'

With the lightest, most tender of kisses, he held her tightly for a moment—and then she was gone. She walked round to open the car door, and lowered herself into the seat, banging the door shut. Lights blazed from the battered old Mini, as she revved up the engine, put the car in gear, and slowly pulled away. Clive watched as she drove up and past the phone box, and on down the High Street. And he stood rooted to the spot long after she was out of sight.

Norman Oates took another gulp from his glass, and settled back comfortably in the sagging sofa. 'The thing is,' he said, his voice booming around the room exactly as it did when he stood in the pulpit to preach, 'we should have organized something like this years ago! We're all Christians, for heaven sake, and we live in an age when we pay lip-service to Christian unity—but that programme was the first time I can remember all the denominations around here worshipping together under one roof! Why on earth did it take a television programme to make it happen?'

'Well, we Baptists aren't proud!' said Stephen Yearling. 'We'd be happy to worship alongside anyone who loves God. As long as we're Christians, who needs labels?'

'So what are you thinking of?' Betty asked. 'Joint services?'

'Why not?' replied Stephen. 'It would save heating four church buildings, if we could all huddle together in just one place, every now and then.'

'We'd have to be very careful how we go about it,' said Norman. 'We mustn't offend anyone, or compromise the spirit of their usual style of worship. But it certainly seems to me it's something we should be talking about.'

'Discussion! That's what we need.' The voice of Charles Waite cut across the room. 'You're treading on very delicate ground here. It will need the most careful discussion and planning, and...'

'A meeting!' Bunty's voice was high with excitement. 'A meeting, and a secretary to organize everything! I volunteer to get the ball rolling!'

'... and a committee!' continued Charles, with a glare in Bunty's direction. 'It will need a carefully chosen, and well-informed committee—and of course, a chairman of the very highest calibre!'

'Then, I know just the man.' Margaret looked towards Jack, and slipped her hand into his.

'Hear, hear!' agreed Bunty. 'What a splendid suggestion!'

Ignoring the snort that came from Charles' direction, Jack looked first at Margaret's hand linked in his, and then round the circle of smiling, enthusiastic faces.

'What I need,' he said slowly, 'is at least a day to get my breath back. And then—I'll get cracking on a seating plan!'